The G
Work _ p

Margaret K Johnson

Margaret K Johnson began writing after finishing at Art College to support her career as an artist. Writing quickly replaced painting as her major passion, and these days her canvasses lay neglected in her studio. She is the author of romances, stage plays and many fiction books in various genres for people learning to speak English. Margaret has an MA in Creative Writing from the University of East Anglia and lives in Norwich, UK with her partner and son.

To find out more about Margaret you can:
Go to her website at www.margaretkjohnson.co.uk
Visit her blog at: www.margaretkjohnson.co.uk/blog
Like her Facebook page:
https://www.facebook.com/MargaretKJohnsonAuthor
Follow her on Twitter -
https://twitter.com/Margaretkaj

One

Janet Thornton pasted on a smile, pushed open the door to the church hall and came to an abrupt halt.

'Goodness!' In front of her, where there was usually a portrait of the Queen, somebody had hung a giant oil painting of a couple with no clothes on. A couple… having sex.

'That's what *we* all said. Or something very like, anyway!'

Janet turned round to see who had spoken. A large, older woman in a fussy floral dress was smiling at her.

'Oh,' Janet said, 'yes.' And then, unable to think of anything else to say, she turned round to look at the painting again, her befuddled brain trying to make sense of what it might have to do with the gardening course she had come to take part in that morning. The painting was so huge the couple in it were life-size, which somehow made the image doubly shocking.

'My name's Reenie,' Fussy Dress was saying to her now.

Janet moved uncertainly into the room. 'Oh,' she said. 'Hello.' She looked around for Gwen, her neighbour, but there was no sign of her, just Reenie and two other women.

As Janet stood there, unsure whether to stay or go,

1

her gaze drifted back once again to the picture. Some- how she just couldn't seem to stop looking at it.

Even more than the size of the man's… *thing*, the most shocking thing about the image was the complete lack of expression on the couple's faces. If ever a couple could be said to mate, then it was this couple. Why, that shockingly open gash of the woman's body was being *ravaged* by the…the *pole* which was the man's penis! Even if it didn't hurt, which surely to goodness it must do, then it should certainly inspire some sort of response in the woman's perfect features. Shouldn't it?

Then Janet thought somewhat guiltily of her lovemaking with her husband Ray the previous evening. While she had been waiting for him to finish, her mind had drifted away to an over-complicated recipe for a raspberry terrine she'd seen on *Masterchef* earlier that evening. Her face had probably been pretty blank too, come to think of it.

'Think it's from the *Kama Sutra*,' the woman – Reenie – said. 'I reckon it must have been painted by a man, don't you? It'd have to be with a you-know-what that size! Why don't you come and sit down, love? Make yourself comfy. No sign of teacher yet.'

'Oh, thanks.' Janet pulled herself together with an effort and moved towards the semicircle of chairs. As she did so, she looked over at the other two women. They were as different to each other as it was possible to be. The one sitting next to Reenie was a large, mannish-looking woman, wearing jeans and a red and white checked shirt, and the one furthest away was a young, perfectly made-up business type in a smart suit and blouse.

2

Both women were looking at her, so Janet smiled back at them uneasily. 'Hello,' she said.

The woman in the checked shirt gave Janet a smile that was more like a smirk than a smile, as if something about Janet amused her intensely. When she spoke, there was definitely a note of laughter in her voice. 'Hi.'

As for the business type, she didn't even bother to speak; just stretched her mouth into a brief, insincere smile and began to examine her manicure with great interest.

Feeling even more uncomfortable than ever, Janet took the seat next to Reenie, realising as she did so that the usual motley collection of church hall chairs had, for some unaccountable reason, been transformed by exotic leopard skin throws.

'I know you, don't I?' Reenie was saying to her now.

Janet looked at her, feeling confused and uneasy. It was difficult to make small talk with that rampaging couple staring at her with their glassy eyes, and she wished Reenie would just leave her alone. She just wanted to sit quietly to wait for Gwen.

'You work in that DIY shop.'

'Carol De Ville Interiors,' Janet said. 'Yes, that's right.'

Business Type looked up briefly from her manicure. 'They sell the most expensive light bulbs in Norfolk in there,' she said in a stuck-up sounding voice.

Janet's response was a reflex action. 'Well,' she said, 'it isn't a lighting shop after all. Mrs De Ville just keeps a few bulbs in for her customers'

3

convenience...' Her voice trailed off as it became clear that Business Type wasn't listening any more.

Janet felt annoyed with herself. Why had she felt she had to defend her horrible boss? And besides, it was true about the light bulbs. They were obscenely expensive. Not that Janet was responsible for the high prices. The closest she got to pricing anything in the shop was by painstakingly writing out the discreet cardboard price cards in the calligraphy-inspired handwriting Carol De Ville insisted upon.

'They have some lovely stuff in there, they do,' Reenie was saying now. 'I said to my Ted, if we ever win the Lottery, I'll be right down there to order a makeover.'

At this, the woman in the checked shirt gave a snort of laughter. Janet looked over at her and saw that the smirk was still on her face.

'*Home* makeover, I mean,' Reenie said, sounding annoyed. 'A complete new look…'

But Janet wasn't listening any longer, because the door that led to the church was opening, and there, at last, was Gwen.

'Hello, Janet,' Gwen said, advancing into the room. 'I've just been checking on the church flowers.'

Gwen started to take her coat off. Her back was turned towards the *Kama Sutra* painting, and Janet waited with bated breath for her to turn round and see it.

'You just can't trust Ruth to do a good job,' she was saying, smoothing down her hair.

'You two know each other then, do you?' Reenie asked.

'Yes,' Gwen told her. 'Janet and I are neigh-

4

bours.'

'That's nice,' Reenie said. 'Live locally, do you? I'm out on the Larkton Estate myself.'

Janet was very familiar with Gwen's opinions of the residents of the Larkton council estate, so she wasn't very surprised when her neighbour chose a seat as far away from Reenie as she could. Gwen patted the chair next to her. 'Come along, Janet,' she said. 'Sit here, next to me.'

As Janet was already settled next to Reenie, it felt a little on the rude side to be picking up her belongings and moving, but somehow she found herself doing it anyway, shooting Reenie an apologetic smile as she went.

'Whatever have they done to these chairs?' Gwen said, and Janet couldn't believe she still hadn't noticed the painting.

Reenie looked as if she was going to say something, and Gwen quickly directed a smile at Business Type, effectively blocking Reenie – and the painting – out with her back.

'I've got an ongoing problem with my primulas,' she said brightly. 'That's why I'm here. How about you?'

Janet saw Business Type give Gwen a baffled stare. Over on the other side of the room, Checked Shirt burst out laughing. 'That's a new name for it!' she said.

Janet looked over at her. What was so amusing? Reenie was grinning broadly too. Janet just didn't get the joke.

'Isn't that rather the point of this course?' Business Type replied at last. 'To find out what our problems are?' Her voice was icy cold, designed to shut off all further conversation, but Gwen didn't seem to take the hint. Janet saw her nod understandingly, giving the rather superior smile that Janet was all too familiar with.

'Just general shedding and rot then, is it?' Gwen asked politely.

On the other side of the room, Checked Shirt gave another snort of laughter, while Reenie let out what Janet could only describe as a whoop of mirth. A muscle flickered in Gwen's cheek. Janet knew from experience that her neighbour was now seriously annoyed, and to be honest, Janet didn't blame her.

'I think it often comes down to whether you spread muck or not,' Gwen sailed on regardless. 'Put something really good in, that's my advice. It's the only way to reap the benefits.'

As Business Type stared back at Gwen, there was such a complete look of disdain in her expression that Janet felt embarrassed for her neighbour. Especially since, behind Gwen, the hilarity was continuing unabated.

Janet felt quite lost. Whatever was going on? Gwen could be quite laughable when she was on her high horse or doing her Countess Gwen-oh-so-pleased-to-meet-you act, but it wasn't *that* funny.

'Do you mind?' Gwen retorted, sweeping round, and Janet saw her eyes widen as *at last* she saw the picture.

But before Gwen could say anything, the door opened and a woman in a swirling, black lace dress swept into the room.

Janet felt her mouth drop open.

'Bloody hell,' Checked Shirt said in a quiet voice that wasn't quite quiet enough. 'What is this?

6

Sodding *Strictly Come Dancing*?'

If the woman had heard, she didn't show it. Sweeping further into the room, she held her arms outstretched in a dramatic gesture of welcome. 'Ladies!' she said in a warm American-sounding voice. 'My name is Jade Gate, and I'm your tutor for the course.'

'Janet!' Gwen whispered to her. 'What *is* that painting doing there?'

Janet shrugged. 'I don't know,' she whispered back, still staring at the woman. *She's like a witch!* she thought, taking in her black clothes and her glorious copper brown hair tumbling down her back. *A beautiful, powerful, frightening witch.*

Jade Gate clasped her beringed hands in front of her and smiled at each of them in turn. When Janet received the smile, she felt as if a powerful laser beam had connected with her. Jade's green eyes seemed to see right through and inside her. It would not be easy to have secrets from this woman, Janet knew it. But, bathed in that emerald green attention, she didn't want to have any secrets from her. She wanted to crumple, to entrust herself entirely into the woman's hands so that she could... What? She wasn't sure.

As Jade's gaze moved on to Business Type, Checked Shirt, Reenie and finally to Gwen, Janet watched their faces to see if they were as affected by it as she had been. It was impossible to tell. And in fact, Jade only looked at each of them briefly. And yet when she had looked at Janet, it had felt as if the moment had lasted ages.

'Welcome to this series of workshops,' Jade said, her smile now taking in all of them. 'By coming here today, you have taken a first bold step to discovering the joyous, sensual women you are.'

Janet wasn't surprised when Checked Shirt gave a grunt, which could have been amusement or disbelief, or a mixture of both. But this time Janet didn't look at her. She didn't want to, because for one thing, Jade was far more interesting to look at, and for another, the woman was starting to get on her nerves. She reminded Janet of her daughter Debbie when she was in a contrary mood. It was far better not to give her the satisfaction of noticing.

'In the coming weeks we shall embark on a thrilling journey together; a roller coaster ride of amazing discovery! Not only will you learn to give yourselves intense pleasure,' Jade continued, 'but you'll gain the self-confidence to tell others exactly what to do to give pleasure to you.'

Janet frowned to herself. Jade's flowery language seemed very inappropriate, even for a horticulture course.

She wasn't surprised when Gwen piped up. 'My husband just leaves it to me at the moment really,' she said. 'He has other interests.'

Gwen always liked to speak at lot at Adult Education classes. Janet knew she ought to be used to it, but it still made her cringe. Gwen just loved the sound of her own voice. It had been the same thing in Yoga First Steps, Beginner's French and Basic Pottery. Gwen always had to put forward her point of view. Occasionally she even disagreed outright with the tutor. Sometimes Janet thought it was Gwen's main motivation for attending classes: to stir things up.

Jade was giving Gwen a sympathetic smile now.

'Well, by the end of the course, your husband will be with you one hundred percent,' she promised. 'I guarantee it.'

Janet watched Gwen frown. 'Oh no!' she said. 'I couldn't stand that! I *like* to do it by myself!'

At that, the other three women all began to laugh. Janet looked at over them, uncomprehendingly. What *was* the big joke? She had to be missing something!

Gwen, meanwhile, was looking annoyed. 'What's wrong with that?' she snapped, glaring at them all, and Jade was quick to smile soothingly.

'Nothing's wrong with that...I'm sorry, I don't know your name,' she said.

'Gwen Chalmers,' Gwen said, her voice sniffy.

Jade's smile was kind. 'Nothing's wrong with that at all, Gwen,' she said gently. 'In fact, mastering the art of solitary pleasure is a first, very important step. And it's entirely a woman's personal choice whether she wishes to build on that with a partner or not.'

Gwen shook her head. 'Oh no,' she said, definitely not. I've had quite enough of building work. I told my husband after the last time: "I'm not putting up with that filthy mess again, Peter," I said. 'So don't you ask me to!'

Janet thought Jade looked somewhat abashed at that, but she quickly hid her reaction with a smile and swept on.

'With such a sensitive subject,' she said, 'it's only natural for you to feel apprehensive, and that's why our first priority will be to create an atmosphere of trust and support within the group. For all of you to truly benefit, you'll need to be prepared to share your most personal secrets with each other – the things you love and hate in bed, for example: what feels good for you and what doesn't.'

Goodness! Janet could feel her face burning. For some reason her gaze was drawn to the fornicating couple in the oil painting opposite again. What kind of a course *was* this?

It seemed Gwen was wondering exactly the same thing. 'Excuse me,' she said, 'but just how is that supposed to help me with my primulas? Every year they wither and dry up!'

Checked Shirt gave another loud guffaw of laughter. 'She thinks this is a horticulture course!'

Janet was transfixed by Gwen's face, which had quickly turned a strong shade of beetroot. 'Well, that's what it said on the publicity!' she said, and Janet watched her as she dug in her handbag for a leaflet. 'A woman's harvest of delight! It says it right here!'

'Different sort of harvest altogether, love,' Reenie told her, not unkindly.

Meanwhile, Jade was reaching out an apologetic hand towards Gwen. 'Oh, I am so sorry, Gwen,' she said. 'I didn't mean to mislead you.'

Gwen was looking furious. 'You mean this *isn't* a gardening course?' she said, and Jade shook her head.

'No, I'm afraid not.' She paused significantly. 'It's an orgasm workshop.'

Two

Oh, my God! The blood pounded in Janet's head. She covered her mouth with her hand, torn between disbelief at what she was hearing and a guilty sense of pleasure at Gwen's humiliation. If she wasn't careful, she was going to burst out laughing.

'Well!' said Gwen.

'The course is aimed at women who have been experiencing dissatisfaction with their sex lives. Obviously I should have worded the poster differently,' said Jade.

'Obviously!' said Gwen, pushing her chair back and shoving her handbag over her arm much as the Queen held hers in the picture the *Kama Sutra* painting had replaced.

She gave a sniff of strong indignation. 'Janet?' she said. 'Come on, we're leaving!'

Janet knew she should move, but somehow found she could not. The blood was pounding in her head. Her mind was suddenly filled with an image of herself from above, lying in bed with her nightdress hoiked up, her mind full of raspberry terrine recipes as Ray pounded away on top of her.

'I shouldn't let her push you around if I were you, love,' Reenie told her, eliciting one of Gwen's best glares.

'Excuse me, but Janet has got a mind of her own,'

Gwen snapped. 'Come *on*, Janet!'

The image of herself and Ray in bed evaporated as Janet became aware of Gwen's bossy voice. Gwen's *perpetually* bossy voice. Janet suddenly realised that everyone in the room was looking at her, waiting to see what she would do. She licked her lips and somehow found her voice.

'No,' she said at last, the word coming out in a squeak.

Gwen glowered at her, as scary as the PE teacher who had once found Janet hiding behind a tree during cross-country. '*What?*'

Over Gwen's shoulder, Janet could see Reenie smiling at her encouragingly. Perhaps Reenie wasn't so bad after all.

Self-consciously, Janet tried again. 'No,' she said a little more clearly. 'I'm sorry, Gwen, but... I want to stay.'

'Good for you, love!' Reenie said, but Gwen was looking horrified now.

'You can't mean it!' she said. 'Janet, this is a small town – everyone will *know*!'

Janet's face was on fire. She knew she would care about that later on, but for now it just felt too good to be standing up to Gwen about something. She lifted her shoulders with feigned carelessness. 'I want to stay,' she said.

Gwen pressed her lips together. 'I see,' she said. 'Well, on your head be it!' And with that, she marched from the room, her back so rigid it looked as if her spine might snap in two.

As the door slammed behind her, every bit of Janet's bravado dissolved. 'Oh dear,' she said, suddenly panic-stricken.

'Good riddance!' said Reenie.

'But you don't understand,' Janet wailed. 'Gwen's my neighbour! She might tell my husband about it!'

Jade's warmth reached out to her from her smile. 'Don't worry, Janet,' she said. 'When the time is right, you will tell your husband yourself. Not necessarily with words, but by your sensual actions. Picture yourself driving him half-mad with pleasure; he won't be interested in the gossip of a busybody when you're doing that.'

A busybody... The description of Gwen was so pleasing Janet found herself smiling slightly, even though the picture of her driving Ray half mad with pleasure was illusive.

'OK,' Jade said. 'Now, as we'll be working together very much as a group, giving each other plenty of mutual support along our individual journeys, it's important that we get to know each other. So I suggest we take it in turns to introduce ourselves. Janet. Why don't you start?'

And once again, all eyes were on her expectantly. Oh God, what had she gone and got herself into?

'Well, er...there's nothing much to say really,' she stumbled. 'I'm forty-two, married with one daughter, Debbie, and I work part-time as a shop assistant.' She paused, but Jade was still looking at her expectantly, so she stumbled on. 'What else? I...like baking. Oh, and my mother's just died. Two months ago.'

Now, why, *why* had she said that?

'Ah, that's a shame, love,' Reenie said, laying a sympathetic hand on her arm, and eliciting an immediate lump of reactive emotion in Janet's throat. She looked down quickly, avoiding looking at anybody while she recovered herself.

'Thank you, Janet,' Jade said warmly. 'On a course like this, it's very important to open up, so well done – you're off to an excellent start! Now, who wants to go next?'

'I will!' Reenie said. 'Might as well get it over with!'

Judging that the coast was clear, and that the focus of attention had moved on from her, Janet looked up again. Reenie was fiddling with one of the flounces on her dress, and looking as uncomfortable as Janet was feeling herself. It was oddly reassuring.

'Well, my name's Reenie Richardson and I'm sixty-two, so I'm the geriatric of the group!' Reenie said. 'I'm married to Ted; he's a bus driver, and we've been married for nearly forty years now, so we must be doing something right! Though obviously not everything, or there'd be no need for me to be here, would there?' Reenie stopped and looked around with a nervous smile on her face.

Across from Reenie, Janet squirmed in her seat, feeling embarrassed for Reenie and more than a little terrified at the thought that she would soon be doing this herself.

'Right,' said Reenie, pressing on. 'I've got three daughters: one of them still at home; the other two married with kids of their own. Got four grandchildren, I have. It's bedlam in our place when they all come for Sunday lunch, I can tell you!'

Once again Reenie looked around, smiling. Janet smiled vaguely back, picturing her own family's Sunday lunch. They always seemed rather strained affairs these days. Debbie often came round with Nigel, her boyfriend, but since she and Nigel always went out on a Saturday night, they usually had hangovers. And Ray always played golf on Sunday mornings, and inevitably seemed to scream up the drive for lunch at the very last minute.

'I've not got a job,' Reenie said. 'I'm what used to be called a housewife.'

She smiled at them all. ' What's the lingo for it nowadays? Homemaker, domestic engineer? Whatever. I kept meaning to try for something, but somehow with that brood it just never happened. And now at the age I am, I don't suppose it ever will.'

There was silence. Reenie, it seemed, had finally run out of steam. Looking at her slightly flushed face, Janet wondered if Reenie minded about not having worked. Janet didn't much enjoy her job, but she couldn't imagine not earning some money of her own. It would be awful to have to ask Ray for everything.

'Thank you, Reenie,' Jade said, her eyes moving on to Business Type. 'Would you like to go next?'

Business Type sighed and pulled her short skirt down further towards her knees. When she spoke, her voice was clear and confident. 'My name's Estelle Morgan and I'm in business locally,' she said.

There was silence while everyone waited for her to say more, but nothing more was forthcoming, and as Estelle just sat there, Janet expected Jade to try to draw her out a bit. She and Reenie had said a lot more than that, after all!

But Jade didn't try to draw Estelle out. Instead she just gave her the same warm smile she'd given to Reenie and to herself. 'Thank you, Estelle,' she said simply. 'You're very welcome here.' And her gaze moved on to Checked Shirt, the last woman of the group.

'And last but by no means least?' she said, smiling encouragingly.

Looking over, Janet saw that the smirk was finally gone from Checked Shirt's face. Now everything about her face and her body language was pure defensiveness, her arms folded across her chest like a rigid barrier, and her eyes focused on a point somewhere to the left of Jade's shoulder as she avoided making eye contact with anybody. 'The name's Kate,' she said. 'Kate Mitchell. I'm thirty-two, and I work at Shelthorpe College as a Catering Lecturer.'

The information she had shared wasn't particularly remarkable, so Janet was as surprised as everyone else when it seemed to inspire a dramatic response from Reenie.

'I can't believe it!' she said, sounding furious. Gone were the friendly smile and the self-effacing humour. It was as if the sun had gone behind the clouds to be replaced by a tempest. 'You're the bitch who just threw my Marcia off her catering course!'

Checked shirt – Kate – turned round in her seat. 'Marcia Richardson?' she said, sounding appalled. 'That little troublemaker is never your daughter?'

Reenie got to her feet. Janet could see she was literally quivering with rage. 'My daughter is *not* a troublemaker!' she declared. 'It's you! She told me about it! You're nothing but an ignorant bully!'

'I suggest you do your research properly before you go throwing accusations like that around!' Kate replied coolly, and something about the calmness of her voice seemed to act like a red rag to a bull to Reenie, because she started towards Kate. When

Kate got to her feet too, it seemed to Janet that violence was inevitable. The two women, who were both on the big side, were squaring up to each other. There was going to be a fight!

But Jade quickly went to stand between them. 'Ladies, please!' she said, and Janet looked at her, surprised by her unexpectedly authoritarian tone of voice. The two squabbling women were momentarily jolted too, and they both looked at her.

'Please, take your seats,' Jade continued, still with the same power in her voice. There was no trace at all of her previous warmth and encouragement, and Janet thought Jade looked almost dangerous. She wasn't too surprised when both Reenie and Kate sat down again, even though they both continued to glower at each other across the space.

'Thank you.' Jade was smiling again now, but her eyes were still dark and glittering as she met first Reenie's and then Kate's gaze. 'Now you two ladies clearly have issues to resolve between you,' she said.

'Too right we do,' said Reenie, 'I won't have that bitch–'

'But,' Jade interrupted quickly, 'out of respect for your fellow students, these issues must be resolved out of this class.' She paused, looking alternately at each woman. Janet waited for Kate to get up again and flounce out of the hall. It seemed inevitable that she would.

But Jade was sweeping on. 'Now, Kate,' she said. 'You are a beautiful woman.'

Reenie made a sound of something like disgust, but Janet didn't look at her. She was too busy looking at Kate, whose face was filled with cynicism and self-loathing. 'Yeah, right,' Kate was saying.

'Ever thought you might need to make an appointment at Specsavers, Jade?'

'No, Kate,' said Jade deliberately. 'There's nothing wrong with my eyesight. You *are* beautiful. All of you are, in your own, unique ways. And if you have the courage to continue with this course, if you can co-operate and open your minds for the benefit of your bodies, then you will come to realise it.'

It would be nice to believe that, Janet thought, although she knew she never would. Why would she? She had never felt beautiful in her whole life.

Jade's powerful gaze was sweeping over them all again. For a moment, it rested on Janet, and she flushed, experiencing the distinct feeling that Jade could read her mind.

'But I say it again,' Jade continued. 'Although you all have individual journeys to make on your roads to fulfilment, you can and must help each other along the way. While you are in this room I want you to be respectful of each other. Mutual support and confidentiality are essential. Each of you must feel she can say whatever she wants to say within these four walls without the fear of being judged, and with the total assurance that nothing she chooses to share will be repeated outside of this room.'

Again she looked at each one of them in turn, and now Janet felt like a misbehaving child in a classroom. 'Is that understood?'

One by one, they muttered something. It was all Janet could do to stop herself saying, 'Yes, Miss.'

Three

Estelle looked disparagingly around at her fellow classmates. Two dull housewives and a closet lesbian. And as for the so-called tutor, she was just a joke. Bloody hell, the woman belonged on the stage, not in a classroom. Why on earth had she ever thought signing up for this workshop was a good idea? What was she doing here with this lot?

Still, the session hadn't been without its entertainment value. The look on that snobby cow's face when she'd found out she'd inadvertently enrolled on an orgasm workshop had been priceless. And then Reenie and Kate almost having a catfight on the floor! It was a shame really that Jade had stepped in the way she had.

And the *way* she had stepped in! Lecturing all of them about respect as if they were a class of misbehaving kids! Estelle didn't appreciate being lumped together with the rest of them. *She* hadn't been the one about to pull a handful of somebody's hair out!

'Now look,' Estelle spoke out. 'I didn't pay to be spoken to like one of *her* brattish college students.' Estelle nodded her head in Kate's direction as she spoke, unintentionally rekindling Reenie's fire.

'My Marcia isn't brattish!' she said. 'I'll have you know–'

But Jade swept in smoothly, cutting Reenie off before she could get going. 'You're quite right, Estelle,' she said. 'It is essential that I respect you too. And let me assure you that I do. I both respect and admire you all.' When she smiled this time, the warmth was back in her face. 'Look, I know it wasn't easy for any of you to come here today. I know you're all probably feeling a little vulnerable and ill at ease. That's only natural. Let's get on with today's session, OK? And if any of you want to leave at the end of it, then I'll refund your money in full.'

Estelle almost expected Jade to add 'I can't say better than that now, can I?' like some used car salesman, but she didn't. In fact, she didn't pause long enough for any of them to comment. Instead she looked at her watch and moved briskly on.

'Now,' she said, 'I assume you're all here because, as yet, you haven't been able to achieve an orgasm. Over the coming weeks, we will be exploring why this might be so. But for now, just in case any of you thinks – quite wrongly – that this is because you're frigid, or not a proper woman, just downright inadequate or for any other false reason, I want to prove to you that this isn't the case.'

Frigid, not a proper woman, inadequate. Estelle wondered if the other women had felt the way she did as the list was read out. Small. Pathetic. *Revealed.* Nobody on earth knew she'd never had an orgasm before. Certainly not the men she'd had sex with.

'So I've arranged a little entertainment for you,' Jade said with a smile, 'something I hope will prove just that. If you'd like to follow me outside, I think we'll be just in time.'

20

Jade walked to the door, her black lace skirts swishing after her. *Like some sort of funereal wedding dress!* Estelle thought.

Jade opened the door, pausing to look back at them all. 'Come on,' she said. 'I guarantee you'll enjoy this experience.'

Estelle was intrigued despite herself, but it was Janet who was first up. Then Reenie, shooting Kate a colossal scowl as she passed her. Kate, meanwhile, had her head down and her arms folded. At first she had seemed to find everything about the class hilarious, but the laughter seemed to have well and truly gone now, and she didn't look as if she was going anywhere. Sighing, Estelle got to her feet. Better get it over with. She could always make a dash for her car while she was out there if things got too bad. Put the whole thing down to temporary insanity.

As Jade led the way out of the room, they had to troop past the *Kama Sutra* painting. Estelle had disliked it at first sight, and had been avoiding looking at it ever since. But now her gaze swept over it, and her stomach instantly clenched unpleasantly. Suddenly she knew what it was she didn't like about it. It was the man – he looked so much like Rashid. Why hadn't she noticed it before? Oh, God; *Rashid*. She definitely did not want to think about him. Or that night…

Janet was saying something to her; Estelle barely registered what. Something like, 'This is all a little strange, isn't it?' but Estelle didn't reply. She was too busy getting outside, away from the painting; stuffing painful memories back where they belonged – deep inside of her.

When Jade came to a halt at the edge of the car

21

park, near some shrubs, Reenie and Janet clustered close around her. Estelle stayed on the sidelines and lit a cigarette. Her hands were shaking a little, but she didn't think anybody had noticed. *That's in the past,* she told herself. *You aren't that Estelle Morgan anymore. You're a successful businesswoman. You're envied. Why, just think about Kate; she must be about the same age as you, and yet just look at the difference between the two of you!*

She didn't realise Kate herself had come out to join them until Jade smiled at her over Estelle's shoulder. Taking a look, Estelle saw that Kate still had her arms folded and was steadfastly avoiding eye contact with anyone. Everything about her body language was screaming 'all right, I'm here, but don't you think that means you've won me over! Don't you think I'm going to take anything you tell me seriously!'

For a moment, Estelle found herself half-smiling in sympathy. But she quickly stifled it.

'Now,' Jade said. 'I'd like you to look up to the second floor of that apartment building – the nearest balcony to us. The one with the French windows.'

As she spoke, the windows were opened by somebody from the inside and a man came out onto the balcony – a young, half-naked man, wearing only clingy boxer shorts.

'Bloody hell!' said Reenie.

'Goodness!' said Janet.

'Mmm…' thought Estelle, having a good look. The man was blond, and as refreshingly different to Rashid as anybody could be.

The man, seemingly oblivious to them standing ogling him from the car park, proceeded to yawn and stretch luxuriously. Even from a slight distance it was possible to see the way his muscles moved beneath the surface of his tanned skin. He definitely looked as if he worked out regularly.

Actually, he reminded her of someone else from her past; a guy she'd met on her trip to Australia a few years previously. A surfing type, with the ubiquitous blond hair, muscles and suntan. What the hell had his name been? She couldn't remember now. But she did remember the effect he'd had on her when they'd first met in a hotel bar. It had been lust at first sight. *Mutual* lust at first sight. She'd really thought that he would be the one. If this Adonis couldn't give her an orgasm, then nobody could. But then, when it had come down to it, his penis had been disappointingly small for someone so well endowed in other areas.

Which definitely did *not* seem to be the case with this guy, to judge by the bulge in those clingy boxers.

'Isn't he a magnificent sight?' Jade said, looking pleased with herself.

There was a brief silence as they all drank him in.

'How did you know he'd be there?' Janet asked.

Stupid cow, thought Estelle. Wasn't it obvious it was all a fix? Jade had obviously slipped him a few quid to come out and pose for them.

'He comes out onto his balcony every morning around this time to greet the day,' Jade told her. 'I spotted him the first time I came to look round the hall and made it my business to meet him. He didn't mind in the least when I asked him if he'd time his ritual more specifically today.' And, lifting her hand, Jade gave the man a wave. Instantly, he smiled and waved back, flexing his muscles for their benefit.

'I think he's been watching too many adverts,' Estelle said waspishly, almost resenting her admiration of him now. He was such a poser!

'I like his taste in underpants,' Reenie said. 'Maybe I ought to get my Ted some like that.'

'You'd think he'd feel a bit chilly,' Janet said. 'It is almost autumn, after all.'

'Don't think of such things,' Jade said. 'Give yourselves up simply to the pleasure of looking. The muscles gliding beneath his smooth, young skin, his sleep-tousled hair and his firm loins and tight buttocks…'

For God's sake!

'Probably a male prostitute,' Kate said from the back, causing Reenie to whirl round instantly and glare at her.

'Surely not!' said Janet timidly as Reenie tutted.

'No,' Jade said, 'that's all right, Kate. Imagine he is. Imagine that as a special gift to you a friend has arranged for him to pleasure you. He's standing in front of you quite naked, and he's bending to kiss the skin of your neck beneath your hair…'

Jade's hands were lifting her own hair as if to clear the way for imaginary lips, and Estelle wasn't sure whether to groan out loud or collapse laughing. The woman was unbelievable! She could easily get a job as a pole dancer. Maybe she did it as a sideline.

'He's going in,' Janet observed, and they all looked.

Reenie sighed a regretful sigh. 'That's made me go all hot, that has,' she said. 'Thought I'd got over the hot flush stage an' all.'

'That's your Inner Sex Goddess speaking to you, Reenie,' Jade said as the French windows closed behind the man.

Kate snorted, still looking cynically up at the window. 'Well,' she said sarcastically, 'it didn't speak to me. Kept on thinking of the diseases I'd be likely to catch if I let him go any further than neck kisses.'

Jade was smiling at Kate. God, how did the woman have the patience?

'Yes, Kate, I quite agree with you,' she was saying. 'Health issues are of the utmost importance and we'll definitely be devoting some time to the subject at a later session. But just for now, we'll be concentrating on the liberation of your senses.' She smiled brightly at them, pleased by the effect of her treat. 'And now, if you'd like to make your way back inside, we'll make a start on doing just that.'

The others started to walk back towards the hall entrance. At the front, Janet asked Jade something, Estelle didn't hear what. Reenie hurried after them, listening in, while Kate dragged behind. Estelle, meanwhile, sauntered along in last place, finishing her cigarette. Her car was just there. If she wanted to make a getaway, now was the time.

And yet... And yet...

She thought again of the man on the balcony - of his perfect body. She'd had too many lovers to be able to fool herself anymore. Even if she managed to meet him somehow, even if she seduced him, she doubted whether she would have had an orgasm.

And I want an orgasm, she thought. *I own a lingerie business, for God's sake! I'm expected to be a sexy, sexual woman!*

OK, so the chances of this charade being able to help her may be minuscule, but she'd paid her fee now. Didn't she owe it to herself at least to give it a little bit longer? If nothing else, there were bound to be plenty more entertaining moments along the way.

Sighing, Estelle threw down her cigarette butt and ground it out with the sole of her expensive shoe. Then she walked briskly to catch the others up. In front of her, Kate's behind wobbled alarmingly in her jeans.

Bloody hell! What if the entertainment included watching Kate bringing herself to orgasm? It didn't bear thinking about.

Four

Heading quickly down the hill towards the town centre, Kate turned up a side street, barely registering the smell of crabmeat from the sandwich stall or the tinny jingle of the amusement arcade. Her destination was the Victorian pub at the end of the road, and her mission was to tell her friend Geoff that there was no way on earth she was going to go back to that workshop next week.

Geoff was at the bar when she went in. They both had Fridays off from their jobs as lecturers at the local further education college because they taught Saturday day schools. As Kate walked towards her friend, she strongly wished this were not the case. If she didn't have Fridays off, then she could never have attended today's workshop.

As she got near, Geoff turned and saw her. Grinning, he whipped something out of his pocket and held it up. Taking a look, Kate saw that it was around ten rows of knitting in baby pink. Her sense of humour returned. 'What's that when it's at home?' she asked, noticing at least three dropped stitches. 'A baby's dishcloth?'

'This,' Geoff announced grandly, 'is going to be a designer jumper.'

'Peep holes the new fashion look, are they?' enquired Kate, ordering herself a pint of bitter.

'Well, I should think they would be on that course you've been doing!' quipped Geoff. 'How was it, by the way? Mine was great. I've learned so much. Did you know that Iris who works in Culver's Chemists has got a fancy man? And blinds are definitely out for window coverings this season.'

Kate laughed and downed half her pint in one. When Geoff had first come up with this hair-brained idea that they challenge each other to do a course, Knitting For Beginners had seemed to be the perfect choice for him. Bearded, hairy and huge, Kate imagined he must have been the complete opposite of all the other class members.

And when Geoff had first come up with the idea, it had seemed like a laugh. Kate certainly hadn't imagined there'd be anything like an *orgasm workshop* taking place in sleepy Shelthorpe-on-Sea. Now she had the distinct suspicion that Geoff had, in fact, been very well aware of this before he'd issued his challenge.

'So?' he asked now, his eager tone of voice seeming to confirm her suspicions. 'What about yours? Tell all!'

Kate sighed and led the way over to a table by the window where other people were less likely to overhear them. 'Remind me once again why this stupid challenge seemed like a good idea?' she said.

'It's what we do,' Geoff said with a shrug, settling himself down in the window seat. 'Dare each other.'

'Yeah. But this is in a totally different league to daring each other to use the word 'circumcised' or 'iguana' in a meeting with the principal, isn't it?'

'You're stalling, Katie,' Geoff said. 'Spill. Or I won't tell you who Iris of Culver's Chemists is

28

seeing. *Or* what's the must have pattern for curtain fabrics this season.'

'And I couldn't live without *that* crucial information, could I?' Kate retorted. Then she sighed, bowing to the inevitable. 'Well,' she said. 'It started off well enough. There was this giant painting on the wall of a couple shagging, and these two women who thought they'd signed up for a gardening course.'

'*What?*' Geoff practically choked on his beer as he attempted to laugh, speak and swallow at the same time.

Kate didn't give him time to recover. 'But then it turns out that one of the other course members is Marcia Richardson's mother.'

Geoff instantly sobered. 'Oh, shit, Katie. That must have been awkward.'

'Just a bit,' Kate agreed. 'She nearly floored me.'

'Ah.'

'Yes, ah. Holds me completely responsible for it all of course.'

They were silent for a moment, thinking back to the incident that had taken place a month previously. Geoff had been teaching in the class next door and had come running in to help when he'd heard the commotion.

'I always thought there must be more to that business than we got to know about,' he said thoughtfully now.

Kate shrugged. 'Wasn't for a want of trying. Silly girl clammed up on me.'

She drank some more of her beer, reluctantly allowing her thoughts to dwell on Marcia Richardson. In the days before her marriage break-up, when Kate had still really cared about her job,

Marcia had been precisely the type of young person she'd enjoyed turning around. A pretty girl with a chip on her shoulder the size of a chip shop, she'd tried to hide her insecurities by causing trouble and giving her teachers grief. 'A challenge,' to use the PC jargon.

'She was waiting for me at the end of the session,' she told Geoff. 'Her mother. Asked me what I meant by flushing her daughter's chance for an education down the toilet.'

'Doesn't she know about the chip pan?' Geoff asked.

'She does now!' Kate said. 'I told her about it.'

Although she hadn't, not really. What she'd actually said, was, 'Why don't you ask Marcia what she did with that chip pan? I don't suppose she's bothered to mention *that*!' And then she'd hurried off, with Reenie bellowing after her, 'What chip pan? What bloody chip pan?'

Kate shifted in her seat, not liking the feeling of guilt that was threatening to settle on her like cling film.

'What's the teacher like?' Geoff asked, returning to the subject of the workshops.

Kate thought about Jade, hearing her passionate voice in her head as she had urged them all to listen to their inner sex goddesses. 'She's like some sinister Christmas tree angel,' she told Geoff. 'All black lace and evangelistically spread arms.' She put down her pint glass and spread her arms wide, attempting to replicate Jade's zealous expression. 'You must learn to hear your inner sex goddess,' she said, making an attempt at an American accent. 'At first her voice will seem like a whisper in an unfamiliar language.

But as the weeks pass, you'll begin to hear and understand her more clearly…'

Geoff was rolling about. 'More,' he croaked. 'Don't stop. More!'

Kate obliged. 'At first I shall tell you what to say to her, but gradually you'll begin to invent your own language; a language intended for you and your Sex Goddess alone!' Kate picked up her pint. 'It was all bollocks, Geoff; absolute bollocks. Know what she wants us to do for homework?' Kate leant in towards Geoff and lowered her voice. 'She wants us to stroke our body in a bubble bath or rub it with a piece of velvet. *And* go out somewhere without any knickers on!'

That was too much for Geoff. He was laughing so much he was holding his stomach. A part of Kate knew she ought to feel offended or fed up with him, but his laughter was, as always, infectious, and soon she was joining in with him, the tensions of the morning slipping away.

'You going to do it?' Geoff asked when he could speak again. 'The no knickers thing?'

'Might do,' said Kate, although she had absolutely no intention of doing so. 'Maybe in the departmental meeting next Tuesday.' She paused as Geoff began to laugh again, then went in for the kill. 'But only if *you* leave off your Y-fronts.' As his shoulders began to heave once more, Kate quickly held up her hand. 'Just kidding! I have enough trouble concentrating in our departmental meetings as it is! Anyway, you haven't told me. Who *is* Iris of Culver's Chemists having it away with?'

Geoff wiped his eyes. 'That guy from the news-agent's next to the museum.'

'The bald one or the one with the lazy eye?' Kate asked.

'Baldy.'

Kate shook her head. 'Poor Stan Culver,' she said. 'Nice, he is. Always got a smile for everyone. Poor bugger! Won't be smiling if he finds out.'

Geoff's expression grew more serious. 'No.' He looked at her carefully. 'You heard anymore about your divorce from PC Plod?'

Kate shrugged. She didn't want to talk about it. *Or* think about it. 'Nothing to hear. Wheels are turning, I suppose. All takes time.' She reached out for his pint glass and stood up, avoiding his gaze. 'Want another?'

'Yes, ta,' Geoff said. He stood up too. 'Just visiting the little boy's room.'

The barman was serving somebody else. While she waited for him to be free, Kate leant back against the bar and looked out of the window. A familiar figure was passing, almost as if her conversation with Geoff had conjured him up: Ian, her lying, cheating, low-life ex-husband. Leaving the glasses on the bar, Kate went quickly over to the window to look out at him. There he was, checking car tax discs, a regulation green PVC jerkin over his uniform.

As she watched him, she saw his face suddenly light up. Obviously he'd struck gold. Kate saw him take his pen out of his pocket and begin to write, his tongue protruding slightly. As he did so, a thousand memories flitted into her brain. Other times when she'd seen him concentrating just like that – making a birdhouse with tongue and groove joints in his shed at the bottom of the garden. Cooking a curry with freshly ground up spices. Wrapping a present with perfect corners.

Geoff joined her by the window, stretching his neck to see what she was looking at. 'Ah. PC Plod himself, is it?' he said.

Kate was still lost in her memories. 'I wish there was somewhere you could go to get your memory wiped,' she said.

'Like in that film? *Eternal Sunshine*, was it?'

'*Eternal Sunshine of the Spotless Mind*. Yeah, just like that.'

Ian was still busy writing. 'My mind's littered with so much bloody crap about that man,' she said. 'The way his face goes red the minute he drinks anything. How his hair clogs up the shower plughole. How he likes his shirts ironed.'

'Should have done them himself,' said Geoff, and Kate shifted her head ever so slightly to give him a smile. 'You're right there – he should. S'pose *she* does them for him now.'

'Poor cow.' Geoff put his hand on her shoulder. 'Come on; leave him to his dirty work. Let's get those pints in.'

Reluctantly, Kate followed Geoff over to the bar. But as usual, a casual sighting of Ian had ruined her day. She didn't feel remotely like laughing about the orgasm workshop, or, for that matter, about anything at all now. She didn't only wish her memories of Ian could be wiped, but her feelings for the bastard too.

And as Geoff changed the subject yet again, talking about some film a bit like *Eternal Sunshine* that was coming out soon, Kate switched off, her thoughts returning to the workshop. Jade had said that the course would help them to find the courage to tell others what to do to give them pleasure. Yeah, right. She and Ian had *never* had those kinds of conversations. The idea of it was completely impossible. They'd talked about work, about domestic stuff and things they saw on the telly. But about sex? No, never. And yet she had loved him so much. And she knew that if he were to turn up at her bedsit and beg her to take him back, she would, despite everything.

'So d'you fancy going when it comes out?' asked Geoff.

'Yeah, why not?' agreed Kate, not having a clue what she was agreeing to see, her mind busy wondering if her lack of ability at sex had played a part in her break-up with Ian. How would she know? She'd never been with anybody else. Would Ian still be with her if she had regular conversations with the inner sex goddess Jade had been banging on about? Was their split, in fact, her fault?

Five

It was six-thirty on Saturday morning, and Reenie was dreaming about the orgasm workshop. Jade had just handed out chip pans to them all and invited them to hit each other over the head with them. Reenie had been paired off with Kate, and now she was wielding her pan with great relish, enjoying the thump, thump, thump every time it collided with Kate's skull.

'Here we go again,' groaned Reenie's husband, Ted, waking Reenie up.

'What's the matter?' asked Reenie, bleary eyed.

'They're at it again!' said Ted, and Reenie realised that the thumping sound was actually the sound of their new neighbours' bed bashing against the wall.

'Bring back Stan and Tracey,' Reenie said, struggling to sit up and unavoidably listening to the escalating screams and groans from next door.

'It's like a porno movie,' Ted said.

Reenie gave her husband's thigh a playful slap. 'And how would you know that, Ted Richardson?' she asked.

A rumble of laughter started up in Ted's chest, and then suddenly they were both helpless with it. As the groans and thumps from next door increased in volume and pace, Ted and Reenie writhed about laughing, hiding their faces against each other or beneath the covers. By the time a final screech indicated their neighbours' mutual climax, Ted and Reenie were both exhausted.

'Gawd,' Reenie said, wiping tears of laughter from her eyes. 'How am I going to look at her when I put the rubbish out?'

'I'll make us a cuppa,' Ted said, swinging his legs out of the bed. 'Won't get back to sleep now anyway.'

'Ta, love,' Reenie said, plumping up the pillows for them both and settling down to wait for him to return.

While she waited, she thought back to her dream, and smiled grimly to herself. She hadn't had the chance to speak to her daughter about what Kate had said yet. Marcia had been out at a friend's house when Reenie had got home yesterday and hadn't got in until late. Though Reenie was one hundred percent certain that it would be something and nothing. Marcia had told her that Kate was a prize cow and a bully, and Reenie hadn't seen anything at the workshop yesterday to make her think differently.

Reenie hadn't told Ted about what Kate had said; she wasn't sure why. They normally told each other everything.

She shifted uncomfortably in bed, wishing for the thousand and twenty-first time that she hadn't given up smoking. Ted didn't need to know anything until Reenie knew whether there was anything to know, did he? No point in getting him all riled up for nothing.

'Here you are,' said Ted, coming back in with the tea.

'Thanks, love,' said Reenie, taking the steaming mug from him. 'Here, let me hold yours while you get in.'

Soon they were snuggled together comfortably, sipping at their drinks, the silence between them relaxed and companionable.

'So,' said Ted casually, spoiling it all. 'You haven't told me very much about the workshop yesterday. Nothing, in fact.'

Reenie tensed up. It was true, she hadn't. And somehow, she didn't want to.

'Well, it's confidential, isn't it?' she said defensively. 'I can't tell you about the girls on it and what they said, can I? It wouldn't be right.'

'So it's all women then, is it?' Ted asked quickly. 'No men?'

Still reluctant to talk about it, Reenie sighed. 'Yes,' she said, 'it's all women.'

'Good,' said Ted, but his expression was still expectant, and Reenie frowned at him.

'*What?*'

'Is that it, then?' Ted said. 'That's all I get to know?'

Reenie felt suddenly irritated. 'Look,' she said, 'you wanted me to do the course, so I'm doing it, all right? That's all you need to know for now, isn't it?' There was no way she was going to tell him about this week's homework, which included going out somewhere without any knickers on. She wasn't by any means sure she was going to find the nerve to do it anyway, and he'd only wet himself laughing.

'All right!' said Ted. 'Keep your hair on! I was only showing an interest!'

Reenie was instantly contrite. She and Ted rarely

exchanged a cross word. 'I'm sorry, love. Only it's just… well, it's a bit embarrassing.'

Ted sighed. 'No, *I'm* sorry. You don't have to go back next week if you don't want to. I was only thinking of you, you know, when I suggested it. Just doesn't seem fair that you don't have any fun.'

Reenie suddenly felt like crying. 'Silly old fool!' she said. 'D'you think I've been lying here suffering all these years?'

Ted put his arm around her and pulled her close. 'Not suffering, no. Just not…well, experiencing the earth moving.'

'I nearly did that time in Blackpool,' Reenie reminded him.

'Nineteen ninety-nine,' Ted confirmed.

Then he caught Reenie's eye and the pair of them burst out laughing again.

Ted gave her another hug. 'I mean it. Don't go back again if you don't want to.'

'No,' said Reenie. 'I'll give it another go.'

Next door, their neighbours had started up again. Reenie gave Ted a nudge. 'And if it doesn't work, I can always go round there and ask those two for some advice, eh?'

Ted groaned. 'Not sure I could keep up with that! Come on, might as well get up.'

When Reenie got downstairs, Ted had made a start on the breakfast and was frying bacon with the back door wide open.

'Didn't want to risk waking up Sleeping Beauty with the smoke alarm,' Ted explained. 'Not sure what time she got in last night, are you?'

'No,' Reenie said. 'It was pretty late though.'

'Might be time for a little father-daughter chat

38

soon,' he said. 'She needs to think about what she's going to do with her life now she's not on that course.' Ted reached over to switch the radio on, filling the kitchen with the over-cheery voice of a DJ on the local radio station.

'Good morning, Shelthorpe! It's Saturday 18th September, and it's a fine day out there, so get up you lazy lot!'

And just like that, as soon as Reenie heard the date, everything changed. The eighteenth of September. Reenie sat down before she fell down, her heart racing.

Over at the cooker, Ted carried on cooking the breakfast, but there was something different about his actions now. They were quieter. He was attacking the preparations with less gusto. Going through the motions. More than anything, Reenie wanted him to reach down to switch the gas off and turn to speak to her. But she knew he wouldn't.

When he did finally turn with her plateful of bacon and eggs, his eyes were deliberately turned towards the crispy bacon.

'There you go, girl,' he said, his voice as artificially cheery as the DJ's. 'Get that down you.' And when he sat down opposite her and began to eat his own food, Reenie experienced, just for a moment, a feeling something close to hatred for him. How could he carry on as if nothing had happened? How *could* he?

With a great effort, she pushed herself up from the table. She was trembling with emotion, but somehow she managed to speak. 'I…I'm not very hungry at the moment. Think I'll… go for a little walk.'

'I'll put yours in the oven to keep warm then, shall

I?' Ted offered, still not making eye contact.

When Reenie didn't answer, he got up and did it anyway, while she stood and waited. But afterwards he just sat down again and carried on eating.

'Do you want to come, Ted?' Reenie asked in a small voice. 'Do you want to come for a walk?'

He smiled briefly, focusing his gaze somewhere over her shoulder. 'No, thanks, love. I think I'll go down to the allotment. Take your coat with you. There's a chill in the air.'

There's a chill in our relationship! thought Reenie, *I don't know about the air!* And she grabbed her coat off the peg without bothering to put it on, closing the door after herself and hurrying off down the garden path without another word.

So desperate was Reenie to reach her destination, she threw caution to the winds and took the most direct route, walking straight down Bartolph Street and turning right along St Mary's Drive. It had been three years since she'd last walked this way. This was where it had happened, and ever since then she hadn't been able to come near. Normally these days she took the long way round, skirting the industrial estate and the shops. But it took a good twenty minutes longer going that way, and today she just didn't have twenty minutes to spare.

But by the time Reenie reached the point of no return, she realised it had been a big mistake to walk through these streets. She was still trembling and now she felt cold as ice as well. She dared not look anywhere but straight ahead. If she could have walked safely with her eyes closed, she would have done. At any minute, she expected to see someone she knew; to hear someone calling out to her,

40

mouthing off. But it was still early, so mercifully she saw no one, which was as lucky as Reenie expected to get that day of all dreadful days.

That blooming, sodding workshop. Thinking about it had driven everything else from her mind. *Everything* else. How could she have forgotten? How could she? She felt ashamed of herself. And so very sad.

At last she reached the ornate gates and turned into the entrance of the cemetery. The grave was in the far corner, much closer to the road and the traffic than Reenie had ever wanted it to be. But its exact location had been, like so many things, out of her hands.

Once there, Reenie knelt down on the ground to be as close as possible. 'Hello, love,' she said. 'Hello, my darling. Dad says sorry he can't be here.'

At the lie, the tears came, sliding silently down her cheeks. She didn't speak again until she heard footsteps behind her; felt a comforting hand on her shoulder.

'Hello, Mum. Knew I'd find you here today.'

Reenie reached up to cover her eldest daughter Gaynor's hand with her own, her sobs deepening at the thought of how she so very nearly *hadn't* been there.

'Three *years*,' Reenie said. 'Can you believe it?'

'No,' said Gaynor, her voice thick with tears. 'I can't.'

'Grandma!' called a voice, and quickly Reenie blew her nose, doing her best to pull herself together before her grandson reached her.

'Hello, Charlie, mate,' she said.

Charlie's face was wearing an expression of

41

puzzlement. 'Grandma,' he asked her seriously, 'why are you wearing your slippers?'

Six

As Janet paid for Carol De Ville's bacon and avocado baguette in the High Street sandwich shop on the Tuesday following the workshop, she heard the unmistakeable sound of Estelle's voice behind her in the queue.

'No, next week isn't soon enough. You assured me they'd be ready by the end of this week.'

Without stopping to think, Janet half-turned from the counter to smile at Estelle, but Estelle was talking into her mobile phone and didn't notice her. So Janet gave her a little wave for good measure.

'Well, I would appreciate it if you would pull out all the stops out and make it possible,' Estelle said with a frown, turning away, and it was only then that it occurred to Janet that Estelle might not want to acknowledge her. *Of course* Estelle wouldn't want to acknowledge her. The workshops were supposed to be confidential. It was just plain daft of her to feel hurt.

'Your change, madam,' the sales assistant said.

'Oh, thank you.' Janet took her change, picked up the baguette and began to creep past Estelle, keeping her gaze on the floor.

'Well, frankly, that's your problem, Mr Short,' Estelle was saying into her phone.

Janet was concentrating so hard on looking at the

floor she forgot to check she was holding the cellophane wrapper of the baguette the right way up. Just as she passed Estelle the baguette began to slip out of its wrapper, ejecting the majority of its contents onto Estelle's foot.

'Oh, no! Oh, God, I'm so sorry!' Quickly Janet squatted, dabbing nervously at Estelle's expensive suede with a tissue from her pocket.

'Leave it!' Estelle snapped at her then spoke quickly into her phone. 'No, not you, Mr Short! Look, I'll have to call you back!'

Estelle's shoe was now free from slices of avocado, but Janet's frantic efforts with the tissue were ensuring that the green slimy mess was irreversibly rubbed into the surface of the suede.

'Estelle, I am *so* sorry.'

People were looking at them now, but Janet was too busy mopping at Estelle's shoe to notice.

'Look, will you just leave it?' Estelle said, attempting to drag her foot away.

'Let me pay for them, Estelle,' Janet babbled. 'I haven't got enough money with me now, but I can bring it to the workshop on Friday...'

At that, Estelle gave her foot an extra tug and stalked towards the door, her face red with fury. Mortified, Janet scurried after her, stopping only to shove Carol De Ville's baguette, minus most of its avocado, back into its cellophane wrapping.

'Estelle!' Janet called after the fast-retreating figure, but Estelle carried on walking, not bothering to turn back.

The mayonnaise-smeared baguette stared accusingly at her from its cellophane bag. Well? It seemed to say, what are you going to do with me?

44

Janet gave the sandwich shop a brief glance. She *ought* to go back in to buy a replacement. But if she did that, she would have to pay for it herself. And, what's more, it was her afternoon off, which Carol had known full well when she'd asked Janet to go and buy her a sandwich at one o'clock.

What would Jade do in such a situation? Would she replace the sandwich or simply smile and hand it to Carol as it was? But Janet couldn't think, because of course, Jade would never have got herself into such a situation in the first place. On impulse, Janet reached into her bag for yet more tissues and wiped the outside of the baguette down. So what if she earned herself another one of Carol De Ville's dirty looks? She seemed preconditioned to be on the receiving end of those, anyway.

But as it happened, when Janet got back to the shop with the baguette, Carol De Ville was talking to John George, one of her suppliers, so she scarcely had the time to give Janet or the baguette a glance. John George, on the other hand, made a point of looking up to smile at Janet. He was a nice man; Janet sometimes saw him at church. In recent months, since his divorce had come through, he'd been on his own.

'I was very sorry to hear about your mother, Janet,' he said now, and Carol De Ville paused in what she was saying, a pained look of politeness on her face.

'Thank you,' Janet said, meaning it. 'I'm just off now to make a start at sorting her things out actually.'

John nodded. 'There's always such a lot to do,' he said. 'When my folks died I couldn't believe the

45

amount of stuff they'd got stashed away in the attic. Yes, it's a grim task.' When he reached out to give Janet's hand a warm squeeze, she was touched.

'See you on Thursday then, Janet,' Carol De Ville told her, and it was such a blatant dismissal that Janet was suddenly very glad indeed she hadn't bought another baguette to replace the one she'd dropped.

In fact, as she gave John a little wave and made for the door, she found herself wishing she had shoved the slimy mess she had mopped from Estelle's shoe back between the French bread. *And* hung around to watch Carol take a bite out of it.

Smiling to herself at the image, Janet got into her car and drove home to get changed. All Janet's life her mother had been over house proud, keeping her home scrubbed to within an inch of its life, but during those last months of lingering illness, the dust had inevitably begun to pile up.

Just as Janet was on her way upstairs to find her old jeans, there was a knock at the door. When she opened it to find Gwen standing on her doorstep, Janet didn't feel very surprised. She wished she had the nerve to say, 'Gwen! How are your primulas?' But in any case, Gwen didn't give her the chance to talk.

'Janet,' she said, coming straight to the point. 'You've been avoiding me ever since Friday.'

'No, I– '

'Don't bother to deny it.' Gwen was inside the house and walking straight past Janet up the hallway and into the lounge before Janet could do anything about it. Sighing, Janet followed her, watching as Gwen strolled around the room inspecting everything the way she always did when she came round.

46

Checking for what? Dust? Expense or otherwise of ornaments? Taste? 'You practically ran into the house with your shopping on Saturday to avoid speaking to me,' Gwen went on. 'I thought you were going to do yourself an injury.'

Bored by the ornaments, Gwen lounged, uninvited, on the sofa; crossing her legs in their tailored trousers. Trousers that – Gwen would no doubt be horrified to know - clearly showed a visible panty line.

'Well–'

'And what I want to know is, how long you intend to persist with this madness. I really don't know what Ray would think. I'm presuming you haven't told him about it?'

Janet fiddled with her necklace. 'Oh, you wouldn't tell him, would you, Gwen?' she said, panicking.

Gwen smiled, gratified. 'Hit a nerve, have I?' she said, and Janet flushed.

'I haven't told him yet as it happens,' she admitted. 'It's… a surprise.'

One of Gwen's immaculately eyebrow-pencilled eyebrows lifted. 'Oh? So you're doing it for *him*, are you?' she said.

'Well, yes.' *Was* she?

Gwen's expression changed to one of concern. 'I had no idea you and Ray were having such problems. You poor dear. You should have told me!'

'Well– ' *Were* they?

'But you don't seriously think that…that…*woman* is going to be able to help you, do you?' Gwen laughed. 'She's a joke, darling! Even you must see that!'

47

It was the 'even you' that finally did it. Janet took a deep breath and lifted her chin. 'Look, Gwen,' she said, 'I'm running late. I only came home to get changed. I really must ask you to go.'

Gwen sighed. 'Janet, don't be offended. I didn't mean… Look, you have to admit, you can be a tad on the naïve side on occasion…' But when Janet just stood there with her arms folded, not replying, Gwen finally sighed again, uncrossing her legs and standing up. 'Oh, all right then,' she said, 'I'll go. But don't think for one minute you've heard the last of this. I can't just sit back and let one of my oldest friends get sucked into some kind of…*sect*, now can I?'

'Well,' said Janet, 'should I find myself at the risk of being brainwashed, you'll be the first to know, OK?'

When Gwen gave an indignant sniff and took herself off, Janet almost felt like punching the air. Yes! She had actually stood up to Gwen! Unfortunately, her bravado only lasted until she reached her mother's bungalow on the edge of town. Sitting in her parked car outside the bungalow, Janet looked bleakly through the window. She'd been dreading this, but Ray was right. She needed to get it done so they could put the house on the market. Then they could pay their mortgage off with the proceeds. Maybe then Ray wouldn't have to work such long hours and they'd be able to spend more time together. And if the workshops paid off, maybe some of that time could be in bed, in the throes of passion…

'You? In the throes of passion?' Janet could almost hear her mother say to her. 'What d'you think marriage is? A Mills and Boon novel?'

48

Janet got out of her car and walked up the crazy-paved pathway to the front door, carrying her mother's voice inside her head. 'And another thing! What do you think you're doing, going along to that *filthy* workshop? It's degrading and pathetic. And you'd better not even *think* of taking your knickers off in public, my girl!'

Janet opened the front door with her key and stepped inside. The house still had its distinctive smell of lemongrass and furniture polish, although they were fading now, becoming eased out by the musty odour of unused rooms.

Janet shut the front door behind her and took a roll of black bin liners from her bag. 'You're too late, Mother,' she said out loud. 'I've already done it. On Sunday! So there!'

Seven

'Anyway, by the time I came out of church, the wind had got up.' Before the start of the next workshop, Janet was describing her adventures the previous Sunday to Reenie.

'There was the vicar waiting outside to shake everybody's hand, but I was clinging onto my skirt for dear life in case it blew up and showed the rest of the congregation *everything*.'

Reenie smiled, but there was something a bit distant about her expression and Janet suddenly wondered if Reenie thought she was showing off. She clammed up, her face going pink with embarrassment, but Reenie asked, 'So, what did you do?' prompting her to continue.

'Well,' said Janet, feeling a bit self-conscious now, 'I sort of bunched my skirt up in one hand and shook the vicar's hand with the other. Only I had my skirt in my right hand, so I had to shake his hand with my left, and it was all a bit awkward. He gave me a bit of a funny look, but I got away with it.'

'Should have let them get an eyeful,' Kate said, examining her fingernails. 'Need a shake-up, that lot do.'

'Oh,' said Janet, surprised. 'Do you know people at St Luke's then?'

'I don't need to.' Kate's tone of voice was unpleasant and Janet felt discouraged. 'They're all the same, church types.'

Janet flushed. Hadn't she just admitted to being a church type herself? Really, Kate was very rude.

Beside her, Reenie was bristling on her behalf. 'Just ignore her,' she said with a scowl in Kate's direction. 'Tell us what it felt like being in church without any knickers on.'

Reenie's expression was back to normal and she looked genuinely interested now. Janet smiled. 'Well,' she said, 'it felt rather wicked actually, I must admit. But wicked in a sort of *good* way, if you know what I mean.'

'Wicked can be very good though, can't it?' Reenie said. 'I'm sure Jade would agree with that.'

Kate let out her breath in an obviously sarcastic way at that, and the sound was bait enough for Reenie to turn on her. 'Look,' she said, 'just what exactly is your problem? Me and Janet are just having a friendly chat. We don't need any of your smart alec remarks, thank you very much.'

Kate spread her hands, all innocence. 'I didn't say anything.'

'If you don't want to be here,' Reenie said, 'why don't you just piss off?'

Estelle arrived at that precise moment, pausing in the doorway for a moment before walking briskly across the room. As her heels clacked against the wooden floor, Janet's gaze went automatically to her shoes. They were burgundy leather, and obviously new.

'I can see I timed my arrival just right,' Estelle said, setting her briefcase down on the floor and unbuttoning her suit jacket.

Overcome all over again with mortification, Janet didn't look at her, and it was obvious that Kate and Reenie, wrapped up in their conflict, had scarcely registered that she had arrived at all.

'Piss off yourself,' Kate was saying to Reenie, but there wasn't much venom in her voice. In fact, Janet thought she sounded singularly unmoved. However, the same could not be said for Reenie. By now she was red-faced and furious and spitting for a row.

As soon as she'd arrived at the hall, Janet had been aware that the tension between Reenie and Kate was still very much present, and now it seemed as if this was just an excuse to get it out into the open. There seemed to be every chance that it was going to spoil the day's workshop when it started.

'Coming here, being unpleasant to everybody every chance you get!' Reenie went on. 'I say we ask Jade to kick you off the course. See how *you* like it, eh? You can always tell everybody you had to leave because of a bloody chip pan!'

'Oh, please, ladies,' Janet found the courage to say, 'don't be like this. Remember what Jade said last week about respect and support.'

'Bugger respect,' said Kate.

'I wouldn't support her if she'd got a broken leg!' said Reenie.

'Now look,' said Estelle acerbically. 'It's not at all easy to free my diary up to allow me to attend these sessions, and I for one don't–'

'What do *you* want with an orgasm workshop anyway?' said Reenie nastily to Kate. 'Not as if you've even got a man, is it? Everybody knows that copper husband of yours dumped you.'

'Yeah? And you've got the marriage from heaven

52

have you?' snapped Kate right back.

'I have, actually,' said Reenie. 'Me and Ted have been happily married for nigh on forty years!'

'So what are you doing here then, eh?'

Janet couldn't stand it any longer. 'Oh, please! Stop it!' she said, but she didn't say it very loudly, and neither of them paid her any attention.

'Your marriage can't be that brilliant if you have to come to an orgasm workshop, can it?' Kate was sniping nastily.

'It's beginning to feel more like a kindergarten than a workshop at the moment,' Estelle said, but they didn't listen to her either.

'At least I'm not a dried-up old bitch like you,' Reenie was saying. 'At least I'm not the type of person who has to take out their disappointments on other people!'

'Meaning your daughter, I suppose?' Kate said.

'Yes!' Reenie shouted. 'Meaning my Marcia! That course was just what she needed it was, and you have to come along and– '

'Want me to tell you what happened?' Kate cut in. 'Want to know what that precious daughter of yours did to get herself expelled?'

'I know what she did,' Reenie spat. 'Nothing! I asked her about it last week. She said you just– '

'She poured hot chip fat over another student's hand,' Kate broke in, and suddenly it was very quiet in the room.

Janet put her hands to her face, feeling shocked. 'Goodness!' she said.

'That's a lie!' said Reenie, but she didn't sound quite so confident now, and when Kate spoke again, her voice was quieter too.

'He suffered third degree burns,' she said. 'His parents were all for reporting it to the police, but Stuart – the boy – wouldn't let them.'

This time it was Estelle who broke the silence. 'Well,' she said, 'now we've got that sorted out, maybe we can concentrate on the real reason we're all here. That is, if our so-called tutor ever deigns to show up.'

Right on cue the door opened, and there was Jade herself.

'Good morning, ladies,' she said, arms spread wide in greeting. 'How very good to see you all again!'

Janet felt relieved to see her. 'Hello, Jade,' she said.

'You're late,' said Estelle, looking at her watch.

Janet saw that Jade was wearing trousers today, but they weren't any old trousers. No, they were figure-hugging black satin with diamante sparkles up the sides, and they were teamed with a halter-neck silver Lurex top that showed off the curve of her breasts and the creamy skin of her arms and her back. Hardly an average Thursday morning in the church hall kind of an outfit, although for all the notice Kate and Reenie took of it, it might just as well have been sackcloth. They were still rumbling on in the background.

'I don't believe it,' Reenie said miserably.

'Believe what you want,' Kate replied. 'But it happens to be true.'

'I was deliberately late today Estelle,' Jade said, advancing into the room. 'I wanted to give you the opportunity to bond as a group.'

Estelle's laugh was cutting. 'Well, as you can

see,' she said, indicating Reenie and Kate, 'your experiment has been a miserable failure.'

Jade stood and looked at them all, hands resting on slim hips. Janet looked back at her fearfully. She was feeling rattled by the tension, as well as more than a little horrified by what she had heard. Reenie's daughter had deliberately poured hot chip fat over a boy's hand? How awful! Surely it couldn't be true?

'It does seem so, Estelle, I agree,' Jade said. 'However, at least we now know exactly what we have to deal with.' Janet watched as Jade drew up a chair and sat down, her long-fingered hands clasped together in her lap, her legs crossed at the ankle. Then she calmly waited without speaking. When Estelle sighed with heavy criticism, Jade showed no sign of having heard. For Janet, the moments ticked by agonisingly slowly. Then, finally, Reenie looked up. And lastly, Kate. Only then did Jade smile. 'Good,' she said. 'And once again, welcome to you all.'

Janet let out her pent-up breath, relaxing. There was something so reassuring about Jade's smile. Something that made Janet feel everything would be all right. That Jade would make it all right.

'You are all so brave to come here,' Jade told them. 'I never underestimate the courage it takes for my students to attend each week.'

Jade seemed impervious to the cynical twist of Estelle's lipsticked mouth, Reenie's flushed face and fidgety fingers or Kate's blank, dismissive stare. She just kept right on smiling at them.

'Now, by its nature, an orgasm workshop has to deal with very intimate material,' she said. 'In order to truly benefit from the sessions, you must each of you be prepared to share your very personal sexual experiences with each other. And I'd hazard a guess that, at this moment in time, none of you would be prepared to discuss such things openly with each other. Am I right?'

'That's the first thing you've said so far I've been able to agree with,' said Estelle.

'Thank you, Estelle,' Jade smiled.

'I, for one, am *never* going to speak about any of that stuff!' said Kate.

This was exactly what Janet had been thinking herself, although she wouldn't have said it outright. But the thought of telling these…*strangers* what she and Ray did in bed was…*impossible*. Why, she and Ray didn't even talk about it with each other! In fact, she had *never* talked about that kind of thing with anyone, ever.

'What you choose to talk about and not to talk about is, of course, entirely a personal choice,' Jade went on. 'But my experience tells me that the level of your openness will correspond directly to the level of your achievement in these sessions. And…' Here Jade's smile got, if anything, bigger. '…Since in this case we're talking about mind-blowing, life-changing pleasure when we talk about achievement, then I would like to suggest that this should be incentive enough for anyone to strive for success.'

They all looked back at her blankly. It was hard for Janet to imagine such a thing as mind-blowing, life-changing pleasure. The phrases just failed so completely to connect up with what she currently experienced with Ray.

Jade seemed to read her mind. She smiled. 'However, I do realise that at the moment, all this might seem to be a slightly abstract concept to you,' she said. 'You're here to learn another language – the language of your Inner Sex Goddess. And so far you've only learnt how to say 'hello' to her.'

Kate made a little snorting sound; whether of disbelief or scorn, Janet wasn't sure.

'Yes, Kate?' Jade said instantly. 'Do you have a comment you want to make?'

'I didn't get any reply when I said hello to mine, so I tried asking if anybody was there. Still nothing.'

Jade was unfazed. 'It takes time to hear your Inner Sex Goddess,' she said.

'Well, what if she never shows?' Kate asked. 'What if you haven't got one? Is there some kind of Inner Sex Goddess Adoption Agency you can go to?'

'Each and every one of you has got an Inner Sex Goddess,' Jade assured them.

'Look,' said Estelle impatiently. 'This is all very interesting, I'm sure, but when are we going to get on with some real work? I've got a business to run. I can't afford to waste my time debating the existence of some alleged Goddess.'

'Our "real" work, as you put it, Estelle, can only begin to start when there is a stronger atmosphere of trust and support among us,' Jade said. She stood up and moved her chair. 'And as a means of encouraging that atmosphere to develop, I'd like us to spend half an hour carrying out some exercises.'

'I didn't come here for a yoga session,' Kate grumbled under her breath, but Jade chose to ignore it and, a few minutes later, she had them all standing up and paired off – Janet with Reenie, and Estelle with Kate.

Then she produced some scarves from her bag and

gave one to Janet and the other to Kate. 'Right,' she said. 'I'd like you to blindfold your partner please. Make sure she's comfortable, but don't leave any gaps for her to see through.'

To Janet's left, she could hear Estelle and Kate muttering to each other with disapproval about what they were being asked to do, but she didn't pay much attention because she was trying to tie the blindfold around Reenie's eyes, and the scarf was slippery and kept falling down. Also, Reenie was very quiet. Janet could tell she was still reeling from what Kate had told her about her daughter.

'Are you all right?' Janet whispered, but there was no time for Reenie to answer, because now Jade had moved on to the next stage of her instructions.

'Now, Janet, Kate; I want you to lead your partner carefully around the room. You may go outside the building if you want to, but remember that your partner is totally dependent upon you, and also remember that it can be a bit frightening not to be able to see. Speak to your partner, tell her where you are, and warn her in plenty of time if you're going to change direction. Remember, while you are her guide, you are totally responsible for her welfare. All right, begin!'

Janet nervously took hold of Reenie's arm. It felt warm beneath her touch. 'OK, er…shall we walk towards the stage?' she said, and Reenie shrugged.

'So long as I don't end up arse over tit, it's all the same to me,' she said.

Over the other side of the room, Estelle and Kate appeared to be squabbling.

'Now, ladies,' Jade told them. 'Remember this exercise is all about developing trust!'

'Stuff trust! If she pairs me up with that cow,' Reenie said malevolently, 'I've a good mind to take her outside and lead her straight in front of a bus! She's a bloody liar!'

Janet doubted personally whether Kate's story could be a complete lie. Surely such an outrageous tale had to have more than a grain of truth in it? But she didn't say so.

'We're nearly at the stage now,' she said instead, 'so we need to start turning to the left.' Guiding Reenie along as she was, it was impossible for Janet not to be aware of the tension in the other woman's body. So she wasn't too surprised, although she was distinctly dismayed, when Reenie's voice began to wobble.

'My Marcia would never do a thing like that,' she said emotionally. 'I know she wouldn't. Deep down, she's a good girl. I don't care what anyone says.'

'I'm sure there's a perfectly simple explanation,' Janet started to say, but Reenie cut in.

'I've told you what the explanation is!' she said. 'That bitch is a bloody liar!'

'Janet! Watch out for the piano!'

Jade's warning came only just in time. 'Oh, gosh, yes!' Janet said, giving Reenie a yank and almost toppling her over. 'I'm *so* sorry, Reenie!'

As Reenie directed what was obviously a filthy look in her direction from behind her blindfold, Janet was filled with a sense of total discouragement. The way things were going, the workshops seemed doomed to certain failure.

Eight

Being led blindfold around the room by the burly Kate was one of the most unpleasant experiences Estelle could remember.

Apart from the fact that Kate was *hustling* her along far too quickly and with only the tersest of instructions – 'left here,' 'right ahead,' etc, – the woman's clothes reeked of cigarette smoke and…*curry*. It was disgusting. But worst of all, a gathering feeling of a total loss of control was starting to make Estelle feel panicky. Her skin was hot and clammy, and she longed to take her jacket off. But it was taking every bit of her self-control just to keep from ripping the blindfold from her eyes, so she just gritted her teeth, succumbing for as long as she could.

But then Kate trod on her foot.

'Watch where you're going, you clumsy idiot!' Tension added more feeling than was strictly necessary to her voice.

'Sorry, Your Ladyship,' Kate said sarcastically.

Something snapped in Estelle's head. 'Don't take that tone with me!' she said, and next minute Kate was enraging her still further by imitating her voice.

'Don't take that tone with me!' she mimicked like a primary school child in the playground. 'Who d'you think you are? Lady Muck?'

'Well, at least I keep my clothes clean!' Estelle said, and then Kate let go of her arm and walked away, abandoning her. 'Hello?' Estelle said. 'Where are you? Come back here!'

'All right, everybody,' Jade said just then, stepping in quickly to prevent total anarchy, 'that's enough of that for now. You may remove your blindfolds.'

Estelle pulled at the scarf with relief, looking angrily around for Kate. She found her leaning against the stage, arms folded.

'You were supposed to be looking after me!' she accused, but Kate only shrugged.

'All right, well done,' said Jade, apparently oblivious to the non-success of the first exercise. 'Now I'd like you all to form a queue opposite me, facing the wall.'

God, this was pathetic. Unless they were forming a queue to collect a vibrator, then what the hell was the point? But somehow Estelle found herself standing in line behind Janet and Reenie, with an even more reluctant Kate behind her.

Baa! Baa! Bloody baa!

'Right,' Jade said, and she was *still* smiling at them. Christ, the woman was going to have some deep laughter lines in a few years' time. 'Now I'd like you to take it in turns to close your eyes and run towards me,' she said. 'My job is to stop you before you reach the wall. Don't worry, I won't let you crash!'

Oh, for God's sake!

'Come on then, Janet. Close your eyes. Good, now run towards me. That's it! That's it! Nearly there! Got you!'

Estelle watched as Janet turned to rejoin the queue, a look of happy triumph on her face. Anyone would think the stupid woman had completed a marathon, not a few metres' trot across a hall, she was looking so pleased with herself.

'It's not as bad as you think it's going to be,' she was telling Reenie.

'Come on Reenie,' Jade was saying. 'Janet's right. There's absolutely nothing to worry about. You're in safe hands.'

Reenie's nervousness was so palpable Estelle could practically smell her fear. But then she was off, waddling across the hall towards Jade in her flouncy dress with her eyes closed, all nervous giggles and bouncy flesh. Or rather, she started off towards Jade, but then she drifted off course a bit, heading straight for the wall. But Jade sidestepped smoothly and caught her.

'Haven't run like that since I last got House at bingo,' Reenie wisecracked with obvious relief, and then it was Estelle's turn.

And suddenly she felt nervous too. Well, more vulnerable really. Everybody was looking at her, which shouldn't bother her, because she was used to chairing meetings and giving talks and having lots of people looking at her. But she was in control of all that. She called the shots. She decided what she was going to do and what she was going to say. This was different.

But she only had to run in a straight line for a few metres, for goodness' sake. How difficult could that be? And it probably wouldn't even hurt very much if she missed Jade altogether and ran into the wall.

'Come on, Estelle.' Reenie's encouragement made

her feel even more self-conscious and tetchy. As if she needed Mrs Flouncy Flop's encouragement to do something so ridiculously easy!

'I won't let you down, Estelle,' Jade said.

'Oh, for God's sake!' Estelle said out loud, and then she closed her eyes and launched herself forwards, a bit like a swimmer in a pool. Before she knew it, she was being clasped in Jade's arms, with Jade whispering words of encouragement to her.

'Well done, Estelle,' she said warmly. 'Very well done.'

Pathetic.

Firmly quashing the ridiculous sense of achievement that seemed to be trying to get itself expressed, Estelle folded her arms and watched Kate have her go. Kate looked as if she were even more cynical about the activity than Estelle was herself, if that were possible. Estelle wouldn't have been too surprised if Kate had deliberately headed off in the wrong direction and then done something drastic like slamming herself against the wall. There was something very destructive and unpredictable about Kate. She was like a ticking bomb. And since the next thing Jade wanted them to do was each to take a turn at the wall to catch everybody else, this was not a very reassuring thought.

'How do we know everybody's going to take this seriously?' Estelle asked, voicing her concerns aloud.

'Yeah!' said Reenie, glaring in Kate's direction.

'Just let go and trust,' Jade told them. 'Everything will be all right. OK, who wants to be first catcher? Janet?'

'Oh!' said Janet. 'Me? Er…all right.'

Janet stood, smiling nervously, her face pink and

her arms already spread like the big mummy she was. As Estelle watched her, a chord of memory suddenly pinged inside her head.

Primary school.

Her friends had always been met by their happy, open-armed, smiling mothers, whereas Estelle had always been met by the nanny. Her mother had never, not once, come to school meet her. God, what the hell was she thinking about that now for?

'When you're ready, Reenie,' Jade said, and Reenie went straight away, with much giggling from both her and Janet as she was enfolded in Janet's arms.

'Well caught, love!' Reenie told Janet, and then all eyes were on Estelle again.

She ought to walk out. Go back to the office. What the hell was she *doing* here running towards a wall with a bunch of losers? If anyone she knew ever got to hear about this, she'd be a total joke.

But suddenly she was closing her eyes and, despite feeling foolish, it was easier this time, not quite so scary.

'All right?' Janet asked her shyly, and Estelle gave her a nod.

'Yes, thank you.'

By the time it was Estelle's turn to be catcher, Jade had started to talk to them while the women took turns to run towards her, her voice necessarily loud in order to be heard over the sound of running feet.

'One of the keys to being orgasmic is finding the courage to let go, just as you're doing now,' she shouted. 'Take that step into the dark. Surrender control of your body and your emotions to another person,' she said, as Estelle caught first Janet – warm, apologetic and smelling of soap, and Reenie – bulky and dressed in those unpleasant artificial fibres – in her arms.

'This doesn't mean you can't have some control over what's happening; sex and lovemaking are very much give and take activities. But you have to truly want to give, and truly want to take.'

Listening to Jade, Estelle knew she had never truly wanted to give to her lover, RT. Or to any of the other lovers she'd had. Sure, she'd acted as if she did; she'd massaged them and sucked them and kissed them and all the rest of it. But the truth was, it didn't give her any real pleasure apart from the odd frisson of power, and she wasn't really sure why she bothered.

Realising just in time that Kate was thundering towards her like a hippo on heat, Estelle put her arms out to catch her.

'You must allow yourself to tip over that edge into that velvet pit of pleasure!' Jade urged them rather dangerously as Estelle and Kate swayed, struggling to keep upright.

Kate was still clasped in Estelle's arms like a lover when the door opened and a short, bald man in a brown work coat looked in.

'Oh!' he said as if he'd caught them doing something downright obscene. 'I just came to check everything was all right and…and…you've got everything you need…'

Over to one side, Reenie laughed. Janet joined her nervously. Estelle quickly pushed Kate away.

The little man was looking at the *Kama Sutra* painting now, his eyes widening, whether with shock or arousal, it was difficult to say.

Jade stepped briskly towards him. 'Yes, thank you, Mr Black,' she said, 'everything's fine. I'll be sure to let you know if there's anything we need.' And with that she hustled the bewildered man out of the hall.

When she came back, she was grinning broadly. Reenie, meanwhile, was in fits of laughter.

'His face!' she said.

'Who was he?' Janet asked.

'The caretaker,' Jade said.

Even Kate had a smile on her face, albeit a small cynical little twist of her lips.

'I think he got more than he bargained for,' Estelle said, and instantly Jade's smile beamed its light her way.

'Yes, Estelle, I definitely think he did! Now, come on, let's finish off here, and then we can have a cup of tea while I talk to you about your vaginas.'

Estelle was to wonder afterwards whether that sentence alone had acted as more of an icebreaker or bonding tool than any of the trust games they had played. Certainly it seemed to defuse what remained of the tension in the room. There weren't even any punch-ups or mentions of chip pans when Kate had to run into Reenie's arms and vice versa. Just the odd scowl or ten.

'Your vaginas are beautiful,' Jade told them, her arms spread in that dramatic, embracing way she had. 'As wondrous as the overlapping petals of fragrant roses or magical, exotic sea creatures.'

Roses? *Sea creatures?*

'That lobster or crab, Jade?' Reenie quipped, and

Jade smiled to acknowledge the quip before continuing.

'I want each of you to become aware of the unique wonder of your vagina,' she told them. 'Familiarise yourselves with it. Be proud of it. Celebrate it.'

Maybe it could become a tradition. Christmas Trees at Christmas. Easter Eggs at Easter. Shamrocks for St Patrick's Day. Sea Creatures for Vagina Day?

'You all right, love?'

Looking up, Estelle realised to her surprise that Janet had begun to cry. Reenie had noticed and was trying to comfort her.

'Oh, I am sorry,' Janet said, scrabbling about fruitlessly in her handbag for a tissue.

'Here,' Reenie said, handing her one from her own bag.

'Thank you.'

'Do you want to talk about it, Janet?' Jade asked, and Estelle's heart sank at the prospect of some emotional wallowing. Could the stupid woman really be crying about the prospect of her vagina looking like a sea creature?

'Oh, it's just…' Janet snivelled, '…well, as I told you, my mother died a few weeks ago.'

Reenie was instantly all gushing sympathy. 'Poor, love,' she said. 'It is an awful time when you lose your mum.' But if anything Janet looked even more upset at that.

'No,' she said, 'you don't understand. I don't feel the way I know I ought to feel about it, you see. I'm *not* sad. Oh, I know that must sound very wicked, but you see we never really got on.'

Ah.

'And…well Mother certainly didn't think a…vagina was an amazing creation of nature. The very opposite, I should say. She always said women were *cursed*.'

'Then she was wrong, Janet,' Jade told her strongly. 'Because just like a fingerprint, no two vaginas are exactly alike. And if that isn't amazing, then I don't know what is!'

Estelle had a date that night with her lover, RT. Normally their meetings were restricted to shagging, so it seemed very ironic to Estelle when he told her he'd booked a table at a well-known seafood restaurant on the coast.

'What's the joke?' he asked, when she couldn't help smiling at her plate of oysters.

If he only knew…

'Nothing,' Estelle said, but in her head she could still hear Jade banging on about sea creatures and celebrating vaginas when she picked up an oyster shell, which then made it seem almost…*perverted* to eat it.

'Well, there's obviously *something* amusing you,' RT said. His voice was sulky, and as she looked at him across the table, Estelle thought he sounded like a petulant schoolboy. Why *did* she still meet up with him?

'Just something someone said to me. You wouldn't think it was funny. You had to be there. How's business?'

The question proved to be an effective diversion. Off he rattled about the boring stationary company he worked for, leaving Estelle to her thoughts.

They were sitting in one corner of the restaurant,

and Estelle had the seat against the wall. Over RT's shoulder, she had a good view of people at all the other tables. *Too* good a view. Mark Turner, her Sales Director, was sitting at a table on the other side of the room with a blonde woman.

Bloody hellfire!

'What is it now?' RT asked, still in the same sulky voice.

'A member of my staff,' Estelle said. 'No! Don't look!'

But it was too late. RT had already turned round to look, even moving his chair slightly to get a better view. 'Where?'

'For God's sake,' Estelle hissed. 'I thought we were supposed to be being discreet?'

'My wife won't know anybody who comes here,' RT said dismissively. 'Who are you looking at?'

But Estelle didn't have to answer, because, at that moment, Mark Turner looked up and saw them, lifting a hand in greeting.

Estelle responded grudgingly, watching Mark as he said something to his companion, causing her blonde head to turn in their direction too. Estelle took her irritation out on RT. 'Can you please not stare?'

'What's the big problem?' RT asked, at long last turning back round.

'I prefer my private life to be private,' she said irritably. 'Not the subject for office tittle-tattle!'

'Sure it's just that?' he said, tossing an empty oyster shell onto his plate. 'Sure you don't fancy him?'

'Don't be so stupid!'

'Why not?' RT asked. 'He's an attractive man.'

Was he? Estelle looked over in Mark's direction

again. He smiled. Sod it! She hadn't expected him still to be looking at her. Scowling, she looked away quickly.

'You are in a really bad mood,' RT said.

He was right. She was in a bad mood. *Now.* But she really hadn't been before.

Against all the odds, the workshop this morning had been quite enjoyable, and in the afternoon, she'd had some good news about a big order from France. All in all, it had been quite a good day.

'Coming here was a mistake,' she told him, giving up on her oysters. 'Maybe this whole thing is a mistake.'

'Oh, don't say that.' RT was instantly contrite. 'You know how much I think of you.'

Did she bollocks. 'I know you like to fuck me when there's a frisson of danger,' she said. Once they had even done it on the golf course in the middle of a round of golf.

'I do,' he agreed, looking at her mouth. 'And I know you like it too.'

Estelle became suddenly aware of something – a shoeless foot – pressing at her crotch. Automatically, she opened her legs.

'So let's cut the boyfriend/girlfriend stuff...' she said vaguely, her voice trailing off as she concentrated on the sensations the foot was arousing.

The foot made probing and rubbing progress beneath the table clothed table. Estelle forgot what she had been about to say.

'No boyfriend/girlfriend stuff. Right.'

RT looked her smugly in the face as he increased the foot's pace.

'And...' The foot rubbed harder, the big toe

70

attempting to penetrate but getting thwarted by her knickers.

It was quite arousing, in the middle of the crowded restaurant, and not for the first time, Estelle wished that the main course would match the hors d'oeuvre. But maybe this time it would?

The waiter came to the table to clear away their plates. 'Could you hold the main course for a moment please?' Estelle asked him. 'I need to go to the lavatory.'

'Me too,' said RT smiling. 'Where is it?'

'To the left of the bar,' the waiter told him, and if his smile was knowing, neither of them noticed.

'The Mile High Club without the mile,' RT panted five minutes later, pounding Estelle's head against the cubicle door as he pumped away energetically, once again completely failing to bring her to orgasm.

Why not? thought Estelle miserably. *You were excited enough back at the table. So what's different now? What is wrong with you?*

Nine

'It doesn't matter who told me. I know, that's all.'

Reenie and Marcia were wedged into Marcia's messy box room with its pop posters and scattering of cheap make-up on the dusty dressing table. Reenie rarely ventured into her daughter's bedroom, usually making it a rule that Marcia cleaned it herself, which, in reality, meant it hardly ever got cleaned at all.

But cleanliness was the last thing on Reenie's mind today as she looked at her youngest daughter, who sat picking at her split ends at the other end of the bed. Reenie had put off this confrontation for as long as she could. Marcia had been out a lot, and Reenie had felt down all week. Somehow she just hadn't managed to find sufficient strength for it. But now it just couldn't be put off any longer.

'Not that I can believe it. A daughter of mine… You could have been arrested. Whatever got into you?' Reenie still hadn't got over the humiliation of finding out about the chip pan incident from Kate, a woman she didn't like. She'd so wanted not to believe it, but somehow she'd known it was true the moment she'd heard it. It wasn't the sort of thing anyone would make-up. Not even a cow like Kate.

'Come on, love,' Reenie said, softer this time. 'Tell me what happened. It must have been something pretty bad to make you act like that. It's just not like you.'

Bingo. Marcia stopped fiddling and burst into tears. 'Oh, Mum…'

'Oh, love, come here.' Reenie took her into her arms and held her, much the same as she had done when Marcia had been a child. In many ways she still was a child, despite all the make-up and bluster. Marcia had always been the most vulnerable of her three girls, and it was small wonder this had got worse in the past three years.

'Shhh. Shhh… Come on now, what did that boy do to you? Stuart was it?'

Marcia nodded. 'He said…he said Craig deserved to die… He said as I was his twin, I should have killed myself too as a…as a mark of respect…'

Reenie gasped with shock, then closed her eyes against an all too familiar wave of pain, clutching Marcia even closer to her. Suffocatingly close. Distressed though she was, it was too much for Marcia. 'Mum, you're hurting me,' she said, pulling away and wiping her nose on her sleeve.

'Who is he?' Reenie said angrily, tears spilling down her cheeks. 'I'll do his other arm for him, little bastard!'

Marcia fingered the bedspread. 'He's one of Louise's cousins,' she said.

Louise. Helplessly, Reenie sighed. 'Oh, love,' she said.

Louise Block had been Craig's girlfriend. She'd died with Craig when the car they were joy riding in had careered off the road and smashed head-on into a wall.

Pretty, popular Louise, with her umpteen brothers and sisters and cousins and aunts and uncles, let alone her parents and grandparents. Not so completely unlikely that one of them would end up in Marcia's catering class. Not completely unlikely, but definitely completely unlucky.

'I'm so sorry.'

'I didn't think,' Marcia said. 'He was going on and on at me. Calling me a murderer's sister. The pan was just there, and I reached for it. It wasn't really hot, Mum! Well, it *was* hot, but not as hot as it might have been. It had been on the side for a little while. But, Mum, he did scream. And…everyone else in the room was really quiet. There was just the sound of Stuart screaming and screaming. On and on…I thought it would never stop!'

Reenie could detect shame as well as horror in her daughter's voice now, and she reached out to squeeze her hand. 'How come I'm only hearing about this now?'

'I thought you'd go mental at me,' Marcia said, and Reenie shook her head.

'No, I mean how come this Stuart's family didn't raise merry hell?'

Marcia shrugged. 'I don't know. I think Miss Mitchell had a word with him. And I was expelled, so I suppose he got what he wanted.'

A wave of heat rose inside Reenie, a heat that had its source in unresolved grief and burning shame. All her children were hugely important to her, but Craig, her only son, had been the light of her life. Good-looking, clever, and popular with his mates, his teachers, everybody; Craig had possessed charm in abundance. With all of that and a loving family, there had been no reason for him to act like some deprived kid with an axe to grind.

74

Sometimes, in moments too lonely to share even with Ted, Reenie wondered whether the after-effect of her son's reckless behaviour would ever go away. Whether she would ever get an answer to the constant 'why?' she lived with night and day.

And whether she'd ever be able to forgive him.

'It's not your fault, love,' she said. 'None of it.' Then she gave her daughter a quick hug. 'Come on,' she said, with a big sniff. 'Let's go into Norwich to do some shopping. Cheer ourselves up a bit.'

It worked, up to a point, even though finances dictated that they keep to the market stalls and bargain shops. At least there was a smile on Marcia's face for a while anyway, and when they passed the seafood stall on the market, Reenie smiled too, remembering Jade going on about seafood in the workshop.

'Something amusing about my crabs, lady?' the stallholder asked her, which had the effect of tickling Reenie even more.

'*Mum!*' Marcia hissed with embarrassment, dragging her giggling mother away. 'What is the *matter* with you?'

'Nothing,' said Reenie, her laughter abruptly tailing off. Nothing. Everything. Because something had to be wrong when beautiful, *favoured* Craig had been wiped out from the world just as if he'd never existed at all, while his mother was still here to laugh at the thought that her private parts might look like some of the more exotic items on display on a Norwich fish stall.

Marcia looked at her. 'Mum? Are you all right?'

Reenie made herself smile. 'Of course I am!' Today was about Marcia. About making sure her

75

vulnerable daughter never again, not for one moment, was allowed to think 'it should have been me, not him.'

'Come on,' Reenie said, linking her arm in Marcia's. 'Time for something to eat. Shopping's hungry work!'

* * * * *

Back in Shelthorpe on Sea, Janet was examining a large conch shell that was part of the bathroom display at Carol De Ville Interiors. The shell was many shades of pink – the scroll of its inside a deep rose graduating down to almost white, its lumpy outside a deep shade of peach.

Cradling the shell in one hand Janet flicked the feather duster over it with gentle strokes. 'What colour am I?' she thought as she looked at the shell. Ray knew, presumably, but he had never told her. No doubt her doctor knew too. But at the age of forty-four, Janet still didn't.

Strange.

* * * * *

In the town centre, Kate was thinking about seafood too. At the fish shop, she splashed out on a pint of unpeeled prawns. Jade's class had given her the idea.

Coming out of the fish shop, she opened the bag and smiled. The prawns did not make her think of her 'secret body.' They made her think of revenge. Prawns stuffed into an ex-lover's hollow curtain rail were an urban myth. Well, she couldn't easily get access to Ian's curtain rails, but his police car, which she had seen parked around the corner with its window slightly open, was a sitting duck.

Nobody was in sight. Carefully posting the prawns through the gap, Kate watched with satisfaction as they slithered down the window and down the side of the seat where they were likely to remain undetected for some time.

Small revenge for someone who had so totally broken her heart, but hey, any revenge was good.

Ten

It was like déjà vu, only this time Estelle was the one at the sandwich shop counter buying a baguette.

Hovering in the doorway, Janet wished she were the type of person to make wisecracks. Then she could casually wait in line until Estelle had finished paying, stick her foot out and say 'Go on then, get your own back, why don't you?' Or something similar. Some-thing wittier, preferably. But as it was, she just wanted to turn and run. Would have, except that Estelle finished paying and headed towards her.

Once again she was on her phone, but this time she interrupted the conversation to call out to Janet. 'Can you hold on a sec, Maria? Janet! Wait a minute.'

Janet waited. Estelle smiled at her. Janet was surprised, both by the smile, and by how much prettier smiling made Estelle look.

'Have you got time for a coffee?' Estelle asked, and Janet was so astonished, she found herself saying yes. And then had to hover like a spare part for a minute or so, while Estelle finished her call.

'Right, sorry about that,' Estelle said at last. 'Shall we?'

Janet followed Estelle to one of the two tables in the window of the sandwich shop and watched as she ordered coffee for them both. Everything about

Estelle was confident and, she had to admit it, intimidating. Estelle's clothes were immaculate – a severe, tailored grey suit with a hint of lace at the neck to soften it, perfect make-up, cheekbones to die for, and sexily chopped blonde hair. Estelle was classy – from the tip of her manicured fingernails to the shine of her new designer shoes.

'Did you ever manage to clean up your other shoes?' Janet found herself asking, the full horror of their last meeting in the sandwich shop returning to her, but Estelle just waved a hand.

'Didn't try,' she said. 'Binned them.'

Janet felt herself flush. 'Oh, gosh, I am so– '

'Sorry,' Estelle finished for her. 'I know. Forget it. I have.'

Janet opened her mouth to say something more on the subject then closed it again. 'All right,' she said at last. 'Thank you.'

'But remind me not to sit next to you if we ever go out for a meal together,' Estelle ruined it by saying, but a quick glance showed Janet that the surprising smile was in evidence once again. 'Just joking,' Estelle said. 'Anyway, I should apologise to you. I was a rude, stuck-up bitch.'

'No,' said Janet, 'that's all right. I should have thought you wouldn't want me to mention the workshops in public.'

The waitress arrived with their coffees at that moment. *Of course* the waitress arrived with their coffees at the very moment when Janet was, yet again, mentioning the workshops in public, but, happily, Estelle didn't seem to be bothered by it this time.

'My lover would be totally astonished if he knew

about the classes,' she told Janet when they were alone again. 'I fake it.'

'*Do* you?'

Estelle nodded. 'Mmm hmmm.'

'And he can't tell?' Janet asked.

Estelle shook her head. 'No. RT thinks he's stud of the century, so he's not hard to fool.'

Janet tried, and failed, to imagine faking an orgasm with Ray. 'So, what do you do?' she asked, adding hastily, 'if that's not too personal a question?'

Estelle thought about it. 'Plenty of groaning,' she said. 'And I sort of make my muscles quiver inside.'

'Oh,' said Janet, absorbing this information thoughtfully.

Estelle laughed. 'Are you trying it out now?' she asked.

'What?' asked Janet, bemused.

'The quivering thing!'

Janet flushed scarlet. 'No!'

'You should. Jade would definitely approve.'

Janet's head was whirling. It was a bit too much to absorb somehow, this sudden difference in Estelle's attitude towards her. And yet…and yet, she was enjoying herself. A lot.

'By the way,' Estelle was saying now, 'I've been doing a spot of research. Guess what our Jade's name means?'

'Isn't it just Jade as in the precious stone?' Janet asked, confused.

Estelle shook her head smugly. 'Nope. It's Chinese. Jade Gate, Honey Pot, Valley of Joy… Get it?'

'You don't mean…?'

Estelle nodded. 'Yes. The woman's named herself

80

after a vagina! She's got some nerve, I'll give her that. Her real name's probably Nancy Harbottle or something.'

'Or...Jane Smith!' Janet suggested, entering into the spirit of it.

Estelle laughed.

'Yes,' she said. 'Jane Orgasmatron Smith.'

Janet sipped at her coffee, shaking her head. 'I'm afraid the course might prove to be a little adventurous for me,' she said, but Estelle kept on smiling.

'You never know what might happen if you– ' Estelle broke off to do a perfect imitation of Jade – 'speak the same language as your inner sex goddess...'

Janet laughed, but sobered quickly, thinking of the reality of making love with Ray. 'My husband says I think about shopping lists when we're...you know.' And she blushed at her temerity of stating such a thing not only out loud, but also in the High Street coffee shop.

'And do you?' Estelle asked her.

'Sometimes, yes. Not always though. Sometimes it's recipes. Or crossword clues.' As an honest answer, it was somewhat sad, but somehow it made both her and Estelle laugh out loud – great snorts of irrepressible schoolgirl mirth that made people look their way.

When they finally sobered, Estelle looked Janet in the face. 'I had a bitch of a mother too,' she told her.

'Did you?' Janet said, wondering whether this was the reason behind Estelle's changed attitude towards her.

Estelle nodded. 'Oh, yes. In fact, neither of my

81

parents were exactly overjoyed when I came along.'

They shared a moment of sympathetic silence.

'There was only Mum and me,' Janet said. 'Dad left when I was little.'

'And I bet she blamed you for that,' Estelle said.

Janet nodded. 'Yes, I think probably she did.'

Estelle sighed, finishing off her coffee. 'Oh well, I should be grateful to my parents really I suppose,' she said. 'Needing to prove something to them has probably got me where I am today.'

Once again they shared an easy silence, and then suddenly Janet noticed the time. 'Goodness,' she said, 'I'd better get back to work, or I'll be seriously late.'

Estelle pulled a face. 'Don't let Cruella boss you around,' she said.

Janet frowned. 'Cruella?'

'Cruella De Ville. That's my name for her. I know her from the local Businesswomen's Guild. A prize bitch. Useless businesswoman too. Sorry, but I only give that shop of hers six months tops.'

But Estelle was only confirming Janet's already established opinions. 'I've always dreamed of running my own interior design business actually,' she told Estelle dreamily. She laughed. 'Silly, isn't it?'

'Not at all,' said Estelle. 'Go for it! We'll talk sometime.' Estelle pushed her chair back. 'Who knows?' she said with a twinkle in her eye. 'I might even have to join forces with you if Jade keeps spreading the word about the benefits of not wearing knickers and my business goes down the pan!'

Janet looked at her blankly.

Estelle laughed. 'Oh dear,' she said. 'You lot

don't even know what I do for a living, do you? Janet, you are looking at the lingerie queen of East Anglia!'

* * * * *

'Now, which of you would like to go first? Get those bad experiences of sex out there in the open so you're free to move on with a completely clean slate?'

At the next workshop, Estelle was aware, without even looking, that Janet and the others were, just like her, studiously avoiding making eye contact with Jade. Somehow, today, Estelle didn't even feel like making the sarcastic quips she would have made the previous week. Because the truth was that it would take weeks for her to talk about all her bad sexual experiences, there had been so many.

'Come on, now,' Jade urged them. 'It won't be so difficult once you start.'

Even though Estelle still didn't accept the challenge of being the first to bare her soul, she knew something had changed within her since the last workshop. She had taken herself by surprise when she had invited Janet to have coffee with her, and the even bigger surprise had been how much she had enjoyed it.

Why *had* she done it? She wasn't entirely sure. It had been an impulse. Janet had been looking at her like a kicked dog, and for some reason Estelle suddenly hadn't wanted her to look at her that way.

It was strange. On the face of it, Janet was her complete opposite – their worlds were poles apart. She owned her own successful business, and Janet was just a housewife with a part-time job. And yet… Estelle hadn't just been saying it when she had mentioned to Janet a connection between them because of the shared coldness of their mothers. Maybe people reacted differently to similar childhood traumas. Or maybe Janet just showed on the outside what Estelle kept hidden away inside. Whatever. Strange as it seemed, there *was* a connection between them now, and that connection seemed to be making Estelle want to try to take the workshops more seriously.

'Well, all right then,' Jade said, 'let me start.'

With the danger of being in the spotlight temporarily averted, Estelle and the others looked up. Jade smiled at them all.

'I lost my virginity at the age of thirteen to a boy I didn't even like.'

'Ditto,' thought Estelle, but kept quiet.

'Why didn't I say "no"?' Jade's gaze scoured along the row as she asked the question. 'Because I didn't like myself enough to say no, that's why.'

Ditto again. Except that presumably Jade had stopped doing such things now, unlike Estelle.

'I had sex quite often after that,' Jade went on. 'But I didn't actually have my first orgasm until I was twenty-five years old. That's a lot of non-orgasmic and sometimes, I have to say, downright unpleasant sex.'

'So, what made the difference in the end, Jade?' In the end it was plump, blousy Reenie who finally got the courage to speak. Although actually Reenie looked a lot better this week. She'd toned down the frills and flounces, and there seemed to be less tension between her and Kate, thank God.

'What made you, you know…have an orgasm?'

'It wasn't just one thing, Reenie,' Jade said. 'It was a combination of several things, the most important being, I think, that I learnt to love myself. I know it's a cliché, but learning to love yourself really is the greatest love of all.'

Estelle wriggled in her seat, holding on to her new spirit of co-operation with difficulty. But Kate supplied the cynical words she was trying to hold back herself.

'That is one hundred percent Whitney Houston,' she said. 'Didn't do her much good, did it, poor cow?' she said.

Jade ignored the comment, her smile refusing to falter. 'Why, thank you, Kate,' she said. 'I love that song. There's so much truth in it isn't there?'

'Yeah,' Kate said cynically, arms folded defensively across her breasts. 'Except for the bit where she says it's easy, but I expect that's just put in to make the song sound right.'

'All love takes work,' Jade told them. 'And loving yourself is no different. So,' and she smiled again, 'that's why we need to clear out all the negativity that might be getting in your way; dump all those depressing experiences of sex right here and start afresh with a completely clean slate. Reenie, why don't you start? It doesn't have to be anything in-depth, a short statement will do. Just something, anything that's had a negative impact on your sexual confidence.'

Reenie was silent for a while. 'Well, I was a virgin when I met Ted, and a virgin when we got married,' she said at last, taking the plunge. 'A complete innocent, in fact. Which wasn't what you'd call a good start to our sex life. Girls these days, they know it all really young, don't they? Take my three, at it almost as soon as they got breasts, they were. Well, they are, aren't they, youngsters today?'

'My mother told me sex was a joyless duty,' Janet said shyly into the pause that followed this statement.

'Mine too!' Reenie said, and then they were off, the stories tumbling out.

Well, Janet's and Reenie's stories were. Kate just sat there with that cynical arms folded body language as if she were bored or above it all, and as for Estelle, a part of her *wanted* to join in, but another part of her felt too embarrassed to do so. Janet's and Reenie's tales of marriage bed disappointments just didn't seem in the same league as her own stories.

'I was eleven years old when a boy first thrust his cock into my face, demanding oral sex,' she could have said. Or, *'once I had sex with twin brothers, but even being pleasured by two gorgeous men at the same time didn't make me come.'* Or, *'once my father caught me screwing a boy in the stables and horse-whipped us both.'*

'I've tried pretty much everything at least once,' was all she said. 'Nothing makes any difference.' And suddenly it seemed to Estelle that her words joined Janet's and Reenie's sob stories and all the things she *hadn't* said to hang in the air like a great big, depressing cloud in the room.

Eleven

Despite the blank, hostile expression, there was actually a lot going on in Kate Mitchell's head as Janet and Reenie spouted on about painful losing of virginities, shock at first seeing an erect penis, the discomfort of sex post-childbirth etc., etc.

She wasn't really sure why she kept returning for another dose of Jade's evangelism. If she'd refused to come back after week one, Geoff would have made her life a misery for a little while, but she could have lived with that. In fact, Kate was fairly sure he'd expected her to drop out. So what was she doing here? Was she really so deluded to think there was a chance that Ian would turn up to ask her to take him back? Was she really trying to increase her allure for that two-timing toerag?

And the truth was, hearing the others yacking on about their bad experiences wasn't doing Kate any good at all. It was making her relive her own worst ever experience connected to sex. Making her picture herself a year previously, on her way home unexpectedly early from work due to a cancelled meeting, with beer and fish and chips for a treat. As carefree and as waggy-tailed as a dog on its way home to its master.

Kate Mitchell didn't do sunsets or wrapped up à deux in cosy blankets watching shooting stars all night. She did impromptu fish and chips and paying attention to dull accounts of the minutiae of arrests. And so she had trotted with the fish and chips back to her marital home with that waggy-tailed walk. Very probably she had been humming a little tune to herself as she made her way up the garden path. Maybe even Whitney Houston, who knew? At the front door, she had reached into her bag for her door key, shifting her warm kitchen-papered burden into the crook of her left arm.

What had come first? The strange sounds coming from upstairs? Or the scent of an all-too-familiar perfume in the hallway? Neither perhaps. Or maybe both. A collusion of clues firing up her instincts, causing her to lay the package of fish and chips down on the hall table and to creep silently upstairs. Her heart had never beaten as quickly before or since. Even standing in the bedroom doorway watching Ian suckle her best friend Jennifer's nipple, when, by rights it should have stopped beating altogether…

When the two people you love most in the world hate you enough to betray you, then how the fuck can you ever hope to love yourself again?

'Well done,' Jade was saying. 'Thank you for sharing those things with us.' The green eyes latched themselves inevitably onto Kate. 'And,' Jade said, 'if, at any point, anyone else feels ready to share their secrets, then the way is always open for them to do so.'

Nobody knew all the details of her break-up with Ian. Not even Ian and Jennifer, for Kate had left the bedroom door as silently as she had crept up to it. Certainly her family didn't know. Never having liked having a policeman for a son-in-law, they had been easily convinced by her 'we grew apart' tale. And not her friends. Oh, no, definitely not Geoff. God, no! Those milliseconds she had stood in the doorway of the bedroom watching Ian suckle the closed-eyed Jennifer's nipple were Kate's own black, poisonous secret.

And the earth would stop turning before she exposed the humiliation of that secret to this shower's scrutiny.

Jade was busy with some sort of diagram now, covering the *Kama Sutra* painting with it, and Kate came to, realising that the other women were sniggering with embarrassed laughter. She soon saw why. The diagram was an explicit and faithful reproduction of the female genital area, blown up many times over.

In your face, so to speak.

'Your homework for this week is to use a hand mirror to study your secret selves: your labia, your clitoris, your vagina, your perineum and your anus.'

Bloody hell! That beat the homework she dished out for the kids on the GNVQ Hospitality and Catering course hands down.

'Sit in good light, and do make sure you take the phone off the hook. This is a special time for you, so you want to avoid interruptions at all costs.'

Though, come to think about it, she would rather do Hospitality and Catering homework any day of the week.

'Put on some relaxing music, and make sure the room is warm enough. Then, when you're ready – and not before – position the mirror between your legs and reach down to gently unfurl the layers of yourself.'

Jade's face was rapt. She had her hands spread again, exactly as Kate had impersonated her to Geoff. 'Then simply look,' she told them earnestly, 'carefully and at length. And, as you do so, try to imagine you're looking through the eyes of someone who's wild about you. Someone who wants to give pleasure to the very areas he's looking at with such close, loving attention. How would this person describe what they see?'

Smelly? Fishy? Bloody difficult to find amongst all the flab that had gained ground since Ian's betrayal?

'And next week I'd like you all to report back on how the experience was for you.'

Fat chance.

On the way out at the end of the session, Reenie waylaid her.

'Look…' she said, making scant eye contact.

Kate decided to make it difficult for her. 'You talk-ing to me?'

The irritated flush on Reenie's face was gratifying to say the least. 'I just wanted to say…' she started up again. 'Well, I tackled Marcia about the chip pan thing, and she…well, she admitted it.'

'And?'

This time the irritation spread into Reenie's voice. 'Look, I'm trying to apologise here!' she snapped. 'Do you have to make it so sodding difficult?'

Yes. Don't you know that making things difficult is my speciality?

Kate sighed. 'Go on,' she said.

Reenie glowered at her, then took a deep breath. 'Like I said, Marcia told me what happened. And there's no excuse for what she did to that boy. She knows that now. But he did say some filthy… *unforgivable* things to her.'

Her eyes flicked opened again. 'Were you aware of that?'

Kate sensed that what Reenie had really wanted to ask was – *Did you bother to even ask her why she did it?* – but was doing her very best to keep a tone of accusation out of her voice. Kate answered the unspoken question. 'If you're asking if I tried to find out what brought it on, I did. Neither of them would talk about it.'

'Well,' said Reenie, and suddenly there was a raw emotion in her voice that Kate couldn't help but hear. 'It's not something that I… care to go into now. But I do want you to know that Marcia was severely provoked by that Stuart. What he said was… Well, it was unspeakable.' Reenie took a deep breath and carried on. 'Look, Marcia's not the kind of girl to do something like this. Not normally.'

Kate thought back to the horror of that day. Stuart screaming, Marcia sobbing. Half the class sobbing, for God's sake! It had been the worst day of her teaching life. But Reenie was trembling now with the effort of holding back tears, and instinctively Kate knew there was something big she didn't know about here.

Inside of her, Kate suddenly felt something slipping, like an ice floe starting up when the temperature rises, trying to connect her with Reenie. Every instinct within Kate rebelled at the thought. She didn't want to connect, not in any meaningful way, with anybody. Frozen, nothing could get at you. She was close to Geoff – they had a laugh together, and that was fine. But when emotions started to get involved, it was different.

Kate sighed heavily. When she spoke, her voice was bordering on being kind. 'I had to report the incident to the principal,' she told Reenie. 'I didn't have any choice.'

Reenie sighed too. 'I know,' she said.

'*She* tried to get the pair of them to explain themselves, but neither of them would talk to her either.'

'No.'

Then Reenie put her shoulders back and gave her a grim smile. 'Anyway,' she said, and nodded. 'I just wanted to say…' She broke off, not finishing the sentence.

Kate nodded.

'See you next week, I suppose,' Reenie said.

'Yes,' agreed Kate. 'See you then.'

Twelve

On the Saturday morning after the diagram of the female anatomy class, Janet and Estelle went shopping together in Norwich. It was Estelle's idea, so they went in her car, and, as it was a sunny day, they had the top down. It was exhilarating and fun, and as they drove briskly along the country lanes, Janet found herself wondering what it must be like to be Estelle, a successful businesswoman, taking success and its accompanying rewards such as this car for granted.

And yet Estelle still felt the need to go to the workshops... Somehow it didn't seem to fit.

'I hope I'm not interfering with what you usually do on Saturdays?' she asked.

'Not at all,' Estelle said. 'I like shopping. Have you thought what you'd like to buy?'

Janet shook her head. 'I'm not very good at shopping. My wardrobe's full of expensive mistakes. Ray's always going on at me about it.'

Estelle smiled. 'Well,' she said, 'I'm an expert shopper,' she said. 'Leave it to me. We'll get you something really stunning.'

It wasn't until the sixth or seventh shop, when Estelle had barely looked at anything for herself, that Janet first began to suspect that the whole shopping trip had been for Janet's benefit. But if she had become some sort of project for Estelle, then that was fine by her. Left to herself she would inevitably have gone straight to Marks and Spencer and then maybe on to BHS on St Stephen's Street. She hadn't even known of the existence of some of the shops Estelle dragged her into.

'Surely all the clothes in there are a bit young for me?' she tried to protest once, outside a trendy-looking boutique in The Lanes that was pumping music out onto the street, but Estelle wasn't having any of it.

'Nonsense,' she said simply and bowled inside, leaving Janet to follow.

And the truth was, Estelle had excellent taste. She was a fast, direct shopper, not a browser, and she seemed to know exactly what she was looking for. Taking skirts, trousers and tops Janet would never have picked out herself into changing room after changing room; Janet was surprised time and time again by the results.

'You've got a good figure, Janet,' Estelle told her once.

'Have I?' Janet was amazed.

'Of course,' Estelle said simply back. 'Don't you know most women would kill to have a bust like yours?'

And another time – 'There you go, Janet. That's an outfit for a trendy Interior Designer if ever I saw one.'

Janet's ego hadn't had such a boost for as long as she could remember. It was fantastic. By lunchtime she was weighed down by carrier bags bearing unfamiliar names and happily wearing a trendy hat Estelle had insisted on treating her to. She felt fantastic, and so far she had successfully kept most thoughts of Ray's reaction to the shopping marathon at bay.

And then they turned the corner next to The Body Shop, laughing together about something, and ran straight into Gwen.

'Janet!' she said, her eyes widening first at Janet's plethora of carrier bags before fixing on Janet's new hat. 'What on earth have you got on your head?'

Instantly Janet's newfound self-confidence began to slip away. Her hand lifted in a reflex action to her head. However, so did Estelle's.

'Something stylish, and *modern*, eh, Janet?' she said, and she pulled Janet's arm down and glared at Gwen's conventional clothes.

Janet watched an angry flush grow on Gwen's carefully made-up face. 'I suppose this means you're still attending those ridiculous workshops?'

'Well,' said Janet, 'actually I– '

'Really, Janet!' Gwen interrupted her. 'I thought better of you than this. What would the vicar say if he knew?'

Janet paled at the thought and might have started to plead with Gwen not to tell him, if Estelle hadn't grabbed hold of her arm, beginning to pull her away. 'Come on, Janet,' she said. 'We've got some hand mirrors to buy.'

And they headed off towards the shopping centre, leaving Gwen furious and red-faced in the slipstream of shoppers.

'You don't think she will tell the vicar, do you?' Janet worried as she hurried along beside Estelle.

'You need to stop worrying what people think of you,' Estelle said, leading the way purposefully towards Boots. 'Especially people like *her*. The woman's a prize bitch. You really ought to introduce her to Cruella.'

'They already know each other, actually,' Janet said. 'They were at school together.'

'Now why doesn't that surprise me?' Estelle said. 'Anyway, two bossy bitches in your life is too many in my opinion!'

* * * * *

Back in Shelthorpe-on-Sea, Reenie was sitting on the edge of her bed dressed in her slip, preparing to do her homework. She usually had the house to herself on Saturday afternoons because Ted was almost always down at the allotment or supporting one of their grandsons at some sporting event or other. But today he was hanging around the house. Just when she didn't want him to.

'If I hold the mirror for you, you'll get a better view,' he was saying.

'No, thank you.'

'Only trying to be helpful,' he said, offended.

Reenie sighed, reaching out to squeeze his arm. 'I know you are, love,' she said. 'It's just…well, it's a bit embarrassing, is all.'

Ted immediately grinned at her, reassured. 'You got nothing to be embarrassed about, Reen!' he said. 'I've seen it all, remember? And it's bloody bootiful, I can tell you!'

Reenie's smile was a little on the wan side. 'Thanks.' She wasn't too sure she appreciated the implied reference to turkeys by his use of part of a local advertising slogan. Her desire to do her homework without interference or assistance increased threefold.

She sat waiting, mirror in hand, but Ted didn't move. 'Look, love,' she tried again, 'I just want to do this on my own, all right? After all, we need to have *some* mystery in our relationship, don't you think?'

He didn't, she could tell, but even so, at last he did as he was told and headed for the door. 'All right, all right,' he said. 'I'm going.'

'Thanks, love.' She blew him a kiss, and finally, finally, he went.

'Thank Gawd for that.' Reenie spoke to the small round mirror she held in her hand, looking into it to pat her hair into shape. Putting off the evil moment.

'Come on, Irene, my girl!' she told herself at last. 'Get on with it!'

And, taking a deep breath, she pulled up the hem of her slip and lowered the mirror into position. Then she looked.

And looked.

'Oh, my good Gawd!' She began to giggle and brought the mirror up again to look at her flushed face. 'So that's what we look like down there!' she said to her reflection, then lowered the mirror back down again to take another look.

* * * * *

Back from her shopping trip with Janet, Estelle was also preparing to get busy with a hand mirror. But unlike Reenie, Estelle didn't have to fight for privacy. Privacy was almost always hers, unless she chose to invite somebody to invade it.

Also unlike Reenie, Estelle already knew very

well what her 'secret body' looked like. She had examined herself in this way before. But she had never done so while wondering whether she looked more like the overlapping petals of a rose or a wondrous sea creature. And she had never tried to do it through the eyes of somebody who was crazy about her.

So, with ambient music in the background and lily-scented candles flickering on the mantelpiece, Estelle carefully lowered her own mirror.

* * * * *

It was Saturday, so Kate and Geoff had been at work all day. Kate hated working on Saturdays, and today's students had all been a particularly irritating bunch of know-it-alls. The 'I don't do it that way myself, dear' types. As a result, she wasn't in a good mood.

'We need a bit of fun around this place,' Geoff said. 'It's all been too serious and boring lately.'

'Why don't you get on with your knitting if you're bored?' suggested Kate, not really listening. She was rummaging around in her desk drawer trying to find a hand mirror she'd confiscated from a student last term. Tina Jamison, touching up her make-up in the middle of a practical session.

'Ha, ha,' said Geoff. 'I'll have you know, my knitting is coming along fine. I was talking about work; making work more fun. In fact, I was thinking we could get the students to have another go at a world record,' Geoff said.

Kate glanced up briefly. Geoff was a larger than life character; the type everybody loved. He was a good friend to her, and sometimes she didn't know how she would have made it without him since her break-up. But there was no getting away from the fact that he was also stark, staring mad. 'After the last time?' she said. 'You're crazy.'

'Well, I can see now a giant Swiss roll was a bit on the ambitious side,' Geoff said, warming to his theme. 'Who'd have known it would end up being too heavy to roll up? But I reckon we could have a go at the world's biggest trifle. I've got it all planned out. We could use a temporary swimming pool to assemble it in.'

Kate shoved her hand right to the very back of the drawer beneath the pile of wayward meeting agendas, recipes and assorted odds and ends of stationery. 'And what would you make the custard in?' she asked sarcastically. 'A cement mixer?'

Geoff's face lit up. 'Brilliant idea, Katie!'

She gave him another scathing look. 'Er...durr, cement and custard ...I'm thinking grey, *solid.*'

But Geoff was inspired. 'We could borrow a new one!' he said. 'I can get us a sponsor from the building trade! It'll be fantastic!'

Kate finally tracked the mirror down inside a bundle of ancient recipes. Pulling it out, she proceeded to clean it on the elbow of her catering whites. Geoff immediately glanced over. 'What d'you want that for?' he asked.

Kate scowled at him. 'Believe me, you do not want to know!' she said.

Geoff's smirk turned into a grin. 'Believe me,' he said, 'I do!'

Which inspired Kate to toss the mirror back into the drawer and to slam the drawer firmly shut.

'Well, tough flaming luck!' she snapped, snatching up her bag and striding for the door.

'Oh, come on, Katie!' Geoff called after her. 'Don't be like that. I was only fooling around. Katie!'

But Kate carried on walking, ignoring him.

* * * * *

Over in her mock Tudor house on the Holly Croft Estate, Janet was struggling to hold onto the euphoria of her shopping trip with Estelle.

Ray had been out when she got home, so she'd gone straight up to the bedroom to put her new clothes away and to use her new hand mirror to do her homework. But then some perverse compulsion had made her strip off to examine her reflection in the full-length mirror instead, and this was an activity guaranteed to make her spirits plummet.

Janet hated her body. Or, to be more exact, she hated her stretch marks and the scars her body bore from her caesarean and her hysterectomy.

It was all very well for Estelle to say she had breasts most women would kill for. Or, for that matter, for Jade to say she was beautiful. But neither Estelle nor Jade had seen her without her clothes on. Naked, it was quite a different story.

OK, so her breasts *were* quite nice. She'd always worn a good bra, and she hadn't been able to breastfeed Debbie, so one way or another her breasts had kept their shape. But the most attractive breasts in the world would look awful above those hideous scars and stretch marks.

Looking at her reflection now, Janet traced the

100

stretch marks with her fingers. She knew Ray thought they were ugly, and he was right, they were. And there was no reason to suppose she would be any less ugly down below.

Who was she trying to kid with all those trendy clothes? She was a scared, middle-aged housewife and mother, and no amount of new clothes was ever going to change that. 'Should have called you Jane, not Janet,' her mother had told the young Janet on many occasions. 'Plain Jane. Get your looks from your father's side of the family, you do.'

Good old Mum. She always had known exactly what to say to make Janet feel inadequate.

Janet sat down on the bed, still looking at her reflection, a lump of emotion in her throat. With her own daughter, she had made it her absolute priority to ensure she had a healthy level of self-esteem. Debbie certainly didn't think she was ugly or plain or stupid. On the contrary. Sometimes Debbie was so sure of herself, Janet even wondered whether she'd taken the ego boosting too far.

'You spoil that girl,' her mother had told her repeatedly, and it was probably true. But if her daughter's self-confidence sometimes seemed to border on arrogance, then Janet told herself that was far better than her being a vulnerable mouse the way she had been herself at the same age.

Suddenly her introspection was interrupted by the sound of a car pulling into the drive. Ray! Sneaking a look out of the window to check, Janet was in time to see her husband climbing out of his car.

Instinctively, she turned back into the room to put her jeans on. But then she stopped, half in and half out of them. To hell with it. Today had been fun.

She'd really started to believe she could be somebody different; somebody confident and attractive. And maybe if Ray saw her in her new clothes, he would see it too.

Rifling quickly through her carrier bags, Janet picked out a new bra and knickers set and a fifties-inspired dress with a cinched-in waist and a closely fitting bodice. Zipped up, the dress fitted Janet's torso like a second skin.

Downstairs, she heard the front door open and close. 'Janet?' Ray called.

Janet smoothed the dress down over her hips, looking at her reflection nervously. 'I'm up here!' she called. 'In the bedroom. Come up!'

As Ray came upstairs, Janet had just enough time to put some lipstick on. Then she turned towards the door with a smile on her face.

'I've been shopping,' she said as he came in. 'What d'you think?'

Ray frowned, looking her up and down. 'It's a bit short for you, isn't it?' he said.

Immediately Janet's smile crumpled. 'Oh,' she said. 'Do you think so?' And she looked down at herself.

'Well, no offence, love,' Ray went on, 'but your legs are hardly your best feature, are they? Not now.'

'All right!' said Janet, feeling hurt and annoyed, reaching behind her to undo the dress zip.

'Well, you wouldn't want me to lie about it, would you?' said Ray, as the dress fell into a fabric pool on the floor.

'Of course not, Ray,' said Janet sarcastically, picking up the dress and starting to fold it up.

'Don't be like that,' Ray said, coming towards

102

her. 'You've got plenty of other assets.' And he began to nuzzle at her breasts with his stubbly face. 'And I do like this new bra. *Very* nice.'

Janet's instinct was to push him away, but she held back, suffering his attentions while she tried to work out how a confident sex goddess would deal with such a situation. It was true that Ray had just paid her a compliment and was making it clear he found her desirable, but that was right on the heels of implying that she had elephant legs. And since that was the part of their conversation her mind was choosing to dwell on, she just wasn't feeling very sexy.

Just then somebody rang the doorbell.

Hooray! thought Janet. *Saved by the bell!*

Ray was pushing her towards the bed. 'Ignore it!' he said, still nuzzling.

But the bell rang once again, persistently.

'Go on, Ray. It must be important,' Janet said, giving him a little push.

Ray groaned. 'Don't move!' he commanded.

Sighing, Janet lay back on the bed, listening to her husband clumping down the stairs. Then, next moment, she sprang up again, as she heard Gwen's voice.

'Ray!' Gwen said. 'I've been trying to catch you! There's something I think you ought to know about!'

Oh, no!

Quickly Janet pulled the discarded dress back on, intending to hurry down to stop Gwen from saying too much. But then, as she went to the door, she paused. It was probably too late anyway; Gwen would already have done her worst by now. And wasn't it best if Ray found out really? After all, he was always going on at her for not enjoying sex, so he should be pleased she was trying to do something about it.

Nervously, Janet sank back down onto the bed to wait for her husband. She didn't have to wait long, because just then the front door closed, and Ray began to bound back upstairs. One look at his face when he had torn the door open was enough to obliterate Janet's fragile bravado.

'Are you trying to make a complete fucking fool of me?' he demanded, eyes narrowed, one hand driving his black hair back from his face in a gesture of complete fury.

'Ray, I just– ' she started, but he wasn't in a mood for explanations.

'The whole fucking estate will think I'm crap in bed!'

'Oh, no, I don't think they– '

'When the fact is, bloody Casanova himself wouldn't be able to make you come! You are frigid, got it?' He stabbed one brutal finger in her direction. 'Fucking frigid!' And with that he turned tail and stormed down the stairs and out of the house.

Janet followed him. 'Ray!'

She reached the open front door just as he got to his car. 'And you needn't think you're going to anymore of those sodding classes, because you're not!'

'But I was only doing it for you!' Janet cried, but too late. The car door slammed behind him and seconds later the engine roared into noisy life.

As Ray drove off with a screech of tyres, Janet looking helplessly after him, a taxi pulled up outside the house from the opposite direction. The door

104

opened and Debbie got out, complete with several heavy-looking suitcases.

'Nigel's a total shit,' she told her mother. 'I've left him. And what on earth are you wearing?'

Thirteen

'Happy birthday, sweetheart.'

Reenie wished Ted would cry. If he cried, then she could *really* cry herself. But he never had, not once. Not three years ago when the phone call had come, not at the funeral, not even when they'd gone to the mortuary to identify Craig's body.

And now it seemed as if Ted's grief would remain hidden forever. At least this time he'd actually come to the graveyard, but he wasn't *really* here, was he? Not next to her while she laid the wreath on Craig's grave. No, he was off with the grandchildren, supervising a game of tag amongst the gravestones.

'He doesn't mean it, love,' she said now to Craig, kneeling on the grass, uncaring of the gathering stains on her tights. 'He loved you so much.'

'Of course he did,' Gaynor said gruffly.

'Yes,' Julie agreed.

The three of them bowed their heads, choking back emotion. Reenie reached out to straighten the wreath. It was an excuse to touch the soil of her son's grave, the nearest she could get now to touching him.

Slimmer than Reenie had thought was good for him, Craig had still been able to lift sizeable Reenie off her feet, swinging her around the kitchen in an affectionate hug, making her squeal and protest. 'How's my best Mum this morning?' he'd say.

'She'd be better if she saw you doing any work towards your exams!' she'd protest back, time and time again. Why had she done that? When she'd always known Craig wasn't the exam type? People like Craig didn't need exams. They made their own way in life.

If they lived long enough.

* * * * *

'He was only nineteen. Passed his test first time. The car was his Dad's old one. Craig worked on it; good with engines he was. First proper time out in it when it happened.'

At the next workshop, Reenie tried to share her grief with the other women. 'Every birthday I think "this year it'll be easier," but it never is. Same with the anniversary of the accident.' She hadn't intended to talk about it, but she hadn't been able to pretend nothing was wrong either. She just felt too emotional.

'Let it all out, Reenie,' Jade encouraged her. 'Let it all out.'

'I wish Janet was here,' she said, sensing that Janet, being a mother, would understand.

'Yes,' said Estelle. 'I wonder where she is?'

There was a pause. Reenie knew she ought to try to pull herself together, but somehow she just couldn't find what it took. The same as she hadn't been able to find what it took to celebrate Marcia's twenty-first the way it had deserved to be celebrated. None of the bright smiles and presents had been able to hide the true focus of all their thoughts, poor cow. Forever afterwards the anniversary of Marcia's birth would serve as a reminder that Craig, her twin, ought to be alive and celebrating his birthday too.

'Would it help to tell us exactly what happened, Reenie?' Jade asked.

Reenie shrugged. 'We don't know, not exactly. The police interviewed most of the young people on the estate, but…nothing. If any of them do know anything, they're keeping quiet. The only clear thing is there was some kind of row that turned into a race. Craig's car ended up wrapped round a lamppost, and both he and Louise, that was his girlfriend, were killed instantly.'

Jade pulled her chair closer to squeeze Reenie's hand. Reenie lifted the other hand to wipe the tears from her face.

'And the worst thing about it,' she went on, voice quavering, 'is because Craig was the one at the wheel, it feels like we haven't got the same right to be cut up about it as *her* family have. Louise's. Been feuding with us ever since, they have, the Blocks. Spit at us in the street and hurl abuse every chance they get.' Reenie sniffed. 'The kids are the worst. Louise's brothers. Marcia gets more stick than any of us. Pick on her any chance they get, they do.'

'Maybe you need to apologise. Either that or do something to make amends.'

It was unfortunate, perhaps, that it was Kate who broke the silence that greeted the end of Reenie's story. Kate, who, no matter what the provocation, was the person responsible for removing Marcia from the college course Reenie had hoped would serve as a distraction and a focus for her daughter.

'Like what?' Reenie's response was automatically hostile.

Estelle, who had been very quiet during Reenie's outpouring, spoke up in her defence. 'The girl's dead. What can Reenie possibly do about that?'

Kate shrugged, keeping her head down. 'There's these projects for young people,' she said. 'Community drama groups.'

'How is some *drama group,*' Reenie spat the words out scathingly, 'supposed to stop that lot having a go at my family?'

'Listen to what Kate has to say, Reenie,' Jade interjected persuasively.

Another shrug from Kate. 'Well, they're specialist youth workers who work with joyriders. Get them involved in video projects and stuff. I saw one film they'd made with some kids. It was quite good.' She paused, then said casually, 'I could find out about it, if you like.'

Reenie wasn't sure how to respond. She was torn between her desire to find some sort of solution to her problem and an instinctive dislike of Kate that made her resistant to anything she suggested. At the end of the last class they'd reached some sort of uneasy truce, but instinctively Reenie still couldn't bring herself to trust her. Or to like her very much.

'That sounds like an excellent idea, Kate!' Jade said. 'Doesn't it, Reenie?'

Reenie shrugged. She didn't want to admit that she was interested in the idea. 'It'd take money though, wouldn't it?' she said grudgingly. 'Something like that?'

'There's grants you can apply for,' Kate said. She paused, then said casually, 'I could look into it for you if you like.'

It was an olive branch, Reenie could see that, but

she still felt reluctant to be beholden to Kate.

* * * * *

'Look at this one, girls!' Later on in the session, Estelle looked as Reenie held up a particularly large vibrator from the pile of vibrators of all shapes, sizes, colours and functions that Jade had laid on a piece of silky cloth on the floor.

Somehow, during the last hour, they had become the 'girls' – a group. Estelle wasn't quite sure how that had happened, but it had. Maybe it had started with Reenie telling them about her son's death, and Kate's suggestion of a community project. Whatever, there had been a general shifting of opinions. Just a slight one, but no less important for that. Enough to allow them to laugh together anyway.

'It certainly puts all the men I've known to shame,' she said of the vibrator.

'Looks like it was modelled on a mule,' Kate added.

Jade took the vibrator from Reenie and switched it on. 'Actually, Kate,' she said, 'it was.'

Laughing, Reenie picked up the vibrator's box, holding it at a distance so she could read the print. 'Hey, get this!' she said. 'It's only called a Mule Rutter!'

They laughed, and Jade passed the buzzing vibrator to Kate, who moved it indecently up and down through the air, inspiring even more laughter.

'Your vibrator is your personal slave,' Jade told them. 'It awaits for your command, its only purpose to provide you with pleasure.'

Reenie was on a roll. 'Doesn't answer you back

either, does it?' she said.

As they examined more of the vibrators, Estelle kept thinking about Janet. Why wasn't she here? She was fairly sure Janet wouldn't have seen a vibrator before, and besides, she was missing all the fun. Estelle was pretty sure something drastic must have happened to keep her away. She knew how important the classes were to her new friend, and she didn't think Janet was the type to stay away on a whim.

'I'm going to phone Janet,' she told Jade, taking her phone from her bag. 'Find out what's happened to her.'

She dialled, listening to the ringing tone against a background of giggling and buzzing vibrators, but there was no answer.

'Perhaps she had to go into work or something,' Reenie suggested, trying a clitoris stimulator attachment against her nose. 'Good Gawd! You could use that to scrub floors with!' she said, and Estelle laughed, switching off her phone.

'It might take you a while to do a whole floor with that,' she said, and then, as she was putting her phone away, something, or rather someone, caught her eye at the window. 'Why!' she said. 'The dirty bastard's spying on us!'

The other three heads swivelled around to look. Bill Black was up a ladder, ostensibly cleaning the window, but clearly doing a lot more looking than cleaning.

Kate's chair scraped back. 'Oy!' she shouted, hands on hips, but Jade was already sprinting across the hall to draw the curtains with the curtain cord.

Swish! And Bill Black was obscured from view.

'Hope he falls off his bloomin' ladder!' said

111

Reenie, and they all laughed as they returned to their examination of the vibrators.

* * * * *

While all this was going on, Janet was in the superstore on the edge of town pushing a loaded shopping trolley with one squeaky wheel bleakly along the aisles.

She was miserable. Ray wasn't talking to her, Debbie was alternately whinging about Nigel and demanding to know what was wrong between Janet and her father, and, worst of all, Janet was really missing the company of her new friends. The workshops had been a bit of light in her life. Even if she never had an orgasm, it was just so nice to talk and to laugh and to try new things.

A few weeks back, she would never have thought it possible that somebody like Estelle would want to be her friend. And yet Estelle had given up loads of her precious time to help Janet choose new clothes – clothes that were now in the back of her wardrobe, probably doomed never to be worn.

'Janet!'

Blinking back into focus, Janet's heart sank even further at the sight of Gwen bearing down on her past the toilet rolls with her trolley. Well, she wasn't going to talk to her. This was all her fault.

'I'm glad to have seen you,' Gwen said, stopping by Janet's side.

Janet turned away, pretending to be very busy comparing the prices of the various toilet roll brands.

'I want to apologise.'

Janet made her choice and placed a large pack of

Supersoft lily white three-ply into her trolley, then moved on to the disinfectant.

Gwen trundled after her. 'I know I shouldn't have gone behind your back like that,' she said, 'but I only had your best interests at heart. Honestly.'

Still ignoring her, Janet reached for an extra large bottle of disinfectant.

'I care for you, Janet, you know that.'

The label on the disinfectant bottle read 'Destroys all lurking germs stone dead!' Janet put it into her trolley next to the toilet rolls, shooting a meaningful glance at Gwen as she did so.

But Gwen didn't pick up on the hint.

'Look,' she persisted, 'it's not too late. We could still enrol on class together. Didn't you want to learn to knit? I think there's a Beginner's Knitting class. Come on – say yes! It would be just like old times…'

And suddenly all Janet's fight went out of her. What was the use? It was like trying to get through a brick wall. She was fated to remain a plain, non-orgasmic, non-exciting, part-time employee and inferior attendee of adult education classes.

'I'll think about it,' she told Gwen flatly, wheeling her squeaking trolley away and quite missing her neighbour's look of triumph.

'You won't regret it!' Gwen said, 'I promise you!'

Janet didn't look back.

But later, lying next to her husband's unyielding back, the tears slid silently down her face.

Fourteen

After trying to ring Janet unsuccessfully a couple of times, Estelle went to try to track her down at Carol De Ville Interiors on her way to a meeting on the Monday morning.

'Estelle! How delightful to see you!' Cruella greeted her unctuously.

It seemed to Estelle that since she had met 'the girls', she had taken to re-examining her first impressions of people. True, Reenie was a bit common, and Kate was difficult as hell, but despite that, Estelle had come to…well, *like* them. Janet too, yes, definitely Janet. And what, apart from having bitches as mothers, had she got in common with timid, homely Janet? Somehow it didn't seem to matter.

So, if she could like such an ill-assorted, *different* bunch of women, then maybe, just maybe, she'd been too quick to judge people previously.

Take Cruella, for instance. No, *Carol.* She'd barely spoken more than a few sentences to the woman at the Businesswomen's Guild, and yet Estelle had her down as being avaricious, insincere, and incompetent in business. Now, why was that?

She scanned Carol's woman's face, noting the heavy make-up that was just a little too orange, the thin lips that were just a little too crimson. It wasn't fair to dislike someone because they were crap at choosing and applying make-up though, so she made an attempt to look beyond these superficial facts. Carol's smile was faltering slightly now beneath the force of Estelle's scrutiny, but had it been a real smile in the first place anyway? Or just an artificial stretch of those thin lips? The woman's eyes were completely unreadable, and it wasn't just because of the sixties-inspired heavy eyeliner and thick mascara.

Carol cleared her throat. 'Is everything all right, Estelle?'

Estelle blinked. 'I was looking for Janet,' she said, and the pencilled-on eyebrows lifted.

'Janet?' she repeated, making it sound as if the name was totally new to her.

'Your assistant?' Estelle prompted.

'Oh, Janet,' Cruella said, and the dismissive tone of voice she used to speak her assistant's name was quite enough to confirm her status as Cruella.

'It's her morning off,' she went on, and now the unctuousness was back in her voice. 'She'll be in this afternoon. But if you'd like to tell me what she was helping you with?'

Cruella stood there, smiling at her, waiting. Estelle believed in the smile about as much as she had ever believed in fairies at the bottom of the garden.

'Umm…' she said, thinking about Janet and their new friendship. 'Being female, I think.' She nodded, satisfied. 'Yes, Janet was helping me with being female and being a friend.'

Since Cruella was quite obviously lost for words after this, Estelle laughed and pulled a gift-wrapped package from her bag. 'Could you make sure Janet gets this?' she asked, holding the package out.

115

Cruella took it in a daze.

'And tell Janet the rest of us are meeting in the pub tonight, would you? The Rose. About eight o'clock. Thanks.' And she made for the door.

'You mean…' said Cruella behind her, 'you don't want anything from the shop?'

Estelle paused, allowing her gaze to roam dismissively around the displays. 'No,' she said. 'I don't think so.' And then she walked out, hearing with great satisfaction as she went, Cruella's 'humph' of indignation.

* * * * *

'You think she'll turn up?' Reenie asked later in the Rose.

'Not if that bitch of a boss of hers has got anything to do with it, she won't,' Estelle said. 'She's bound to have "forgotten" to give her the message.'

The Rose was neither a wine bar nor the select bar of the golf club. In short, it was not the type of licensed premises Estelle frequented. It was, in fact, Kate's local, complete with pool-playing youths and cribbage-playing old men.

Meeting here tonight had been Kate's suggestion, a suggestion that had taken both Estelle and Reenie by surprise. Estelle had agreed to come before she'd had a chance to think about it, and, walking into the pub at the appointed hour, she had paused, feeling suddenly panicked, asking herself whether she was going out of her mind. But then Reenie had spotted her.

'Estelle!' she called over-loudly, attracting the

attention of at least half the youths and all of the old men. 'Over here!'

And so, after a few seconds' more hesitation, Estelle had attached a rather Cruella-style smile onto her mouth and walked over to join Reenie and Kate at a table by the window.

That had been three gin and tonics ago. Now the cribbage-players were long gone, and the youths had lost their sense of menace due to familiarity. And although she still wasn't entirely sure how she had ended up there, Estelle was... well, much to her surprise, enjoying herself.

* * * * *

'You see all these hunks on TV, don't you?' Reenie was saying. 'All bristling muscles and jutting out jaws.'

'Minuscule dicks though, probably,' Kate said.

At the beginning of the evening, Kate was pretty certain Estelle would have flinched at such common talk, but the G & Ts seemed to be smoothing out some of her stuck-up ways. Thank God. At first she'd been a bit like aristocracy at a jumble sale. 'How good of me to stoop so low as to meet *you* two *here*,' that tight-arsed smile of hers had said. *Now* she was saying: 'Hey, don't destroy the fantasy, Kate, please!' as if the three of them were regular girly-girly mates or something.

'And they don't giggle when they have sex, do they?' Reenie said.

Estelle laughed. 'Well,' she said, 'they don't giggle on television, anyway, Reenie.'

Reenie pulled a face. 'Oh, ha ha, Estelle, very

117

funny.' she said. 'I meant in real life. I bet they don't giggle during sex in real life.'

'No sense of humour, that's why,' Kate chipped in. 'No brain, come to that!'

Estelle laughed, but Reenie was determined to have her say. 'They swagger in, all cleft chins and what d'you call it? *Ambidextrous* expressions, and get the girl swooning straight off.'

Kate grinned. 'Think you mean ambiguous, Reenie,' she said.

There was a fragment left of Reenie's original resentment towards Kate in the way she glared at her. 'Well, whatever,' she said with dignity. 'Ambidextrous or ambiguous, the effect's still the same on the girl.'

'Pussy as wet as a November weekend,' Estelle said, and there was a second of surprise before they all burst into noisy, drink-spraying laughter.

'Estelle!' Reenie said at last.

'Well, it's true, isn't it?' Estelle asked.

'You certainly don't see the actresses lathering on the KY,' Kate agreed.

Reenie's eyebrows rose towards the ceiling. 'I've needed tubes and tubes of that bloody stuff since the change, I have,' she told them.

Kate shook her head. Too much information. Definitely too much information!

'Maybe if there were more good-looking men about then none of us would have a problem,' Estelle said. 'I mean, take a look around here. Not one attractive man in sight.'

She had a point, Kate had to admit, though she was pretty certain she and Estelle wouldn't go for the same type anyway. No, Estelle wouldn't notice a

118

bloke like Ian unless he'd stopped her for speeding in that posh car of hers and she was buttering him up to try to get let off.

'D'you think it's all down to looks then, Estelle?' Reenie was asking doubtfully.

Estelle shrugged. 'The brain's the biggest erogenous zone, isn't it? It must be a lot harder for it to kick in for a balding bloke with a beer belly and body odour.'

Although she joined in with their laughter, Reenie was looking sceptical. 'Well,' she said, 'I think there's more to it than that. In his day, my Ted was really good-looking, but it's like...' She broke off unhappily. 'It's like we're buddies, not lovers. We get all giggly when we try something new, and giggly's not sexy, is it? And we're terrible at talking about it too.'

So, she wasn't the only one who found it nigh on impossible to speak about sex then. Sighing, Kate swished the last inch of her pint around in her glass, unable to find much comfort from the fact. She hadn't had a shag, been made love to, had sexual intercourse, whatever you wanted to call it – for a year, giggly or non-giggly. And she was beginning to wonder if she ever would. Or, for that matter, if she'd ever want to.

Just then the pub door opened, and in walked Geoff. Geoff, who was the real reason she was here tonight in the first place. Not content with making her join the class, he now wanted to meet her classmates.

'Just want to check them out, Katie,' he'd said winningly. 'So I can picture who you're talking about when you give me all the juicy gossip.'

119

But actually, Kate was starting to feel uneasy about doing that anyway. It was easy to promise to dish the dirt when people were strangers, but Reenie and Estelle *weren't* strangers anymore. Besides, if they ever repeated anything *she* told them, she'd fucking kill them.

Not that she had told them anything yet. To talk about her sex life with Ian would feel like breaking the Official Secrets Act. Worse still, she'd probably start howling.

No way.

Geoff was hesitating on the threshold. Kate knew full well he was waiting for her to look up and invite him over, so she shifted in her seat to give him a good view of her back.

Reenie spotted him. 'Now *there's* a halfway attractive bloke,' she said, nodding her head in Geoff's direction.

That made Kate look up. Geoff? *Attractive?*

Geoff took the look as the invitation he'd been waiting for. Over he bowled, grinning from ear to bloody ear.

'Hi Katie!' He'd ironed his shirt, by the looks of it, which had to be a first. *And* he'd trimmed his beard and rediscovered his hairbrush.

'Geoff.'

It was all Kate was intending to say, but when he kept on standing there, grinning at Reenie and Estelle like a shaggy, expectant dog, there was nothing to do but introduce him. 'This is Geoff, a friend of mine from work,' she said grudgingly. 'Geoff, this is Estelle and Reenie.'

Geoff took first Estelle's hand, then Reenie's. Kate half expected him to kiss them, but was very

120

relieved when he didn't. 'Delighted to meet you, ladies,' he said.

'You a teacher too then, Geoff?' Reenie asked.

Geoff nodded. 'Yes,' he said, 'bakery.'

Kate shot him a glare, and he smiled, finally taking the hint. 'But I'll leave you ladies to it.' He winked at Reenie. 'Remind me to tell you all about my French sticks another time.'

Reenie giggled. 'Kate, he's *gorgeous*,' she whispered after he'd gone to the bar.

'He isn't!' she protested.

'He fancies you,' Estelle told her.

'He doesn't!'

'She's right,' Reenie said. 'He does.'

Kate looked over at Geoff. He had a pint in his hand by now, and he raised it towards them in a toast. She looked quickly away, studying her own drink and feeling confused.

'He does not fancy me,' she said. 'We're just mates. And besides, I'm through with relationships.'

'You're far too young to say that,' Reenie told her.

'I am not,' Kate said. 'Anyway, what's the point? Get involved with someone, and they want to change you. So you change, and it's not enough, so you change something else. On and on until you've forgotten who you were in the first fucking place. And then they end up pissing on you anyway.'

Whoops. She hadn't intended to sound off like that. And now Estelle and Reenie were looking at her with silent sympathy.

'*What?*' she said defensively, and when Reenie reached across the table to pat her hand, she snatched it quickly out of reach. Fuck that! She didn't want their pity!

'Look, Kate,' Reenie said. 'What I said in class the other week – w ell, it wasn't a nice thing to say, and I'm sorry. I haven't got a clue why you and your husband split up, and it's none of my business either. Just so long as you know you can always talk about it if you want to.'

Kate knocked back some of her pint. 'What is this?' she said sarcastically. 'Another workshop session?'

Estelle looked her straight in the eyes. 'I don't know, Kate,' she said. '*What* is this? Tell us. After all, meeting up tonight was all your idea.'

Kate avoided Estelle's gaze. She didn't quite trust herself to speak. Her sarcastic, 'fuck you all' mask was threatening to slip again, and the seething quagmire lurking beneath it was still just too terrifying to contemplate.

'Does it have to be anything?' she asked quietly.

'I thought it was just for us to get to know each other better,' Reenie said.

'Yes,' Estelle said, 'but why?'

She was still looking at Kate, and Kate was still looking at her drink.

'Well,' said Reenie, 'because of how Jade says. If we're going to talk about stuff, then we've got to trust each other.'

'*If* we're going to talk about stuff,' Estelle said.

'Well,' said Reenie, 'trust like that doesn't come overnight,' she said. 'I'm sure we'll all talk when we're good and ready.'

'The truth is,' Estelle said, 'we probably all of us need shrinks more than we need sex therapy.'

Kate's GP had offered her counselling after the

122

split with Ian, but she'd told him where to shove it. The last thing she'd wanted to do was rake over the red-hot coals and bring the fire back to leaping light. No, she'd wanted the choking dust to settle on the embers, and that had been best achieved with a prescription for brain-numbing drugs.

Except that even the very strongest dose hadn't seemed able to wipe out the image of Ian suckling on fucking Jennifer's nipple.

'So, what's your story then Estelle?' Reenie was saying. 'Why all the affairs?'

Kate watched the same defensive expression she was wearing herself appear on Estelle's face. 'It's obvious, isn't it?' she said. 'I'm a commitment phobe with severe attachment difficulties. I have no intention of being *owned*, ever.'

'My Ted doesn't own me,' Reenie said, sounding startled.

'Doesn't he?' Estelle asked. 'Are you sure about that? Whose idea was it for you to go to the workshops in the first place?'

Hostility was suddenly bristling in the air. 'Maybe we shouldn't try playing at being amateur shrinks,' Kate said.

'Yeah,' Reenie said, glaring at Estelle. 'Maybe we shouldn't at that. But for your information, it was *my* decision to go to the workshops. Ted had the idea, but there was no force involved. Ted's never forced me to do anything.'

Estelle sighed. 'I didn't mean to offend you, Reenie,' she said.

'Maybe you should ask him to use force,' Kate said. 'Might be just what you're lacking. Some people swear by a spot of S and M, don't they?'

Reenie turned her glare in Kate's direction for a moment, but when Estelle started to laugh, the tension suddenly lifted.

'Hark at us lot,' Reenie said. 'More defensive than bloody Colditz.'

'Well,' said Estelle, reaching for her purse. 'Maybe another drink will help us to escape. Same again?'

'She needs bringing down a peg or two, that's her trouble.' Reenie said of Estelle as she went up to the bar. 'But she's all right really, I suppose.' She looked at Kate. 'And you.'

'Yeah?' said Kate sceptically. 'Forgiven me, have you?'

Reenie pulled a face. 'Wouldn't go that far,' she said, but Kate recognised it for the apology it was and smiled.

Reenie smiled back. 'So,' she said, 'it was that Geoff who challenged you to do the course, was it?'

Kate nodded, glancing over at Geoff, who appeared to be in deep conversation with Estelle. 'It was, actually, yes.'

Reenie's grin was wicked. 'Wonder why he did that then, eh?' she said.

Kate didn't reply. She had thought it was just Geoff, taking their dare games to another level. But had he really had a very different motive?

Nah, that was a crazy thought.

Wasn't it?

Fifteen

Janet hadn't got the message about going out for a drink with the others, and she was feeling thoroughly depressed. It was as if she had never experienced the excitement of workshops. Life was back to depressing normality, with Carol De Ville being her usual nagging and critical self, Debbie sulking about Nigel, and Ray still being cool towards her. Although one distinct advantage of this was that he didn't want to have sex.

Escaping to the toilet out the back of Carol De Ville Interiors for five minutes, Janet knew she oughtn't to be thinking of avoiding sex as an advantage. She was hardly likely to become a sensual woman in tune with her inner sex goddess if she did.

Because Janet had decided that, classes or not, she definitely *did* want to become such a woman. Not only so that she could experience the pleasure of sex, but also because she was pretty sure that the confidence and sense of well-being such pleasure would bring would spill over into all areas of her life.

Surely?

Jade said it would, anyway, and Jade certainly seemed to be very confident. Look at the way she had handled that caretaker. And Estelle, Kate and Reenie, come to that, because they were all very strong personalities. *And* they didn't much like each other. Without Jade's authority, the workshops would soon disintegrate into chaos with the girls squabbling with each other.

The girls. How she missed them all. Did they think about her? Wonder where she was? And had any of them had an orgasm yet?

Estelle, at least, had tried to phone. When Janet had switched her mobile on, she had seen several missed calls from her. She'd tried to ring her at home too. Debbie had taken the call.

'Some woman phoned yesterday while you were out, Mum,' Debbie had told her.

'Who?' Janet had asked.

'I dunno.' Since returning to her parents' home, Debbie seemed to have adopted the same offhand tone of voice she had used as a teenager. 'Some posh woman.'

Janet had kept meaning to call Estelle back, but somehow she didn't get round to it. Estelle was young, single and strong; she wouldn't understand why Janet couldn't find the courage to just to defy Ray and return to the workshops. Come to that, she probably wouldn't understand why Janet was with such a dyed-in-the-wool chauvinist as Ray in the first place.

Flushing the toilet, Janet washed her hands, wondering how she could further her plans to become more sensually aware without the workshops. Going without knickers and having luxurious baths was all very well, but she was hardly likely to have an orgasm that way, was she?

No, she was just going to have to have another bash at masturbation. She had tried it before, of course, with no luck, but maybe if she tried again?

126

Perhaps she could buy some sort of book to help her. Although she would have to keep it hidden from Ray. And it might not be that easy to find the privacy to try it out. Debbie said she had flu now, and she was off work, lounging around the house.

Janet's conscience bit her. Poor Debbie. If she said she had flu, then she *did* have flu. Why should she pretend? And she had just split up with Nigel too. *Of course* she was going to mope about. What sort of a mother was she, wishing her daughter were out of the way so she could practise masturbating?

'*Selfish,*' her mother's voice told her inside her head. '*You are a very selfish and uncaring person.*'

'Janet!' Carol De Ville greeted her with a frown when she finally returned to the shop. 'There you are! I've been rushed off my feet with customers, and Mr George is waiting to have his delivery checked! See to it, would you?'

John George's eyes twinkled at her over the pile of boxes on the shop counter. The last time Janet had seen him had been on that very windy day at church – the day she hadn't been wearing any knickers. Not, of course, that he'd known that, but even so... She smoothed her skirt down over her hips, doing her best not to blush.

'Thinks she's Lady Muck, she does,' John whispered to her out of the side of his mouth.

Janet smiled. 'She does rather,' she whispered back. She liked John; it was difficult not to. He was such a friendly, good-humoured man, especially since his divorce six months previously.

Janet had never liked John's wife, Audrey. She was one of life's backbiters, never happy with her lot and determined that nobody else should be either.

127

Easy-going John had always been first in the line of fire for her poison, and over the years, Janet had often wondered why he didn't leave her.

But in the end it had been Audrey herself who had done the leaving, running off with a neighbour in the village where they lived. The affair had lasted a total of three weeks before Audrey realised that the grass *wasn't* greener and returned to her husband, blithely expecting to be able to pick up the reins again. But by then it was too late. John had experienced the heady delights of freedom, peace and quiet and beer and curry in front of the TV. In short, he had come to his senses, so he had politely, but very firmly, refused to have her back.

'Settles her accounts like the aristocracy too,' John said of Carol De Ville. 'Months behind, she is.'

Carol De Ville always settled her bills and accounts late. It was an unofficial part of Janet's job to stall suppliers about their invoices. She absolutely hated doing it, and she got no thanks for it either.

'Whoops!' said John, 'Best get on, she's looking daggers at us.'

Stifling a giggle, Janet picked up the checklist for John's order. John dealt in Victoriana, and today's order was for door furniture. 'Two dozen brass finger plates, assorted designs,' she read.

John opened a box, picking out samples to show her. 'Ten basket weave, six cherub and eight figurine.'

Janet placed a tick by the side of brass fingerplates. John replaced the plates in the box and put it to one side.

'Brass door knobs,' Janet read next.

'Egg-shaped, quantity twenty.'

128

Janet ticked brass doorknobs and moved her pen down the list. 'Free-hanging robe hooks.'

'French-style, quantity one dozen.'

Tick.

'Cast iron door hooks.'

John rearranged the boxes to get to the right one. Janet reached for the ticked off boxes and shoved them beneath the counter to make some space for him.

'Ram's head design, quantity two dozen,' he said, holding one of them up.

Janet placed a tick next to 'Cast iron door hooks,' becoming aware as she did so of a strange buzzing sound nearby. Puzzled, she swivelled round, searching for the source.

'I think it's coming from beneath the counter,' she said.

John George paused in the act of closing the box of door hooks. 'Sounds like your electrics,' he said, leaving the box and coming round to take a look.

Carol De Ville bustled over, frowning. 'What *is* that noise?' she asked.

'We're not sure,' Janet said, just as John brought out Estelle's gift-wrapped package from beneath the counter where it had been jogged by the boxes Janet had just shoved there. The package was making a loud, mysterious buzzing sound.

'That's yours,' Carol De Ville told Janet irritably. 'Estelle Morgan brought it in for you yesterday.'

Mystified, Janet took the package from John's hand.

'Well,' said Carol De Ville, 'you'd better open it!'

And so, watched by both her boss and John George, Janet did so. And brought out... a box.

Whatever was causing the buzzing was clearly inside it, and, even without the vivid full-colour pictures and the emblazoned name of 'Mule Rutter!', it was patently obvious what it was.

'Well, really!' said Carol De Ville, scandalised.

John George began to laugh. 'Mule Rutters, life-size,' he announced. 'Quantity one.'

* * * * *

At lunchtime Janet was alone in the shop, a still outraged Carol having gone out on an appointment. The Mule Rutter was burning a hole in Janet's handbag beneath the counter. If the thought of finding the privacy to masturbate had been difficult, then Janet had no idea how she was supposed to use something that buzzed quite so loudly as the Mule Rutter.

But remembering once again her boss's scandalised face, Janet couldn't help letting out a snort of laughter. A woman who was browsing through some colour charts looked over at her. Janet 'sneezed', pretending to dust a display. 'Don't know where all the dust comes from, do you?' she said, but then she caught sight of Estelle's package poking out of the top of her bag and snorted again, louder this time.

She wasn't too surprised when the woman left shortly afterwards.

Whoops! For all Carol De Ville's earlier protes-tations about being rushed off her feet, trade had been pretty slack lately. Carol really needed all the customers she could get.

Smirking to herself, Janet reached down to her

130

bag to tease the gift-wrap aside. Whether she ever used it or not, the Mule Rutter was so fantastic, she just had to take another peek. Next thing she knew, the wrapping paper was off, the box was open and she was holding the 'veined' shaft of the Mule Rutter in her hand.

Blimey. It was incredible, absolutely incredible. Were mules really so well endowed? Poor lady mules! Or was it *enviable* lady mules?

As Janet was pondering this question, the shop door pinged.

'Oh!' Hastily thrusting the Mule Rutter under the counter, Janet stood up, red-faced, to see…Estelle, Reenie and Kate, striding determinedly towards her like characters from a western.

'We've come to order you to come back to the classes,' Estelle told her.

Kate stepped forwards. 'Yeah,' she said, hands on hips. 'And we're not taking "no" for an answer.'

Reenie tried, and failed, to keep the same straight face as her friends. 'You'd better believe it, sister…' she managed to say before her voice dissolved into giggles.

Janet looked at the three of them – her new, her *dear* friends, and her eyes filled with tears. 'But what about Ray?' she said tremulously. 'You see, Gwen told him all about it and he banned me from going again!'

Estelle shrugged. 'Sod Ray,' she said.

Sod Ray. She wanted it to be as simple as that, but it wasn't, was it? If she went behind Ray's back and he found out, then she would be in big trouble. *Their marriage* would be in big trouble.

Isn't it in trouble anyway, though? asked a voice

inside her head, and suddenly Janet remembered her husband's expression after he'd been confronted by Gwen. He'd been so furious, mouthing off at her and not even giving her the chance to explain herself. He'd acted towards her like some sort of stern parent.

For some reason Janet found herself suddenly thinking of another man's expression: laughing, affectionate, and about as different to a stern parent as it was possible for anyone to be. John George, when she had pulled the buzzing vibrator from its packaging earlier that day.

'You've already got me into big trouble today,' she told Estelle, pointing a finger at her and beginning to smile.

'Me?' asked Estelle, mock innocent, and Janet wiped a tear away, reaching below the counter for the Mule Rutter. She held it aloft, grinning.

Reenie burst out laughing. Janet flicked the switch to make the vibrator buzz. Kate cheered.

'So?' asked Estelle cheekily. 'Are you coming back to the classes?'

'I want to,' Janet said. 'But I'd have to go behind Ray's back if I did.'

'Well,' said Reenie. 'Look at it this way. He's the one who's likely to benefit if you're transformed into an all-singing all-dancing Sex Goddess, isn't he? In my exper-ience men don't always know what's good for them!'

'That's true,' Janet said thoughtfully.

'Come on, Janet,' Estelle urged her. 'Say yes. You know you want to!'

Janet smiled. She still didn't like the idea of going behind Ray's back, but it served him right for reacting the way he had. 'All right, then. Yes,' she

132

said quietly. 'Yes, I'll come back to the classes.'

Estelle grinned at her, thrilled. 'Don't you mean, "Yes! Yes! Yes"?' she asked, her voice getting louder and louder with every word, and Janet laughed and came round the other side of the counter to give her a hug.

Sixteen

'Remember, ladies, don't neglect your perineum!' Jade told them in her usual over-the-top style. 'Caressing this delicious soft spot will be a revelation, believe me. And your man will love it if you caress his too.'

'Didn't even know I had one!' Reenie whispered out of the side of her mouth to Kate. Which was the truth. Well, almost the truth. She'd known about the bit of skin between her vagina and her anus, but not what it was called. And definitely not that it might hold the secret of untold pleasure…

'Sure you don't mean primula, Jade?' Kate said, and everybody laughed.

'You can call it what you like, Kate,' Jade said. 'Just don't let it go to waste!'

Kate grinned in Reenie's direction. The pair of them had become halfway matey with each other, against all the odds. A few more weeks and Reenie had decided to have a go at persuading her to try to fix it to let Marcia go back to college, but she didn't want to push it. Best to be subtle; let her think it was all her idea.

Maybe she should use the same principle to get Ted massaging her perineum. Because the fact was, even though the classes had been Ted's idea, ever since she'd been attending, he'd been having a spot of trouble in the bedroom department. Kept on about not finding the whole business intimidating, but since the evidence kept on saying something quite different, that didn't quite wash with Reenie. In fact, a couple of times lately she thought he might have been hinting that she could pack the classes in if she wanted to. Not that she had any intention of doing *that.* The classes were a real bright spot in her week.

'Before you all go,' Jade was saying now, 'here's this week's tip for getting you in the mood for raunchy sex. It has the added bonus of keeping you fit at the same time.' And she reached into a bag to pull out a glittery, jingly piece of fabric.

'Belly dancing,' she announced, tying the fabric around her hips and giving them a quick wiggling demonstration. 'Here, have a go yourselves.'

Which was how Reenie and the others ended up with a glittery scarf thing tied around their hips, attempting to shimmy along with Jade to some Arabian-sounding music from Jade's iPod.

'Liquid spine, sensual hips,' Jade kept on saying, making it look easy. 'That's the way, Reenie.'

It was? Blimey. Though, come to think of it, those sultan types liked a woman with a bit of flesh on them, didn't they? Maybe she should have become a belly dancer earlier on in life.

'Where d'you get these scarf things from, Jade?' she asked at the end of the session.

'I send away for them, Reenie,' Jade told her. 'But you can borrow that one, if you like.'

'Thanks. I think I will.'

Jade was reaching down into her bag again. 'There's a bra to match if you'd like,' she said, and held out a large, tasselled bra to Reenie.

'That'll get your hubby going,' Kate said as Reenie jiggled the bra about, making the tassels swing.

'I hope so,' Reenie said, wrapping the bra in the glittery shawl.

'Remember, Reenie,' Jade said. 'If belly dancing *doesn't* get your husband going, as Kate puts it, it doesn't matter. The really important thing at this stage is that it gets *you* going. After an erotic belly dancing session, you should feel ready for pleasure. And it doesn't matter whether that pleasure is provided by your husband or yourself…'

Later that evening, dressed in both bra and glittery scarf, Reenie jiggled and gyrated like a good 'un, doing her best not to feel like a total prat, while Ted just sat there at the head of the bed, arms folded, a big stupid grin on his face.

'Wait 'til I tell the lads about this,' he said, 'they'll be green with envy.'

'Don't you dare, Ted Richardson!' she said, slightly breathless, stopping to take a breather. 'Don't you dare!'

After five solid minutes of belly dancing, Reenie's back was killing her, her heart was pumping like billy-o and, by the looks of him, Ted was just amused, not aroused.

'Only joking, love,' he said, laughing.

'You'd better be!' Reenie said, but beneath the bantering tone, she felt disappointed and let down. Where were the results Jade had promised? By the looks of things, Ted wasn't about to fall on her anytime soon, and it was difficult to tell whether *she* was feeling aroused when all she felt like was a figure of fun.

136

Stomping irritably across the room, Reenie took her battered old dressing gown from the back of the door and put it on. Ted looked crestfallen. *Now* he looked crestfallen.

'Oh,' he said. 'That the end of the show then?'

'Yep,' Reenie grunted.

'Sorry, love,' Ted said. 'I was taking the mickey, wasn't I?'

'Just a bit, yes,' she said, sitting on the side of the bed to brush her hair.

'Come on,' he said coaxingly. 'I didn't mean anything by it. You looked fantastic.'

Reenie didn't reply. Sparks fairly flew from the hairbrush.

'You always look fantastic to me, Reen.'

Then why in almost forty years had she never, not once had an orgasm? And why, when they were supposed to have such a good, strong marriage, couldn't they talk about it properly?

'Reen?' he said, sounding worried now.

The doorbell rang downstairs. Reenie tossed down her brush and went to answer it, grateful for the interruption.

* * * * *

It was the first time Kate had ventured onto the Larkton Estate; she'd never had any reason to go there before. Walking through to Reenie's house, she felt self-conscious, waiting to be recognised. Half her students lived on the estate. But in the end she saw nobody she knew, and she reached Reenie's house without incident.

Reenie's house stood out from the others around

it, mainly because of the garden. Even in the half-light of evening it was obvious someone spent loads of time on it.

She and Ian had done a lot of gardening. Trips to the garden centre, propagating seedlings in the greenhouse, neat rows of onions and potatoes, moss killer on the lawn – the lot. The day after she'd caught Ian sucking on Jennifer's tits, Kate had filled a gallon can with petrol at the local petrol station, taken it back to that pristine patch of green and used it to spell out the words 'cheating bastard.'

Then she'd set fire to it.

Ever since then, she hadn't so much as tended a houseplant.

Kate quickly knocked on Reenie's door before she had the chance to change her mind. Three weeks ago, two weeks even, she would never have dreamt she'd be doing this. She'd had zero intentions of getting involved on any level whatsoever with any of the other workshop attendees. A lot of sad women without enough to do, that's what she'd had them down as, not individuals with feelings and problems of their own.

And now here she was, come to do something she knew would please Reenie. She was going to have a word with Marcia with a view to her returning to college. Just like the old Kate would have done. She was going soft; had to be.

'Kate! Hello!' Reenie opened the door in her dressing gown, which seemed to suggest to Kate that she'd come at a bad time, but Reenie's smile seemed genuine enough, and there had been warmth as well as surprise in her voice.

'Sorry,' Kate said. 'You're having a bath or

138

something.'

Reenie smiled, unfastening her dressing gown to give Kate a flash of – belly dancing outfit. 'Or something,' she said. 'But I'd just called a halt anyway. But don't just stand there! Come on in!'

Wiping her feet carefully, Kate crossed the threshold to be welcomed into an interior that was all peach paint, plush carpets and family photos. Very Reenie.

'You're in luck. I was just going to put the kettle on,' Reenie said, bustling ahead, presumably towards the kitchen.

'I came to have a chat with Marcia actually,' Kate told her, and Reenie instantly stopped and turned back, her face emotional.

'Oh, Kate, that *is* good of you!' she said. 'As luck would have it the little minx happens to be in tonight, which is a very rare thing, I can tell you! Backtracking along the hall, Reenie yelled up the stairs. 'Marcia! Somebody to see you!'

Above their heads, there was the sound of a bed creaking as someone got down from it, then footsteps. A door on the landing opened.

'Who is it?' Surly voiced and snaggle-haired, Marcia appeared at the top of the stairs. 'Fuck!' she said when she recognised Kate.

'Less of that talk, if you please!' Reenie told her. 'Come on. Get down here. Kate's come all this way specially to see you.'

'Needn't have bothered,' her daughter said sulkily, but she traipsed down the stairs anyway.

Like her mother, Marcia was also wearing a dressing gown, but somehow Kate doubted whether it was concealing evidence of belly dancing activity.

139

The girl looked ill. Ill and depressed. And suddenly, Kate was glad she'd come.

After that, it was easy. Kate had always been good at communicating with the kids she taught. *Wanting* to communicate was seventy percent of it. Interpreting the sulks, pouts, nail-biting and stumbled words made up the other thirty percent. Before her marriage blow up, Marcia and Stuart's chip pan altercation would never have happened. Kate would have been on the case at the first warning signs.

Which made the whole ugly incident partly her fault.

'I didn't decide to do it, Miss,' Marcia said, after a long, pouting, nail-biting pause Kate patiently waited out. 'It just sort of happened.'

Kate nodded. 'I can buy that,' she said. 'Dickhead saying hurtful things, hot chip pan close by…yes, I can buy the whole "just happening" thing. Thing is,' she said, looking Marcia in the eye, 'what if it had been dickhead saying hurtful things and a loaded gun close by?'

Marcia coloured and looked down.

Kate sighed and took pity on her. 'Look,' she said, 'I know my arrest after I split up with my husband is common knowledge with you lot.'

Marcia looked up again, interested.

'And I know that probably means you think I've got no right to tell you what you can or can't do with hot chip pans.' She paused for a moment, and then went on. 'But just because *I* was a vengeful, stupid cow, doesn't mean you have to be, Marcia,' she said. 'The Stuarts of this world just aren't worth messing up your life for.'

Or the Ians.

Kate knew she would never forget the ensuing interview with the College Principal. Ian didn't press charges; even *he* couldn't morally do that, but the local press had a field day nevertheless. After all, it isn't every day a scorned woman almost sets fire to the marital home by burning vengeful words onto her front lawn. The whole town knew about it in no time. Kate even found herself held in high esteem by other women who had suffered a similar fate. But none of that washed with the Principal.

'This simply isn't the example we want our lecturers to set to our students, Kate,' she'd said.

She'd been right, of course, although Kate hadn't been thinking about her students as she stood, arms folded, watching those two blazing words with intense satisfaction as Ian panicked about, alternately calling the fire brigade and trying to beat out the flames with the welcome doormat.

'I think it was cool, Miss, what you did,' Marcia said now, and Kate carefully hid a smile.

'I don't think so, Marcia. And as for what you did; if that chip fat had been any hotter, you'd be in prison by now. Really. As it is…' Kate looked into the vulnerable dark eyes of Reenie's youngest daughter. 'I've spoken to the Principal and explained the background to…what happened. I've also spoken to Stuart. I don't think he'll give you any more trouble.'

Marcia looked sceptical at that, so Kate looked at her sternly. 'Look, if you're going to come back to college, Marcia,' she said, 'you're going to have to put this whole thing completely behind you. Which means forgiving and forgetting. Is that understood?'

Marcia looked right back at her. 'Is that what

you've done, Miss?' she said. 'Forgiven and forgotten?'

It was a fair question, and it deserved an honest answer. 'No,' she said. 'I haven't. But I'm hoping you've got more strength of character than I have. Because if you have, you can come back to college.'

Marcia's whole face lit up. It was touching really. 'Can I, Miss?' she said, a sudden glow wiping the surly expression right from her face.

Kate smiled. 'But only for one month's trial to start with, OK?'

* * * * *

'Thank you *so* much, Kate!' Reenie said emotionally when she heard the news, enveloping Kate in a fluffy dressing-gowned hug.

'It's only for a probationary period at first, Reenie,' Kate said, but she might just as well have not spoken.

'Thank you, thank you!' Reenie said again. 'Thank you *so* much! You're a real star, you are!'

And so, when Kate walked back through the council estate towards home, that's how she felt – like a star. Or at least, more like her old self. So it was a shame when entering the High Street that the first thing she saw was Ian in a clinch with Jennifer outside the kebab shop.

The next day at work, Kate had a hangover to end all hangovers, having gone straight from the scene of the Ian and Jennifer mega snog to the Black Horse.

At break time, Geoff brought her a giant mug of coffee and a Mars bar. 'Look, Katie,' he said kindly, 'if doing these workshops is messing with your head,

142

you can always give it up, you know. I won't take the piss. Well, not much, anyway. And I can always give you an especially difficult word to drop into a meeting to make up for the fact that I'm still doing Beginner's Knitting. Orgasm, maybe. Or vagina.'

Kate lifted her head from her hands for long enough to give him a look. 'Get lost, Brannigan,' she said.

* * * * *

The next workshop was the most risqué yet. There they were, knickers off, actually *touching* themselves, in front of each other! OK, the curtains were tactfully drawn and they'd taken the precaution of wedging furniture in front of the door to stop anyone coming in, but even so…

'Remember, no direct contact just yet. Our aim here is just to tease and tantalise until your clitoris is crying out for attention.'

Kate was following Jade's directions along with the others, even though she had absolutely zilch expectations of having an orgasm or even of becoming aroused. Mind you, she suspected the others felt exactly the same way she did. Janet had looked shocked as hell when Jade had told them all to whip their knickers off. Reenie had made some wisecrack or other, but she'd blushed scarlet while she was doing it. Even Estelle had been uncomfortable about it, for all her cool exterior. Well, who wouldn't? Masturbating in public just wasn't natural unless you were wearing a stained beige raincoat.

'That's it,' Jade was encouraging them. 'Now, try

applying just a little more pressure.'

When the door handle suddenly began to rattle as someone tried to get into the hall, it was almost a welcome interruption.

'Somebody's trying to get in!' Janet shrieked, and then all four of them were all scrabbling about for their underwear.

Pulling on her jeans as she went, Kate shunted the piled-up pair of tables out of the way and yanked the door open. The diminutive figure of Dick Black, the caretaker, peered at her from the other side of the door.

'What d'you think you're playing at?' Kate growled, enjoying the confrontation.

'You…you can't block a fire exit like that!' Dick Black blustered fearfully, and then Jade was at Kate's shoulder.

'It's all right, Kate,' she said. 'I'll deal with this, thank you.' And Jade manoeuvred the caretaker from the hall and out into the vestibule.

'Well done, mate!' Reenie said, clapping Kate on the shoulder.

'Can you imagine if he'd got in and caught us in the act?' Janet said, horrified.

Outside the room, Kate could hear Jade talking to the caretaker with persuasive charm. It was all too easy to imagine her 'accidentally' popping a button on her blouse to dazzle him with her cleavage. Jade, Kate thought, was definitely not above using feminine wiles to get what she wanted from a man. It was something she'd never done herself, and could never imagine doing either. For one thing, she would need to be a feminine kind of woman, and she had never been that.

'Right,' Jade said, coming back into the room, metaphorically dusting her hands. 'He shouldn't trouble us again. Knickers off again, ladies! We've got work to do!'

As she followed the others back over to the chairs, Kate thought about Geoff. He would definitely appreciate Jade's turn of phrase. It was right up his street.

Seventeen

As she looked at her reflection in her bedroom mirror, Janet felt self-conscious in a skirt and top she'd never worn before. Estelle had helped her to pick them out on their shopping trip, but now, when she looked at herself in the mirror, Janet could hear Ray making disparaging remarks about her legs. He wasn't around to do the same thing this evening; ever since their falling out and Debbie's arrival back home, Ray had been taking himself off to the golf club a lot. But whether he was around or not, Janet could still hear his discouraging tone of voice loud and clear.

The top looked all right, didn't it? Or was it a little too *obvious*, for someone of her age? Normally she didn't wear red. The colour was just too attention catching. Though it did suit her, she had to admit.

Oh, it was all so difficult, this image business. And if she didn't get a move on, she was going to be very late indeed meeting up with Estelle.

'Bloody hell, Mum! You're not seriously going out in that, are you?'

The moment Janet set foot in the living room, Debbie, who was sprawled on the sofa dressed in a pair of cutesy bunny-patterned pyjamas watching an ancient repeat of *Who Wants to Be a Millionaire*, trampled on her mother's already flimsy self-

146

confidence.

Janet immediately went over to the mirror to look yet again at her reflection. 'What's wrong with it?' she asked.

'Well, even I don't wear my skirts that short,' Debbie barged on. 'And I'm

not–'

'All right!' Janet interrupted, hurt.

'Well come on, Mum,' Debbie continued only slightly more kindly. 'What's got into you lately? You're out all the time, you're dressing like…like… And you're not even *trying* to make things up with Dad!'

Janet pressed her lips together stubbornly. 'Your father's hardly ever in these days, in case you haven't noticed!' she snapped. 'And even when he is, I don't see *him* trying to make things up with *me*!'

'You won't even tell me what you've fallen out about!' Debbie said accusingly. '*And* I thought you'd want to spend some time with me while I'm here!' Debbie's voice had turned whiny and self-pitying, and Janet slumped down onto a chair, feeling instantly guilty.

'Debbie,' she said, 'it's Saturday night. I know you've been ill, but you're better now. You should be out with your friends if you're not going to try and patch things up with Nigel.'

'And *you* should be at home watching TV!' Debbie accused.

She was probably right too. Most people of her age would be. Or at least, they wouldn't be on their way to some trendy wine bar dressed in clothes too impossibly young for them. Maybe she ought to get changed and stay at home. After all, she didn't want

147

to embarrass Estelle in front of her business friends.

She might have done just that, but before she could, her new mobile phone began to ring. It was the first time it had, and the jaunty ring tone filled her with panic. It was so much more complicated to use than her old one had been, and she searched for it desperately in her handbag, anxious to shut it up.

'And since when did you have a mobile as flash as that?' Debbie asked, sounding scandalised.

But Janet was squinting at her phone, trying to remember what button she was supposed to press to answer a call, so she didn't reply. In the end she took a guess, which turned out to be right.

'It's me,' Estelle said on the other end of the line. 'Just phoning to check you weren't thinking of bottling out.'

The sound of her new friend's voice lent Janet some much-needed courage. 'No,' she said resolutely, turning her back on the mirror. 'I'm just on my way. See you in ten minutes.'

And she put the phone back in her bag and stood up, resisting the urge to pull her skirt further down towards her knees. 'Right, I'm off then,' she said brightly to Debbie. 'See you later.'

Debbie stared at the TV screen, her arms folded mutinously. Janet walked past her to the door. At the very last moment, she looked back. 'And remember,' she said, 'you could always phone a friend.'

It wasn't until she had nearly reached the wine bar that she realised how the comment could have been taken, bearing in mind the programme her daughter had been watching.

* * * * *

148

Had her friends always been such shallow bitches, or was she just seeing them as they truly were for the first time?

In the Last Wine Bar, waiting for Janet to arrive, Estelle listened to the chatter of the other three women at the table. Marie, Rosa and Cora were all businesswomen like her; she knew them from the local Businesswomen's Guild. Marie ran a travel agency, Rosa managed the family catering empire, and Cora was an executive for a hotel chain. All three were extremely successful in their particular fields. But had they always been so bitchy? Normally Estelle let their sniping wash over her, but tonight she listened to it properly. Anyone they knew seemed to be fair game. It wasn't difficult to guess that this same policy would be extended both to her and to each other.

Was that what she was like herself?

When Janet appeared in the doorway, dressed in some of her new clothes and obviously nervous as hell, Estelle was pleased to see her. But she was also aware of a huge sense of responsibility. Poor Janet, she was so genuine and good. It was like throwing a lamb into a lion's den, exposing her to this lot.

'Janet!' Estelle got up to kiss her, a gesture of impulsive and genuine warmth. 'You look nice.' It was only halfway true. The clothes suited her, yes, but Janet was sort of *shrinking* inside of them. Nerves, no doubt. And her make-up was a bit on the clownish side. Not to mention her hair... Estelle longed to persuade Janet to move on from her rather starchy image, but it hadn't seemed a good idea to try to do too much at once.

149

But now, as she drew Janet forward to introduce her to her friends, she wished she had been a bit more insistent. The bitches were already clocking her hair and make-up dismissively.

'Everybody,' Estelle said, still in the same artificially bright voice, 'this is a new friend of mine, Janet. Janet, this is Rosa, Marie and Cora.'

There were polite murmurs of greeting, and then Estelle sat Janet next to her and poured her a very large glass of wine.

'Janet works with Carol,' she told the others to forestall any awkward questions about how they knew each other.

'Oh,' said Marie. 'Then you're an interior designer?'

Estelle jumped in quickly before Janet could speak apologetically about her job. 'Yes, she is,' she said, smiling encouragingly at Janet.

Janet drank some wine.

'How interesting,' said Marie, gazing speculatively between Estelle and Janet, her shrewd mind obviously busy at work.

'So Janet,' Cora said. 'What d'you think the next big design trend is going to be? Where should we all be heading?'

This time there seemed little choice but to let Janet fend for herself. Willing her not to make a complete tit of herself, Estelle waited with the others while her friend drank some more wine and finally put her glass down.

'Belly dancing,' she said.

Belly dancing?

'That is, the harem. Bringing the harem right into the living room.'

Excellent!

Estelle was so pleased with the startled reactions of her friends she shot Janet a broad grin. 'Fantastic, eh?' she said to the others. 'Because how many of us restrict our lovemaking to the bedroom anyway?'

There was a moment or two more of stunned silence, and then Marie began to laugh.

'Good point,' she said. 'Good point.'

And suddenly everyone was laughing.

'What about another bottle of wine?' Estelle said, putting in an order, and then she sat back to relax, confident that everything was going to be all right.

* * * * *

If she *were* an interior designer, about to launch a collection inspired by the harem onto a receptive public, would she be like these women, Janet wondered? They were so well groomed. It looked as if a make-up artist had done their make-up. And their hair! It was so shiny, so well cut and styled! Not a grey hair in sight, although Marie and Rosa were older than Estelle and Cora. Had they had to learn how to look so immaculate, or had it always come naturally?

You couldn't look at them and be in any doubt that they were highly successful women, all of them. White-toothed, perfectly manicured, carefully displaying exactly the right amount of jewellery; Janet thought they were positively terrifying. And Estelle looked right at home with them all. But Janet wasn't afraid of Estelle. Not anymore anyway.

Where on earth had that harem idea come from? Still, it seemed to have worked anyway, which was a stroke of luck. She had spoken so totally off the top of her head, it could just as easily have been disastrous. What if she'd said: 'cartoon characters. Bringing cartoon characters into the living room from the television.'

The idea made her laugh out loud. Fortunately, it happened when the others were laughing at something – Janet had no idea what – that Marie had just said, so she got away with it without comment. But later, after she and Estelle had left the others with much air kissing and 'nice to meet yous' and were walking a little drunkenly along the High Street, Janet told her about it.

'You *are* taking the mickey,' Estelle said, and suddenly they were both hooting with laughter. 'The idea is downright *Goofy*.'

Janet's stomach hurt. 'Oh don't!' she said, stopping to clutch it, laughing helplessly.

'Thanks for tonight,' she said after she'd recovered enough to walk on. 'It was fun. Your friends are– '

'Absolute bitches,' Estelle interrupted.

It was nothing but the truth. 'Well…' she said, but broke off as Estelle pulled a face.

'It's all right,' she said. 'I know what they're like. More than ever perhaps since I met you.'

Drunk as she was, Janet still detected an edge of emotion in Estelle's voice. She linked her arm in hers affectionately. 'You're nice to me,' she said. 'Really nice.'

'I'm not sure I know how to do nice,' Estelle said as they walked along together companionably.

'Don't run yourself down,' Janet wanted to say, but it seemed such a ridiculous thing to say to confident, successful Estelle that she didn't.

'Of course you do,' she said instead. 'You're a natural.'

'My female employees wouldn't agree with you.' Estelle said. 'They loathe me.'

'Oh, I'm sure they don't!'

'Believe me,' Estelle assured her, 'they do.'

Janet suddenly remembered when Estelle had regarded her as if she were some sort of insect deserving of being ground underfoot the time she had dropped the baguette on her foot in the sandwich shop. 'Perhaps they're just jealous,' she said. Because *she* had been jealous of Estelle. Still was, really. She couldn't even begin to imagine what it would be like to be so self-assured and successful. 'Anyway,' she said, 'what about the men who work for you?'

'There aren't too many of them,' Estelle said. 'Only my sales director, Mark. Haven't got a clue what he thinks of me.'

They had reached the taxi rank. Janet stopped. 'Well,' she said, 'I'm sure he likes you.'

Estelle smiled at her. 'Maybe,' she said. 'Look, don't go yet. Come back for a nightcap.'

Janet hesitated. 'I don't know,' she said. 'Debbie was quite upset about me going out tonight.'

'She'll be in bed by now then,' Estelle said.

That was true. But there was still Ray. 'I'd better not. Ray will be wondering where I am…'

Would he though? He still wasn't even really speaking to her. Stuff him, as Kate would say! 'Well, all right,' she said in an abrupt change of mind. 'I will!'

Estelle looked at her with pleased surprise.

153

'Great!' she said. 'I thought I was going to have to work on you.'

Estelle wasn't nearly so surprised as Janet was herself. What was happening to her lately? Here she was, going behind Ray's back, *defying* him even by still attending the workshops. And the thing was, it felt…well, good.

'You know,' she said to Estelle, linking her arm in hers, 'I think you're good for me.'

'Glad to hear it,' Estelle said.

Estelle's apartment was the opposite of harem style. Decorated in minimalist pristine white with splashes of tasteful colour here and there, it was a tranquil, sophisticated space. A space that went with perfect make-up, manicures and understated, designer clothes.

Janet looked at the acres of white with trepidation. 'I'd better switch to white wine if you have any,' she said when Estelle offered her a drink. 'I'd be terrified of spilling red on this sofa.'

'Nonsense,' Estelle said, opening a bottle of red in the kitchen area.

The room was large and open-plan, with a vast window overlooking the sea. Janet couldn't imagine what it must be like to have such a room all to yourself. No television on unless you wanted it to be on, no nosy neighbours popping in on any flimsy pretext, no husband reading the paper and demanding meals …

'What's your husband like?' Estelle asked as if on cue, handing Janet her wine.

Janet held the glass carefully. 'Oh, he's very hard-working,' she said loyally. 'An efficient provider.'

Even to Janet, it didn't sound very exciting, and Estelle obviously agreed.

'Bossy?' she asked.

'Well...'

'Come on,' Estelle persisted. 'Is he bossy?'

'Yes.' God, *how* bossy he was.

'Parental?'

Janet traced the rim of her glass with her finger. She found it difficult to say bad things about Ray, even if they were true. 'I suppose he is, yes.'

Was Ray as loyal about her? Or did he say, 'My wife's hopeless. Absolutely hopeless.' Well, one thing was for sure, he wouldn't be saying: 'you'll never guess what she's gone and done now! Only joined an orgasm workshop! Can you believe it?'

'But I can be pretty useless sometimes, you know,' she said. 'I expect I encourage such treatment.'

Estelle ignored this comment as not being worthy of acknowledgement. 'Ever thought of getting shot of him?' she asked casually.

'No!' It was an instinctive, truthful reply. She hadn't. 'How would I manage?' she asked.

Estelle looked at her cynically. 'You mean, how would you manage without being bossed about and bullied?' she asked. 'Very well, I imagine.'

Janet sipped her wine, feeling suddenly depressed. Estelle was right of course. She *wouldn't* miss either of those things.

But it wasn't as simple as that. She'd never lived on her own. She'd swapped her mother's house for Ray's house. It was the only way of life she knew, and if she lived as Estelle did, with only her own thoughts and inefficiencies to keep her company,

155

she'd probably go crazy.

Wouldn't she?

'Feel free to tell me to mind my own business if you like,' Estelle said, putting her bare feet up on the other sofa. 'What do I know? Never married, never in a relationship for longer than six months; a proper emotional defective, I am.'

Janet responded to the carefully hidden sorrow in Estelle's voice. 'Oh, Estelle…' she said. 'I'm sure that isn't true.'

Estelle smiled cynically. 'You haven't met my lover,' she said. 'Or you might revise your opinion. Look, just don't underestimate yourself, that's all I'm saying. Anyone who can work for Carol De Ville for six months without chucking a bathroom fitting at her must be a bloody tough cookie.' She took a sip of her wine. 'Anyway, you haven't told me how you got on with your mirror. Were you a rose or a sea creature?'

Janet smiled, grateful for the change of subject, and the rest of the evening was fun and light-hearted. That was, until Janet got home. When she did, Ray was waiting for her, his expression anything but light-hearted.

'What time do you call this exactly?' Tie askew, whisky in hand, he regarded his wife sternly from his armchair.

Janet had never had a father to give her grief about late nights out during her teenage years, but she imagined it might have felt quite a lot like this if she had.

The room was swaying ever so slightly, so she planted her feet firmly on the carpet and used slow, careful movements to look at her watch. 'Two a.m.,' she said, an edge of defiance in her voice.

Ray's expression was scathing. 'You look like a prize slut,' he said dismissively, and instantly Janet felt most of her confidence begin to slip away.

Feeling suddenly old and ridiculous as well as distinctly unsteady on her feet, she flopped down onto the sofa. 'Well,' she said. 'At least it's got you talking to me again.' She closed her eyes. When she laid her head back the room began to spin.

'Don't count on it,' Ray said with contempt. 'I'm going out.'

Janet quickly opened her eyes. Too quickly. The room gave a dangerous lurch. 'Where?' she asked, clutching her head. 'It's the middle of the night!'

But Ray just stormed from the house without bothering to reply. Not that it was likely that Janet would have heard him anyway; she was too busy running to the downstairs loo to be sick.

* * * * *

Estelle was still up. For some reason, she didn't feel relaxed enough to go to bed yet. The events and the conversations of the evening were still running through her mind. In a way, Janet was lucky. OK, so she had a pig of a husband and a whiny daughter, but even so, the world was hers to discover, provided she could find the courage to do it. Janet was raw material waiting to be developed.

The same could hardly be said for herself. The material she was made of had been modelled and shaped and shoved in the back of a kiln to cook for so long it was hard as rock. She was solid; solid and flawed. And sometimes she thought the only way she was going to be able to move forward was by smashing herself into pieces.

The door buzzer rang. Maybe it was Janet back again. Maybe she'd had a Road to Damascus moment on the way home and decided to leave that shit of a husband of hers.

But when Estelle looked at the image provided by the entry camera, she saw it wasn't Janet at all. It was RT. She pressed the buzzer to let him in.

'Hope it's not too late,' he said. 'I saw your light.'

In Estelle's drunken, philosophical mood, his words seemed charged with significance. Was it too late? Or was there a chance of light at the end of the very long, dark tunnel of her life?

'That's OK,' she said. 'It's nice to see you.' It was, actually, if only to save her from being alone.

This wasn't the reply RT had expected, she could tell. He was far more accustomed to her being cool and condescending; the type of woman who grants favours rather than begs them. His glance was suspicious. 'Are you all right?' he asked.

'Sure,' she said, filling her glass up again. 'Never been better. Want a drink?'

'What I want,' he said, 'is you.' And he reached out to take her glass from her, putting it safely out of the way on the coffee table before taking her into his arms. Lowering his mouth, he got stuck in.

He needed a shave.

Estelle moved away, taking a slug from her glass and putting it down again. 'All in good time,' she said. 'First of all, I want to entertain you.'

'There's only one sort of entertainment I want right now,' he said, reaching out to pull her hand into his crotch.

158

'Ah,' she said, swirling out of his reach. 'But that's because you haven't seen me belly dance before. Look.' And she pushed her top up and her skirt down onto her hips and began to wiggle her pelvis, arms lifted above her head.

'You're pissed,' RT said.

'Not at all,' she said, wriggling and twirling in front of him.

'As a proverbial newt.'

She ignored him, concentrating on getting her hip movements right.

'What is it with you women these days?' he said. 'It used to be the men who got wasted on a Saturday night.' And he went over to her glass and quaffed the contents in one.

Sulky bloody bastard. Suddenly running out of steam for belly dancing, Estelle sank back on the sofa. Which was exactly what RT wanted. The predatory smile returned at once and he sank down beside her, his mouth tasting of her wine as he moved in for another snog.

Giving up, Estelle lay back and let him get on with it. But RT didn't even seem to notice that she was more passive than usual. And by the time her lover gave his final orgasmic grunt, Estelle was right in the heart of her dark tunnel and the light at the end of it looked too dim to be reachable.

Eighteen

'Imagine you're in your bedroom. The curtains are drawn, gently flickering candles light the room, and the temperature is perfect. Instead of your usual bed, there's a sumptuous four-poster covered in exotic, shimmering drapes...'

Seated next to Reenie and the others in the church hall with her eyes closed, Kate tried her hardest to visualise the scene Jade was describing. It was difficult to imagine a four-poster in her cramped bedsit though, try as she might. And even if she did have a four-poster, the covers would still be an ill-assorted collection of rumpled sheets strewn with crumbs, cat hair and the paraphernalia of in-bed TV watching. That was simply the way her life was. Or at least, the way it seemed to have become, post-Ian.

'You're dressed in silk lingerie,' Jade was continuing. 'A soft, sexy basque perhaps, and French knickers. Clothes to reveal and to skim and to tantalise.'

Oh yes, the kind of clothes she had drawers and drawers of! *Not.*

'And you're kneeling at the foot of the bed, observing the man you've invited for the occasion...'

Moving on in her mind from a very vague picture of her lumpish body clad in outsize lingerie, Kate looked towards the head of the 'bed' to see who was

160

sitting there watching her make a complete dick of herself. It was Ian, inevitably, dressed in his police uniform, oddly with one sock off. One bare foot and one dirty great policeman's boot defiling the sumptuous bed; an expression of utter scorn on his face as he looked at her cavorting in her skimpies. Yes, that'd be true to life, the slimy, treacherous bastard!

* * * * *

'He's naked, his body is glistening with oil, and you've tied his wrists to the bed frame with silken scarves, making him powerless to move.'

Next to Kate, Reenie was also having trouble imagining the scene. At least, she could imagine it all right, because she liked wearing lingerie, so long as it was comfortable, and she'd always fancied a four-poster. No, it was Ted she was having trouble picturing, or at least, Ted as macho hero, anyway.

'Your man is helpless; completely at your mercy,' Jade said. 'He can only lie there and watch as you begin to pleasure yourself.'

The Ted in Reenie's head just wasn't being obliging. He was doing the helpless bit all right, but it was laughter he was helpless with, not lust.

'Sorry, Reen,' he was giggling. 'Sorry! I just can't help it!' And off he went again; giggle, giggle, giggle. More silly-schoolboy than aroused stud.

* * * * *

The four-poster in Janet's mind was one she'd seen on a visit to a stately home once; all gilt and

161

golden canopy, probably too small for a comfortable night's sleep, since it was common knowledge that people had been shorter in those days. Maybe because of the period the bed came from, Janet was wearing a white muslin chemise instead of silk or satin, and her hair was longer than it was in reality, tumbling down over her shoulders in sexy, youthful waves.

'Slowly and gently, you begin to stroke your body through the silk of your lingerie,' Jade said. 'Your hands smooth their way delicately over your ripe breasts…'

As if in an out-of-body experience, Janet watched as she stroked herself through the gauzy fabric of her chemise, her pink nipples standing out clearly through the fabric, tingling as her hands came into brushing contact with them.

'…and down to the soft swell of your stomach…'

The woman in Janet's mind moved her hands down from her erect nipples. But instead of the soft, sexy swell Jade was describing, they encountered her stretch marks and then her operation scars, causing the hands of her imaginary self to spread in an instinctive act of concealment.

'You have no thoughts of any imperfections,' Jade said, just as if she had read the imaginary Janet's mind. 'No thoughts of being too fat or unattractive in any way. You accept yourself utterly as you are.'

Eyes tightly closed, Janet forced the woman in her mind to move her hands, lifting the chemise until the blemishes were in full view.

'You have never felt so good about the way you look in your entire life.'

The woman's hands glided over her less-than-perfect stomach.

'You feel inspired. Beautiful. Powerful. You are a temptress, a goddess, perfectly confident that, when the time is right for you, you will drive your man to the heights of ecstasy.'

Janet didn't allow her imaginary self to look up towards the head of the bed. She didn't want to see Ray and his cynical, impatient expression or to hear him say 'for God's sake, cover yourself up, Janet!' She wanted to be free of Ray. She wanted to enjoy the moment.

'Finally,' Jade said, 'with your man avidly watching your every movement, you reach down to your well of delight.'

The real Janet's face was hot. The impulse to open her eyes to see how caught up the other three women were in this fantasy was almost overwhelming, but she resisted it. Before she had started this course, Janet had never seen her 'well of delight.' It had just been something Ray pounded into once or twice a week. Something, prior to her hysterectomy, into which she had had to insert sterile white tampons during her period. Something that smelled if she didn't wash herself carefully. A place unmentioned by name by herself or anybody else on the earth, least of all by the doctor who had delivered Debbie.

'I'm afraid it will have to be a Caesarean, Mrs Thornton,' he'd said, and that had been that. No discussion, no arguments.

But now, because of the course, Janet had studied this place very thoroughly with her hand mirror.

'Your fingers are knowing and utterly tender. You love this person you are making love to; really love her. And why shouldn't you? She's gorgeous.'

163

Nobody had ever loved Janet like that, least of all herself, and there was a part of Janet that could have just buried her face in her hands and wept and wept at how very sad that was.

* * * * *

The scenario Jade had been describing was not unfamiliar to Estelle. She didn't have a four-poster bed, but she did have a king size, and she always wore sexy lingerie. With her own lingerie company, it wouldn't make sense to do anything else. Besides, she liked it.

She had also masturbated for the delight of many different lovers. She enjoyed the performance of it; she even enjoyed, in a perverse kind of a way, the fact that not one of them had ever guessed that it *had* been a performance.

And so it was very easy for her to imagine herself performing the actions Jade was describing. But it was a lot less easy to imagine the feelings side of it all. Impossible, if she were honest.

Estelle knew she had a good body. She was an attractive, successful woman with enough guts to get it on in front of a man. But she did it all from behind a kind of force field, a force field she had erected at an early age in order to be able to cope with the constant rejections from her parents.

'She is wondrous,' Jade was saying.

Estelle knew she was *not* wondrous. How could she be, when as a child she had been packed off out of the way to a series of nannies and boarding schools? She was the child of parents who obsessively adored each other, and they hadn't wanted her around, cramping their style. And, as the years passed, and she had blossomed into a surly and dangerously attractive young woman with boys constantly trying to get hold of her on the phone, they hadn't liked it at all.

Was it any accident that her father's work had suddenly taken her parents abroad with increasing frequency? Whatever, Estelle had chosen to stay with various school friends during the holidays. She had learned to be self-sufficient and to stand on her own two feet. She had also learned to keep her true feelings deeply hidden. It was safer that way. If you didn't have feelings, you couldn't be hurt. The other night with RT would probably have hurt if she'd had feelings, for instance. The rough way he'd torn into her without regard for her own arousal; using her body to get his own back on his wife, feel more of a man, whatever. RT didn't want her to be a person, or not a real one anyway. He didn't want her to belly dance for him, or tell him what to do or make any demands of him whatsoever. He came to her to escape.

'This woman deserves the best loving in the world,' Jade was saying. 'And this is what you proceed to give to her, with your man watching every thrilling, electric movement of your hand.'

What must it be like to *really* feel like that about yourself? Not only on the surface, but also deep inside of you, in your soul?

'How was that for you all, ladies?' Jade asked a few minutes later with a twinkling smile, and Estelle stirred herself from her gloomy thoughts to look round at the others. Kate was looking her usual cynical self, while Reenie appeared to be a bit down.

Janet, on the other hand, was red-faced, looking somewhere between excited and embarrassed.

'It was very…er unexpected,' she told them all, avoiding eye contact.

'Unexpected?' Jade asked, her perfectly shaped eyebrows lifting quizzically.

'Yes,' Janet said. 'You see, when I… looked up at the man tied to the bed, it… well, it wasn't Ray!'

Jade smiled kindly at her. 'It was your fantasy, Janet,' she said. 'You're allowed to fantasise about whoever you like. It isn't being unfaithful if it's only in your head.'

Janet looked doubtful. 'It *felt* as if I was being unfaithful,' she said.

'Who was it?' Jade asked. 'A movie star? A sports personality? They're the ones women most commonly fantasise about.'

Janet pulled an embarrassed face and shook her head. 'No,' she said. 'It wasn't either of those.' She hesitated. 'Actually, it was somebody I know.'

Reenie seemed to perk up. 'You dark horse you, Janet!' she said.

'Go on then, Janet,' urged Estelle. 'Tell us who it was!'

Janet licked her lips, clearly very embarrassed. 'It was a man I know from church,' she told them at last. 'John George. He supplies things to the shop, so I see him quite regularly.'

'Tasty, is he?' Reenie asked.

'No!' Janet said, scarlet-faced. 'At least, yes, I suppose he *is* quite good-looking, but– '

Janet fancied the man, Estelle could tell. Good for her! She deserved a bit of fun.

'Is he single?' Kate was asking.

Janet looked thoroughly uncomfortable. 'Well, yes,' she said, 'he's recently divorced, actually. But that's beside the point.'

'We're only having you on,' Reenie told her soothingly. 'We all know you're not the type to play around.'

'More's the pity,' Estelle said, and Janet frowned at her.

'What d'you mean?'

Estelle hesitated. A few weeks ago she would probably have just come right out and told Janet that she thought her husband was a wanker who didn't deserve her loyalty, but now, true though it might be, she didn't want to hurt her new friend's feelings.

'Nothing,' she said. 'Don't listen to me.'

Reenie filled the slightly awkward silence that followed this. 'Jade,' she said, 'you aren't expecting us to do that for real for our homework, I hope?'

Jade smiled. 'No, Reenie,' she said. 'Though if you want to, that would be fantastic, of course.'

Estelle smiled at the hasty way Reenie shook her head. 'I'd love to, Jade,' she said. 'Only I'm a bit busy this weekend.'

'I'm a bit busy forever,' Kate said, and although everyone laughed, Jade gave them all one of her piercing looks.

'You must never be too busy for the sensual side of yourselves,' she told them. 'When you're in tune with your inner sex goddess you'll feel confident, optimistic and warm-hearted.'

As they left the hall at the end of the session, Estelle felt anything but confident, optimistic and warm-hearted. Another weekend stretched ahead of her– a another two days to fill with work and chores in an effort to stave off loneliness. And although this had been the pattern of her life for just about as long as she could remember, suddenly – she had no idea why – she seemed to feel less equipped to deal with such solitude.

She turned impulsively to Reenie who was bustling along behind her. 'Are you really busy this weekend?' she asked. 'Or was that just an excuse to get out of the homework?'

Reenie smiled. 'I'm busy on Sunday,' she said. 'Got my family coming over. But that's all. Ted's got a darts match on Saturday night, so he'll be busy with that.'

'What about you two?' Estelle asked Janet and Kate. 'Are you free on Saturday night?'

'Well,' Kate said sarcastically, 'I was going to ask Daniel Craig out on a date, but I'll blow him out for you if you've got a better offer, Estelle.'

Kate's sarcasm would have irritated the hell out of her a few weeks back, but now Estelle smiled, recognising it for the defence mechanism that it was. 'What about you Janet?'

Janet shrugged, looking fed up. 'Ray's not talking to me,' she said. 'Remember?'

'She's free,' Kate said.

'What have you got in mind, Estelle?' Reenie asked.

Estelle smiled, already feeling some of that warm-heartedness Jade had been on about. 'A lingerie party at my place,' she said. 'You bring the wine, I'll supply the frillies.'

Nineteen

The night before the lingerie party, Janet attempted to make things up with Ray.

Still feeling guilty about being 'unfaithful' to him in her fantasy, she was more motivated than previously to try to bridge the icy gulf between them in their double bed. She had never enjoyed sex with him, but neither did it repel her; it was just one of the things they did together as a couple.

Now, without it, Janet was aware of how very few things they actually did do together as a couple. Certainly not shopping – Ray saw that as being very much Janet's domain. Often they didn't even eat together because Ray was working late or out at some golfing social event. Janet had gone along to those years and years ago, but she had never felt as if she fitted in, and Ray hadn't put up a fight when she asked if he minded going on his own in future. In fact, she suspected he'd been relieved.

Lying in bed now with her back to him, Janet could tell he was still awake, and impulsively she turned to face him, reaching out a tentative hand to stroke his back. His body tensed beneath her hand.

'Ray?' she said cautiously, but he wriggled out of reach. 'Ray,' she tried again. 'Don't let's be cross with each other.'

'Janet,' he said coldly, 'I'm afraid you can't just

emasculate a man one week and expect him to be able to perform the next. That isn't how it works.'

Rejected, Janet moved her hand quickly away and lay on her back, staring at the ceiling. She didn't want to cry; she just felt empty and helpless. And surely she should want to cry? She had been married to Ray for twenty years – almost half her life. They had a child together. And now sometimes she could hardly remember how or why they had got together in the first place. At least, she could remember the sequence of events and the accompanying feelings of that first meeting and their ensuing courtship, but it all felt like a story she had heard once, a story about somebody else's life. Reality was this cold, bossy, egocentric man she didn't understand and who didn't understand her either. But why should he understand her? When she didn't understand herself? She didn't even *know* herself for heaven's sake. Oh, she knew the bumbling, timid never quite up-to-scratch Janet that Ray and most other people on the planet thought she was, but she didn't know the Janet who had, just lately, been trying to claw her way to the surface. The new Janet who had a friend like Estelle and who fantasised about masturbating in front of another man. Had this Janet been there all the time? Carefully shut away in some dark, unrecognised recess of herself?

Goodness knows, life would be a lot easier if this new Janet had stayed shut away, leaving her as the placid, malleable woman she had always been; a woman without big hopes or expectations. But try as she might, Janet just couldn't climb back into that box. It was too late for that. Her life was set on a new course, and she had a strong sense that she was hurtling towards some very big changes in her life. Although, at the moment, she wasn't ready to dwell on what those changes or their consequences might be.

Beside her, Ray began to snore, oblivious, and Janet turned on her side. A long while later, just as she was drifting off to sleep herself, a dream image filled her mind – an image that was accompanied by a swift surge of pleasure. Janet's eyes flicked open as she tried to keep hold of the image. For a moment it eluded her consciousness, but then there it was in glorious Technicolor – a shop sign. 'Janet's Dreams.' That was all, no shop, just the sign with her name on it. Janet's Dreams…

She had dreamed about her dream – a shop of her own. How wonderful.

This time, when she dropped off to sleep, there was a smile of contentment on her face.

* * * * *

'What is this supposed to be?' Next night, in Estelle's apartment, Kate held up a scrap of black and red lace.

'It's a teddy, Kate,' Estelle told her, pouring them all more wine.

'Estelle, that wouldn't fit my granddaughter, let alone me,' Reenie said. 'It's tiny.'

'Might fit your granddaughter's teddy,' Kate joked, tossing it back onto the heap of lingerie on the floor and having another sort through.

'There are some larger sizes amongst that lot,' Estelle told her. 'Keep on looking. You'll find something.'

Kate wasn't sure she wanted to. She wasn't exactly a lingerie person, and even if she found something that fitted, it was a safe bet it would look ridiculous on her. In fact, Estelle was probably the only one it would look good on. And Janet of course, if she ever got the nerve to wear any of the stuff, which Kate doubted. And if she ever turned up to have a look in the first place, because so far there was no sign of her.

Just at that moment the door buzzer went, and Estelle jumped up to answer it.

'Hi, Janet,' she said into the intercom. 'Come on up. It's Janet,' she told them unnecessarily, crossing to the door to open it.

Kate was impressed by Estelle's apartment. It was the kind of place she would never live in herself, or, if she did, it would never look like this. It would get cluttered up in no time, and would end up becoming a much larger version of her bedsit. Well, almost.

Kate's bedsit had only ever been intended as a temporary arrangement; a bolt- hole while she got herself together after the split with Ian. Presumably the fact that she was still there a year later meant that she hadn't got herself together yet.

Well, she hadn't, had she? Not if she had to go and get totally off her face just because she saw Ian snogging Jennifer in the street. Sometimes Kate was convinced that what she needed to do was move right away somewhere new, make a new start. But so far she just hadn't got enough energy together to do it. And besides, she didn't want to give Ian the satisfaction. He'd be fucking thrilled if she left. Which was a thoroughly excellent reason to stay put.

'Hello everyone,' Janet said, arriving in the

172

apartment. 'Sorry I'm late. I waited until Ray went out so he wouldn't ask where I was going.'

'What about doleful Debbie?' Estelle asked, and although Janet put on a stern expression, Kate could tell she was amused. Good old Janet. She was sound, she was.

'Now that's not very nice, Estelle,' Janet said, and Estelle smiled.

'Ah,' she said, 'but I'm not a very nice person. Haven't you realised that yet?'

Kate hadn't liked Estelle at all at first. She'd thought she was really up herself with her pristine bloody business suits and her superior attitude. But just lately she'd mellowed a lot. Maybe they all had.

'Debbie's actually gone out tonight, I'm happy to say,' Janet said, accepting a glass of wine from Estelle and joining Kate and Reenie on the carpet. 'I don't know where, but anywhere's better than lounging about watching TV in her dressing gown the way she has been doing.'

'Tell me about it,' Kate thought, bringing to mind countless evenings spent in exactly that fashion.

'Anyway,' Janet said brightly, 'has anyone found anything suitable for me to try on?'

Janet was looking good tonight. She hadn't overdone it; her jeans and T-shirt were casual but not scruffy, and she had obviously taken some time over her make-up. Kate wasn't wearing any make-up herself. She *had* thought about her clothes though, if only because she knew everybody else would and Estelle had a rather exclusive address. But in Kate's opinion, if you were a bit on the big side, it didn't really matter what you wore anyway. And Kate *was* a bit on the big side. In fact, she had been quite shocked to discover that half the clothes she'd dug out from the back of the wardrobe hadn't fitted her properly anymore. Maybe she ought to add dieting to her list of things she ought to do.

And suddenly, she had no idea why, she thought of Geoff. Big, jovial Geoff the baker. It might be a cliché, and yet somehow it was impossible to imagine him any other way. A big man with a big laugh and big appetites. Or at least, she assumed his appetite for sex was as big as his appetite for food; he was a man, after all.

'More wine, Kate?'

'Yes please.' Kate downed her refreshed glass almost in one. What was she doing, for God's sake, thinking about Geoff's appetite for sex?

'Come on then,' Estelle was urging them. 'Make your choices. Then you can try them on.'

'Best give me a drop more wine too then, Estelle,' Reenie said, holding out her glass, and Kate held her glass out too.

'Me too, please, Estelle,' she said.

* * * * *

'This is fun, Estelle, this is,' Reenie said.

Dressed in a basque top made of some sort of black netting with touches of red ribbon decoration, Reenie was sprawled comfortably back against a floor cushion watching as Janet paraded unsteadily around the room in an ivory silk teddy. Janet's cheeks were flushed from the wine, and Reenie knew it was the only reason she had the nerve to totter about in a pair of high heels borrowed from Estelle, showing off her figure, which was, incidentally,

174

fantastic.

Not that Janet seemed aware of it. The poor cow had been dead shy about trying on the underwear at first, retreating to the bathroom and keeping her jeans on. Now look at her! Turns out she was self-conscious about showing her stretch marks and operation scars, or so she'd confessed to them all when everyone else had started to get really stuck into the modelling.

'Operation scars?' Kate had said unsympathetically. 'With a fantastic figure like you've got?'

'She's right, Janet,' Estelle said. 'If there were any men here, I can assure you they wouldn't be looking at your scars.'

It was true. They'd be looking at her breasts, Reenie knew it. Worthy of a Page Three girl they were, for all that Janet was knocking forty-five. Looked a treat with that plunging ivory neckline they did.

'It's nice of you to say so,' Janet said politely, 'but I can't help feeling the way I do. My scars repulse me.'

'Well they shouldn't,' Reenie had told her firmly. 'They're proof you're a woman.'

Janet pulled a face. 'Half a woman, you mean,' she said. 'Since one of the scars is from my hysterectomy.'

'Don't talk to me about being half a woman,' Reenie said. 'I was done and dusted with the menopause by the time I was forty-one.'

That had impressed them.

'Isn't that a bit early?' Estelle asked.

'Runs in my family,' Reenie said. 'My mum was

the same. And her mum. Good job I got started early with the babies.'

Reenie looked at Estelle and Kate. It seemed to her they were looking a bit thoughtful. 'But you don't have to worry,' she told them. 'It's very rare for women to finish that young.'

Estelle shrugged. 'I don't intend having children anyway,' she said.

Reenie was shocked and showed it. 'Oh, Estelle, why ever not?' she asked.

'Because it's hard enough living my own life,' she said. 'Besides, do I seem the maternal type to you?'

Reenie shrugged. 'Well maybe not, on the surface, but that's what it's all about, isn't it? Us going to Jade's classes? Finding out what we're capable of?'

'Fulfilling our potential,' Janet said.

'Yeah,' Reenie agreed. 'That an' all.'

'Achieving an orgasm is hardly the same as giving birth, Reenie,' Estelle told her with just a touch of warning frost in her voice.

Reenie surged right on, ignoring it. 'Don't know whether Jade would agree with you there, Estelle,' she said. 'When you have a child, it's like you're stripped completely bare. There you are, legs spread, some doctor shining a light up you and what feels like your insides being pulled out. Nowhere to hide then, is there? You just got to act on your instincts. Same kind of thing when you have an orgasm, I shouldn't wonder. Least, that's how Jade makes it sound.'

Estelle looked as if she'd like to argue, but drank some of her wine instead. Reenie wondered why. Perhaps she'd hit on a nerve or two.

'D'you think Jade's got a family?' Janet asked,

176

and they all looked at her.

'She hasn't said, has she?' Reenie said.

'It's amazing how little we do know about her,' Kate observed, and Reenie had to admit this was true.

'We know nothing about her,' Estelle said. 'She could be a complete fraud for all we know.'

'Oh, but she isn't, is she?' Janet said with that anxious frown she had sometimes. 'I'm sure we'd know if she was. She seems completely genuine to me.'

'She certainly seems to believe what she says, I'll give her that,' Kate said. 'As to whether it's a complete load of bollocks, that's a different matter entirely.'

'I think she's all right,' Reenie said. 'A bit weird, but I don't mind that. I for one, am prepared to give her advice a try.'

'So why are you here instead of at home strutting your stuff in front of your fella?' Kate asked.

'Because I want to have a go on my own first, Kate,' Reenie said with as much dignity as possible, bearing in mind the subject matter. '*If* I can find the chance to have a bit of time on my own. Never know when somebody's going to drop in at our place, you don't. Still, at least our Marcia's a bit more cheerful these days, thanks to you.'

'I wish I could say the same for Debbie,' Janet said worriedly. 'Oh, she's gone out tonight, I know, but I don't think her heart was really in it.'

'She'll be all right,' Estelle said. 'Forget about her for a while. Have some more wine and enjoy yourself.'

Which was precisely what Janet did. And, a few

more glasses of wine later, she had found the confidence to take her jeans off, thereby revealing the stunning full effect of the ivory silk teddy.

'Your Ray would soon start speaking to you again if you wore that for him, surely, Janet?' Reenie said, but soon wished she hadn't, because the mention of her husband's name wiped the smile off Janet's face.

'I wouldn't like to count on it, Reenie,' she said.

'Well he bloody well should do.' Kate, as she so often did, said what the rest of them were thinking but were too polite to say.

'You look fantastic, Janet,' Estelle told her.

'Yeah,' Kate agreed. 'And I bet that bloke in your fantasy would agree.'

Janet coloured up so brightly at that they all laughed. Even Janet herself.

'I quite shocked myself,' she said. 'I shan't know how to look him in the face the next time he comes into the shop.'

Reenie thought about her own fantasy again. Ted had been there in hers all right, but only in body, not in mind. Did that count? Reenie wasn't sure that it did. Not that she'd tried it out on him for real yet of course. Maybe she should. And maybe, if she did, it wouldn't be the same as she'd imagined it at all. After all, she loved Ted. Adored the stupid idiot. So just why exactly they had never quite managed to get it right in bed was a complete mystery to her, it really was.

Estelle put some music on, and suddenly it was a party. Reenie resolutely put all morbid thoughts about her sex life with Ted to the back of her mind and got up to have a bit of a bop. Reenie had always loved dancing, and she could never resist shaking it about a bit, even though she was now pushing sixty.

'Come on girls!' she encouraged the others.

Janet and Estelle got to their feet. Janet was a bit all over the place – you could tell she didn't get much practice at it – but Estelle was really quite a good dancer in a tight, controlled sort of a way.

'Come and join in!' Reenie tried to persuade Kate, but Kate wasn't having any of it.

'No way!' she said, smiling. 'Do you realise how bloody kinky you lot look prancing about together in your undies?'

'It's a good job no one can see us,' Janet said.

'Haven't got any hidden cameras, have you, Estelle?' Reenie asked.

'Not this time,' Estelle smiled.

'Shame,' said Kate. 'I could earn a fortune in blackmail money once you lot have sobered up.'

Reenie laughed. 'You just bloody try it!' she said.

By the end of the evening, they were all very drunk, and Reenie was glad she'd arranged for Ted to come and pick her up. It was going to be worth his while anyway because she had bought the black and red basque top and a pair of matching knickers from Estelle.

'We should have another get together, soon,' she said, as they got ready to leave. 'What about a big day out? Weekend after next? A bit of a drive up the coast and a spot of lunch? That'd be a real treat, that would.'

'Good idea, Reenie,' said Janet, who was looking a bit unsteady on her feet. She and Ted were dropping Janet off, and by the looks of her, it was just as well.

'We can go in Estelle's car and have the roof

down,' Janet went on. 'We can all wear headscarves and sunglasses and be terribly glamorous!'

'The sunglasses I can do,' Kate said, 'but the headscarf is a definite no-no. I'll look like Princess Anne!'

Reenie laughed. It had been a great evening, and she was sad when it came to an end. But Estelle had one more surprise for them. 'Here,' she said, giving them all a bag. 'A party bag for you all.'

Reenie opened hers and took a look. Then she put her hand inside and pulled out a wisp of silky fabric. The others were doing the same.

'Estelle,' Kate said, examining the flimsy red knickers she was holding. 'These appear to be damaged.'

Reenie examined the crotch of her own pair of knickers. There was a slash running the whole length of it. A *neatly sewn* gash. 'Oh my gawd!' she said. 'It's deliberate!'

Estelle was grinning. 'Of course!' she said. 'The ultimate in seductive briefs. It's one of our most popular lines.'

'I'm sure Jade would approve,' said Janet.

'I'm sure my Ted would approve!' said Reenie, though secretly, she wasn't sure she was going to show them to him just yet.

Twenty

Next morning, as Janet staggered past Ray en route to the toilet, the giveaway lurch of her body and the hand she had clutched over her mouth were finally enough stir him into speech.

'What the hell's wrong with you?' he growled, but Janet didn't stop to answer. She couldn't.

Five minutes later she crawled back to bed, her forehead cold and clammy, her mouth tasting disgusting.

Ray was dressing in his golf clothes. 'Where the hell did you get to last night?' he snapped, his angry voice kept mercifully quiet because Debbie was in the next bedroom.

'Out with friends,' Janet said weakly, keeping her eyes closed. 'Must have had one too many…'

'One too many? *One*? It smells like a bloody vineyard in here!'

Desperately wanting to block him out by burying her head under the duvet, Janet nevertheless kept completely still, not daring to move in case she inspired a fresh wave of nausea.

'Who are these friends? You're not telling me Gwen's in this state too, because I don't believe it!'

If she hadn't been dying, Janet would have laughed out loud at that; the thought of Gwen at last night's do was so ludicrous. Gwen in her bra and knickers in high heels and a feather boa! Hell would freeze over first.

Despite her fragile condition, her amusement must have shown itself in some minuscule facial flicker, because Ray was down on her like a ton of bricks.

'It is not fucking funny, Janet!' he shouted, forgetting all about keeping quiet for Debbie's benefit. 'I do not expect my wife to be out getting pissed up on a Saturday night like some common slapper!'

Janet licked her lips and attempted to open her eyes, her voice coming out as hoarse as if she'd been singing karaoke all night. 'It was only one night, Ray.'

'And it had better stay that way!' he said, snatching a diamond-patterned zip-up top from the chest of drawers. 'Because next time I won't be so understanding!' And with that he stormed from the room, his feet like hammer blows on the stairs, the front door slamming closed behind him.

Janet felt too ill to worry about Ray's temper just then. She was just incredibly grateful that he was gone, and sank instantly into a much-needed healing sleep.

'Mum?' A few seconds or a few hours later – Janet was incapable of detecting which – Debbie woke her. 'What *is* wrong with you and Dad?'

Maybe if Janet hadn't felt so ill she would have been able to detect the genuine concern in her daughter's voice. But as it was, the room swam crazily from having opened her eyes too quickly, and she was forced to push the duvet back and attempt to struggle to her feet.

'Mum?'

'Get out of my way!' Janet shouted, but too late. As she vomited into Ray's discarded slippers, Janet was only dimly aware of her daughter's horror.

'Mum!'

* * * * *

Across town, Estelle wasn't faring much better. OK, so her hangover was limited to a throbbing headache that had kept her blinds securely drawn against the sunny day outside, but it was bad enough.

Still, it had been worth it. Last night had been a lot of fun. When her mobile began to ring she picked it up to see who was calling. RT. No doubt he was at the golf club. Come to think of it, she did vaguely remember arranging to meet him down there. Well, he could forget it. She was going back to bed with a glass of orange juice. Sex was the very last thing on her mind.

* * * * *

Things were unusually quiet in Reenie's house for a Sunday morning. Marcia was still asleep of course – nothing unusual about that – but it was almost unheard of for both of her other daughters to be busy all day and not be coming round for Sunday lunch. However, it did mean that Reenie and Ted had some time to themselves. *If* she could persuade him not to go down to the allotment.

As they sat up in bed together drinking their tea, Reenie could already sense her husband's attention turning towards his purple sprouting – the broccoli sort – and a very different type of purple sprouting to the one she wanted to discuss.

'I reckon the girls will be a bit hung-over this morning the way they were knocking them back last night,' she said brightly to make conversation.

Ted blinked and smiled at her. 'You always could hold your drink, love.'

'Don't know if that's a good thing or a bad thing,' Reenie told him, but he just nodded, and she could tell he was floating back to his veggies.

'They're great girls,' she said and reached out to pat his hand. 'Best thing you did, persuading me to join those classes.'

He looked at her then. *Really* looked. 'Having an effect then, is it? Apart from you making a few friends?'

Ted's eyes were what had first drawn Reenie to him all those years ago. They were a striking shade of pale blue, and these days they stood out in contrast to his white hair, whereas once they had stood out in contrast to his black hair. When they'd first met, when Reenie had been seventeen, she'd sometimes had trouble holding Ted's gaze for very long because he had such beautiful eyes. She didn't have that problem now, of course, except on the rare occasions she was trying to hide something from him.

'Eh, Reen?' he prompted her. 'Is it making a difference?'

'I don't know, love,' she said evasively. 'What do you think?'

Ted turned to put his mug of tea down on the bedside table. 'Well,' he said, 'if you don't know, I'm sure I don't.'

Reenie was uncharacteristically silent. Ted began to caress her shoulder beneath her nightdress. 'Why

184

don't you show me a thing or two of what you've been learning?' he said.

'All right.'

Reenie thought about it. What *had* they learnt exactly? She had a feeling Ted would just collapse laughing if she started going on about – what was it? Recapturing the essence of Aphrodite with her own inner sex goddess. 'Well,' she said at last, 'we've talked about the different, you know, *erogenous* zones and that, but mainly it's been about thinking so far,' she said.

'Thinking?' he asked.

Reenie traced the pattern of the duvet with her finger. 'Yes, you know; *thinking* yourself sexy.'

'You mean like a pool player might think about himself winning before he starts a frame?' Ted asked. 'Or a darts player might see the arrow landing in the double twenty?'

Reenie nodded. Typical of a man to have to think about sport to make sense of anything. 'Something like that.'

'I see.' There was a suspicious pause after that, and, flashing a quick glance in her husband's direction, Reenie was just in time to see him hiding a smirk. Irritated, she pretended she hadn't noticed.

'Last lesson we had to do this whatya-ma-call-it,' she told him. 'A visualisation thing.'

'Seems to have increased your vocabulary anyway, this class,' he observed dryly. 'That a posh word for seeing the dart go in the double twenty?'

'Sort of,' Reenie said, refusing to respond to his amusement. 'Only a lot more complicated, with a four poster and… rope and stuff.'

Ted's jaw dropped. 'Rope?'

185

'Yes. You were tied up to the headboard while I…' She broke off, embarrassed.

'While you what?'

'*Saw* to myself.'

'You saucy beggar!'

He was openly laughing now, and Reenie glared at him. 'That's what you did in the visual thingie too,' she told him.

Ted's blue eyes opened innocently. 'What?'

'*Laughed.* It really messed it up.'

'Sorry, Reen,' he said, and something about his tone of voice *almost* made her see the funny side of it.

'Not your fault what you do inside my head, I suppose,' she told him grudgingly.

Ted kissed her, giving her a quick squeeze. 'Go on, show me what it was like,' he said. 'Before I messed it up laughing.'

Reenie looked at him doubtfully. 'Sure?'

'Positive,' he said. 'Go on.'

So, taking him at his word, Reenie tied him to the headboard with scarves, popped on the lingerie she had bought the previous night and began to caress her breasts through it, exactly as she had done in her fantasy. Except that it felt weird rather than sexy because she felt so self-conscious and, although she was careful to avoid looking at Ted, Reenie just knew he was really having to concentrate to keep himself from laughing. Not at *her*, but just at the whole ridiculousness of the situation.

So there was no way on earth then that she was going to move on from caressing her breasts to caress her *you know what*; it simply wasn't possible. In the end she sighed and gave up.

186

Ted, his arms still tied to the headboard, watched her. 'What's up, love?' he asked kindly. *Too* bloody kindly.

'Nothing,' she said irritably. 'I just can't do it, that's all.'

'Well,' he said, 'it doesn't matter, does it? Untie me and I'll give you a cuddle.'

Some unreasonable part of Reenie didn't want to co-operate. It wasn't Ted's fault she felt like a stupid prat, but somehow she wanted to blame him anyway; leave him there, tied up and helpless, while she got dressed and made a start at lunch.

'Come on, love,' he asked patiently, and at last Reenie swallowed her irritation and started to untie the scarves.

'Might as well get dressed, I suppose,' she said when he was free, but Ted made a grab for her.

'Hey,' he said. 'Not so fast.' And he pulled her back to him to kiss her thoroughly, one hand stroking her body through the black net of her lingerie just where she had been stroking herself. 'Your mate sells some very sexy underwear,' he whispered into her ear, and finally Reenie relaxed, kissing him back as she reached out to unbutton his pyjamas.

* * * * *

Like Reenie, Kate didn't have a hangover that morning. She had drunk a fair amount, it was true, but these days her body was used to dealing with copious amounts of alcohol. Her head was still throbbing though, but this was more due to the disturbed night's sleep she'd had.

Kate had been dreaming all night long – a series

187

of short, frustrating dreams, and every single one of them about Geoff. After each one she had woken up, feeling disorientated, the bedclothes drenched with sweat. And as soon as she went back to sleep, a new dream started up straight away. It was weird. Whatever had happened to make her start to think of Geoff like that? Where had it come from?

In one of the most vivid dreams, Geoff had been standing with his back to her in his baking whites, engrossed in rolling up a giant Swiss roll. As she hovered, not wanting to disturb him in the middle of such a delicate procedure, he turned and beckoned to her. Then, as she moved closer, he picked up the finished Swiss roll and held it out to her – all three feet of it. That was all; she'd woken up at that point.

Although Kate very definitely wanted to avoid any phallic interpretations of that particular dream, she was extremely hard pressed to come up with any interpretation beyond the blatantly obvious. But exactly why she was dreaming about Geoff and giant cocks in the same context, Kate had no idea. It was all very disturbing, especially since she was supposed to be meeting up with him at the pub that lunch time. Geoff would piss himself laughing if he found out she had been dreaming about him in *any* capacity, but this! If he ever got wind of her phallic Swiss roll, she would never hear the end of it. Which he wouldn't, obviously, because there was no way she was going to tell him.

It was all Geoff's fault anyway, persuading her that the workshops were a good idea. There was no way she'd have been dreaming about giant Swiss rolls pre-Jade.

She almost didn't turn up at the pub. When she

did, Geoff had nearly finished his first pint. 'I thought we could go for a walk,' he astounded her by saying.

'A walk?' she repeated, stunned. 'Since when did you want to go for walks?'

Geoff stuck his belly out and gave it a resounding slap. Kate did her best not to look. 'Since I decided I need to lose some weight,' he said, and then frowned at her. 'What's up with you? Your face is all red. You coming down with something?'

'No! Nothing's wrong,' she said hastily. 'Where d'you want to go for this walk then?'

'I thought by the sea. It's a lovely day.'

Kate hadn't even had the chance to buy herself a pint yet. He'd sprung the walk idea on her the minute she arrived. 'Doesn't usually inspire you to sample the great outdoors,' she said, transferring her beer money from hand to hand.

'No,' Geoff agreed, downing the rest of his pint and hitching his trousers up. 'But maybe it's time to change. Come on.'

So off they went, without Kate even getting a drink first, down to the seafront to join the couples and the families out taking the air. And Kate, who usually rattled away to Geoff sixteen to the dozen about anything and everything, suddenly couldn't think of one thing to say.

A tractor was pulling a fishing boat up onto the beach from the sea. Kate saw the name painted on the side of the boat. *Sultry Sue.* Sultry Sue! Any other time she'd have given Geoff a nudge and they'd be laughing. But today she couldn't even find the resources to do that. It was like she was in a play. Or floating in the air somewhere, looking down on

189

herself. Nothing seemed natural.

'World record trifle soon,' Geoff said after the silence had gone on forever.

'I know.'

'S'pose you do,' he said. 'All I've talked about at work lately, I expect.'

'Yes.'

'Got the TV coming. And the radio.'

'I know.'

'Should raise quite a bit for charity, I reckon.'

'Yes.'

'And you don't mind being in charge of fruit and jelly?'

'No.'

'Good.'

And that appeared to be the end of the giant trifle as a topic of conversation. They walked in silence along the promenade, leaving the tractors and the lifeboat station behind them and on past the area of beach Kate guessed Estelle must be able to see from her window.

'How are the girls from the course?' Geoff tried again.

'Fine.' She was aware of him smiling, doing his best to get her to look at him, but she kept looking straight ahead to where a man and a child were flying a kite on the beach.

'Good,' Geoff said. 'I never did meet that other one. What's her name again?'

'Janet.'

'Yes, that's it. Janet. She all right too?'

'She's getting there.'

Suddenly Geoff stopped to look at her. 'Are you all right, Katie? Only you seem a bit fed up.'

And suddenly that was exactly how Kate felt. Fed up. No, more than fed up. Depressed. Ever since the split with Ian she'd been so angry; angry with an anger so red-hot it had soothed the edges of her pain. Anger had made her drink herself unconscious, lark about with Geoff and other friends, plot petty revenges on Ian and Jennifer and scream and shout at her layabout students. Anger had become her pastime, a satisfactory time-filler against the unspeakable alternative – an abyss of raw, unprocessed pain.

By the side of a shelter long ago decorated by school children with paintings of dolphins, Kate came to an abrupt halt and looked at Geoff – her friend, her ally, her lifeline for the past ghastly twelve months. And he looked right back at her, frowning.

'What's up with your eyes, Katie?' he asked. 'They look all sore.'

'Too much fresh air,' she said abruptly, turning away before she burst into tears. 'I'm calling it a day.'

'Katie!' he called after her, but she powered on, as fast as her bulky body would let her – back up the promenade, on past the amusement arcade, sharp left by the café and out of Geoff's sight.

* * * * *

In Reenie and Ted's bed, their lovemaking was proceeding along very familiar lines. After caressing her breasts for a while, Ted had gently removed her French knickers and moved on to caress her private parts. Private parts! Reenie chided herself. Her vulva, vagina and her clitoris. Mostly her clitoris. Which should be all right – after all, the clitoris was supposed to be her love bud, her key to untold, incomparable pleasure. So why did it just feel…well, uncomfortable when Ted got stuck in with it?

Lying back with Ted caressing her, Reenie racked her brains to remember exactly what Jade had suggested to them about clitoral stimulation. It had been a few weeks back, the day they'd almost had that pervy old caretaker crashing in on them; the first time, in fact, that they'd taken their knickers off in front of each other. That was it – Jade had encouraged them to concentrate their caresses on everywhere *but* their clitorises at first. The odd teasing touch to it maybe, but no more than that, not until it was screaming for attention. Not that her clitoris had exactly screamed during the lesson, but it had spoken a bit, at least. Which was a lot more than it was doing now.

Ted was getting ready to stop the caresses and climb on board – Reenie recognised the signs. If she didn't speak now, it would be too late. 'Love,' she said gently, and Ted literally jumped, he was so unused to her speaking at all during sex.

Caresses of all kinds instantly stopped altogether. 'What?'

'Nothing,' she said, suddenly feeling as nervous as a teenager. 'Just… well, d'you think you could touch some of my other places as well?'

Ted pulled back to look at her. 'What places?'

'Well,' she said, 'round and about. You know.'

'Show me,' Ted said.

'Oh, well…' Reenie lifted the duvet up and pointed into the darkness. 'There and there…'

192

Ted smiled. 'No,' he said, offering her his hand. '*Show* me.'

'Oh.' So, feeling like a fool and wishing she'd never said anything in the first place, Reenie attempted to guide Ted's hand. And, once his hand was in place, Ted very obligingly caressed.

'That better?' he asked.

'Yes, much thanks,' she said, even though it wasn't at all. Or rather, it might have been, if she hadn't felt so self-conscious, and if she wasn't extremely aware of Ted's erection deflating by the second.

Time passed. Reenie was pretty sure Ted was no longer feeling aroused, and she certainly wasn't herself. 'It's all right, love,' she plucked up the courage to say at last. 'Thanks.'

Sighing, Ted rolled over onto his back. Reenie cuddled into his side in an attempt to be reassuring, looping one arm around his waist.

'Never have been good at talking about sex, have we?' he said at last. 'Funny, really, when we're so good at talking about everything else.'

But Reenie thought with sudden pain about their son and how he had become almost a forbidden subject between the two of them. 'Well, I don't know if that's strictly true,' she said. 'I don't really think we are good about talking about everything.'

Ted turned to look at her. 'What d'you mean?' he asked, but Reenie's eyes were full of tears, and when he saw them, Ted instantly stiffened.

'We never speak about Craig,' she persisted, but she saw the shutters immediately come down on his face.

'What's to speak about?' he said. 'The boy's

dead. End of subject.' And with that, he swung his legs out of bed. 'I'm off down the allotment,' he said, grabbing some clothes and going to the bathroom to get dressed.

* * * * *

Estelle had gone into work finally, more for something to do than anything else. The thought of seeing RT was still unappealing, especially since he seemed so desperate to see her – he'd phoned at least five times in the past hour. So that meant golf was out. There was nobody she fancied seeing, except perhaps for Janet to gossip and chat about the previous evening, but it was Sunday and Janet would be busy with her family, undeserving of her as they may be. So, work it was.

But when she pulled into the car park, another car was already parked there – Mark Turner's. Frowning, Estelle let herself in and went through to his office.

He looked up, surprised to see her. 'Estelle! Hi!'

'What are you doing in?' she asked, not sounding over-friendly.

But Mark just smiled. 'Don't worry, I'm not doing any out-of-hours embezzling,' he said. 'Just needed to get a few things ready for Paris.'

The Paris sales conference. Of course. Estelle nod-ded. 'Oh,' she said. 'Good.'

She turned to go out again, but Mark stopped her. 'What about you?' he asked. 'What brings you here on a fine day like this?'

'I'm bored,' she could have said. *'I'm bored and lonely, and I'm trying to avoid my lover. Hell, I don't even like my lover, so what sort of a person does that*

194

make me?'

'Oh, just a bit of paperwork to do,' she said instead.

'Right,' Mark said. He looked at her, a searching kind of look that gave her the impression there was something else he wanted to say. She raised an eyebrow, waiting, but then he seemed to bottle out. 'Well,' he said brightly, 'I won't be here long. I'm meeting someone at the Hampton for lunch at one.'

His girlfriend, no doubt. The blonde she'd seen him with that night at the seafood restaurant. And suddenly it seemed to Estelle as if everyone in the entire world but her had someone they wanted to spend this sunny Sunday afternoon with.

As if on cue, her mobile began to ring again. Taking it out of her bag she looked to see who was calling. RT again. She was *almost* tempted to answer it, to show Mark she had someone who wanted to spend some time with her as well, but the reality of meeting up with RT hit her just in time, so she switched her phone off again. She did not feel like an afternoon of unfulfilled shagging today. In fact, it was high time she finished her affair with RT, but she didn't want to do that today either.

Turning her back on Mark, she headed off towards her office. 'Well,' she said, 'make sure you shut the outside door firmly behind you on your way out, won't you?'

'Of course,' he said, but she had already gone into her office.

* * * * *

Janet had spent the majority of the day in bed –

either there or in the bathroom anyway. She had staggered down to the kitchen at one point in a failed attempt to cook Sunday lunch, but it had proved completely beyond her. Debbie, thoroughly disgusted by the vomit in the slippers incident, had gone off somewhere, so Janet couldn't ask her to do it. But in the end Ray didn't come back for lunch anyway.

In fact, the next time Janet saw him was when he came to bed later that night.

'Ray?' she said croakily into the darkness. 'Is that you?'

'Who else were you expecting?' he said sarcastically, and even through her own hangover, Janet could tell he had been drinking.

The bed sagged as he climbed in, and then she could smell his beery breath close up. Instinctively she turned away, afraid of feeling sick again, but Ray put a hand out to turn her roughly back again. 'Getting it off with the church warden behind my back, are you?' he said in a slightly slurred voice. 'Faking a hangover so as to get me out of the way for a bit of righteous rumpy pumpy?'

'Ray! Of course not! Don't be silly!' she said, but suddenly Ray's mouth was clamped painfully to hers, shutting off any further words. It was a hideously brutal kiss of possession that was echoed in the rough way he divested her of her nightdress and clamped his hands onto her breasts.

Sensing what was to come, Janet tried to shrink back, her body rigid with rejection, but Ray carried on regardless, entering her with a grunt, his greedy penis tearing at her unprepared flesh.

Twenty-one

The weather was bright and sunny that week, though for all Janet noticed, it might just as well have been snowing. She felt depressed and lethargic. Ray, on the other hand, seemed to be in a particularly good mood. There was chirpiness about the way he shook his newspaper out and bit into his toast at the breakfast table. Once or twice he even hummed tunelessly, something he never did unless he was pleased with himself. Evidently he thought he had taught Janet a lesson. He was talking to her again anyway, and didn't seem to notice that she didn't have very much to say in return.

When Friday morning came round, Janet considered not going to the workshop. She knew she wouldn't find it easy to hide how she was feeling from the girls – especially Reenie and Estelle. But in the end she did go, if only because it felt as if the unsuitably jaunty sunflower yellow walls of her kitchen were closing in on her.

Because of her indecision, she was uncharacteristically late arriving at the hall, but, as she quietly pushed the door open, she soon discovered that her misery was unlikely to be detected after all. A full-scale row appeared to be taking place.

'I'm sorry, Jade, but I've had a bellyful of the "importance of connecting with my inner sex god-

197

desses"!' Estelle was saying unpleasantly. 'It's just too wishy-washy! It's week five, for God's sake, and none of us is any closer to having an orgasm. Are we girls?' Estelle looked round at Reenie and Kate for con-firmation.

'Think I'm further away from it than ever, actually,' Reenie said miserably.

Estelle nodded in an 'I told you so' kind of a way. 'And you, Kate?' she prompted.

Kate shrugged. 'Me? I'm just fucking losing it,' she said, her voice unnaturally quiet and subdued.

'There you are,' Estelle said to Jade triumphantly, and Janet shrank instinctively into the shadows, not wanting to become the next focus for Estelle's attention. 'Even Kate's dissatisfied with the way the course is going.'

'It isn't just what we're learning,' Kate said. 'It's all the constant bickering as well. *You* bossing everyone around. I'm sick of it.'

'Oh, that's right,' Estelle said nastily. 'Blame everyone else because things aren't going right for you. You've been set on failure since Day One. And not just for yourself either – for all of us.'

'You're the one who's carping on at Jade about the uselessness of these classes!' Kate pointed out aggressively, and Janet hunched her shoulders, attempting to sidle out of the hall again while she still hadn't been noticed.

Except that somebody had noticed her. Jade. While Estelle and Kate continued to squabble, Jade silently got up and drifted over to Janet, putting a welcoming hand on her shoulder.

'Hello, Janet,' Jade said warmly and, to Janet's surprise, she bent to kiss her on the cheek. 'It's good

198

to see you. As you can see, we're in the middle of a debate. Do come and join us.'

Short of wrenching herself away and making a bolt for it, Janet had no choice but to be drawn towards the hostile trio. And as she didn't have the energy for either wrenching or bolting, she sat down meekly, avoiding all eye contact, while Jade stood at the front to address them all.

'Ladies,' she said. 'I can see that you're not happy, so let's talk about it.'

Estelle tore her glance away from Janet. 'We've done quite enough talking!' she said. 'What we need are techniques!'

But Jade seemed determined not to become ruffled. Instead she sat down, carefully arranging her skirts before looking up and smiling. 'All the techniques in the world won't help you if you aren't truly prepared to take a risk,' she told them calmly.

It was like a red rag to a bull.

'Oh, for God's sake!' Estelle retorted.

'Excuse me, Jade,' Reenie said, 'but last weekend I did what you suggested – I tied Ted to the flippin' bedstead and... *stroked* myself in front of him! If that isn't risky, then I'd like to know what is!'

Janet could sense Estelle's gaze moving on to her, urging her to make a contribution to the argument, but she continued to hang her head. She had nothing to say.

'You're doing wonderfully,' Jade told them, still in that same calm voice. 'All of you. I am so proud of you, I really am. And I *know* you've all taken personal risks. Even coming to these classes in the first place was a risk. But...' Jade paused, looking at them all in turn. 'It isn't enough.'

Estelle coloured up. She looked angry enough to spit.

Jade carried on swiftly. 'Being orgasmic is about being free of all barriers and inhibitions.' She held up her hand to forestall interruptions. 'And yes, I know that what you did with your husband must have seemed uninhibited, Reenie, but tell me, did it really *feel* uninhibited? Or were you uneasy? Did you feel like someone on stage with an audience watching her every move?'

Reenie's gaze dropped. She began to fiddle with the hem of her dress.

Jade gave them another sweeping glance. 'You aren't actresses,' she said. 'To be effective, sensuality must come naturally to you. And until you face your personal demons, I honestly don't think that it will.'

There was a pause as everyone absorbed this. A lorry went past outside, causing the windows to vibrate. When Estelle spoke, her voice was deeply sarcastic. 'Go on then,' she challenged Jade, 'tell me what my personal demons are.'

Jade looked her full in the face. 'Your fear of commitment, Estelle,' she said. 'Whatever it is that drives you to settle for affairs rather than relationships.'

Jade's gaze moved on to Kate. 'And you need to dismantle that force field of yours, Kate. Be open to the possibility of meeting somebody new.'

Kate sneered and folded her arms defensively across her chest, but neither gesture quite hid the despair that seemed to ooze from her.

Jade's gaze moved on to Reenie, and softened. 'And I think you know what I'm going to say to you,

Reenie,' she said kindly. 'Before you can fully devote yourself to your sexual awakening, you and your husband need to finish grieving for your son.'

The seconds passed. Even though Janet didn't look up, she knew that Jade was now looking in her direction. And not only Jade, but everybody else, with the exception perhaps of Reenie, who was probably still reeling after Jade's last pronouncement. The blood rushed in Janet's ears. Out of nowhere she remembered the precise sound of Ray's grunt as he had entered her unwilling body on Sunday night.

'And as for you, Janet,' she heard Jade say with infinite gentleness. 'You have to stand up to people and stop doing things you don't want to do.'

* * * * *

The argument continued on the Big Day Out, when it came round. Janet had almost decided not to go. She was still feeling low, and she didn't relish the thought of more squabbling. Also, after Jade's declaration to Janet that she had to stop doing things she didn't want to do, she was feeling even less sure of her own mind. Did she really even *want* to go out for the day with the girls? Or was she just going along with it to avoid upsetting people?

The atmosphere in the car was fractious. Estelle was driving, with Reenie in the front passenger seat and Janet and Kate squeezed in the back. The sun roof was down to make the most of the sunshine, but even with the clean fresh country air swirling around them, there was a pervading atmosphere of claustrophobia in the car; an atmosphere that was a lot more to do with everybody's moods than a lack of space.

'I say we seriously consider stopping going to the classes.' With her sunglasses and headscarf, Estelle might have looked straight out of a Grace Kelly movie if it hadn't been for her grim expression. Janet glanced at the back of her friend's head with dismay. The thought of not having the lifeline of her weekly meetings to look forward to was too much to bear.

Reenie seemed to agree with her. 'Oh no, Estelle,' she said. 'We can't do that!'

'Why not?' Estelle said. 'It's not as if they're having the desired effect anyway.'

'Waste of flippin' time,' Kate agreed grumpily.

Encouraged, Estelle swept on. 'And if it isn't bad enough that none of us has had an orgasm yet, now we have to be subjected to Madame Jade's attempts at amateur psychology! It simply isn't good enough! What right has she to tell me what I should or shouldn't do in my love life?'

'She only meant you're more likely to have orgasms in a committed relationship, Estelle,' Reenie said bravely. 'Makes sense to me.'

'Well it doesn't to me!' Estelle said irritably. 'Plenty of people only have casual sex and still manage to have a rip-roaring time. This isn't the Dark Ages. Besides, what about what she said to you? A load of complete illogical rubbish!'

'Oh, yes?' Janet could detect a seam of vulnerability in Reenie's defensive reply. 'Why's that?'

'Because you weren't having orgasms before your son's death either, were you?'

'But I wasn't trying to do anything about it then,

was I?' Reenie snapped. 'Maybe I should have done, eh? Maybe that little bit of extra contentment at home would have made all the difference! Made my Craig stay home more, instead of gallivanting about with fast-driving yobbos.' Reenie was clearly upset now, but Estelle didn't seem to have noticed.

'I wasn't saying that, Reenie,' she said. 'Don't be so stupid.'

'Don't you call me stupid, you smug cow!' Reenie shouted.

'Fucking great day out this is turning out to be,' Kate said with a scowl.

Too late, Estelle tried to make amends. 'Look, Reenie, I'm sorry if this is upsetting for you, but all I'm saying is that I think you should– '

But Reenie had had enough. 'I'm not interested in what you think I should or shouldn't do, Estelle Morgan,' she shouted. 'In fact, I'm sick and tired of being bossed about by the likes of you. And maybe you're right; maybe we should stop going to the workshops. Who needs orgasms anyway? Hardly important in the big scheme of things are they? Not a matter of life or death!'

The car was just driving past a sign to the Holkham Bay car park. Janet, whose head had begun to throb with tension, had a sudden, overwhelming urge to get out. 'Stop the car!' she said.

Startled, Estelle immediately slowed down, looking at Janet anxiously in the driving mirror. 'Are you all right?' she asked.

'No,' Janet said in a small but determined voice. 'I want to get out.'

'All right.'

Indicating right, Estelle turned into the car park

and stopped. Everybody looked at Janet, as she struggled with her seatbelt, her fingers clumsy in her anxiousness to escape.

'Janet?' Estelle asked again, 'what is it? Are you feeling ill?'

Janet opened the car door. 'I just need some air,' she said, but when she got out she began to walk quickly away along the track that led to the beach.

Somebody called after her – Reenie, it sounded like – but Janet didn't turn back.

In days gone past, Janet had come here to Holkham a lot. Romantic walks with Ray through the pine trees and down past the brightly-coloured row of beach huts to the beach before they were married; hand in hand, talking about hopes and dreams and plans, or not talking at all; comfortably silent together. And later, when they had Debbie, there had been family picnics, games of beach cricket and walks across the vast swathe of wet sand in search of the sea edge, always just too far away for toddler legs eager for a paddle. They had been happy days, but now they seemed so distant they could almost be dreams, not memories.

When was the last time she'd been here? She honestly couldn't remember. And neither could she remember the last time she and Ray had talked about hopes and dreams and plans together. As for silences, well, there were plenty of those, only these days they weren't comfortable, they were lonely emptinesses she no longer felt equipped to fill. The truth was, she and Ray had run out of things to say to each other a very long time ago.

Emerging onto the beach from the sandy path bordered by swishing pine trees, Janet realised that this was no longer true. They *did* have a topic to discuss now. Sunday night.

Janet knew Estelle would describe what had happened between Janet and Ray as rape, if Janet were to tell her about it, and maybe she would be right. After all, she hadn't wanted to have sex with Ray; with her hangover and him still not speaking to her properly, it had been the very last thing on earth she had wanted. But she hadn't actually said no, had she? So technically it couldn't have been rape. *Yes,* said a voice in her head. *But he knew you didn't want to have sex, didn't he? He couldn't help but know. And he went on and did it anyway.*

Rape or not, it had definitely not been an act of love or respect. And the harsh truth was that Ray neither loved nor respected her. He couldn't do – not if he treated her like that.

Walking on across the sand, Janet wiped the tears angrily from her face. She didn't want to think about this. If she did, she would have to think about what she was going to do about it, and she didn't feel strong enough for that.

And suddenly she wished she hadn't run off the way she had. She didn't want to be on her own anymore, and she wondered whether the others were following her down to the beach. She hoped so, or it was going to take her a very long time to get home. Feeling chilled despite the sunshine, Janet was about to turn to look for them when a man on the nearby dunes called over to her.

'Lovely afternoon, isn't it?'

Automatically Janet looked over at him. 'Er...yes...' she started to say, but then gave a gasp of surprise. The man, who was standing facing her with his hands on his hips, was stark naked. 'Oh!' Janet exclaimed, horrified yet still unable to drag her gaze away from the large swell of the man's belly and a set of genitals that looked disproportionately small in comparison.

Mercifully a posse arrived at just that moment – a posse in the form of Estelle and Kate, with Reenie puffing along at the rear. Janet had never felt as glad to see anybody in her life.

'He's got no clothes on!' she hissed to Estelle and Kate as the man continued to pose and smile, obviously under the impression that he was giving her a treat.

'This part of the beach is for nudists, love,' Reenie told her, puffing up to her side.

'Goodness!' said Janet, still not moving.

'Come on,' said Kate, giving her a little shove. 'Let's get away from here before I lose my lunch.'

Janet responded to the shove, and they wandered on towards the sea. When Estelle and Reenie began to giggle, it was difficult not to smile.

'Feeling better now, love?' Reenie asked her kindly, and Janet nodded.

'A bit, yes thanks,' she said, and it was true, she was. She had only known these three women for a short time, but they were all so dear to her. In a funny kind of a way, they were almost like a second family.

'Well,' Estelle was saying, grinning at them all, 'I can think of something to cheer us all up,' she said. 'Not to mention Droopy over there!' and with that she threw her bag down onto the sand, kicked off her shoes and began to strip.

Everyone looked at her as if she'd lost her mind.

'Come on!' she said, looking straight at Janet.

'After all, Jade accused us of not being prepared to take risks!' She whipped her shirt off and started on her jeans.

Nobody else moved.

'Our inner sex goddesses will get hypothermia in that sea, Estelle,' Kate pointed out dryly.

Estelle didn't bother to reply. By now she was down to her underwear and reaching behind her back to unclip her bra.

Suddenly Reenie burst out laughing and started to pull her T-shirt over her head. 'I'm with you!' she said, and Estelle smiled approvingly.

'Well done, Reenie!' she said, looking in Kate's direction. 'Kate?'

By now Reenie was stepping out of her trousers, a huge mischievous grin on her face. Janet never dreamed Kate would join them, but suddenly she did.

'Oh sod it!' she said, and next minute she was unbuttoning her shirt so fast the buttons almost flew off.

Laughing with approval, Estelle unclipped her bra to free her breasts. Reenie wasn't far behind her, and suddenly Janet didn't know where to look.

'Come on, Janet,' Estelle said. 'All for one?'

Reenie was in the process of whipping her knickers off. 'And one for all!' she shrieked and began a bouncy-fleshed run towards the sea.

Estelle watched Reenie go, smiling as she removed her own knickers. Then she looked up one last time for Janet's response. Kate, meanwhile, had left her clothes in an untidy heap and was careering down the beach after Reenie, determined to get to the sea first. Shrieking, Reenie stepped up her pace.

'Wait for me!' shrieked Estelle after them, leaving

Janet behind as she headed fleet-footed across the sand.

Alone on the beach and uncomfortably aware of the naked man on the dunes only a matter of metres away, Janet hesitated, watching her three friends as they braved the waves, screaming as the cold water made contact with their flesh. Did she want to join them, or would she just be a sheep without a mind of her own if she did? And what about her stretch marks and operation scars? She never let anybody see them, not even Ray if she could help it.

'I say!' the naked man called over to her and she turned to glare at him, suddenly making up her mind.

'Get lost!' she shouted, and then she began to strip off, leaving her clothes in an untidy pile with the others.

'I'm coming!' she yelled to her friends.

And, with Estelle and Reenie cheering and Kate giving her loud wolf whistles, Janet ran naked down to the sea.

Twenty-two

'I don't want all this to end, Estelle. I want an orgasm.'

Janet was slightly tipsy, Estelle decided. Her cheeks were flushed, and she was being more outspoken than usual. She hadn't even really bothered to lower her voice when she'd said the word orgasm, despite the fact that they were in a fairly busy pub.

'I know Jade can be a little *unconventional*,' Janet continued, seemingly oblivious to the fact that several people at neighbouring tables were now listening in to the conversation. 'But I'm sure she's completely sincere. And in my case, I know what she says is right. I do need to stop letting people tell me what to do. I have to start thinking for myself.'

There was a cheer from the other side of the bar where Kate and Reenie were playing the fruit machine. Evidently they had won the jackpot. Now that their differences had been sorted out, they seemed to have become firm friends. Estelle had never seen Kate smile so much, and both she and Reenie had really entered into the spirit of the skinny dip. Running from the sea, Kate had even done a detour to give the posy nude guy more of an eyeful than he had bargained for.

Estelle smiled at Janet. Two months ago she

would never have dreamed that any of these women would have become her friend, but now she genuinely cared for them all, especially Janet.

'I think you're stronger than you realise, Janet,' she said. 'I think if you make your mind up to something then that's it, you do it.'

Janet looked doubtful. 'Do you?'

Estelle nodded. 'Of course. Look at the way you decided to join the workshops.'

Janet pulled a face. 'I think I sort of slid into that,' she said. 'I hadn't got a clue what I was getting myself into.'

'Well maybe,' Estelle said, 'but once you did find out, you stuck with it. Even when that husband of yours tried to forbid you to go.' Estelle did her best to keep her feelings about Janet's husband from her voice, though she found this hard. The man sounded like a total prick.

Janet was looking so thoughtful that Estelle regretted ever suggesting that they should all stop going to the workshops. Jade had really annoyed her at the last session with what Estelle had seen as her arrogant proclamation of their faults, but clearly the workshops meant an awful lot to Janet. Something about Janet just inspired a sort of…tenderness in Estelle. It was like nothing she had really experienced before. Estelle wanted to protect Janet; to make things all right for her and to help her to realise her potential. And somewhere in the back of her mind, Estelle knew that Jade would approve of the caring, nurturing feelings Estelle had for Janet. 'Well done, Estelle,' she would say. 'You're making a real connection with another human being. And every connection you make brings you a step closer to connecting with yourself.'

Or something like that.

Janet looked up. 'Do you know,' she said, 'in twenty years of marriage, I've never been the one to, you know, start things off sexually. I'm hoping that if I continue with the classes I'll finally have the courage to do it.'

'Initiate sex?'

Janet nodded. 'Yes. I'd like to be able to, but somehow when I try to imagine it, it never quite works out.'

Estelle, who had frequently initiated sex, tried and failed to imagine what it must be like to be completely passive. 'Well, how do you imagine doing it?' she asked.

Looking slightly embarrassed, Janet sipped some more of her wine. 'Well, funnily enough, I never imagine us being in bed together when I think about it. We're always in the living room, and Ray's reading the newspaper with his slippers on.'

'Sexy,' Estelle said, and it was impossible to keep a note of sarcasm out of her voice.

Janet didn't seem to notice. 'Well, not really,' she said. 'He has quite skinny legs you see, and he always has them crossed when he reads the paper. His trousers ride up, and there's at least six inches of leg showing above his socks...' Janet's voice faded momentarily as she pictured the scene. 'And he holds his newspaper up like this.' Janet lifted her hands to indicate a broadsheet barrier.

'Even sexier,' Estelle smiled, and this time Janet laughed.

'It's not terribly, is it?'

'Well,' said Estelle, 'let's just say that I'm not

surprised you can't imagine initiating sex in those circumstances.'

'No. Although in a funny kind of a way, those are exactly the kind of circumstances I would *like* to be able to initiate sex in.'

'Why?' asked Estelle. 'Because it would be a challenge?'

Janet looked at her drink. 'In a way. But also because…married life can be so very dull. All those shared meals, all those evenings with the television on and Ray reading every inch of the newspaper. Sometimes I just get this impulse to…oh, I don't know, do something completely crazy just to put a spanner in the works!'

Estelle looked at her friend with affection. 'Go for it, girl!' she felt like saying. 'Show the pompous git what you're really made of!' But she didn't.

'Well, today was a good start, I should think,' she said instead. 'You didn't know you were going to be swimming naked in the sea when we set out this morning.'

Janet smiled. 'I still can't believe I did it!' she said. 'Mind you, I'm not sure I'll be doing it again. The sea was a bit on the cold side.'

'A *lot* on the cold side,' Estelle corrected her. 'There were goose pimples on my goose pimples.'

Janet laughed. 'But it was fantastic. And you're right. It could be the start of me being more daring altogether, if I let it.'

'Before you know it you'll be turning your back on *Coronation Street* and ripping that newspaper out of his steely clutches,' Estelle joked.

'Ray would have a fit if I did that,' Janet said. 'He hates his *Times* to be creased.'

212

They giggled. 'You'll be too busy kneeling on the carpet unbuttoning his flies prior to fellatio.'

Janet's wine went down the wrong way and her coughing and spluttering caused Reenie and Kate to glance over from the fruit machine.

Laughing, Estelle slapped Janet on the back. 'Sorry.'

'You have no idea how impossible *that* is to imagine,' Janet told her after she had recovered.

'Don't you do oral sex?' Estelle asked.

'No!' Janet said, red-faced. 'Well, at least, we *did*. Once or twice. Ray wanted to. But I didn't know what I was supposed to do, and I don't think I was very good at it. And... when Ray did it to me, I remember feeling so... *embarrassed*.'

Estelle frowned. 'Why?'

Janet's face was red. 'Well,' she said. 'I suppose I wasn't very confident that I tasted very nice. And of course, I still didn't have an orgasm anyway, so he got discouraged. Anyway, for one reason or another, we eventually stopped doing it.'

The flat tone of Janet's voice conjured up an image of functional sex with very little foreplay. A pretty joyless part of the week's routine, along with the viewing of particular television programmes.

Poor Janet.

'I asked my lover what I tasted like once,' Estelle said to cheer her friend up.

Janet glanced up, looking astonished and embarrassed. '*Did* you?' she asked. 'Oh my goodness!'

Estelle grinned, remembering the moment well. The bedside lamp had been on, and for a few seconds RT's expression had been totally transparent. 'Well, he *said* I tasted like "dusky musk", whatever that is.'

'Dusky musk,' Janet repeated, fascinated.

Estelle nodded. 'Yes. Mind you, his face said something entirely different.'

Janet was agog. 'What?' she asked.

'Fish!'

When Janet burst out laughing, Estelle joined her. It was funny now, looking back on it.

'What are you two creased up about?' Kate returned to the table, flushed with success from her jackpot win.

Reenie wasn't far behind. 'Yes!' she said. 'Share the joke!'

Estelle explained.

'Blimey!' Reenie said with a grin.

And suddenly they were off again, Janet clutching her stomach she was laughing so hard, drawing glances from everyone nearby. Then somewhere in the middle of it, Reenie's mobile began to ring. Shoulders still shaking, she got it out of her capacious handbag and answered it semi-incoherently.

'Oh, hello, Ted. Sorry, one of the girls just told a joke. No, I can't tell you what about now. It's too rude. I'll tell you later. What's that?' Reenie began to laugh again, looking at the others, her eyes dancing merrily. 'He wants to know what we're having for tea,' she told them then spoke into her phone again. 'What about a nice bit of fish?'

Even Kate had to hoot with laughter at that. It was the end to a good day. Or almost the end.

'So, you'll carry on coming to the classes Estelle?' Janet asked her later, and Estelle smiled.

'I'll carry on coming,' she said, but Kate swiftly

214

corrected her.

'No, Estelle,' she said. 'You'll *start* coming. We all will!'

'I'll drink to that!' Reenie said

'To coming!' they all said, clinking their glasses together.

Twenty-three

Estelle didn't sleep well that night. In the end she got up, made herself a cup of decaf and stood looking out of the lounge window in her silk dressing gown to drink it. The sea was invisible in the darkness, but somehow the knowledge that it was there was soothing. Or at least, it was usually soothing.

Today had been fun, lots of fun. Those who knew Estelle as a hard-nosed businesswoman would have been astounded to have seen her laughing with the girls in the pub, a bona fide paid-up member of a girlie gang. She definitely hadn't been somebody who kept people at arm's length today. She had felt warm towards all of the girls, not just Janet. They had all unwound with each other, even Kate. She was a very funny woman, Kate, when she forgot to be quite so hostile and cynical.

Yes, today Estelle had certainly made connections, and she knew Jade would definitely approve. But the trouble with making connections was that you got used to it. Then, when it ended, when you were out of that bath of warm humanity and back into the cold, real world again, everything seemed just that little bit colder, that little bit more lonely. Coming back to her pristine, immaculate flat with the rest of the evening stretched out before her had been a thoroughly deflating experience.

Normally Estelle enjoyed being on her own, having some space away from the bustle of running her own business. But that evening, as she sat flicking restlessly through the television channels with a glass of wine, she found herself thinking about Reenie. Judging by what Reenie said, the Richardson household was at its best chaotic, and at its worst, bedlam. Estelle couldn't imagine what it would be like to constantly surrounded by people the way Reenie was, with her grown-up daughters and their children constantly popping in and out of the house. It sounded like an endless cycle of meal preparation, clearing up and noisy chatter, and it was a safe bet that Reenie didn't have time on her hands to think the way Estelle sometimes did. It was obvious too that Reenie had a very good marriage, despite her lack of orgasms.

No, that level of bustle and human involvement wasn't what Estelle wanted for herself. But…a small piece of it might be nice. Not having ever really experienced it, she wasn't entirely sure, but just lately she seemed to have been developing an increasing desire to find out.

Suddenly Estelle realised her cheeks were wet, and she brushed the tears away angrily. She was tired of feeling sorry for herself. OK, so she hadn't had a happy childhood. So what? She was hardly the only person in the world who could say that. And what good did dwelling on that kind of stuff do after all? The past was dead and buried.

Yet somehow it didn't seem to want to remain that way any longer, and when Sunday turned out to be another sunny day, Estelle decided on impulse to do something about it. Snatching up her car keys before

217

she had a chance to change her mind, she quickly left her apartment and drove off towards Cambridge to visit her parents.

It was ten years since she'd last seen them. The occasion had been their silver wedding anniversary, and when Estelle had received the formal printed invitation to a celebratory dinner party, she had thrown it away. There hadn't even been a scrawled note on the back of it; nothing. It was as if she were a business colleague or a distant relation, not their daughter. But then, on the night of the party, she had somehow found herself rifling through her wardrobe for something to wear and phoning Rashid, her lover of the time, to tell him to get into his dinner jacket.

Rashid's jaw dropped when he saw her. She was wearing a long dress of ivory satin with a plunging neckline, and her red hair was piled up on top of her head with sexy escaping tendrils framing her neck. The whole look was classily set off by the ruby pendant she had bought for herself to celebrate the first substantial deal of Estelle Morgan Enterprises, and Rashid was all for forgetting the party and getting her out of the ivory satin as quickly as possible. But now Estelle's mind was made up about going to the party, she wasn't about to back down, so they set off in her car. When it quickly became clear that Estelle wasn't in the mood for conversation, Rashid settled down for a sulky sleep, his long, attractive black eyelashes closing over his beautiful dark eyes.

Although Estelle had no desire for Rashid to be anything more than her lover, he was definitely a stunning man, and the perfect trophy escort. Rashid turned heads wherever they went, and with his easy

218

charm he was inevitably popular at parties. Rashid and the ruby pendant were both intended to say the same thing to her parents – 'Look how well I've done without you!'

But as they neared Cambridge, a feeling of dread began to creep steadily over her. Rashid was still soundly asleep, so there was no one to maintain a front for – because there was no way Estelle would have confided in her lover about the sick feeling in her stomach or the clamminess of her skin beneath the ivory satin. Real emotion wasn't a part of the unspoken deal she had with Rashid – the deal was sex and entertainment, that was all.

Real emotion wasn't normally part of the deal Estelle had with herself either. She preferred to be task and achievement orientated rather than reflective and sentient. It was safer that way.

So what the hell are you doing coming here? a nagging voice had asked her. *Why don't you turn round and go back before it's too late?*

But somehow she hadn't turned back; some masochistic compulsion had kept her en route to her parents' house. And the same compulsion kept her en route now, ten years later. She was an adult after all – a successful woman with a thriving business who had achieved far more than her parents ever had. They couldn't hurt her. Though she remembered thinking much the same thing ten years previously with Rashid asleep by her side, and it hadn't been true then, so no doubt it wouldn't be true now.

Despite all the years she had spent in boarding school, the countryside was very familiar as she approached Langley Bottom, the village outside which her parents had lived all their married lives.

Over the years, a succession of nannies had walked Estelle along these dull lanes bordered by stark agricultural land on the way to the village shop in an effort to relieve the tedium of rural life, and it was round about here too that Rashid had woken up, stretching his long legs and peering disapprovingly into the impenetrable blackness out of the car window.

'Mother of God,' he said. 'You've brought me to the very back of beyond, Estelle.'

He hadn't been far wrong either, Estelle thought dryly now, eyeing the desolate countryside with dislike. But she remembered how his attitude had changed when she'd turned into the drive of Hopkins, her parents' home, and he'd caught his first glimpse of the impressive frontage of the house.

'Now that's more like it,' he said, sitting up straighter in his seat, suddenly all beady-eyed and eager.

Estelle hadn't cared whether Rashid approved or not. In fact, she was half regretting bringing him along at all. If she'd been hoping for a man to hide behind, then she was sure she would be quickly disappointed. Rashid was the type to spread his charm widely rather than to reserve it for her exclusive use. Very likely she wouldn't see much of him at all after the first ten minutes or so.

But after Estelle had parked the car, Rashid surprised her by offering his arm to escort her into the house, making her wonder whether if, somewhere within his not overly intelligent interior, Rashid was aware of his chief role – that of assisting her to make the maximum immediate impact. And with his black hair and his dark eyes, and her all cream-and-gold-glamour and sophistication, that was precisely the effect they had as they made their entrance. Though they might just as well have been dressed in sackcloth for all the notice Estelle's mother took of them.

Sonia Morgan was standing by the grand piano talking to a group of friends – a piano that Estelle was quite sure had never been played in all the years it had been in the house. Deep in conversation as she was, Sonia spotted Estelle immediately, but true to character, she continued with her conversation, despite a long moment when her gaze locked with her daughter's. Of Estelle's father, there was no sign at all, and it was only when one of Sonia's oldest friends rushed forward to greet Estelle with over-the-top enthusiasm that Sonia finally broke away from her group to come and greet her.

'Hello, Estelle,' she said coolly, offering her cheek to be kissed. 'We weren't expecting you since you didn't RSVP to your invitation. I'm afraid you won't be able to sit with us at dinner; it would be far too difficult to change the seating plan at this late stage.'

Estelle flushed. 'Hello, Mother,' she said. 'Happy Anniversary.'

Sonia nodded coolly, her gaze washing over every inch of her daughter's appearance, and settling at last on Estelle's ruby pendant.

Before she could make any comment, Rashid, who wasn't used to being ignored, thrust his hand out in Sonia's direction. 'I'm Rashid,' he smiled. 'And seeing that you have the same drop dead good looks as Estelle, I'm assuming that you must be her mother.'

Poor Rashid. Even he withered slightly beneath the frosty response this innocent comment inspired. Regarding him as if he were the lowest species of pond life, Sonia Morgan didn't even bother to honour him with a reply.

'Excuse me,' she said coldly. 'I must attend to my other guests. I'll catch up with you later, Estelle.' And off she went.

'What a bitch,' Rashid said under his breath, and suddenly Estelle felt glad she had brought him along after all.

'Oh, yes,' she agreed, taking his arm. 'Come on, let's get ourselves a large drink.'

Ten years on, as Estelle approached the turning for Hopkins, there was no Rashid at her side to soften the ordeal. She didn't even really know what had happened to him after they'd split up, beyond a rumour that he had hooked up with a wealthy older woman. Rashid always had been allergic to work.

Despite his shallowness, Rashid hadn't been that bad really, and Estelle smiled briefly, remembering the way he had yanked her around the dance floor that night, subjecting her and her sophisticated cream ivory to wild rock and roll twirls more suited to a bawdy wedding reception than to her parents' refined silver wedding anniversary celebrations.

The turning to Hopkins was up ahead. Estelle's heart suddenly began to race. She indicated right, but as she began to turn into the drive, she saw the estate agent's sign.

Sold.

Shocked to the core, Estelle braked sharply, stopping the car halfway across the road. The car behind her had to swerve crazily in order to avoid hitting her, and its driver shouted obscenities at her out of his window before roaring away.

Somehow Estelle managed to pull herself together enough to drive on past the turning until she reached a lay-by up ahead. There she sat, gripping the wheel, fury swiftly overtaking the shock. OK, so there was no love lost between her and her parents, but she was still their daughter. Were they even going to bother to tell her they were moving away?

Frustration followed hard on the heels of the shock and the anger. She had come all this way to confront the ghosts of her past, and now it seemed as if that was all she was going to find at Hopkins – ghosts. Though maybe they hadn't actually moved yet? Taking the car keys from the ignition, Estelle grabbed her handbag, got out of the car and began to walk quickly back down the road towards the entrance to Hopkins to find out.

The house was set back from the road at the end of a long, winding driveway, and as Estelle walked along it, it began to rain, slow, large drops that bounced off the laurels on either side of the driveway. She carried on walking oblivious, but it wasn't until she got round the final bend that she saw the cars parked out the front of the house – a gaudy yellow sports car and an antique Rolls-Royce, neither of which were her parents' style. So they *had* moved, but presumably fairly re-cently, since the Sold sign was still up.

Estelle paused, uncertain what to do next, but then the heavens really opened and she acted on instinct, heading for the nearest shelter, which happened to be the summerhouse. Nobody came out to stop her, so she let herself in and closed the door. Inside, the room was empty apart from a couple of neglected plants in plant pots, and although it was logical that her parents' battered old sofas would have been removed, the stark emptiness still came as a shock. The summerhouse had been the same for as long as she could remember.

Estelle looked around her, feeling suddenly cold. It had been a mistake to come in here. Bad memories were swooping down on her, and she was powerless to stop them. Her fourteenth birthday party – she and Scott, a boy from a class, sneaking out to the summer-house together. Kissing, giggling, the moon shining down on them where they lay on the sofa. Then suddenly the door had opened, and she and Scott had sprung apart, thinking it was her father. But it hadn't been her father; it had been Tim Lawrence, her father's business friend.

'What's going on in here?' he'd said. 'Something I ought to tell your father about, Estelle?'

'Please don't,' Estelle begged. She really liked Scott, and her father would just ruin everything. He'd never let her see him again.

Tim Lawrence looked in Scott's direction. 'You;' he said. 'Out.'

'Yes, sir,' Scott said, and went.

Estelle made to follow him, but Tim put out a hand to stop her. 'Not so fast, Estelle,' he said. Then he held her by the arms and looked at her, his eyes travelling over her body in a way that made her flesh crawl. Just minutes before, Scott had looked at her in the same way. But that had been different. Nice. But this… Estelle felt afraid.

'Let go of me,' she said, struggling to get free.

'I don't think I will,' Tim said. 'You obviously

came in here for a reason. I think you should get what you came for.'

And suddenly he was kissing her, his tongue forcing its way into her mouth and his fingers digging into her flesh. He smelled of cigar smoke and booze, and with his repulsive tongue thrusting into her throat, Estelle felt as if she couldn't breath. One hairy hand delved lower, pressing its way between her legs, pulling up her skirt. Desperately, Estelle kicked out with the heel of her shoe and made contact with his shin.

'You little bitch!' Tim's grasp loosened enough for her to make her escape, and she managed to break free from him, fleeing from the summerhouse and running back to the safety of the house and the party. Her hair was streaming down her back, her make-up was smudged, and her eyes were wild. Her parents were dancing together in the big hallway. They looked up as she tore through the door. There was no time to compose herself.

'Whatever's the matter, Estelle?' Her mother sounded annoyed to have been interrupted.

Suddenly, Estelle wanted comfort more than she wanted Scott, who had run off and left her there without so much as a backward glance.

Tears filled her eyes. 'It's Tim,' she sobbed. 'He attacked me!'

'He *what*?'

There was disbelief in her father's voice even before Tim Lawrence came into the hall behind her.

'For goodness' sake, Estelle, it was just a cuddle to wish you a happy birthday! What vivid imaginations girls have these days!'

And that had been that, apart from a hissed

reprimand from her father for humiliating him in front of his friend.

Looking back now, Estelle thought that evening marked the end of her innocence. Something had hardened within her after that. She had always craved more love and attention from her parents. But after that evening, she had given up on them. But that hadn't made the hot feelings go away. Perhaps that was why she had picked the summerhouse as a venue to have wild, noisy, party-disrupting sex with Rashid ten years ago.

She'd been very drunk. Not that she'd planned it that way, but the party had been too much of an ordeal to face stone cold sober. Wedged at dinner between a vicar and a dull academic, Estelle had watched her parents lording it on the top table while she worked herself through the best part of a bottle of wine and Rashid flirted with all and sundry.

And then, after dinner, when she was making her swaying way back from the bathroom, Estelle came face to face with her father in the dimly lit corridor.

'Estelle,' he said, seeming to loom out of the shadows. 'We didn't think you'd come.'

Nobody else was around. It was years since they'd been alone together. Years during which she'd built up a successful business. Any other father would have been proud of her and shown an interest in what she was doing. But not hers. 'It was a surprise to me too,' she said sarcastically.

'You're looking well,' he said.

Estelle flushed. She wanted, suddenly, to hurt him. 'You're not,' she said. 'The extra weight doesn't suit you.'

But Edward Morgan just laughed, patting his

stomach. 'I was always a man of healthy appetites,' he said.

Oh yes, that was certainly true. Her mother and father had never been able to get enough of each other. She'd grown up with a constant feeling that she was in the way of their fun. She could remember the look of irritation on her father's face whenever she had made any demands on his time. Just like when she'd run into the hall from the summerhouse the night of the party.

'I must go and speak to Rashid,' she said, moving away.

'Oh yes, your pretty Indian boy,' her father. 'Yes, you're probably wise not to leave him alone for very long.'

Estelle didn't respond to the bait; she just kept right on walking. She needed air, but she needed not to be alone more, so she went to seek Rashid out. Sure enough, he had an admiring crowd – mostly of women – around him, but she stepped into the throng, taking his arm possessively and surprising him so much she almost put him off the punchline of the joke he was telling.

'I need to see you outside for a moment, Rashid, darling,' she said as soon as the joke was finished and the laughter had died down, and although he looked surprised by her use of the endearment, he went with her without a fuss.

'What's so urgent, Estelle *darling*?' he asked sarcastically as she led him outside and into the summer-house.

'This,' she said, reaching up to kiss him while simultaneously grabbing his cock through his trousers.

Rashid wasn't one to argue in such circumstances, and they made love without even bothering to close the summerhouse doors. And later, with her fake cries of pleasure so loud they could be heard by anybody and everybody who happened to be taking the air on that hot, balmy night, Estelle heard her mother's icy voice.

'Don't worry,' she said. 'That's just my daughter. She always was a little slut.'

And that had been the last time she had seen her parents.

Now, ten years later, Estelle looked around the bare interior of the summerhouse again. The passing years hadn't been enough to erase the bad memories of the things that had happened to her there, and neither had her lovemaking with Rashid. Perhaps there were some bad memories that nothing could erase.

There were stones mixed with the soil in the pots of the withering plants. Someone, at some point, had cared enough about them to want to give them sufficient drainage. The stones were redundant now, because the plants were too far gone for them to be of any use. But Estelle could think of a perfect use for them.

Picking up a handful of the stones, she began to throw them at the summerhouse windows; one at a time at first, but then by the handful, in an increasing pebbledash frenzy. The glass began to break, quietly at first, but as she put more force into it, with satisfyingly loud splintering and cracking sounds. The stones ran out while there was still glass intact, and long before Estelle's fury was spent. So she took off one of her shoes and began to beat at the windows with the heel, scarcely noticing when shards of glass splintered into her face.

'What the fuck do you think you're doing?' Estelle ignored the burly man who tore in from the rain outside. He had to grab hold of her and drag her outside as she continued to kick and scream, still attempting to smash the remaining glass with her shoe.

The rain was torrential. Flailing about helplessly in the man's grasp, her hair plastered to her face, Estelle dimly heard him bellow to someone near the house. 'Call the police! There's a fucking lunatic on the premises.'

Twenty-four

The atmosphere in the catering classroom was as tense as a Wild West saloon pre-shoot-out. Feeling like a sheriff, Kate stood between Marcia and Stuart, the boy who had been on the receiving end of Marcia's chip fat. The normal boisterous hubbub of the classroom was silenced, and every pair of student eyes was focused on the trio at the front.

Kate was as tense as the rest of them. She had stuck her neck out to get Marcia back on the course; it had taken hours of negotiation with the Principal, Stuart and even Marcia herself. Reenie had been endlessly grateful for her efforts, but she wouldn't be so grateful if Marcia failed to keep to her word and Kate was forced to sling her out again.

Marcia was currently gazing at the floor, her expression unpromisingly sullen, toeing the pattern of the lino with a grubby trainer. Kate felt like shaking her, but resisted the temptation, restricting herself instead to a firm squeeze of the girl's shoulder. Marcia ought to know what was expected of her. Kate had spelt it out to her clearly enough. It was up to her now.

Just when Kate had begun to think all her efforts had been a waste of time, Marcia lifted her head and – miracle of miracles – looked Stuart directly in the face.

'I'm sorry,' she told him in a halfway audible voice. 'I'm sorry I …you know.'

As apologies went, it wasn't world class, and Kate held her breath, knowing it was the best they were going to get, and hoping it would be good enough. Stuart took his time responding. Obviously aware of his power, he was making the most of having the normally over-feisty Marcia humbled, and while in one sense Kate didn't blame him, she also had a strong urge to give him a good slapping.

She gave his foot a little kick instead, and he blinked. 'And I'm sorry I said what I said about– ' he started, but Kate swiftly cut him off.

'No need to rake all that up again,' she said. 'Now, shake hands.'

Obediently, the two young people shook hands, inspiring a loud cheer from the rest of the class, and Kate smiled and gave them both a little shove away from her. 'Right, go and get on with your work. And the rest of you! That pork won't cook itself!'

It was only as the students drifted off towards their chopping boards and pans, still chattering excitedly, that Kate realised Geoff was grinning at her from the doorway of the classroom. For some unaccountable reason, she felt embarrassed. 'How much of that did you see?' she asked.

'All of it,' he smiled, leaning against the doorframe with his arms folded, watching her. 'You did good, Katie.'

Geoff had flour up to his elbows as well as a smudge of it on his nose, and his baker's hat was jauntily askew on his head. As for his baker's whites, they were buttoned up wrongly and straining over his paunch so badly the buttons looked in severe danger of popping off.

The man could be irritating as hell, but he had been there for her all through the last long, painful year. Without the thought of him here at work, a friendly face to greet her amongst the sea of spotty-faced, unmotivated youths and the pinched-faced, over-motivated college management team, Kate doubted whether she'd have been able to keep rolling up day after day.

Geoff levered himself away from the doorframe. 'By the way,' he said, just before he turned away, 'like your new hairstyle. It suits you.' And then he was gone, strolling across the corridor to the bakery and leaving her to face the catcalls of her students.

'You're in there, Miss!'

'Like your hair, Miss!'

Kate slapped on the scowl she'd perfected over fifteen years of being a catering lecturer. 'That will do, thank you,' she said. 'Get on with your work.'

Why had Geoff paid her such a public compliment? He of all people knew what the students were like, and anyway, it wasn't like him to pay her compliments at all. That wasn't what their relationship was like; normally he wouldn't even notice if she'd had her hair changed. Not that she *had* changed her hair recently. Or in fact as long as she could remember.

It had been Reenie's idea. Her daughter Gaynor was a hairdresser, trying to start up a mobile business following a break to have her children.

'Go on, Kate, give her a go,' Reenie had persuaded her. 'My treat for what you've done for Marcia. It'll give you a bit of a boost and it'll be a customer for Gaynor too.'

232

Kate had been doubtful, and not just because it was a very long time since she'd bothered much about her appearance. 'I don't know, Reenie,' she said. 'I'd have to spend weeks clearing up my place until it was fit to have a mobile hairdresser round.'

They were sitting in Reenie's pristine kitchen drinking tea. 'Well, come round here then,' Reenie said. 'Gaynor's always round here anyway. There's almost as much hair cut in this kitchen as there are meals cooked.'

So that was what Kate had done, and she had to admit she was pleased with the results. Gaynor had not only given her a younger-looking hairstyle, but she had persuaded her to have a dark auburn tint put in. So far the new cut had stayed sleek and manageable, and it definitely made her look younger. She got a jolt of surprise every time she looked in the mirror.

But for Geoff to notice and comment... Well, that felt weird, very weird.

But things were to get even weirder later on.

Kate was on her own in the catering staff room catching up on some paperwork when Geoff came in, minus the flour smudges and the jaunty baker's hat.

'Glad that class is over,' he said, dumping a bag of books and equipment onto his desk, which was adjacent to Kate's. 'Felt like shoving Trevor Barton and his ugly gob right into the dough mixture. Little bastard's far too fond of his adjectives for my liking. Especially since the only ones he knows are the ones beginning with F.'

Kate, normally quick off the mark coming up with one-liners about students, could think of absolutely nothing to say to this. Somehow Geoff's unexpected compliment about her hair had made her feel shy and awkward with him. He was still her funny, no-hope pal; the guy who still hadn't noticed by three o'clock in the afternoon that his bakery whites were buttoned up wrongly, one side yanked up a good six inches higher than the other, but at the same time… Well, he wasn't as well. To the newly sensitised Kate, there seemed to be something just a little bit false about her friend's tone of voice.

When Kate didn't say anything, Geoff raised his eyebrows at her. 'You all right?'

She nodded quickly and got back to her work. 'Mmm hmm,' she said. 'Apart from a ton of marking to do.'

She could tell Geoff was still looking at her. 'Now I know something's wrong with you,' he said, reaching out playfully to put a hand on her brow to feel her temperature. 'Not like you to be so conscientious.'

His hand was hot, and Kate flinched away from it. Geoff noticed. He couldn't help it – she'd wrenched away from the bodily contact as decisively as if his hand was coated with poison.

He looked at her. 'Seriously, Katie,' he said at last. 'Are you all right? Really?'

The genuine concern in his voice made her feel emotional. 'Yes!' she snapped. 'I'm all right, OK? How many times do I have to say it?'

Geoff sat down abruptly at his desk. 'OK,' he said, sounding offended. 'Keep your hair on.' Picking up his bag, Geoff upturned it, emptying its contents out as noisily as a child having a tantrum. Kate glared at him, but Geoff ignored her, proceeding to swipe everything he didn't want to one

234

side of his desk, opening a large book with a thump and generally, it seemed to Kate, making as much noise as he possibly could.

Kate's face was turned in the direction of her NVQ Level Two Catering students' workbooks, but very little of their incorrectly spelt and poorly punctuated scrawlings permeated her brain. Geoff had started to hum a little tune now, although humming was quite a generous term for the tuneless vibration issuing from his throat.

Kate sighed heavily, attempting to return her attention to her workbooks. Geoff turned a page noisily and crossed his leg, his foot almost coming into contact with her knee. Kate gritted her teeth, shifting in her seat.

Thus they had sat, free period after free period, for five years, she and Geoff – ever since he had first started to work at the college. Not that they had often sat like this, both supposedly hard at work. Normally they were engaged in a paper dart throwing competition or sneaking a crafty fag or just bitching to each other about the staff or the students.

'Worse than the flaming students, you two are,' Tom, a colleague had said once, on an impromptu visit from the more earnest Humanities Department. And Kate and Geoff had just grinned at each other, not denying it, simultaneously chucking paper darts at Tom's head.

But now those carefree days seemed like an invention or an aberration of memory, and finally the tension was more than Kate could stick. Scraping back her chair, she stood up and shoved her workbooks into her bag.

Geoff looked up. 'You off?' he asked, sounding

surprised.

'Yep,' she grunted, snatching up her coat from the back of her chair.

'Well look,' Geoff detained her as she headed for the door. 'I was going to say… Well, ask really I suppose…'

She paused, looking at him suspiciously. 'What?'

'Well,' Geoff continued awkwardly. 'How about going for a meal later on?'

She looked at him as if he'd lost his mind. 'A meal?'

He cleared his throat, keeping his eyes on his books. 'Dinner,' he said. 'In a restaurant.'

He looked at her then; the merest flicker of a glance, and Kate realised all of a sudden that he was…embarrassed. Alarm bells went off in her head.

'Is Tom coming?' she asked, and now he looked at her, surprised. 'Or anyone else?'

'Wasn't going to ask anyone else, no,' he said.

'Oh.' Kate was confused to say the least. First the compliment, and now an invitation that seemed almost like… a date. What was going on?

The pause while Geoff waited for her reply and she struggled to make sense out of what it all meant lasted for quite some time. Too long. Suddenly Geoff stood up, tucking his book under his arm and sweeping past her on his way out of the door. 'It was just a thought,' he said gruffly. 'Doesn't matter.'

And then he was gone.

* * * * *

In Reenie's house, it was uncharacteristically quiet with Marcia back at college. True, she had only

236

been off for three months, but Reenie had got used to having her around, even if she had usually been asleep in bed or shut away with her music. But now she was back at college, and Gaynor was busy getting her business off the ground, Reenie knew she was going to have to get used to spending a lot more time in her own company. Funny how you could be totally glad for people and miss them like crazy too. But then everybody on the planet wanted to have their cake and eat it, so why not her too?

It was like the song said though: if you loved somebody, you had to set them free. Even if there was a great big festering place inside of you that knew only too well what could happen when you went about handing freedom out willy-nilly.

'This won't get the windows washed, Reen.' Reenie spoke to herself, trying and failing to spur herself into action.

Normally she wasn't the type to be idle. She liked her home to be spick and span, and with the amount of people who passed through the house, there was always something to do.

But somehow today there seemed little point to it all. What did it matter whether the windows were washed or not? Nobody noticed anyway; it was only her with her mental rota of jobs that got them done at all. Every fortnight of her married life, weather allowing. Her mother had washed her windows every fortnight, and no doubt *her* mother had done the same before her. But it didn't seem likely that any of her three daughters were going to carry on the family tradition; none of them seemed to make housework her priority.

What would her mother have made of her three

girls now they were all grown up? They'd been kids really when her mother had died, but even then they'd been starting to get on her nerves with their teenage tantrums and sulks. She'd have disapproved of Marcia of course. It was a blessing really that she had been saved the stress of dealing with her mother's disapproval while Marcia had been in trouble. Reenie's mum had been a forceful traditionalist, a woman never scared of voicing her opinions on any given subject. While Reenie had always known that her parents loved her, her upbringing had been very strict, and as a result she had always tried to give her own children more freedom than she'd had herself.

It was a different matter trying to do the same for herself though; if she didn't keep constantly busy, a nagging voice bearing a remarkable similarity to her mother's started up inside her head, giving her a hard time about it. 'Who d'you think you are? The devil makes trouble for idle hands!'

The voice was there now, but somehow today even that wasn't enough to motivate her. Reenie had woken up feeling unaccountably depressed, and somehow she couldn't seem to shake the feeling off.

Sitting at her kitchen table with a cooling cup of coffee in front of her, Reenie allowed herself the painful luxury of thinking about her son. Handsome, vital Craig, with a lot of her energy and all of Ted's laid-back charm. Right from a toddler he had done everything and anything he wanted and somehow managed to persuade her that was the way it should be. He'd even managed to win her mother over, more often than not.

What would he be doing now, if he hadn't died?

Would he be at college like Marcia? Working? Married even? In her imagination, Reenie pictured him in each role, mentally changing his clothes to suit, a bit like the mix and match people game one of her grandsons had. Both she and Ted had always had high hopes for their son, especially Ted. A bus driver for the majority of his working life, Ted had wanted more for Craig; a trade of some sort; something skilled. Reenie had just wanted her son to be happy. And he had been happy. She knew that ought to be some sort of compensation for his short life, but it wasn't.

The phone began to ring. Reenie sat and stared at it, wanting to have the guts to ignore it for once. She didn't want to speak to anybody. She didn't want to be happy-go-lucky Reenie, always available for a chat. If she ignored it, then whoever it was might give up and go away.

But they didn't. On and on it rang, until she began to think about all the bad news it could be bringing – Ted's coach crashed, Marcia flipped again at college, something wrong with one of the grandchildren – and she snatched the receiver up.

'Reenie? It's Kate.'

Marcia then.

'What's she done?'

There was a pause on the other end of the line. 'Who?' Kate sounded confused.

'Marcia,' Reenie said. 'That is why you've rung, isn't it? To tell me she's lost it again?'

'No!' Kate said sounding surprised now. 'Marcia's fine.'

'Oh,' Reenie said doubtfully.

'Honestly, Reenie, she is. She's settled back in

239

just as if nothing ever happened.'

'Right,' said Reenie. 'Good.' But she still wasn't convinced. There was definitely something wrong; she could tell from Kate's voice.

'It's Geoff,' Kate told her at last, her voice unusually quiet for her.

Reenie frowned. 'He hasn't had an accident has he?'

'No, nothing like that.' Kate paused, and this time Reenie waited. 'He's asked me out.'

'What?'

'He asked me out to dinner. On a *date*,' Kate said miserably.

Reenie closed her eyes and sighed. No accidents then, just a bit of love angst. 'Well, that's good isn't it?' she said, feeling the adrenalin drain away from her body.

'*Is* it?' Kate said miserably.

Reenie summoned up a smile from somewhere. Kate suddenly sounded about Marcia's age or younger. 'Of course it is,' she said encouragingly. 'He's a nice man; you like him; I can't see what the problem is.'

'He's my mate!' Kate said miserably. 'My best mate. What if we go out and it doesn't work out?'

'Well think about it the other way,' Reenie said patiently. 'What if you go out and it's the best thing that's ever happened to you? You'll never know if you don't try, will you?'

There was silence as Kate turned this over for a while. When she spoke again, her voice was sulky. 'I don't think I want to go out with anyone ever again,' she said, and Reenie suddenly remembered what Jade had told her friend about needing to let go of the past.

240

'Why don't you go, love?' she said. 'Geoff isn't like your Ian; he's not going to hurt you. If it doesn't feel right, you can just go back to being friends, can't you? Look, I've got to go – there's somebody at the door. Let me know how it turns out, won't you?'

Kate still sounded miserable. 'All right,' she said and hung up.

It wasn't like Reenie to tell lies, especially to friends; there was nobody at the door. But thinking about Jade's advice to Kate had reminded Reenie of what Jade had said to *her* about needing to finish grieving for Craig.

And suddenly she knew exactly what she had to do.

* * * * *

Kate replaced the telephone receiver despondently. She'd thought Reenie of all people would understand how she felt, but why should she? Married to the same man for God only knew how many years; OK, so she'd had a bad time with her son dying, but she'd never experienced divorce. Reenie had married Ted expecting to be with him for the rest of her life, and that was exactly the way it was panning out for her.

Ted hadn't gone off with Reenie's best mate. Shagged her in the marital bed. Didn't look down his nose at her as if to say 'I can't believe I was ever married to you.' Ted cherished Reenie, loved her. All right, he couldn't give her orgasms, but he wanted to.

Reenie didn't have a clue what it was like to have to learn to trust all over again. She didn't know how difficult it had been for Kate to let down her barriers

241

enough to become *friends* with anybody post-divorce, let alone contemplate being anybody's lover. And not anybody, but *Geoff.*

And worst of all, it was already too late; that's what she would have said if Reenie hadn't been so eager to get off the phone. Even without her having gone out on a date with Geoff, everything had already changed. Because he'd asked her out, whether she went or not, things would never be the same between them again. They'd be all awkward and strange with each other. The days of playfully taking the piss and being able to be herself with Geoff were gone forever.

Kate was meant to be teaching a class late afternoon, but instead she rang in sick and headed for the pub.

'All alone today?' the barman asked her, pouring her a pint. 'Where are your partners in crime?'

Kate just grunted, downing the pint and gesturing for a refill.

'Like that is it?' the barman asked, raising his eyebrows, but she ignored him, paying for the drinks and going to sit in a corner on her own. It was all Ian's fault. He was the one who had made her so distrustful, so allergic to relationships. Even if Reenie was right, and Geoff was the man she should be with, she was so pathetically insecure these days she was one hundred percent certain to mess it up.

She was damned if she went out with Geoff and damned if she didn't.

* * * * *

It was harder to put the loft ladder up than Reenie

242

had expected. Ted always managed to do it in about two seconds flat, but Reenie had never tried before, and it took her a while to realise how to slide the extension bit up so the ladder was long enough to reach the hatch cover. She finally managed it, but the minute she put her foot on the bottom rung, the extension part slipped down again, bringing the whole ladder down with an almighty crash. Fortunately Reenie wasn't hurt, though she was shaken, but she was so determined to get up into the roof she made herself try again.

Most of Craig's belongings were in boxes in the roof, exactly where Ted had stored them a few months after the funeral. They'd cleared them from his bedroom, but they hadn't been able to face throwing anything away. The boxes had been up there ever since. Too long. And now she'd decided to do some-thing about them, Reenie was in no mood to wait until Ted came home to help her. It was best if she did it on her own anyway. Ted would be too upset. She fully expected to be pretty upset herself, but it had to be done, and now was the time to do it. It was the only way she could think of to try to get some peace.

So she picked up the ladder and took a little time to examine it, noticing as she did so a couple of clips on the sides – presumably for securing the extension part into place. Then she tried again, this time testing the ladder carefully by pushing the rungs firmly with her hands before putting any weight onto it.

When she was sure it was safe, she climbed up slowly and pushed at the loft hatch, sliding it across just as she had seen Ted do. Then she squeezed herself up through the space into the darkness, trying not to think about spiders.

Sitting there, panting, Reenie resisted the temptation to look down, trying to remember where the light switch was. Too late she realised she should have brought a torch with her, but there was no way she was going back down again now. Feeling around carefully with her hand, she finally located the switch and pressed it. The loft was instantly filled with light.

Yes! But Reenie's sense of satisfaction was short-lived, swamped by far messier feelings as she gazed at the neat stack of boxes on the other side of the roof space. The boxes were all that was left of her son; that and his gravestone and the ongoing feud with Louise's family.

Drawing in a ragged breath, Reenie got up and began to walk across the roof space. But unfortunately her thoughts were so entirely focused on the boxes she forgot about the limited roof clearance. Bumping her head sharply on a rafter, Reenie fell with a little cry, her ankle turning painfully beneath her.

Twenty-five

Estelle couldn't stop shivering on her way home from Cambridge Police Station. It had all been so...*tawdry*: that thug manhandling her out of the summerhouse, the indignity of being bundled into the back seat of the police car, the interrogation in the bleak interview room with the compulsory WPC in attendance, and finally a night in the police cells. She felt as if she'd lived through sixteen episodes of *The Bill* and been the accused in every one of them.

'Is there anyone you'd like to phone Ms Morgan?' the cold-eyed sergeant had asked her, placing a deliberately sarcastic emphasis on the word Ms.

'No thank you.' Estelle had sat bolt upright on the hard wooden chair, her blood-flecked hands folded in her lap and with no outward sign of the total turmoil going on inside her head. Who could she ring? In the whole world, who could Estelle Morgan phone to say 'I've done something really stupid. Please, come and help me.' No one. Not even her new friends. Nobody knew her like this. *She* didn't know herself like this. Dangerous. Depressed. *Vulnerable*.

And so she'd listened and responded as required, all with that icy cool demeanour, even while her intelligent mind knew full well that she would be much more sympathetically treated if she could only break down and cry; blurt out the truth about why she'd done what she'd done. They'd probably even have let her off if she'd done that. Even that brute at the house might have thought twice about pressing charges if she'd been a heartbroken, unstable female in the throes of a nervous breakdown.

But as it was, she had been charged with criminal damage in the presence of an unsympathetic lawyer and forced to pay bail in order to be set free. And in the future there would be a court case; her name in the papers. But worse than all of that was the bitter knowledge that none of it had done any good anyway. She hadn't left the past behind, and maybe she never would. Not even if she could smash every pane of glass in East Anglia.

'Cold, crazy bitch,' she heard the sergeant say to a colleague under his breath as she walked with dignity from the police station, and Estelle knew he had a point. She was damaged goods. Deficient. And she always would be.

* * * * *

Janet had spent most of the day at work thinking about oral sex. Cruella (Janet always thought about her boss as Cruella these days) had been out all day, and business had been slow, so there had been plenty of time to think. As far as Janet could remember, those distant times when she and Ray had tried oral sex were the closest she had come to having an orgasm. There had been a definite flicker, she remembered, even if it had quickly been extinguished when Ray had thrust his penis into her face, silently demanding 'his turn.'

She could remember she hadn't enjoyed doing it

to him very much. He hadn't seemed to appreciate the fact that she had tonsils in the back of her throat, and had become irritated when she gagged what he con-sidered to be once too often. And she really hadn't known what she was supposed to do. Why should she? He didn't tell her, and she had never done it with anybody else. It was hardly the kind of thing to discuss with friends like Gwen. Of course if she'd known the girls in those days, then it would have been quite another matter.

But she *did* know them now, and although they hadn't as yet covered oral sex at the workshops, surely it couldn't be too difficult? As the dull day at the shop went on, Janet decided she wanted to have another try. If she did it to Ray, then he might do it to her. And maybe this time she would be lucky. If not, then she would at least have something to discuss with the girls. She might even pick up some helpful tips… Somehow she thought Estelle was probably something of an expert at it.

Janet smiled to herself naughtily. She was changing. *Had* changed. And it was about time Ray knew about it.

* * * * *

Estelle's answer phone message light was flashing crazily when she got back to the flat. Automatically she pressed the play button. The first two messages were from Charlotte.

'Ms Morgan? It's Charlotte. I'll try to reach you on your mobile.'

'Ms Morgan, it's Charlotte again. I've left a message on your mobile as well. The clients from

Stockholm have arrived and I was wondering when we could expect you.'

Shit! How the hell could she have forgotten? She'd been weeks setting up the meeting with the Larssons! The deal was potentially very lucrative and she had let it slip her mind. Frantically Estelle looked at her watch. Almost three o'clock. Maybe there was still time. Maybe the Larssons hadn't left yet.

The voice of Mark, her sales manager, suddenly filled the room. 'Estelle, it's Mark. Just to say I've taken Freda and Artur to the Saracen Hotel for a late lunch. I told them you've been unavoidably detained and will join us as soon as possible. Call me as soon as you get this message.'

Snatching her mobile from her bag, Estelle quickly dialled Mark's number. 'Mark? It's Estelle.'

'Estelle! Hi! We've been worried about you.' She could hear the sound of laughter in the background, but couldn't tell if he was in a bar or just back in the office with the staff laughing and bitching about her.

'Where are you?' she asked.

'Still in the Saracen. Are you joining us?'

Estelle paused. Her face and hands were covered with cuts and her clothes were splashed in blood. She desperately needed a shower.

'Freda and Artur would *really* like to meet you.' Even in Estelle's fragile state she could detect the meaning behind her sales manager's words. 'Get here or the deal's off.'

'OK,' she said. 'Give me half an hour.' And she hung up.

* * * * *

Up in the loft, Reenie sat in the dust with her swollen ankle stuck out in front of her, looking through a box of Craig's toys. They were all there – he'd never wanted her to throw anything away. Sentimental as they come, he'd been. All his Action Men and his toy diggers and his remote control racing car... Even his teddy bear from his toddler days; a poor excuse for a bear now, all threadbare and grimy with one ear torn off.

Hugging the bear to her face, Reenie thought about her bright, happy son at age two, trying to conjure him up from the smell of the bear. Whereas Marcia had been content to amuse herself a lot of the time, when she wasn't being dragged into one of her brother's games, Craig had been into everything. It had been a full-time job keeping tabs on him. Right from the start he'd been determined to live life with a capital L.

But there was no trace of all that vitality left here. The bear just smelt old and musty. Like decay.

Very gently, Reenie put the bear back in the box and moved on to the next one. A stamp album. A school project about leaves, Craig's juvenile writing sloping down towards the right of the pages. Copper Beech with Beech spelt Beach and crossed out and corrected. Running out of space for the word Willow, the final W continuing on the line underneath. A fragile brown leaf crumbling beneath its covering of clear sticky back plastic. A board game about pirates that Craig had started to make one rainy weekend, with pictures of guns and cannons and cutlasses.

Tears running down her face, Reenie traced the X that marked the location of the pirate treasure on a crudely drawn island. How could any of these precious, priceless things be thrown away? Ever?

* * * * *

Estelle's clothes were crisp and fresh, but there was nothing she could do about the state of her face and hands. Entering the bar at the Saracen Hotel, she saw Mark and the Larssons straight away. Switching on a smile, she walked as steadily as she could across the room.

'Freda, Artur; I am so sorry to be late.'

They were all looking at her with shock, especially Mark. Freda took Estelle's outstretched hand automatically but clutched it rather than shook it.

'Estelle!' she said. 'What has happened to you?'

Estelle shifted her gaze to locate a chair, quickly disentangling her hand. 'Oh, just a little car accident,' she said as breezily as she could. 'Nothing to worry about.'

Mark's eyes were boring into hers. 'Are you sure you're all right, Estelle?'

There was genuine concern in his voice, and unwan-ted emotion rose in her throat. She did what she always did in such circumstances – took refuge in hostility.

'Of course I am,' she said coldly. 'It's just a few scratches, that's all.' She turned back to the Larssons and smiled again. 'I'm only sorry it's held you both up. Now, please fill me in on what you've been discussing so far.'

And so the meeting progressed, but Estelle found it almost impossible to keep focused. While she listened and nodded, she felt oddly adrift, as if she might float away from the table unless she kept hold of it. For-tunately Mark seemed to have done some very good groundwork for the deal, so there were only a few loose ends to tie up to finalise everything.

'We must be leaving now Estelle. We have an appointment in London this evening, and tomorrow we fly back to Sweden,' Artur Larsson said at last.

'And you must rest Estelle,' Freda told her, patting her hand.

'Oh, I'm fine,' Estelle told her, smiling with a great effort and standing to shake both their hands. It was a lie. After a night without sleep and precious little to eat all day, she was feeling hot and faint, despite the air-conditioning in the bar. She wasn't entirely sure how long she would be able to stand up. If they would both just go...

'I'll see you both out,' Mark said, taking control of the situation. 'Can I leave my things with you for a moment, Estelle?'

'Oh, yes,' she said vaguely, sinking back down into her seat gratefully. 'Goodbye Freda. Artur.'

'Goodbye, Estelle. Take good care of yourself...'

Alone, Estelle closed her eyes. Behind the bar, somebody dropped a glass. Her eyes flicked open again, her heart suddenly racing.

Mark was back. 'I've just seen your car,' he said. 'There isn't a scratch on it. Why don't you tell me what really happened?'

* * * * *

By five o'clock, Kate was drunk, though not, as far as she was concerned, drunk enough. But she had run out of money, so she lurched out of the Rose and

251

Crown and wove along the High Street towards the cash machine to replenish her funds. There was a small queue of people waiting. The man at the front of the queue turned round.

'No cash,' he told them, frowning.

'Not again!' the woman in front of Kate said.

'Fucking hell!' said Kate more expressively, attrac-ting disapproving stares. 'About sums this fucking two horse town right up!' The queue began to disperse.

Without her audience, Kate continued along the High Street, still muttering insults about the town, intending to call into the supermarket to buy something so she could get some cash back. But on her way there she passed Carol De Ville Interiors, recognising it as the shop Janet worked in. On impulse she pushed open the door and went inside. Janet would lend her some money. Maybe she'd even come for a drink with her.

But Janet wasn't there, only her stuck up five-facelifts boss. 'I'm terribly sorry, but we're just about to close,' she said as soon as she saw Kate, one manicured hand on the telephone as if she were about to call the police.

'Don't want to buy any of this poxy load of old tat anyway,' Kate duly informed her, lurching towards the door again. But then she changed her mind and turned back. 'But since I'm here,' she said, stabbing an aggressive finger in Carol De Ville's direction, 'I want a word with you about Janet.'

'What about her?' Carol De Ville said, shrinking back behind the counter.

'You're not nice enough to her,' Kate said. 'In fact, you're a total bitch, that's what you are.'

'Now look here,' Carol De Ville started, but Kate pushed her face across the counter and Carol De Ville had nowhere else to shrink to.

'No,' Kate said, still stabbing that finger, 'you look here! You'd better be nice to Janet in future or else you'll have me to answer to. Got it?'

Carol De Ville didn't answer.

'*Got* it?' Kate said even more aggressively, and the other woman nodded.

'Yes,' she said with as much hostility as she dared. 'I've got it.'

Kate retreated. 'Good,' she said, and left the shop.

Outside she stood for a moment on the pavement, collecting her thoughts. Now where? Oh yes, the shop. Cash. Back to the pub. More booze. But in the end she just bought a bottle of whisky and drank from the bottle as she walked towards the seafront. Maybe Estelle would have a drink with her. Yes, she'd call in and have a chat with Estelle. At least she was as allergic to relationships as Kate was. She'd understand about Geoff.

But Estelle wasn't there. Kate kept her finger pressed on her door buzzer for ages, but there was no answer, just the sound of seagulls squawking on the roof above. None of her so-called friends was available. They were all much too busy with their own lives to have any time for her.

Lurching even more than ever now, Kate pushed herself away from Estelle's exclusive apartment building and made her way unsteadily down some steps to the promenade. It was colder here; a strong wind was blowing straight from the sea and the tide was right in, the water edging and booming against the sea wall. So Kate sought the relative protection of

253

an old brick-built shelter, sitting right in one corner with somebody's old chip papers, out of the wind.

'Fuck 'em,' she thought as her eyes closed. 'Fuck 'em all to hell.'

* * * * *

'I'm perfectly capable of driving myself home, Mark,' Estelle said irritably.

'And I don't think you are,' he said calmly, and the maddening thing was, he was probably right. She felt exhausted.

'I'll take you home. We can pick up your car tomorrow. I just need to have a cup of coffee first.'

We can pick up your car? Since when had he started making her decisions for her? But he left before she could argue, returning with two cups of coffee and a supply of biscuits.

'Sugar?' he asked.

'No. Thank you.' He was being very nice to her. She didn't deserve it; she was always such a bitch to him. And the rest of her staff. Why was that? Why couldn't she be nice to them? It wasn't as if she wanted to be generally hated by her employees, it was just the way it had turned out. The only way she could feel in control was by being bossy, but she knew she took it too far sometimes. In truth there probably wasn't that much to choose between her and bloody Cruella in the popularity stakes, which was a very depressing thought indeed.

Mark offered her the plate of biscuits. She wanted to refuse them, but even she wasn't that masochistic. She was absolutely starving. Five biscuits later, Mark was smiling at her. She wished he'd stop.

254

'What?'

'Nothing,' he said, cramming a biscuit into his own mouth.

'I thought you'd had lunch?' she said sarcastically.

'You know what the food in these places is like,' he shrugged. 'Beautiful to look at, but very little actual content. Besides, I was busy entertaining Fred and Artur.'

She could tell he hadn't meant it as a dig, but her own conscience made her take it like that anyway. 'I'm sorry you were landed in it,' she said, her voice grudging even though she meant it.

Mark shrugged. 'No problem.'

Now would be the time to tell him what had happened the previous night if she were ever going to tell him, which she wasn't. The silence stretched on, filled only by the sound of biscuit crunching. Suddenly Estelle couldn't stand it any longer. She put her cup down onto its saucer.

'I really must get back,' she said.

Mark stood up straight away. 'Of course.' He offered her his hand to help her up, and for once she didn't argue.

'Thank you,' she said, and the hand became an arm, ready to support her should she need it. And all the way home to her flat she kept her face turned to the window so he wouldn't see the stupid vulnerable tears that were just clamouring to be let out.

* * * * *

'Reen? Reenie? Where are you, love?'

Reenie had no idea how long she had been stuck

in the attic. It felt like hours and hours; long enough for her to relive her son's entire life through the contents of the boxes anyway.

'Up here!' she shouted to Ted as loudly as she could. 'In the roof!'

She heard the ladder creak under his weight. 'What on earth are you doing up there?' he asked, but then he stuck his head through the hatch and saw the chaos which had previously been a neat stack of boxes. With her bad ankle, she'd been forced to pull and topple the boxes rather than unpack them carefully, and it showed. Their sacred contents were strewn untidily all over the dusty floor.

'I've hurt myself, love,' she said, her heart sinking at his grim expression. 'Been stuck up here all afternoon. Couldn't get back down.'

'Serves you right for being so daft as to come up on your own,' he said gruffly, but he came the rest of the way up anyway and bent over her. 'What have you done to yourself?'

'Twisted my ankle. Sprained it, I think.'

Ted sighed. 'Well, I think you're going to have to put some weight on it,' he said. 'Don't know how we're going to get you down otherwise.'

'All right,' she said. 'So long as you're here to help, eh?'

He didn't meet her eyes. 'Yeah.'

An hour later they were in the minor injuries unit at Cromer Hospital, waiting to be seen by a doctor. Ted had hardly spoken two words all the way, and after a while Reenie had stopped trying to keep a conversation going. After the afternoon she'd had, she didn't feel like speaking anyway. And besides, she was sick and tired of the constant chat, chat, chat she did to fill the spaces of life. Who the hell had given her the role of chief entertainer/counsellor anyway? She didn't want it anymore. She was sick of it. She perishing well resigned.

But now, sat in the hospital with her ankle throbbing, she couldn't keep silent any longer. Jade was right. She and Ted did need to finish grieving for Craig if they were ever going to move on. Not to have orgasms – bugger orgasms. They weren't the priority. Normal life; that was the priority. And how could you live a normal life when both you and your husband were avoiding talking about the very thing that most needed a good airing?

'I was thinking this afternoon – we need to find homes for some of Craig's better things,' she said.

Ted wouldn't look at her, and she sighed and pressed on. 'It can't all stay up there forever, love.'

He picked up a newspaper and opened it, blocking her out.

Reenie touched his arm. 'Ted…'

'*No.*'

She was shocked by the violence in his voice. 'What d'you mean "no"?'

'I am not giving his belongings away to all and sundry.'

Other people in the waiting room stopped their conversations to look at them. Aware of the attention they were arousing, Reenie deliberately lowered her voice. 'But we can't just– '

'I don't want to talk about it, Reen.'

Reenie looked at her husband, forgetting about their audience. 'No,' she said, 'you never do, do you?' Sudden tears filled her eyes. 'You never do want to talk about anything important. I should have liked to have remembered him, I would. Talked about him. So would the girls.' She started to shout. 'But we're not allowed to, are we?'

Ted threw the newspaper down and got up, striding quickly towards the exit.

'It's as if he never existed!' Reenie yelled after him, but he carried right on walking.

A nurse materialised in front of her. 'Is there a problem here?'

Tears began to slide down Reenie's cheeks. *A problem? I've broken my flippin' ankle and our son's died and he won't talk about it. What could possibly be the problem?*

Reenie's ankle wasn't broken, just badly sprained. After it was strapped up, they lent her some crutches and she found Ted back in reception, waiting for her. Wordlessly, he took her handbag from her so she could cope with the crutches more easily, and they made their silent way out to the car.

* * * * *

Janet knew that if she didn't act soon, Ray would fall asleep. There was a certain pattern about the sounds and movements he made when he was settling down at night; a series of snuffles, throat clearings and head positionings that rarely varied.

But could she really do it? Lying there listening to Ray's third throat clearing, Janet doubted herself, despite the fortifying glasses of wine she had downed at speed while Ray had been in the bathroom.

Normally at this stage, Janet would say 'goodnight,' Ray would answer, and then roll over onto his side. Ten seconds later he would be asleep.

It was now or never.

Yanking the duvet up, Janet suddenly took the plunge, venturing into the warm darkness of beneath the duvet land and reaching for Ray's pyjamas.

Taken by total surprise, Ray leapt like a fish. 'What are you *doing*?'

Janet heard her husband's voice coming to her dimly through the duvet, but she had come this far, so she did not allow herself to be deterred now. She had done some research on Ray's computer into fellatio, and she frantically tried to remember what she'd read now as she got to work. The duvet lifted slightly as Ray took a surprised look. 'Janet?'

She carried on without replying, and was gratified to receive a twitching response. Very soon afterwards Ray let the duvet fall back again, submitting to her administrations. Perhaps it was the element of surprise, or else the information on the Internet had been particularly good, because it didn't take very long for him to climax.

Swallowing valiantly and flushed with both success and heat, Janet emerged from beneath the duvet. Despite his post-orgasm breathlessness, Ray was already looking at her quizzically. Janet spoke quickly. 'Will...will you do it to me, Ray?' she asked. 'Please?'

For a moment she thought he wasn't going to. His gaze locked with hers almost resentfully. 'What has come over you, Janet?' he asked.

She shrugged. 'Nothing,' she said. 'It just seemed a while since we tried it, that's all.'

He stared at her for a while longer, and then, reluctantly it seemed to her, he finally slid down beneath the covers. Lying back against the pillows expectantly, her body sensitised to every movement he made, Janet felt Ray's hands slide her nightdress up, and the warmth of his breath on her private parts as he began to lower his face. She realised she felt…excited. For the first time in a very long while, she was actually looking forward to a sexual act. And if she was looking forward to it, then maybe, just maybe…

But almost immediately Janet knew it wasn't going to work. As Ray set to with his tongue and mouth, Janet immediately felt unclean. And she wasn't; she had deliberately had a bath that evening. But something about the way Ray was administering to her made her feel as if she were being…*hoovered.* She wanted, almost immediately, to tear his head away again, but instead she lay back and suffered the indignity of having another person's tongue washing out her most private places.

She wasn't in the least bit surprised when he finally gave up.

'Thank you, darling,' she said. 'That was very… nice.'

He gave her an almost scornful look, reaching for a tissue from the bedside cupboard to wipe his face and not bothering to reply. Then he rolled onto his side away from her, leaving her staring open-eyed into the darkness.

Janet was deeply disappointed. It had most definitely not turned out how it had suggested it would on the Internet. But her curiosity demanded to be satisfied about one more thing. 'Ray?' she said.

'What?' His voice was irritable.

Janet's heart beat quickly at her daring. 'What do I taste like?' she asked.

260

There was a pause. She thought he'd fallen asleep.

'Ray?' she said, and finally he answered.

'Musk,' he said, his voice resentful and sulky. 'Dusky musk.'

Twenty-six

'There are now three weeks left until Orgasm Night,' Jade told Janet, Kate and Reenie.

Beside Janet, Kate snorted; a sound of deep scepticism which, after the other night, Janet agreed with wholeheartedly.

Jade ignored the grunt. 'I have every confidence in you all,' she gushed on.

'Well, it's more than I do, Jade,' Reenie said despondently.

Jade smiled kindly at her. 'You've all come a very long way since the course started,' she said. 'Fulfilment can and will be yours. Now, does anybody know if we can expect Estelle today?'

Kate shrugged. She looked ill to Janet, and she was definitely less talkative than she had been of late. In fact, she looked a lot like the surly Kate of old, and Janet wondered why. Maybe something had happened.

'Haven't heard anything from her, Jade,' Reenie said, adjusting her leg with a wince. Poor Reenie, something had certainly happened to *her*. That ankle looked really painful. Imagine getting stuck in the attic for all that time. It must have been horrible.

'I haven't heard from Estelle either,' Janet told Jade. 'Perhaps she's busy at work.'

Jade nodded. 'I'll phone her later,' she said. 'She

needs to know the date of Orgasm Night, and the work we're going to do in the next few weeks is vital to your success.'

'What exactly are we supposed to do on this Orgasm Night?' Reenie asked, and Kate's laugh was mocking.

'Duh…!' she said, and Reenie flushed.

'All right,' she said, 'I'm not stupid. I know we're supposed to have an orgasm on Orgasm Night, but I just don't know how it's supposed to happen when none of us has had one yet, that's all!'

'Yes,' Janet said. 'That's what I was thinking too.'

Jade was still smiling. For the first time, Janet felt a flicker of irritation. It was all very well for Jade to stand there like the proverbial cat who'd got the cream, but none of *them* had had so much so much as skimmed milk yet!

Unless Estelle had struck lucky? Unless that was why she wasn't here today? Because she was at home being made love to by her married lover, on the receiving end of stupendous, mind-blowing orgasms?

Janet was really disappointed Estelle wasn't at the workshop; she was desperate to tell her about the 'dusky musk' coincidence. In fact, she had tried to ring her to tell her about it several times that week, but with no luck. And somehow it didn't seem quite the same to share it with either of the others. Reenie might be shocked, and very likely Kate would just laugh cynically. She could tell Jade, she supposed, if she could get her alone.

'Orgasm night will be a culmination of everything we have been working towards on this course,' Jade told them. 'A chance to practise all the self-pleasuring techniques you have learned in a safe, sensual environment.'

'I'd hardly call this place sensual,' Kate said, and yet again, Janet had to agree. Try as Jade might to sex it up with the *Kama Sutra* picture and the cushions and throws, the hall was still really just the hall, complete with its shadows of pensioners' lunch clubs and bring-and-buy sales.

'Sensuality is all in the mind,' Jade told them. 'And to illustrate this, I've brought along a treat for you today.' She took something from her bag. It was a DVD.

'A porno movie!' Kate said sarcastically, and Reenie looked taken aback.

Jade wheeled the television set over from the edge of the hall. 'No, Kate,' she said patiently, 'not a porno movie; an erotic film.'

'Porn,' Kate mouthed silently to Janet and Reenie.

Jade put the DVD into the machine. 'Now I want you to rid your minds of all negative thoughts about erotica. Contrary to popular belief, it isn't only long distance lorry drivers who watch it. In my opinion erotic films have, or should have, a place in everybody's sex lives.'

The DVD began to play. Janet, who had never watched such a film in her life, felt a frisson of excitement. The film opened with an idyllic tropical beach with lapping waves and palm trees gently swaying in the breeze. Then a luxurious yacht came into view, with the film title superimposed over the top – *The Captain's Mate*. Either side of her, Reenie sniggered and Kate snorted. But Janet...well, Janet felt that initial frisson stirring into something more, and, unconsciously sat forward in her seat so she wouldn't miss anything.

The camera was swooping towards the yacht now, picking out the figure of a young woman who was standing looking out to sea, her long hair blowing gently around her shoulders. Suddenly a dolphin leapt out of the water close to the boat, bringing an expression of joy to the woman's face. As she laughed out loud with the joy of it, the camera panned back to reveal a man watching her as he coiled a long rope. Naked from the waist up, he was muscular and deeply tanned, his dark, curly hair making him look like a pirate.

As the woman remained transfixed by the dolphins, the man began to move stealthily closer to her, holding the rope in both hands. The woman gave no sign that she knew he was there, and the music became suddenly sinister and urgent. He was nearly at her side; surely she would notice him before it was too late? Suddenly the man put the loop of rope over the woman's head until it was beneath her breasts. She gave a token squeal, but as he tugged her back against his body, she submitted. And when he slid his hand beneath her sarong, she closed her eyes and spread her legs in-vitingly.

Kate gave another one of her mocking snorts, but Janet licked her lips, staring at the movement of the woman's sarong as the man caressed her beneath it. The woman was whimpering now, the dolphins forgotten.

'Georgio,' she breathed. 'Oh, Georgio...'

Janet didn't blame her. The man was smiling wickedly. He was gorgeous.

'You like?' he enquired lazily in a sexy Italian

accent.

'Oh yes,' the woman said. 'Yes…'

'You want to show Georgio how much you like?' he said, and the woman turned, pouting up at Georgio provocatively as she unclipped her bikini top.

As the woman's breasts were exposed in all their thirty-six double D glory to Georgio's gaze, Janet was so absorbed she didn't realise at first that the sudden sound of voices wasn't a part of the film.

But when Jade quickly stood up, pressing a button on the remote control to stop the film, Janet suddenly realised there were three other people in the room with them – the caretaker, the vicar and… Ray.

'Ray!' Janet stood up, instinctively clutching at her chest just as if she'd been the one exposing her breasts in the film. Ray's expression was both accusing and triumphant at the same time. As for the vicar, he was open-mouthed and red-faced with shock, outrage or both.

Janet couldn't meet his gaze. But she was uncomfortably aware of him absorbing the leopard skin throws, the *Kama Sutra* painting and, worst of all, the DVD, paused at the moment when Georgio's tongue had just made contact with one of the woman's erect nipples.

'There!' Ray was saying to the vicar. 'You didn't want to believe it, but I told you this was what was going on. Filth! Utter filth!'

In the circumstances, Jade's expression was very calm. 'Gentlemen,' she said. 'How can I help you?'

'Is that your husband?' Reenie whispered to Janet, and Janet could only nod miserably. She wanted the parquet floor to open up and swallow her whole.

266

'Miss…Miss…' the vicar stuttered to Jade.

'Gate,' Jade said smoothly. 'My name is Jade Gate.'

'Miss Gate, I cannot believe my own eyes!' the vicar went on, as Ray stood there, nodding in agreement beside him, hands on hips. 'That you could think it an appropriate use of the church hall to show such… such…' He broke off, words failing him, his confused gaze moving from Jade to Janet and finally on to Bill Black. 'Did you *know* this was happening, Mr Black?' he asked.

'No, Vicar!' Bill Black replied quickly, looking flustered. 'The booking was for a women's health course!'

Ray's sarcastic grunt sounded a lot like Kate's had earlier on. 'Prescribing pornography on the National Health now are they?' he said.

The vicar looked at him irritably. 'Yes, yes, thank you, Mr Thornton,' he said. 'I'll deal with this now.'

'That wasn't pornography,' Jade said calmly. 'It was erotica. But that's a good point actually; I'm sure we'd all have a lot fewer health problems if erotica were something we could get a prescription for.'

Reenie gave a hastily stifled laugh. Even Kate was grinning. The vicar's face deepened a shade from magenta to beetroot.

'I'm sorry, Miss Gate,' he said, 'but I cannot sanction the use of this hall for such purposes. I'm afraid you and your er…' His gaze swept over them all and lingered slightly longer on Janet, '…*students* will have to find alternative premises in future.'

Ray looked at his wife. 'Well,' he said, 'for one student there isn't going to be any future. Come on, Janet. We're going home. *Now*.'

Just as she had hesitated at the first workshop when Gwen had ordered her to leave, Janet hesitated now that it was Ray giving the orders.

'Janet!' Ray said again, but in the end it was the vicar's obvious disapproval that made up her mind for her, and she picked her bag up from the floor.

'I'm sorry, Jade,' she said, 'I'll have to go.'

Jade smiled. 'It's all right, Janet,' she said. Then, as Janet passed, she whispered something so that only she could hear. 'Keep in touch with the others. They'll tell you where to go in future.'

'Come on, Janet,' Ray told her bossily, and as she followed him from the hall, she was aware of the vicar watching her every step of the way. She would never be able to go to St Luke's again.

Outside in the car park, she speeded up, anxious to get away from Ray.

'You've only got yourself to blame, Janet,' he said, trotting to keep up with her. 'I told you to stop going to those classes.'

She paused, turning to look at him. 'How did you know I was still going?' she asked.

His smile was unpleasant. 'Janet,' he said, 'we haven't had oral sex since 1997. And even then, you didn't ask for it!'

Janet dearly wanted to shout something to wipe that smug expression off his face. She wanted to hit him. She wanted… She wanted to be anyone other than dull, mousy Janet Thornton, too afraid to stand up to her husband.

'Now,' he said, sighing patiently, 'get in your car like a good girl and go home.'

It was the jolt she wanted. 'Why does it really bother you, Ray?' she challenged him. 'Me coming to these classes?'

'Why does it bother me?' he repeated, the patient expression vanishing. 'Why does it bother me that half the town knows that my wife, *my wife* has been sneaking off to the church hall to watch dirty videos behind my back? The very fact that you have to ask the question shows how pathetic you are, Janet.'

And off he strode to his car, driving off with an angry squeal of tyres. Janet watched after him resentfully. She didn't want to go home with her tail between her legs the way Ray wanted her to; she was far too full of restless energy for that. But neither could she go back into the hall while the vicar was there. Suddenly she thought of Estelle. Yes, she would go and see Estelle and fill her in on everything she'd just missed.

But when she arrived at her friend's office, it was to discover that her Estelle was off sick.

'Ms Morgan hasn't been in all week,' Estelle's secretary told her.

'Oh,' said Janet, concerned. Somehow it didn't seem very like Estelle to take time off sick. She must be really ill. But then why hadn't she let Janet know?

A handsome, dark-haired man was just leaving some papers on the secretary's desk. He looked at Janet. 'I spoke to Estelle on the phone this morning,' he told her. 'She's on the mend I think, but I'm sure she'd like to have a visitor.'

The man's tones were warm and friendly. Janet decided she liked him. 'I'll go round to see her now,' she said.

* * * * *

'Estelle, it's Janet. Can I come up?'

Estelle hesitated for a second, and then spoke into the entry phone. 'Yes, OK,' she said finally and pressed the buzzer to open the downstairs door. She hadn't seen anybody at all since Mark had dropped her off after Monday's meeting, but her cuts were healing now; or at least the outward ones. Her instinct was still to hide away, but she knew she would have to face the world again soon. She might just as well start with Janet.

But the minute her friend stepped into the apartment, Estelle realised it had been a big mistake to let her in. 'Estelle! What on earth have you done to your face?' Janet asked with a gushing concern that was just too much.

'It's nothing,' she said coldly, but Janet didn't take the hint.

'Of course it isn't nothing,' she said. 'You're covered in cuts! Your hands as well! Oh, you poor thing!'

Tears filled Estelle's eyes; tears she couldn't cope with. She blinked them back furiously. 'I don't want to talk about it, OK?' she said, and Janet, who had been moving quickly towards her, stopped in her tracks.

'Well, all right,' she said, 'but…'

'No buts.' Estelle told her firmly. 'I don't want to talk about it.' She made an attempt at a smile. 'How did you know I'd be here, anyway?'

'I popped in to see you at work,' Janet told her. 'There was a very nice man there who told me you'd appreciate a visit.'

Mark. Crossing the line between helping and interfering. *Again.* He'd rung her several times since

Monday. The first couple of times she hadn't answered the phone, but then on Wednesday he'd mentioned a problem at work so she'd picked up. The problem had turned out to be something and nothing, an excuse for him to ask how she was. She had no idea why he even cared.

Estelle decided to change the subject. She could tell Janet was hurt that she wasn't being more forthcoming, but she couldn't help that. 'How was today's class?' she asked, sitting down on one of the sofas.

Janet's face cleared. She sat on the sofa opposite. 'Well,' she said dramatically, 'that's what I came to tell you. We were *invaded*!'

Listening to Janet's tale, Estelle felt herself begin to relax a little. By the end of it, she was even smiling. 'It isn't funny,' Janet protested, but Estelle could tell she was glad that the atmosphere between them had lightened. 'We haven't got anywhere to meet now, and even if Jade manages to sort somewhere else out, Ray's not going to let me go.'

'Well, stand up to him then!' Estelle could have said. 'Tell him where to get off!' But she didn't have the energy, so she kept quiet. Besides, Janet already knew what she thought about Ray anyway.

'I know,' Janet said ruefully, backing this belief up. 'If I want to go anyway, I should just go.'

Estelle's phone began to ring. Janet, who had been about to say something else, paused.

'It's all right,' Estelle told her. 'It's probably only the office. I'm not going to answer it. Go on.'

'Well,' Janet said, 'I was just going to say, I don't even know why I'm going to the workshops anymore.'

271

Estelle's voice filled the flat as the answer phone clicked into action. 'Sorry I'm not here to take your call right now.'

'I mean,' Janet said over the voice, 'at first it was partly for Ray, but after last weekend... Oh, that's the *other* thing I wanted to tell you about!'

'Leave your name, number and the time you rang, and I'll get right back to you.'

'You will *never* guess what happened the other night...' Janet said.

The answer phone gave a beep, and suddenly RT's voice filled the room. 'Hi, Estelle, it's me. Just wondering if you were free tonight? I'd *love* to see you. It's been ages. I'll try you on your mobile. Bye.'

Janet had stopped talking. She seemed frozen to the spot. 'My God,' she said.

Estelle's mobile began to ring. Estelle reached for it and switched it off, looking at Janet with concern. 'What is it?' she asked.

But now Janet was looking across to one corner of the room. Estelle glanced round and saw her bag of golf clubs, which was propped against the wall where she'd left it after the last time she'd been to the golf club.

'My God,' Janet said again, and covered her mouth with her hands.

'Janet?' Estelle was worried now. 'What's wrong?'

'All this time I thought your lover's name was Artie,' Janet said slowly. 'A-R-T-I- E. I thought...I thought it was short for Arthur.'

'No,' Estelle said, confused. 'It's RT. R-T. I've got no idea what his name is. That's what everyone calls him down at the golf club.'

'Raymond Thornton,' Janet told her, picking up her handbag and heading towards the door. 'It stands for Raymond Thornton.'

And then she left.

Twenty-seven

It was the day of the college record-breaking trifle attempt. Kate was inside one of the kitchens supervising jelly production and fruit chopping. Geoff was outside in the car park with the media, simultaneously being interviewed and keeping an eye on the custard mixture that was being prepared in the brand new cement mixer lorry borrowed especially from a sponsor for the occasion.

Kate could see Geoff out of the kitchen window. He was totally in his element in front of the local TV station cameras, the giant boy's toy rotating beside him, a walkie-talkie shoved in the pocket of his overalls.

'Project Control to Jelly Production. Over.' He'd used the walkie-talkie to summon her earlier on, his voice crackling from the walkie-talkie he'd allocated to her and which she'd slung on the side somewhere. She'd wanted to ignore him, but there were students with her and he wasn't about to shut up.

'Project Control to Jelly Production. Over.'

'Yes, Geoff,' she'd said, emphasising his name. There was no way she was going to call him Project Control. It was just too tragic.

'What's your best estimate for jelly setting, Jelly Production? Over.'

'Oh,' she said airily. 'An hour or so; give or take.'

'Thirteen hundred hours?' came the crackly voice. 'Repeat for confirmation, please, Jelly Production. Was that thirteen hundred hours? Over.'

Kate clenched her teeth. 'Give or take,' she said, refusing to use the appropriate call signs as he'd instructed her to.

'Copy that, Jelly Production. Project Control over and out.'

Geoff was well and truly up himself, and in other circumstances, Kate would have been taking the piss out of him big time. But these weren't other circumstances. A week had gone by since he'd asked her out on a date, a week in which she and Geoff had avoided each other wherever possible, or spoken to each other like polite strangers when it wasn't.

'What is it with you two?' Tom asked after Kate had turned down an invitation for a pint and a game of pool. 'When I invited Geoff he wanted to know if you were going or not, and now you're saying you won't go because you know *he's* coming. I thought you were supposed to be mates.'

The knowledge that Geoff didn't want to spend time with her hurt, even though she didn't want to spend time with him. 'Geoff moved the goalposts,' she told Tom.

Tom looked exasperated. 'So the man asked you out,' he said.

Kate looked at him. 'He told you?'

Tom nodded. 'Yeah, he told me,' he said. 'And so what? Geoff's a nice guy. You could do a lot worse.'

'I don't want to do worse!' Kate protested. '*Or* better. I don't want to *do* anything at all! He's ruined everything.'

'No,' Tom said. 'You're ruining everything. By

275

being so…so flippin' female!'

Kate was outraged. '*What?*' she said, but Tom was already walking away, being utterly *male* and refusing to explain himself. That had been two days ago, and things were still no better now. Kate was feeling so mad with Geoff she wanted to hoik him up in front of the TV cameras and shove him feet first into the cement mixer.

A student interrupted her fantasies. 'Miss, there's no more oranges left.'

Through the window Kate could see a satellite TV station van arriving. Geoff's head was going to swell so much there could soon be a real danger of his baker's hat not fitting him any longer.

'Well, get some oranges out of the cold store,' she dismissed the student irritably. Why didn't they ever, *ever* use their own initiative? God help the restaurants that employed any of them. Most of them were well and truly hung-over today anyway; they'd all been out celebrating the engagement of two first-year students. *Engagement*. At age seventeen. Sheer bloody madness.

'Hey!' shouted a student excitedly. 'It's the Norwich City Football Club team!'

Kate looked out of the window again. Sure enough, the Norwich City Football Club coach was just pulling up. Geoff had said he would try to get them to come and support the event, and it looked as if he'd swung it. As she watched the Principal practically elbowing Geoff out of the way to shake hands with Delia Smith, the football club's chairman and famous TV chef, Kate noticed two policemen standing discreetly to one side, checking that the growing crowd stayed orderly. One of them was Ian, her ex-husband.

'Bloody hellfire!'

'What's up, Miss?'

Kate realised all of the students were looking at her. Several were giggling.

'All right,' she snapped. 'That'll do. Get on with your chopping.'

On impulse she snatched up the walkie-talkie and took it into the neighbouring classroom, closing the door behind her. Looking out of the window, she pressed the button to speak. 'Jelly Production calling Project Control.'

The walkie-talkie crackled into life. 'This is Project Control,' Geoff said. 'Go ahead, Jelly Production.'

'The tall, blond cop with the sticking-out Adam's apple,' she said. 'That's my ex. Don't trust the slimy bastard as far as you can throw him.'

There was a crackling silence from the walkie-talkie. In the car park, Geoff turned towards the catering block, flapping his hands up and down warningly. Too late Kate realised that everyone within a few metres of Geoff, including the Principal, Delia and no doubt Ian himself, had heard what she'd said.

'Fuck!' she said, realising – once again too late – that she had depressed the button, once again making her voice audible to all.

'Over and out, Jelly Production,' Geoff said, and as her walkie-talkie fell silent, Kate saw the Principal excuse herself to Delia before beginning to walk towards the entrance to the catering block.

Oh, shit. She was dead meat.

* * * * *

Reenie and Ted were attempting to make a Big Effort. It was their wedding anniversary, and they were celebrating it the way they always did. Ted had taken the day off and they were having lunch out, just as if they hadn't spent most of the time since the ankle-in-the-attic incident tiptoeing around each other.

So far the Big Effort wasn't going very well. The meal – in an Italian Restaurant – had been a quiet affair. Normally Reenie would have kept Ted entertained with little observations about the other people in the restaurant or chattered on about family things. At least once during the meal they would have got the giggles about something or other and Reenie would have had to wipe her eyes on her napkin.

But today Reenie didn't feel either chatty or giggly, and as for the other people in the restaurant, she couldn't care less about any of them. Deep down she was still angry with Ted, and that anger kept on leaking out, corroding any good intentions she might have. Whenever she said anything that wasn't about the subject foremost in her mind, Reenie felt like a fraud, and she wasn't used to feeling that way. Ted seemed to think his feelings and coping strategies, *his* grief; were all more important than anyone else's, and they weren't. Ever since Craig's death, they'd all had to keep their pain bottled up because Ted couldn't cope with it. But hiding things away just wasn't helping her, *or* the girls.

For Reenie, that afternoon in the attic had been a turning point, and she just wouldn't, *couldn't* pretend any longer. No matter what that might mean for her

278

marriage.

'Fancy going for a drink on the way home?' Ted asked after he'd paid the bill. They always went for a drink on the way home from their anniversary lunch. It was another tradition. Reenie didn't know why he was bothering to ask her.

She smiled stiffly. 'Why not?' At least it would delay the evil moment when they were alone together without the sound of other people's conversations to mask their silence.

The Red Cow was on the Norwich Road, at the edge of the council estate. The Nelson was closer to home, but Louise Block's family and friends always used the Nelson. Or rather, they usually used the Nelson, because as Reenie and Ted walked into the Red Cow, they saw them – a whole table of Blocks, finishing off a meal.

'Well, look who it is,' Carl Block, one of Louise's two brothers said to the rest of the group, putting down his knife and fork to stare aggressively at Ted.

Ted came to an abrupt halt. 'Come on, love,' he said, 'let's go.'

Reenie hitched her bag further onto her shoulder and walked on her crutches straight past him towards the bar. 'No,' she said. 'We're staying.'

* * * * *

'…Keep your personal life at home…' '…a high profile event such as this…' '…no example to set to impressionable young students…'

Blah, blah, bloody blah.

After the Principal had finally completed her dressing down, Kate watched her walk away down

279

the corridor, her slim, affronted bum moving from side to side beneath her size ten, tailored suit.

Stupid bitch.

The woman had been married since 19 fucking 96. What did she know about a lust for revenge that was so strong it was like it was tattooed on your soul? So strong it caused you deliberately to cock up any chances for happiness that happened to fall your way?

Kate wished suddenly and very fiercely that the Principal – and every other smug married sod on the planet – would experience, if only for twenty-four hours, the searing pain of betrayal; the arctic reality of simultaneously losing your best friend and the partner you thought you would be with until you died. See if *she* wouldn't want to grab the nearest walkie-talkie to spout poison into after that!

Stomping her way furiously back to the kitchen, Kate was surprised to find, not the anarchy she had expected, but a pile of chopped fruit and the sympathetic glances of her students who, she realised, must have heard every single word of the Principal's dressing down through the connecting door.

'You all right, Miss?'

'None of us like her, Miss.'

'Stuck-up cow!'

Kate knew she ought to be grateful for their support, but the truth was it was simply more than she could cope with just then. She would not, *could not* blub in front of her students.

'Go and check on the jelly, Fisher,' she snapped. 'They're going to be needing it any minute.'

'Yes, Miss.'

Martyn Fisher scurried off on his mission while the rest of them exchanged glances then kept their heads down, busying themselves with yet more fruit chopping or tidying up.

Until, that was, Martyn returned, his face red and frightened-looking. With one look at him, Kate's feeling of doom tripled.

'What is it, Fisher?' she asked warily, and the boy licked his lips.

'It's the jelly, Miss…' he said. 'It's…melted…'

* * * * *

At the bar, Reenie ordered a double vodka and drank it there and then, ignoring Carl Block's continuing taunts.

Ted was still hovering at her shoulder. 'Come *on*, love,' he said. 'Let's go home.'

'No,' Reenie told him. 'This has gone on long enough.' And with that she picked up her crutches and hobbled over to the Blocks' table. One seat was empty, the half-finished drink and empty plate on the table in front of it suggesting that its occupant had gone to the toilet.

Reenie sat down. The Blocks were all so startled they did nothing to stop her, and seconds later Reenie was face-to-face with Thora, Louise's mother. The last time they'd been this close had been a year ago during a slanging match in the local Co-Op. On that occasion, Thora had become totally out of control, spitting and screaming and hurling things from the shelves at Reenie until the police had been sent for. As a result, both women had been barred from the shop; an inconvenience sorely felt by Reenie, since it meant the nearest food shop was in the town centre.

Reenie had heard on the grapevine that since then, Thora had been receiving psychiatric treatment, and certainly the woman in front of her looked a lot calmer than the harridan from the Co-Op. Though actually, calm wasn't the right word to describe the way Thora Block looked. Tired, old and defeated were much more accurate descriptions. A lot like Reenie felt herself.

'You aren't welcome at this table, bitch!' Carl Block persisted. 'Fuck off!'

'I will,' Reenie said calmly. 'After I've had a word with your mother.'

'We've got nothing to say to each other,' Thora told her blankly.

'You heard her,' Carl said. 'Go on, piss off!'

Someone, one of the young nephews at the end of the table, threw something – a half-eaten bread roll – in Reenie's direction. It landed on the table in front of her, showering crumbs.

Carl laughed. 'Good one, Fin,' he said, and picking up the remains of his cheesecake, tossed it straight at Reenie. His aim was better than the nephew's – the cheesecake landed on the side of her face.

'You leave her alone!' Ted said over Reenie's shoulder.

Carl stood up. 'Oh yeah?' he said. 'Or else what, Granddad?'

The biscuit crust from the cheesecake fell onto the table next to the bread roll. The blackcurrant mush remained smeared on Reenie's face.

Encouraged by Carl's approval, the nephew at the end of the table was searching about for more

282

ammunition. Soon pieces of fruit and cake were being hurled enthusiastically towards Reenie up the table, quickly drawing the attention of the pub manager.

'Hey, you lot,' he said, bustling over, 'pack it in!' But even before he had finished speaking, a splodge of Neapolitan ice cream flicked from a spoon hit him full square in the chest.

'Right!' he said. 'That's it! Out, the lot of you!'

Some, though not many, of the Blocks stood up. Reenie and Thora stayed put, eyeballing each other across the table.

'Reen...' Ted appealed to her desperately, but she shrugged his hand off her shoulder.

'So,' Thora said unpleasantly. 'What have you got to say?'

Reenie wasn't sure. She hadn't rehearsed any of this.

'I said, get out!' The bar manager yelled. '*Now!* Or I'm calling the police!'

The police. They'd had enough of the police to last them a lifetime, them and the Blocks. Enough conflict and grief too. And pretence; above all enough pretence.

'Well?' said Thora, the sardonic twist of her lipsticked mouth daring Reenie to do her worst.

When Reenie started speaking, she still wasn't sure what she was going to say. Certainly not what she ended up saying, anyway. 'It was Craig's fault,' she said. 'It was Craig's fault your Louise died.'

* * * * *

Kate walked slowly past the temporary swimming

283

pool Geoff had had erected in which to assemble the record-breaking trifle. Poor Geoff. This whole idea was – and always had been – totally bloody crazy, but she knew better than most how hard he'd worked on it.

And now, either because a careless student had left the cold store door open or, in her mixed-up frame of mind she'd somehow got the proportions of jelly to water wrong, the project seemed doomed. And she was the one who was going to have to break the bad news to him, in front of the TV people, Delia and the Norwich City Football team and, worst of all, Ian.

By the time she reached the cement mixer, Geoff was up a ladder checking the custard with a giant ladle, smiling foolishly down at the cameras all the while.

'Geoff,' she called to him, keeping her voice deliberately quiet in a vain attempt not to attract too much attention.

He spotted her and grinned, their recent awkwardness with each other evidently forgotten in all the excitement. 'Jelly Production!' he boomed at her delightedly and, out of the corner of her eye, Kate saw Ian's mouth twitch. As she turned to glare at him, Geoff climbed down the ladder.

'Ladies and gentlemen,' Geoff announced to the media, the members of the football club and, no doubt, the viewers at home, 'this woman is my right-hand man, so to speak! Without her talents with jelly making, there would be no trifle today!'

Cameras clicked. Microphones were shoved in her direction. Kate closed her eyes. 'Geoff,' she said again, but he was still grinning foolishly at the

284

cameras, any ability he might ever have possessed to detect trouble obliterated by his five minutes of fame.

'The jelly hasn't set,' she whispered to him, but not quietly enough. A reporter with good hearing was onto her immediately.

'What's that?' he said loudly. 'Did you say the jelly hasn't set?'

'What?' At last Geoff looked at her, quickly drawing her away from the crowd. But the crowd followed. As a fun feature for the local news, this was solid gold.

'I'm sorry,' Kate said miserably to Geoff. 'The jelly; it hasn't worked. It's still liquid.'

Geoff's face paled. 'Ah,' he said, digesting this bit of bad news. Kate felt totally miserable. Before, when Geoff had been over-bouncy, he'd been irritating as hell, but now she really wanted that Geoff back again. She hated being the cause of his disappointment.

Geoff clapped a hand onto her shoulder and gave it a reassuring squeeze. 'Well don't worry,' he said kindly, trying to be upbeat. 'These things happen.' Fixing a smile on his face, he turned to face the media. 'Ladies and gentlemen, I'm afraid there's been a slight setback. The attempt to break the record will still be going ahead, but unfortunately there will be a short delay.'

'How short?' somebody asked.

Geoff floundered. 'Er...approximately three to four hours,' he said.

Only one person in the whole crowd seemed to find this news anything but annoying.

Ian.

Standing next to his colleague with his arms

285

folded across his chest, he was openly smirking with amusement, and suddenly something snapped inside Kate's head. Leaving Geoff's side, she charged over to her ex-husband and slapped him sharply across the face.

'Don't you dare laugh at Geoff!' she shrieked. 'Don't you dare! You aren't fit to clean his boots!' And she slapped him again.

Ian's colleague got hold of her and dragged her away. 'Assaulting a police officer is a very serious offence, madam,' he said, pulling her hands behind her back while the cameras from the local TV news hungrily filmed away. 'You're under arrest!'

As he bundled her towards the police car, Geoff hurried over. 'Leave her alone!' he yelled.

Not wanting him to get into trouble, Kate spoke quickly. 'Leave it, Geoff,' she said. And the last thing she saw as they drove her away was his big, dismayed eyes.

* * * * *

'I cannot believe I heard what I just heard in there.' Outside the Red Cow, Ted strode furiously towards the car, not making any allowances for Reenie's bad ankle.

'It had to be said.'

He turned on her. 'Why? *Why*, for God's sake?'

Reenie rested for a moment. Her ankle was killing her. 'Because it's the truth.'

Ted turned angrily away to unlock the car, getting in. Sighing, Reenie followed him.

'You know I'm right,' she told him, fastening her seatbelt after she'd stowed the crutches onto the back seat with difficulty.

Angry with her, Ted had watched her struggling but hadn't offered to help. 'I know no such thing! He didn't force her to go out with him, did he?'

'We don't know what happened, do we?' she said. 'We weren't there. But we do know he was the driver.'

'She'd have egged him on. She was that type.'

'It doesn't make any difference. It was his car, and he was driving.'

'Oh!' Ted started the engine and pulled away with a screech of tyres his late son might have approved of. 'There's no talking to you!'

For the first time since their row at the hospital, Reenie's eyes filled with tears. 'Well,' she said. 'Now you know what it feels like, don't you?'

They drove – too fast in Reenie's opinion – in silence. Reenie wiped her eyes with the backs of her hands.

'I just want an end to this silly feud,' she said. 'I want to put the whole awful business behind us so we can move on.'

'And that's reason enough to suck up to that bitch, is it?'

'Thora Block isn't a bitch, Ted. She's just a– '

'They're back in there now, just revelling in it. You humiliated yourself, Reenie. I was embarrassed for you.'

It had been an exhausting day, after an exhausting week. 'No, you weren't, Ted Richardson!' she snapped. 'It was *you* who you were embarrassed for. You! It's always bloody well about you! Well, I am sick and tired of pussyfooting around you so your feelings don't get hurt!'

'Oh yes?' Ted turned to look at her. 'And you think I don't have to bite my tongue to save your feelings, do you?' he shouted. 'Well, let me tell you, sometimes I think I'm going to bite it clean off!'

The car was starting to veer across the road. A bus was coming.

'Look out!' Reenie shouted, but too late. There was a massive crash as the car hit the bus.

Reenie heard the sound of a horn blaring. 'Ted?' she screamed, and then she fainted.

* * * * *

In an interview room at the police station, Kate was being reprimanded by a policeman and Ian's friend, Clive.

'Oh, piss off with your Ms Mitchells, Clive,' Kate told him. 'It was me who cleaned your vomit up at our New Year's party in 2010. In case you've forgotten!'

Clive sighed. 'Kate, it's been a year since you and Ian split up. You have to move on.'

'I know how sodding long it's been!'

The door opened, and Ian appeared. 'It's all right, Clive,' he said. 'I'm not going to press charges. But I would like a word with Kate before she goes.'

'Sure.' Mightily relieved, Clive left them to it.

As the door clicked shut behind him, Kate kept her eyes fixed on the table. It was a long time since she'd been alone with Ian.

'I had to do a lot of persuading to get you off,' he told her. 'Assaulting an officer is a serious offence. And your "friend" hasn't done you any favours, hurling abuse over the counter.'

Kate's heart leapt. She looked up. 'Geoff?' she said. 'Geoff's here?'

Ian sniffed. 'Not anymore. The Sergeant had him ejected.'

Geoff had been here. Kate smiled, warmed by the knowledge. Then she remembered the trifle. If the whole thing were a failure, it would all be her fault.

Ian sat down opposite her. 'Kate,' he said, 'I know you still have feelings for me, but you really must try to control yourself.'

He sighed. 'Perhaps it's my fault. Perhaps Jennifer and I should have done the decent thing and moved away. But I'm up for promotion here soon, and besides, Jennifer's mother isn't a well woman, as you know… Look, I'm not going to press charges this time, but I can't promise to keep on…' Ian's voice suddenly tailed off as he realised Kate wasn't listening any longer.

'I don't,' she said, and then she clapped her hands together and began to laugh.

Ian frowned. 'You don't what?' he asked.

'I don't have feelings for you anymore!' she said, grinning all over her face because she had finally realised it was true. 'I am over you, you insignificant, pathetic little prick!'

Twenty-eight

Janet didn't plan to go to her mother's house after the scene at Estelle's flat; it was simply where the car took her. And once there, she didn't get out of the car straight away. Turning the engine off, she stayed behind the wheel, staring straight ahead. Every scrap of energy had deserted her. The only thing alive was her mind, and that was on overload, processing everything that had happened.

Ray was Estelle's married man. Ray was sleeping with the woman who had become her best friend.

One of her mother's neighbours was out the front clipping his hedge. He looked at her oddly, obviously wondering why she was just sitting there in the car. Janet forced herself to open the door and get out.

'Hello there, Mrs Thornton,' he said. 'Looks like rain later.'

She pretended to look at the sky. 'I think you could be right,' she said politely and opened the garden gate. Her world had fallen apart, and yet she was still ex-changing social niceties. How very British. How very *good*.

Fishing her key out of her handbag, she opened the front door and went inside. Leaning back against the front door, she spoke to her mother. 'Well,' she said. 'You were right about Ray after all. I hope that makes you very happy.'

There was no answer.

To fill the silence, Janet went into the living room and switched on the television. There was a cookery competition on. One of the contestants, a nervous, over-anxious woman in her mid-twenties; reminded Janet of herself in her early days of being married. Cooking had never come naturally to her, but she had slaved and stressed over recipes with ingredients she'd never heard of anyway, all to impress Ray and the business colleagues he invited home from work.

The nervous woman had thirty seconds left to complete her dish. In the top right-hand corner of the screen, the seconds were counting down. Her male competitor was whizzing about efficiently, straining, arranging and garnishing. The nervous woman was perspiring. She started to carry a pan of sauce across to some rather charred-looking meat on a plate, but somehow… she managed to drop it. Sauce went flying in all directions, and a horrified gasp went up from the studio audience.

Janet's hands flew up to cover her mouth, exactly like the poor cow's on the television were doing.

'Oh no, Mandy!' the presenter said, rushing over to clasp her. 'Mandy, Mandy, Mandy!'

Yes, that was exactly what she'd been like herself in those fraught early days of marriage. Dropping things, burning things, forgetting vital ingredients. Ray had found it endearing at first, but his indulgence had soon turned to exasperation, and finally Janet had stopped trying to cook anything elaborate.

Thinking about it now, she knew she had never felt as if she came up to scratch in any aspect of her married life with Ray, or at least not in any aspect

291

that he considered to be important. Ray didn't award points for interior decoration, listening skills or child rearing; he awarded points for those skills that satisfied his appetites – namely those of use in the kitchen and the bedroom.

And when she had failed so blatantly on both those fronts, he had ordered takeaways when he fancied something more exotic than the plain food that was all she could cope with cooking, and had affairs when he wanted more than an acquiescent body.

But he had chosen someone who was as inadequate as she was herself at letting go in bed...

If her marriage and the whole structure of her life hadn't been in tatters around her feet, Janet might have found it funny. No, she *did* find it funny. Ray had turned to someone else because he thought Janet was frigid, and without even realising it, he had chosen somebody else with exactly the same problem. It wasn't only funny; it was hilarious.

So why was she crying?

Suddenly her mobile phone began to ring. Wiping her eyes on her sleeves, Janet took it from her bag to see who was calling.

Estelle.

She switched the phone off.

* * * * *

When Kate left the police station, she found Geoff sitting on the steps outside, waiting for her. He was still dressed in his bakery whites, minus the hat, and as she walked towards him she focused on the splatters of custard on the front of his tunic, feeling shy.

'You all right?'

She nodded. 'Thanks for coming.'

'Couldn't have kept me away.'

She risked a glance at his face and saw that he was smiling. 'What about the trifle?' she asked.

He shrugged. 'Sod the trifle. They charge you?'

She shook her head. 'He decided not to press charges.'

'Just as flaming well! He'd have had me to deal with if he had!'

Now Kate was looking at him, she found she couldn't look away. He was so very dear to her, custard splatters and all.

'Come on,' he said, 'let's get you home before he changes his mind.' He held out his hand and looked at her. She hesitated for just a moment then put her hand in his. He smiled and they started to walk along the High Street in the direction of her bedsit.

'I'm scared, Geoff,' she said after a while.

Geoff didn't pretend not to know what she was talking about. 'I know you are, Katie.' He stopped by a fish and chip shop to look down at her. 'But I will never, ever hurt you. Got that?' When tears filled her eyes, he used his free hand to brush them away from her face. 'I mean it, Katie,' he said. 'I think the world of you. Always have. Ever since we first met. If I wasn't such a klutz where romance is concerned, I'd have made my move the minute you split up with PC Plod.'

Kate dropped his hand to fish in her pocket for a tissue. 'If you'd said anything then, I'd probably have run a mile. In fact, if you'd said anything *this morning* I'd probably have run a mile.'

293

'But it's all right this afternoon?' he asked with a smile.

She smiled back. 'Somehow, yes, it is.'

'Nothing like being arrested to put things into perspective,' he said.

She smiled some more. 'No, it wasn't that,' she joked. 'It was seeing you up on the cement mixer with that giant ladle.'

'Sexy, huh?'

She laughed. 'No. Just…significant.'

When he pulled her close to kiss her, he smelt of custard. 'Significant,' he said. 'I like the sound of that.'

* * * * *

The telephone rang. Estelle snatched the receiver up. 'Janet?'

'No,' a male voice said. 'It's Mark. I need to talk to you about something. I was wondering if I could come round.'

Estelle closed her eyes. The last thing she needed right now was to have to pretend to be all right when she wasn't. 'It's not a very good time, actually, Mark,' she said.

'Oh,' he said. Then he spoke again. 'Look, Estelle, it's something pretty important. I think you'd want to know about it.'

Something about his voice made an impression on her. She sighed. 'All right,' she said. 'You can come round.'

Mark arrived five minutes later, clutching a newspaper. It must have been obvious she'd been crying, but although he looked carefully at her face, he

294

tactfully didn't mention it.

'Come in. Can I get you a glass of wine? I'm sorry the place is such a mess…' Estelle realised she was bumbling about the way Janet might.

Janet.

'Estelle? What's wrong?'

Suddenly she couldn't stop crying. The split with Janet seemed to have opened the floodgates to thirty years of suppressed tears.

Mark led her to the sofa and sat her down, his arm around her. 'Shh,' he said very tenderly. 'It's all right. It's all right.'

'No, it's not.' Estelle spoke raggedly through her tears. 'It's not all right at all. I've lost the only real friend I've ever had, and I didn't even *know!* I'd never have done anything to hurt Janet. I care about her too much. And I don't even *like* him really. God knows why I got involved with him in the first place. It's all such a bloody waste!'

She cried until she had no tears left, and after she'd finished, she still lay in his arms, too exhausted to move. Besides, what was the point of feeling self-conscious now? Her barriers were well and truly down. And so, when Mark began to ask her gentle questions about what was wrong, she told him.

Afterwards, he was quiet for a moment. 'I'm sure Janet will understand when she's had a chance to think about it,' he said. 'She'll see that you had no idea this RT was her husband.'

'Yes,' Estelle said miserably, 'but will that make any difference? I'll still be the one who broke up her marriage.'

'It might not come to that,' Mark said. 'She might forgive him.'

295

That had Estelle sitting up. 'She'd better not,' she said, her eyes flashing with the strength of her feelings. 'She deserves so much better than that…that *arsehole*.'

Mark looked at her. 'So do you,' he said, and the stupid, weak tears flooded back into her eyes.

'No,' she said, 'I don't.' But suddenly she felt as if Jade were there in the room.

'You are beautiful Estelle,' she was saying. 'You deserve only the very best from life.'

It would be so nice to be able to believe that.

Mark shifted slightly in his seat. Estelle looked at him, worried he might have had enough of looking after the maudlin female she had somehow transformed into.

'Why don't we have some of that wine now?' he suggested.

Why not? Why not get utterly, totally pissed out of her brains? 'All right.'

While he was gone, Estelle picked up the newspaper he had brought with him. It was turned over to page seven and she saw the report straight away.

Shelthorpe Lingerie Trader in Vandalism Charge.

Shit.

Mark came back with the opened bottle and two glasses. 'Ah,' he said, putting the glasses down onto the coffee table and starting to pour. 'That's what I came over to tell you about. I thought you should be prepared.'

The article gave her name and her age, but mostly it dwelt on her business and the scale of the damage she'd done to the summerhouse. They'd even managed to find a photograph of her from

296

somewhere. It was an old one; her hair was different and she was dressed in a bikini, holding a cocktail.

'Shit.' This time she spoke the word out loud.

'Here.' Mark offered her a glass of wine. She took it from him, still squinting at the photograph. Vaguely she remembered it being taken by a long-ago boyfriend on holiday on his boat. God only knew how the press had got hold of it.

'They'll know,' she suddenly thought. 'Mum and Dad will know.' And suddenly she resented that more than anything else – the fact that her parents would now be aware of the impact they still had on her life.

'Want to tell me about it?' Mark asked gently.

Estelle took a large slug of wine. 'It's a long story,' she warned him.

'I'm in no hurry,' he said.

* * * * *

'So these workshops,' Geoff said. 'They been doing you any good?'

They were lying, fully clothed, on Kate's double bed. Because the bedsit was so untidy, it was the only place with enough space for them both. Or at least, that was the excuse they were both sticking to.

'Wouldn't you like to know?!' teased Kate.

'I would,' Geoff said. 'That's why I asked!' He was leaning back against a pillow propped against the wall, and she was kind of nuzzled into his side. It wasn't that comfortable, but there was no way on earth she was going to move.

'I don't know really,' she told him. 'Haven't really put all the techniques we've learnt to the test yet.' She looked at him closely. 'I've always wondered,' she said. 'Why *did* you challenge me to do the course? Was it just for your seedy little kicks, or…?

Geoff looked suddenly embarrassed. 'Well,' he said. 'There *was* that, of course.'

'Of course,' smiled Kate, then waited for more.

'But I also thought…well, that it might help you to get close to people. I thought you'd have to with a class like that. And since your break-up, you'd virtually shut yourself off from people.'

Kate knew that only a short while ago such an observation would have hurt her, angered her even. But now it didn't. 'Hmm,' she teased. 'Quite the psychologist, aren't you?'

Geoff grinned at her and gave her a kiss. 'I'm not bad, am I?' he said. 'For a baker.' Then he stroked her hair back from her face, his expression growing more serious. 'I didn't have any idea if you *needed* to do a workshop like that of course, but I figured with PC Plod as a husband, it was fairly likely.' He paused, then asked, 'Was I right?'

It was Kate's turn to blush. 'Yes,' she mumbled, avoiding his gaze. 'You were right. Didn't think it mattered at the time, but now, I think…Well I think it probably does.'

'Definitely,' agreed Geoff.

Kate sighed, snuggling even closer to him. 'Anyway, I don't know whether there'll be any more classes or not now we've been chucked out of the church hall.'

'You could use the function room at the pub,' Geoff suggested, and Kate laughed.

'Yeah, right,' she said. 'And have you lot perving

in the bar next door!'

'We wouldn't do that,' he lied.

Kate pulled a sceptical face. 'It's supposed to be Orgasm Night in three weeks' time,' she said. 'Orgasm Night? When we're all supposed to have an orgasm together? I don't think that'd go down very well with the brewery somehow.'

'We could organise karaoke in the bar at the same time. That'd drown the sound of you lot out, especially if Tom gets up to sing.'

Kate laughed. 'Or you!' she teased.

'Hey, watch it!' Geoff said, and began to tickle her. She squealed, attempting and failing to wriggle away.

'Stop! Stop!' she panted.

'Only if you kiss me,' he said.

Kate was glad Tom wasn't around to see them. She knew he'd be pretending to hurl by now. She and Geoff were behaving like a couple of teenagers and it felt good. Very, very good.

'They'll never believe this at work,' she said when they finally broke away from each other. Then she looked at him. 'Hey,' she said. 'Do I still have a job after this afternoon?'

'Well,' he said, 'if you don't, then I don't, because I'll walk if she sacks you. And I'll make sure the whole catering department goes on strike into the bargain.'

Kate smiled. 'My hero,' she said, and although the teasing note was still in her voice, she meant it.

Geoff seemed to know that because when he gathered her close again there was something more urgent about the way they kissed. Very gently and very tenderly, he began to stroke her through her clothes. Kate felt a shiver of delicious desire right down the length of her body. Reaching out, she began to undo his custardy buttons.

* * * * *

'Are you sure you're OK, Mum? The state the car's in, I can't believe you and Dad aren't hurt!'

Reenie smiled grimly. 'I know. Certainly looks bad, doesn't it? But honestly, we're fine. Dad's got a bit of whiplash, but that's about it.'

'So why's Dad so angry then?' Marcia persisted.

'Probably fed up about the car,' Reenie said, and was relieved when Marcia nodded, seeming to accept this explanation.

'Well, I'm glad you're both all right,' she said, and turned to go upstairs. Then she remembered something and turned back. 'You know what?' she said. 'This is one crazy day. First of all Mrs Mitchell gets arrested at college, and then you and Dad– '

'Kate's been arrested?' Reenie interrupted, and Marcia smiled, cheering up a bit.

'Yeah,' she said. 'She hit a policeman. It was really cool! It'll be on the news tonight for sure. There were loads of TV cameras.'

Reenie looked at her watch; it was just after six o'clock. She switched the television on to the local news. And there, staring out at her from the screen was a picture not of Kate, but of Estelle.

'Bloody hell!' Reenie said. 'She's a friend of mine too!'

Marcia listened to the report with her. 'Shit, Mum,' she said, 'all your friends are criminals!'

'Shh!' Reenie said. The reporter was outside

300

Estelle's work now, catching people as they left.

'Excuse me, can you tell me what you know about Ms Morgan's arrest at the weekend?' she asked, but everybody kept their head down and kept on walking, so finally the reporter addressed the camera again.

'At her company headquarters, Ms Morgan has a reputation for being quite a stern employer, and as you can see, everybody here is too frightened to speak to me today. We may not know exactly why Ms Morgan smashed up the summerhouse, but the truth about one thing is now well and truly out, and that's the real nature of the business of Estelle Morgan Enterprises. I can exclusively reveal that *this* is what they deal in behind these doors.'

Grinning, the reporter held up a skimpy, transparent bra and an incomplete-looking pair of panties. 'This is Clare Walker reporting from Estelle Morgan Enterprises in not so sleepy Shelthorpe on Sea.'

'Blimey,' said Reenie.

The back door opened.

'Dad!' Marcia said. 'One of Mum's friends is a pros-titute! She's just been on the telly!'

'Estelle is not a prostitute,' Reenie said. 'She's a businesswoman. A what d'you call it. Importer. Exporter.'

'Yeah of kinky knickers! Bet she wears them for her clients!'

'For the last time, Marcia, Estelle is not a prostitute!'

Reenie whirled round to glare at Marcia and was just in time to see her husband's back as he left the room. So, he wasn't even speaking to her now then.

No doubt he was blaming her for the car being written off.

'Mum,' Marcia was saying, pointing to the television. 'This is it. About Mrs Mitchell punching that copper.'

Reenie looked bad-temperedly back at the television, but instantly forgot all about Ted as she saw Kate running alongside a cement mixer and straight towards a policeman. Pulling her arm back, she socked him one right across the face.

'God almighty,' Reenie said. 'Kate, girl, what have you gone and done?'

* * * * *

When the cookery competition was over, Janet watched a soap. But the storylines seemed tame after the reality of her life, and when the news came on, she switched the television off. She couldn't cope with the problems of the world. She had too many of her own to deal with.

She still hadn't decided what she was going to do. There were only two real options: to go on as normal for the moment and pretend nothing had happened, or to confront Ray with the truth.

In the end, mainly because her brain felt full of fog, she decided not to say anything for now. There was no point, not until she knew what she wanted to happen. Ray was so clever with words he was bound to tie her up in knots, and she needed time to think. Ideally she would have liked to have gone away somewhere to do her thinking, but where could she go without arousing his suspicions?

'You're late back,' Ray greeted her from behind

his newspaper when she got back.

'I went to Mum's.'

'Good.' He lowered the paper and caught sight of her face. 'It had to be done. But I realise it can't have been easy, sorting through your mother's things.'

She stood looking at him, fiddling nervously with her handbag. 'No.'

'Why don't you sit down for a bit before you make tea?' he suggested. 'I'll make you a coffee.'

She knew she might have been moved by this uncharacteristic thoughtfulness if today hadn't happened.

She sat. 'Thanks. Where's Debbie?'

'Gone out.' He stood up. 'I'll get that coffee.'

While he was in the kitchen, she just sat, staring straight ahead.

'Here you are.' Ray returned with the coffee.

She took it automatically. 'Thanks.'

He sat down, picking up the newspaper again, but paused before starting to read it. 'Listen,' he said, 'about these workshops.'

She looked at him. 'Yes?'

'I've been thinking.' He paused to clear his throat. 'I know I was angry with you, but I've been thinking about it, and I appreciate you were probably only going for my sake. I ought to be flattered, I suppose.' He reached out with this free hand to pat her arm. 'But, hang it all, Janet, if you really want to learn about sex, then you don't need any pathetic workshop; you only have to look closer to home, all right?'

She turned her head to look at him; the man she had been married to for more than half her life. What an ignorant person he was. How pathetically arrogant.

'Right,' she said.

* * * * *

Kate had never felt anything quite like this before, a kind of gathering and *clamouring* in her body.

She had ripped all of Geoff's clothes off by now, but he was taking his time with hers; she was naked from the waist up, and he had caressed her breasts and sucked her nipples for what seemed like ages, but she still had her trousers on. And the thing was, the way he was caressing her clitoris and vulva against the trouser seam – here was no possibility of not using the right words for her private parts after the sessions with Jade, especially in her most fevered thoughts – was driving her absolutely crazy. She was straining frenziedly against both his hand and her trouser seam, and she was afraid she was going to come like that. *Afraid she was going to come like that...* A particle of her mind registered the humour in that, but was swept rapidly aside on the torrent of her feelings.

'That's it, girl,' Geoff said softly, 'go with it.'

And so she did, pushing and shoving and jerking against his hand until she cried out.

When she was finally still and silent, Kate felt the low rumble of Geoff's laughter against her and looked up at him. 'But you didn't... you know,' she said worriedly, and he laughed again.

'Who cares?' he said. 'I can "you know" some other time.' And he pulled her closer.

Kate could feel herself getting all emotional. 'Why hasn't that ever happened to me before?' she

304

asked, and he kissed her.

'Because you haven't encountered The Geoff before,' he said, and she smiled.

'Is that right?' she said. 'And how do I know that wasn't a one-off?'

'Listen,' he told her, mock stern, 'have you ever known my bread not to rise?'

Twenty-nine

The morning after she had spewed her heart out to Mark, Estelle woke up and recalled the events of the previous evening with dismay. It was like having a massive hangover and remembering the ludicrous things she'd done while under the influence.

Except that this time she had managed to make a total arse of herself on two small glasses of wine.

She had told Mark about everything. Tim Lawrence, her parents' disbelief, Rashid in the summerhouse, *everything*. How was she ever going to face him again? Work with him? But she had to; she'd had far too much time off as it was.

She could do it. She'd been wearing a mask for most of her life after all. She could do it again. She just had to be strong.

Estelle was dressed in her suit, make-up on, car keys in her hand, ready to set off, but she stopped to look at herself in the mirror, feeling exhausted by the idea of needing to be strong. It had been such a relief last night not to have to pretend. Mark had been so sweet and understanding, listening and holding her, sym-pathetic and non-judgemental, and after she had un-burdened herself she had felt more at peace than she had done in a very long while.

Now, looking in the mirror, Estelle's fingers stroked across her shoulder where Mark's fingers had tightened their grip when she spoke about her parents' reaction when she'd told them about Tim Lawrence.

'You poor thing,' he'd said gently. 'You were their daughter! They should have listened to you.' He reached out to touch her face, and for a moment, she thought he was going to kiss her, but he didn't. And why would he? A woman who had just been arrested for criminal damage? A woman who had just lost her best friend because she was having an affair with her husband?

Still looking at her reflection, Estelle deliberately hardened the lines of her face. Last night had been last night. OK, she had been vulnerable; OK, so she was human after all. But vulnerable was no way to run a business. Vulnerable was no way to keep the pain of the past from hurting her.

When she reached the car park of Estelle Morgan Enterprises, she almost bottled out of going inside. It wasn't just the prospect of facing Mark, it was also the fact that she knew everyone would know about her arrest by now. Her mask had never had such a big job to do before, and she wasn't sure it was up to it.

But what was the alternative? Never go into work again? Emigrate?

Taking a deep breath, she got out of the car. The stairs to the second floor had never seemed so steep and the buzz of conversation behind the door to her offices never so loud. As she reached out to push open the door, her hand was shaking slightly. She pretended not to notice.

'Good morning, Charlotte.'

There was no buzz of voices; her PA was simply on the phone. Charlotte lifted her hand in response to

Estelle's greeting and carried on talking. Estelle walked towards her office. Along the corridor, somebody laughed. She hesitated for a moment and then carried doggedly onwards until she reached her sanctuary.

Breathing a sigh of relief, she closed the door and sat down behind her desk, dumping her briefcase onto the floor. She could do this. She *could* do this.

There was a knock. Charlotte popped her head round the door. 'Can I get you a coffee, Estelle?' she asked.

It was the same question her PA asked her every day. Estelle could detect no difference in the way she had asked it either. 'Yes, please, Charlotte,' she said. 'That would be very nice.'

Charlotte blinked. 'Right,' she said in a bright voice. 'Coming up.' Only after she had gone did Estelle realise that it was *she* who had spoken differently, not Charlotte. When was she ever so polite and appreciative? Especially first thing in the morning?

The phone rang, the tone indicating an outside call. Estelle snatched it up gratefully, anticipating the life-saving hurly-burly of business. But it wasn't a business call at all.

'Ms Morgan, this is Adele Reason of the *Eastern Daily Press*. I wonder if I could ask you a few questions?'

Estelle hung up.

Charlotte came in with her coffee with a smile on her face, a smile that vanished as soon as she caught sight of Estelle's grim expression. Estelle saw Charlotte hesitate as if she were wondering whether to ask Estelle if she were all right. But at the last minute she obviously didn't feel confident enough to do it, because she just put the coffee down on the desk and went out, closing the door behind her.

A text came through from Kate on Estelle's mobile. *Workshop Friday in back room of Rose pub on Fye Street*. In the back room of a pub? If the press got hold of that, they really would have a field day. It would be best not to go. But if she didn't go, then she might miss a chance to see Janet. But Janet probably wouldn't go anyway. Why would she? She had only been going to the workshops for Ray, and she would hardly be very keen to see Estelle.

'Hi.' Mark came in without knocking, as if he owned the place. As if he owned *her.*

Estelle flushed. 'Good morning, Mark,' she said formally, busying herself with the papers on her desk.

'How are you today?' The gentle tone of voice implied intimacy.

She didn't look up. 'Fine. Busy.'

There was a silence. She guessed he was absorbing her tone of voice. 'Right,' he said. 'It's like that, is it?'

'Like what?'

'We pretend last night never happened?'

She still couldn't look at him. 'Nothing did happen,' she said.

'If you say so,' he said coolly.

The sulkiness of his voice gave her courage. She could deal with sulky a lot more easily than she could deal with kind or loving.

'I'm sorry, Mark,' she said coolly looking him in the face now. 'I wasn't myself last night. I can't apologise enough for inflicting all that on you.'

He was about to interrupt; to reassure her that it was all right, but she held up her hand. 'But as you can see, I'm fine today; absolutely fine. There's no need for you to worry about me at all. Now, fill me in on the research you've been doing for our new lines.'

Mark looked at her searchingly. She managed not only to hold his gaze but also to keep a calm smile on her face.

'Can we schedule a meeting to discuss it?' he asked her. 'I'll prepare all the information for you to look at.'

'Certainly,' she said. 'What about Monday morning?'

'That's fine,' he said and walked towards the door. 'See you later.'

As the door closed behind him, Estelle experienced a pang of emptiness in her stomach. But it wasn't anything; just a lack of breakfast, that was all. She'd send Charlotte out for some croissants. That would soon sort it out.

* * * * *

Janet was also attempting to carry on as normal, listening to some tedious account of one of Ray's work meetings, telling Debbie she ought to eat more for breakfast, taking the kitchen rubbish out to the dustbin. She wasn't due in to work until the afternoon, and traditionally Thursday morning was her main time for housework. But when Debbie and Ray left for work, she didn't venture upstairs with her cleaning products and the radio as she usually did. Instead she sat at the kitchen table with a cup of coffee and wished she had a cigarette even though

310

she had given up smoking some twenty years previously.

There was a knock on the back door. Before she could decide to ignore it, the door opened and Gwen let herself in.

'Knew you wouldn't let me in if I came to the front,' she said in her usual matter-of-fact style, helping herself to a mug from Janet's mug tree. 'May I?' she asked, lifting the cafetière enquiringly.

'What do you want, Gwen?' Janet asked.

Gwen poured herself a coffee and brought it over to the kitchen table. 'I've come to help you,' she said.

Janet took a slug of her own coffee. 'Oh yes, and you've been so very helpful towards me lately, haven't you?' she said sarcastically.

'I've honestly only acted in what I thought were your best interests, Janet,' Gwen told her.

'Well, in future *I'd* like to be the one who decides what my best interests are, thank you very much,' Janet said.

Gwen nodded, unabashed. 'Point taken. Peter's always telling me not to stick my nose in where it's not wanted.'

Janet was surprised. Peter, Gwen's husband, was so hen- pecked the term must have been invented especially for him.

'Anyway, I've found something out I think you ought to know about,' Gwen said. 'Don't worry, it's got nothing to do with that Jade or those workshops; it's something else entirely.'

Janet's heart sank. Ray. Gwen had found out about Ray and Estelle.

'It's Carol,' Gwen said.

311

For a moment Janet was confused. Surely Gwen didn't think Ray was having an affair with Carol? Even he wouldn't go that far. Would he?

Gwen's eyebrows lifted. 'Carol De Ville? Your boss?'

'What about Carol?

'Well,' Gwen said, leaning in closer, 'you know my friend Mavis who works at Shaws?'

Shaws was a local estate agent. 'Yes?'

'She says Carol's looking to sell the shop. Had the valuers in last week.' Gwen sat back in triumph. 'So,' she said, 'you might be out of a job soon. Just thought you'd like to know. Pre-warned is pre-armed, as they say.'

Gwen finished her coffee then turned to go. At the door, she looked back. 'Oh, just more one word about those workshops, Janet,' she said. 'I don't know if you realise it, but that workshop leader of yours is living in a dilapidated caravan up at the caravan site. And no, before you say anything, I wasn't nosing around. I just happened to be up that way walking the dog when I saw her. I just thought you should know, because you have to wonder why she's living in such circumstances if she's the bona fide person she makes out she is, don't you?'

When Gwen was gone, Janet didn't wonder any such thing; she was far too busy dwelling on her bombshell about the shop. It seemed to Janet that her entire life would soon consist entirely of nothings – no job, no orgasms, no marriage worthy of the name, no confidence, no self-respect… Unless…Unless she could be brave enough to do something so drastic, so life-changing that things as Janet Thornton knew them would never be the same again.

What have you got to lose? She asked herself as she cleaned the upstairs toilet with a vigour it had never before experienced. What *have* you got to lose?

The answer was another nothing, but this time the nothing was a positive – if frightening – nothing. *Nothing.*

As soon as Janet had begun to think that the impossible might in fact be possible, ideas and plans blossomed with quick fertility inside her head. And later that day, when she parked her car in the High Street car park and walked to the shop, she was already halfway to being a new person. She just hoped Gwen's information was right, because if it weren't, then that would be the end of all her plans and hopes. But Gwen was always right about what was going on in Shelthorpe On Sea; she was head of a kind of gossip mafia in the town, with her positions on various committees and her connections with the WI. And, squaring her shoulders, Janet pushed the shop door open, preparing to take on Carol De Ville.

* * * * *

Since Kate's arrest, she and Geoff had barely ventured out of Kate's bedsit apart from to go to work. And work had largely consisted of clearing up after the failed trifle attempt (Geoff), receiving another dressing down and a final warning from the Principal (Kate), caretaking their students and taking full advantage of any times that the catering staff room was empty (Geoff and Kate).

Tom had come in one time when they were in a clinch. When they pulled quickly apart, not realising at first that it was him, he laughed. 'About bloody time!' he told them, but when he tried to persuade them to go for a drink to celebrate, they turned him down. For the moment they wanted to use every spare minute of their time for research activities. They had a lot of catching up to do.

By the time Friday's workshop came around, Kate had had four orgasms; none as yet as the result of sexual intercourse, but hell, it was still four orgasms in less than four days, and both she and Geoff were overjoyed.

'It's hard to believe I was so scared about you and me,' she told him, lying in his arms in her bed early on the Friday after yet more fieldwork. 'I can't wait to tell the girls. They are going to be so chuffed for me!'

Kate had held back from saying anything to them before now because she wanted to see the look on their faces when she told them.

Geoff gave her right breast a gentle squeeze. 'All right for some, swanning off for a session with a sex guru,' he said. 'Some of us have got to give a theory lesson to twenty-five demotivated day releasers.'

'Don't worry,' she said, 'I'll make sure whatever I learn this morning will have a direct pay-off for you.'

'See that you do.'

Though actually, much to her relief, Geoff seemed to have no complaints so far with anything she had done for him. And if she had had four orgasms, then he'd probably had double that. Not that she was counting.

They walked out together and kissed long and hard by the side of Geoff's car.

'Oh,' he said when he finally broke away.

314

'Almost forgot. I've got something for you.' And he reached into the car for a carrier bag, which he handed to her with a big grin.

Kate took it. 'What is it?' she asked.

'Take a look,' he said, still grinning. Then he gave her another kiss and got into his car. 'See you later, honey,' he said. 'Enjoy!'

'Later,' she said, and stood and waved as he drove away. She didn't mind him calling her honey. She, Kate hard-woman Mitchell wouldn't even have minded if he had decided to call her his doughnut or his sugar dumpling.

Still smiling, she opened the carrier bag. Inside was a very badly-knitted pink jumper. Kate held it up, smiling at every dropped stitch. She loved it.

She wore the jumper to go to the workshop that morning, but when she took her jacket off, nobody mentioned it.

'Reenie,' Kate collared her friend, a big smirk on her face. 'Something's happened.'

Reenie didn't look at her properly, so she didn't cotton onto the smirk. 'Oh no,' she just said irritably, 'not something else! We've had enough happen this week already; me and Ted aren't speaking, Estelle's got to go to court, and she and Janet have fallen out about something – they won't tell me what.' She sniffed, arms folded, obviously very put out about this. 'I thought we were supposed to be a *group*. I didn't know we could take it or leave it as the mood takes us.'

By this time, Kate's smile had vanished. Things certainly did seem tense between Estelle and Janet; they were sitting about as far apart from each other as it was possible to get, and Janet had her arms folded with a sort of mutinous expression on her face. Estelle, on the other hand, kept on sneaking glances Janet's way. Kate had never seen her like that; she looked kind of...hunched. Meek, even.

'Anyway,' Reenie said, 'what has happened to you? Apart from you hitting that ex-husband of yours? Saw you on the news. You were lucky to get off, I reckon.'

It was all so totally different to the way Kate had imagined it, that she just shrugged. 'Oh, nothing special,' she said. 'I'll tell you about it later.'

'Ladies,' said Jade in her usual extravagant style. 'It's lovely to see you all as usual, and very many thanks to Kate for organising this alternative accommodation. Now, without further ado, allow me to introduce the topic for today's session. The G-Spot.'

Normally they'd all have been looking at each other after an announcement like that, but when Kate cast a sideways glance, first at Reenie and Estelle, and then at Janet, she saw that they were all either staring straight ahead or looking with great interest at the swirly pattern on the carpet.

'Now I know you've probably heard all kinds of tales about the G-Spot,' Jade continued. 'There is a great deal of debate about its exact location, and there are even rumours that it doesn't exist at all. Well, let me assure you it most definitely does exist, and by the end of this morning's session, you will have undisputable proof of that fact.'

Beside Kate, Reenie shifted uncomfortably in her seat, but remained uncharacteristically silent. Kate felt obliged to make some kind of contribution to the session.

316

'Why is it called the G-Spot?' she asked, and Jade smiled at her.

'It was named after a German gynaecologist called Ernst Grafenberg in the 1950s. He was the first person in modern times to research and write about it, although there is evidence that ancient cultures were fully aware of its existence. Unfortunately, in more recent times, that knowledge seems to have fallen by the wayside. Until Grafenberg.'

'It's not a very sexy name, is it?' Kate said. 'The G-Spot.'

Once again, Jade smiled. 'No, Kate, I agree with you. Which is why I'd encourage you to think of your own name for this special place once you've become familiar with it. Personally, I call mine my Source, simply because it's the source of my deepest orgasms.'

Kate smiled to herself, thinking about Geoff. They could name her G-Spot together; it would be fun.

'The reason why all of these myths and uncertainties have developed is because, of course, the G-Spot is hidden inside the vagina.' Jade smiled. 'It's always easier to believe in something you can actually see, particularly for members of the male sex.'

Jade paused, but the banter this comment might normally have inspired was not forthcoming, so she pressed on.

'The precise location of the G-Spot is different for each woman, as is each woman's experience of an orgasm as a result of G-Spot stimulation. Some women have several G-Spots, some women have one; some say they have a short, sharp sensation of pleasure, while others speak lyrically of overlapping waves of rapture lasting for several minutes. Today we'll be taking a first step in discovering what the case is for all of you.'

Jade turned to point to her diagram of a woman's anatomy. 'Now, the most likely locations for your G-Spot are here, around the urethral opening, here, along the bladder tube, and here, around the vaginal canal. You have some very sensitive tissue around all these areas, and when you're aroused, your G-Spot becomes engorged with blood, exactly as happens with your clitoris.'

'Or the penis,' Kate said, once again thinking of Geoff.

'Yes, Kate,' Jade said, 'also like the penis. Although it's worth remembering that a man's penis has to serve a dual function, whereas a woman's pleasure spots exist only to give her pleasure.'

'And we've got two places, whereas men have only got the one!' Kate said.

'Yes, indeed.'

Kate saw Jade's gaze sweep quickly over Estelle, Reenie and Janet. Their lack of participation was becoming increasingly obvious as the session went on. Next door, somebody began to hoover the bar, getting it ready for opening time. Kate looked carefully at Jade's face, wondering whether she was beginning to feel the strain, but Jade merely smiled and crossed to a portable CD player.

'Let's create a little ambience,' she said, and the room was filled suddenly with some sensual music they had heard once before, when they'd had a go at belly dancing.

Remembering the time she had gone round to Reenie's house to speak to Marcia and had

318

encountered Reenie in a belly dancing outfit, Kate smiled at her. Or at least, she tried to, but Reenie was still sitting there like a grumpy, unresponsive block of wood.

In truth, Kate was beginning to feel irritated by the lot of them. All right, by the sound of it they all had problems, but nobody had forced them to come today, had they? And it couldn't be easy for Jade having to teach in here with that hoover going off. They could at least make an effort, miserable shower.

Jade adjusted the volume of the music to a steady background level so that she would be heard over it, but unfortunately whoever was doing the hoovering next door started a shouted conversation with somebody at the same time.

'Want me to tell her to keep it down?' Kate offered, but Jade shook her head.

'Thank you, Kate,' she said, 'but I'm sure they'll be finished soon. Now, something you may not be aware of is the fact that it is common for women to ejaculate a liquid as a result of a G-Spot orgasm. This liquid does not come from the vagina, but from the urethra.'

The old Kate might have made some sarcastic crack about them pissing themselves, but the new Kate was simply fascinated.

'But it has been scientifically proven that this liquid is not urine. I am told that the taste of this liquid varies from woman to woman; some people describe it as being sweet, others as bitter or tangy.' She smiled at them all. 'You will have to ask your men to describe yours to you.'

Reenie grunted cynically. 'Fat chance,' she said grumpily to herself, and Kate saw that Jade was debating whether to investigate this statement further or to pretend not to have heard it. Kate felt the latter was the safest course of action. It seemed Jade agreed with her.

'Now,' she said brightly, and the bright tone of voice told Kate better than anything else that their tutor was indeed starting to feel the strain, 'if you could make sure the door is locked for me, Kate? I'll see to the lighting.'

Kate got up to check the Yale lock. It was closed, but she slipped the catch up to stop anybody being able to open it with a key. 'Right,' she said. 'All secure.'

'Thank you, Kate.' Jade had swiftly drawn the curtains and was now lighting candles around the room. 'If you could just hold on over there to switch the lights off for me when I'm ready?'

The last candle was lit. 'OK,' Jade said. 'They can go off now.'

Kate flicked the switch and made her way back to her chair. The room had a totally different feel to it now, especially when the hoovering suddenly stopped next door.

'All right, ladies,' Jade told them, 'the time has come for you to carry out your own investigation into your G-Spots. 'She handed them all a wispy, chiffony piece of fabric. 'If you'd like to remove your underwear if you're wearing a skirt, or your bottom half if you're wearing trousers, then if it makes you feel more comfortable, you can use the piece of material to cover your modesty while you explore.'

Jade tactfully turned her back, finding another candle to light from somewhere and adjusting a curtain that didn't really need adjusting. Behind her on the chairs, nobody moved. Kate had her hand on her trouser zip, but with everyone else just sat there like statues, she didn't quite dare to pull it down.

Jade finally noticed their lack of activity. 'Come, come,' she said. 'There's no need for any of you to feel embarrassed; we're all friends here now. And besides, you'll be doing a whole lot more than this in front of each other on Orgasm Night.' Her gaze ranged across them all, finally settling on Reenie. 'Reenie?' she prompted.

But Reenie just shook her head. 'I can't do it, Jade,' she said. 'I'm sorry, but there you are. I'm just not in the mood. And there's no point anyway; Ted and I aren't even speaking to each other at the moment, let alone making love.'

'I'm very sorry to hear that, Reenie,' Jade told her. 'But don't forget, your inner sex goddess wants to experience sensual pleasure for her own benefit, not simply for the sake of her man.'

'Right now my inner sex goddess just wants to go home and have a nice cup of tea,' Reenie said stubbornly. 'Or, better still, a large gin. I'm just not in the mood, and that is that.'

'Me neither, I'm afraid, Jade,' Janet said. It was the first time she'd said anything all lesson.

'Or me,' Estelle added.

Kate watched as Janet glared in a most un-Janet-like way at Estelle. 'And even if I were in the mood,' she said, 'some of us have had our man *appropriated* by another woman.'

For once Jade seemed at a loss for words. Kate got to her feet.

'You lot are really pissing me off,' she said.

321

'Miserable shower! I felt really good today on my way here. I was bursting to tell you my good news; couldn't wait. But you're all so wrapped up in your own little glooms, you wouldn't have got excited if I'd come in here to tell you I'd won the fucking Lottery!'

'Have you won the Lottery, Kate?' Jade asked her kindly.

Most of Kate's joy instantly came flooding back to her. 'No,' she said, grinning from ear to ear. 'It's way better than that.'

They all looked at her.

'I've had an orgasm!'

* * * * *

Janet was the first on her feet to give Kate a celebratory hug, though no doubt this was partly because Reenie was hampered slightly with her bad ankle and her crutches.

Everybody hugged Kate, and then they demanded more information – full, uncensored information. But first of all, Jade insisted on going next door to buy a bottle of champagne. And as they all raised their glasses to toast Kate, Janet looked across the group at Estelle.

Despite her remark about appropriating men, Janet couldn't hate Estelle. In fact, it was hurting her to see her friend looking so chastened and defeated.

'Just goes to show,' Reenie said, looking distinctly brighter than she had done for the rest of the session, 'there's hope for us all! Cheers, Kate, mate! Congratulations on being the first!'

'And may the rest of you quickly follow my

example!' said Kate.

'Speaking of which,' Jade said, 'are any of you in the mood to discover your G-Spots now?'

Thirty

'Do you have to go straight back to work? Or have you got time to talk?'

When the session was over, Janet approached Estelle.

'No,' Estelle said immediately. 'That is, yes, I'd like to…talk. Shall we go for a coffee?'

'What about a walk by the sea?' Janet said, and Estelle nodded.

'A walk by the sea's fine.'

And so they said their goodbyes to the others and walked off together along the High Street in the direction of the seafront.

'Carol's selling the shop,' Janet said as they neared her place of work.

Estelle looked at her. '*Is* she?' she said. 'I had heard from various people that she wasn't doing so well, but… I'm sorry. You'll miss your job. But perhaps whoever buys it might take you on…' Her voice faltered, and once again Janet experienced a pang of sympathy for her friend. And love. Yes, love. She cared for Estelle more than she had ever cared for any female friend.

'I offered to buy it,' she said, and Estelle stopped walking.

'Janet, that's fantastic!' she grinned.

Janet shrugged. 'She wouldn't agree straight away

of course; said she'd have to think about it.'

'What did you offer?'

'Ten thousand below the asking price. That's the value of my mother's house less inheritance tax.'

'She might have to accept your offer, no matter how much it goes against the grain to be bought out by her assistant! If not, you can always get a business loan.'

'Yes,' said Janet. 'I know.'

They carried on walking.

'You'll make a much better job of it than she has,' Estelle told her.

'I know that too,' Janet said, and realised suddenly that she *did* know it. Goodness, she had changed if she could be so sure about something like that.

Estelle cleared her throat. 'What does…Ray think about it?' she asked in that new subdued voice she had acquired.

Janet smiled at her friend. 'I haven't got round to mentioning it to him yet.'

Tears filled Estelle's eyes. 'Janet,' she started to say, but Janet took her arm and urged her on towards the promenade.

'Shh,' she said.

* * * * *

'So, d'you think you found yours?' Janet asked Estelle later on the beach.

'I think so,' Estelle told her. 'I found this little lump anyway, and if it isn't my G-Spot, then I'm seriously worried!'

Estelle didn't feel as if she deserved Janet to

forgive her, but she so hoped she would. It was great to be to-gether chatting like this again.

Janet smiled. 'I think I've got two,' she said. 'One low down and another much higher up.'

'Well,' said Estelle, 'if it's *that* high up, your Ray's penis will never find it!' The instant she'd said it, she clamped her hand over her mouth, afraid she'd gone too far, but Janet burst out laughing.

'You're right there,' she said. 'Mind you, as he's the only man I've ever made love to, I haven't got anything to compare him with. Is he small then?'

Estelle pulled a face. 'No, not small; just average.'

'Average,' Janet said. 'Yes, that sounds right.' She looked at her friend. 'Why did you stick with him?'

Estelle picked a pebble up from the beach and examined it. 'I don't honestly know,' she said. 'Because there's something lacking in me? Because I'm not brave enough to have a real relationship?' She laughed humourlessly and chucked the pebble towards the sea. 'Maybe I need to see a therapist.' She paused, thinking about recent events. 'Correction, I definitely need to see a therapist.'

'Want to tell me about it?' Janet asked.

And so, for the second time that week Estelle told somebody her story. This time it was slightly easier; and perhaps it would get easier every time she did it. The gag about her needing a therapist had been a throwaway line, but maybe it made sense. She didn't want the past to have such a claim on her. She wanted to be able to move on and begin to lead a normal life.

Whatever that was.

'I've never thought about other people very

326

much,' she said. 'I've just gone all out for what I want without considering what effect that might have on anyone else. Before RT...*Ray*, there have been loads of married men. Loads. I'm a selfish bitch, Janet, I really am.'

Oh, God, the tears were coming again. Would they ever be finished? Estelle felt the comforting warmth of Janet's hand on her back. She cried harder.

Janet held her in her arms for a while. 'Don't you know what you've done for me, Estelle?' she said. 'You have helped me so much. You've believed in me and you've helped me to make the most of myself. Do you really think I'd have gone to see Cruella to offer to buy her out if I'd never met you?'

Estelle wiped her eyes, smiling through her tears. 'I so wish I'd been there,' she said. 'I'd have loved to have seen the look on her face.'

Janet smiled. 'I shall think of it whenever I feel down in the future,' she said.

Estelle thought about the recent TV reports. 'But you see,' she said, 'I know that's probably just what my staff have been thinking about me lately; absolutely rapt that I've been in all this shit.'

'You don't know that,' Janet said.

'No, but I know *I* would be, if I was them. I'm not a very good boss.'

'You could change.'

Estelle sighed. 'I could try.' Starting by trying to make up for her recent coolness to Mark. If it wasn't already too late for that.

'Listen,' said Janet, 'I was wondering. Have you told Ray yet? About me knowing?'

'No,' Estelle said, 'I haven't told him.'

'Me neither.'

'Are you going to?'

Janet looked at her. 'Only when I tell him our marriage is over,' she said, and then Estelle realised how much her friend *had* changed since they'd met. She was very, very glad.

'You deserve so much better than him,' she said, and remembered Mark's response to her when she'd said that to him. 'So do you,' he'd said. 'So do you.'

Was her 'something better' Mark himself? And if it was, could she cope with that?

'I don't think I want anybody for a while,' Janet was saying. 'In the future, yes; a relationship where I was loved and respected and…' She smiled saucily, 'had *lots* of amazing orgasms; yes, that would be good. But for now… I think I just want some time for me. I've never had that, you see; I went straight from my mother's house to being married to Ray, and then Debbie came along… I just feel as if I want to find out…well, more about myself, I suppose; what I want, what I'm capable of. That sort of thing.'

Estelle smiled at her friend. It was funny really; they each wanted what the other had. Oh, she didn't want a joyless marriage to a bastard like Ray, but she did want a life that was more centred around other people. And Janet didn't suddenly want to become a ruthless business tyrant, but she did want independence and a sense of self-respect and confidence that comes from a successful career.

'Does that sound ridiculous?' Janet asked, and Estelle shook her head.

'No,' she said, 'it doesn't sound ridiculous at all. It sounds fantastic. And if there's anything I can do to help, anything at all, please do ask me.'

Janet smiled. 'Thank you, I will,' she said. 'But before that, there's another project I thought we could work on together.' Janet's smile changed subtly. She chucked a handful of small pebbles up into the air and caught them again.

'Oh?' said Estelle, 'and what project is that?'

Janet laughed. She looked about six years old. 'Well,' she said, 'it's more of a plan than a project. A plan to help me get even with Ray.'

* * * * *

More often than not, Ted finished early on Friday afternoons. Without Kate's news about her orgasms, Reenie would probably have been infuriated by the way he snatched a quick cup of tea, mumbled something about the allotment and went straight back out again.

But that afternoon his hasty departure just made her determined to sort things out between them. Ted could be a stubborn B, but he was her stubborn B, and she loved him. What was more, she was pretty convinced she could have an orgasm with him; they just had to change how they did things, that was all. Starting with talking.

Hurrying upstairs, Reenie put on the black and red basque and matching knickers she had bought from Estelle, then securely buttoned and belted a raincoat over the top. A pair of high-heeled shoes would have set it all off a treat, but there was no way she was hobbling down that track to the allotments on high heels. Bugger that; she intended to use her energy for more important things.

* * * * *

'Afternoon, Reenie.'

'Nice weather, Reenie.'

Sod it; she hadn't given a thought to the fact that most of Ted's allotment cronies would be around too.

'Hello, Sam. Gerry,' she said, walking quickly on.

'Think you'll find him in the shed,' Sam called after her.

Perfect. 'Thanks, Sam.'

Ted was sitting in the semi-darkness with a mug of tea, staring into space and, she realised after she had gone inside and shut the door behind her, he was crying…

Reenie had intended to bolt the door, strip off her raincoat and get down to it, but the sight of Ted crying into his tea erased all such ideas from her mind.

'Oh, love…'

Ted quickly put his mug down, sloshing tea everywhere in the process, hiding his face from her as he wiped his eyes on the sleeve of his mucky gardening top. 'I'm all right,' he said. 'Been sneezing, that's all. Dusty in here.'

Tears filled Reenie's eyes too. She felt so much love for the stupid old fool there wasn't enough room inside of her to contain it. She wanted to scoop him up and squeeze him until it hurt, but instead she forced herself to hold back.

'Yes,' she said thoughtfully. 'I know just what you mean. Did a lot of sneezing myself the day the police came to tell us Craig had died.'

Ted glared at her. 'You just can't stop going on about it, can you?' he said, and she shook her head sadly.

'Nope. Not that it was what I came here to talk about. Talking wasn't first on my list at all, as it happens.'

Ted remained stubbornly silent, and she sighed. 'Love,' she said, 'I can't believe you want us to split up, not after all these years.'

That got him looking at her. 'Course I don't!' he said.

'Well then, we've got to talk, haven't we? We can't just ignore it when things aren't right. That's always been the trouble with our marriage I reckon, not being able to talk properly.'

'So now we've got a problem marriage, have we?' he said crossly.

'No,' she said gently, 'of course we haven't. But...we haven't always been able to talk about things as well as we ought. And I'm not just talking about Craig either.'

'What else then?'

Reenie felt embarrassed, but she knew if she didn't say it now, then she never would. 'Well, sex,' she said. 'Oh, I'm not blaming you; I blame myself mostly. I've always been a bit...well, passive, I suppose. I've never really told you what I wanted and that, partly because I was embarrassed, but also, to be honest, because I was afraid of hurting your feelings. But then I got to thinking, it was you as told me about these workshops, so it's daft of me to think like that. I mean, you'd hardly have told me about them in the first place if you were bothered about me making demands of you in bed, would you?'

Ted seemed to be thinking about it. 'Well,' he said cautiously, 'no, I...I s'pose not.' Then he looked at her, frowning. 'What demands?'

Reenie smiled and began to undo her raincoat. 'Well,' she said, holding the coat open, 'I thought we could start with…' And bending forwards to give him a generous view of cleavage, she whispered something into his ear.

* * * * *

It was almost four o'clock by the time Estelle got back to the office. Driving there from the beach, she burst out laughing every time she thought about Janet's plan. It was priceless, absolutely priceless. And best of all, it proved more than anything else could have done that Janet had forgiven her.

'Ms Morgan!' Charlotte greeted her the minute she walked in the door. 'Did you forget about your meeting? I've been trying to get you on your mobile all afternoon.'

'Have you?' Estelle took her phone from her bag. It was still switched off from the workshop. 'Sorry, I didn't have it on.' She racked her brains, trying to remember what the meeting had been about.

'Andersons?' Charlotte prompted her. 'You asked them to quote us for the new lines.'

Whoops. 'Oh well,' she said. 'I'll phone them and grovel. If they want our business, they'll forgive me.'

Charlotte looked at her. 'Ms Morgan?' she said. 'It's none of my business, but… are you all right?'

The prickly retort that automatically sprang to her lips belonged to the past, and Estelle duly suppressed it. 'Thank you for asking,' she said instead with a smile. 'And yes, I'm fine. I just had a more important meeting to attend this afternoon, that's all. Plus, of course, I completely forgot about Andersons!' She started to walk on, then looked back briefly. 'Is Mark in his office do you know?'

'Yes,' Charlotte said, sounding slightly stunned by the pleasant way her boss had spoken to her. 'I think so, Ms Morgan.'

Estelle turned back one last time. 'Why don't you call me Estelle from now on, Charlotte?' she suggested. 'Ms Morgan makes me feel like a head teacher in a girls' boarding school.'

Charlotte began to laugh, but quickly stopped herself. 'Yes, Ms...Estelle,' she said.

Estelle didn't bother to go to her office. There was no point because she wasn't going to be able to do any work until she'd spoken to Mark anyway. It was all she could think about. What she was about to do was so scary that she had to do it while the impulse was with her.

She pushed his door open. 'Mark?' But the office was empty.

Disappointed, she backed out again. Rachel, her finance clerk, was walking past along the corridor. 'Are you looking for Mark, Ms Morgan?' she asked. 'I just saw him downstairs at the photocopier.'

Estelle smiled her thanks. 'Thank you, Rachel,' she said.

'No problem, Ms Morgan.'

She would have to put the head teacher at a boarding school joke in a company email or something.

'Have a nice weekend, Rachel,' she said and hurried on towards the stairs.

'Thank you, Ms Morgan,' Rachel said, but Estelle was already through the doors and taking the stairs two at a time.

'Mark?' She tore round the corner and found him deep in conversation with Cheryl, his assistant. 'Oh.' Judging by the way Cheryl was twirling a piece of her hair around her finger, the conversation wasn't about business.

Mark looked at her. 'Good afternoon, Estelle.' he said. 'Did you want me?' Cheryl melted away, probably in fear of her job. Did they really think she was that much of a tyrant? Though actually, she did want to sack the girl on the spot for flirting so shamelessly with Mark.

'Estelle?'

She realised she hadn't answered him. She wanted to run; either that or start a conversation about sales figures.

'I've decided…' she started.

'Yes?'

'I've decided I…' She lifted her chin. 'I can't wait until Monday for you to tell me about your research into new lines. Can you bring what you've got so far to show me now please?'

Mark looked at her. 'Very well,' he said. 'I'll be with you as soon as I can.'

In her office, Estelle paced up and down, unable to sit. This was way more frightening than that night in the police cell; way more frightening than anything else she had ever done in her life. What if he rejected her? What if she stripped herself emotionally naked in front of him and he just laughed? Where would she go? What would she do?

Then suddenly she thought about Janet, remembered her mischievous face. If Mark rejected her, there would still be the plan. There would still be

334

Janet. And Reenie and Kate. And Orgasm Night.

The door opened. Mark came in, carrying a pile of papers, his expression serious. 'I was planning to produce a proper report for Monday's meeting,' he said, 'but I haven't finished typing it up yet.' He moved past her to lay the papers out on her desk.

Before Estelle could look at them, there was a knock at the door. Charlotte came in cautiously. 'Er...Estelle,' she said, 'I was wondering if I could go home slightly early. Only I've just had a call from my son's childminder. She says he's not at all well and I– '

Was Charlotte always this terrified of her and she just hadn't noticed before?

'Yes, of course, Charlotte,' she said now. 'You get off. I hope he's all right.'

Charlotte smiled with relief. 'Thank you!' she said. 'I'll make up the time next week.'

Estelle knew there must be countless times when her PA had worked late. 'Forget it,' she said, feeling ashamed by Charlotte's gratitude. She couldn't be Estelle, the inhuman bitch any longer. She couldn't. Wouldn't.

'OK then,' Charlotte said. 'Thanks again. Have a good weekend both of you.'

Charlotte left. Mark seemed to have forgotten all about his papers. Estelle crossed the space between them and met his gaze steadily. 'I'm sorry, Mark,' she said. 'I am so sorry.'

* * * * *

Over on the allotments, Sam and Gerry leant on their spades and stared at Ted's shed. It appeared to

335

be shaking.

* * * * *

Despite the fact that Janet had never felt better in her life, she was in the pharmacy stocking up on throat sweets. Being ill was a sure-fire way to avoid sex with Ray, and as she had no intention of having sex with Ray again, ever, then it was absolutely essential to avoid even the possibility of it before she and Estelle had the chance to put their plan into operation. A cold would be too difficult to fake, but a sore throat and a potential throat infection couldn't be too hard. Ray almost always slept in the spare room if she had anything infectious.

Trying to decide between honey or cherry flavour (menthol were too disgusting unless you really had a desperately sore throat and were prepared to try anything to relieve it), Janet suddenly realised just how many 'lasts' there were going to be. This coming Sunday would be the last time she would cook a Sunday roast for him. Tomorrow would be the last time she washed his clothes… The reality of the situation suddenly hit her. Her marriage was about to end; it was really about to end.

'Janet? I thought it was you. You all right?'

Janet blinked. Looking up, she saw John George standing beside her. He was holding a hairnet and a packet of pink rollers.

'Oh, hello, John,' she said vaguely.

He smiled. 'Don't worry,' he said, 'these not for me. I'm shopping for my elderly neighbour.'

Janet looked at the luxuriant waves of his hair. 'I didn't think you needed rollers,' she said.

John looked at the sweets she was holding. 'I hope you're not ill?' he said.

'Oh no,' she said, looking down at the sweets herself. 'Just stocking up. In case of...emergencies, you know.'

'Advance planning?' he asked, one eyebrow raised.

'Something like that,' she said. It occurred to her that it would be great fun to confide in John about what she was actually up to, but of course she couldn't. So she smiled at him warmly instead. Perhaps she would tell him, after it was all over. Yes, she rather thought she would.

'I'm glad I ran into you actually,' he was saying.

'Oh yes?'

He pulled an apologetic face. 'Not fair to mention this to you really, I know. You're only an employee at the shop. But the fact is, Carol's seriously late with her payments this time. And the word is I'm not the only one. Should I be worried?'

Janet nodded. 'Yes,' she said. 'I think you should. Look, have you got time for a coffee? I can bring you up to speed. I'll just pay for these.'

So over coffee Janet told John about Carol's plans to sell the shop and also about her own hopes to buy it.

'OK,' he said after he'd listened to everything she'd got to tell him, 'let's see if we can't think of a way to help both of us.'

By the end of the conversation, they had a plan of action.

Plan NumberTwo, thought Janet. It was almost as good as Plan Number One.

'I did,' Reenie panted. 'I nearly came that time. I definitely did.'

Ted held his wife close on his lap. 'Nearly's not good enough,' he told her.

'We'll get there,' she said. 'After all, these are hardly the most comfortable of circumstances for two people pushing sixty.'

She kissed him, overjoyed that the tension between them had gone. And she *had* felt a definite flicker of building excitement; she wasn't making it up for his benefit.

'I can't believe I've been doing it all too hard and too fast for you all these years,' he told her. 'Why on earth didn't you say before?'

She kissed him. 'Daft, isn't it?'

They held each other. Ted buried his face in the side of her neck. 'Listen, I'm sorry for how I've been about Craig. I… I haven't let you grieve for him properly.'

Tears filled her eyes. 'You haven't let yourself grieve for him either,' she told him.

'I know,' he said. 'You're right. I've had my head shoved firmly in the sand. About all sorts of things. But it'll be different from now on, I promise.'

'All in good time,' she said, but he shook his head.

'No, there's been enough waiting around,' he said. 'We'll go and see Louise's parents together; thrash things out with them. Maybe we could pay for some sort of memorial for her.'

'That's a great idea, love,' she said, and they looked at each other. By now they both had tears

338

streaming down their faces.

'We'll be all right, Reen,' he told her.

'Yes,' she said, 'I know we will.'

He smiled through his tears. 'That's if Sam and Gerry don't decide to break the shed door down to check we're all right.'

She laughed. 'Maybe I'd better go home and get dressed.'

'Maybe *we* ought to go home and get you *un*dressed more like,' he said. 'I haven't finished with you yet today. Got plans for that G-Spot of yours, I have. Some slow, persistent plans.'

Reenie felt a flicker of excitement in her groin. She kissed him on the mouth. 'Come on then,' she said. 'What are we waiting for?'

And roughly an hour later, after a quick dash home and up the stairs and a leisurely and thorough period of caressing, fondling, sucking and kissing, Ted Richardson entered his wife as slowly as possible, millimetre by tantalising millimetre. Reenie was making little moaning noises and moving about restlessly, her hands on his buttocks, trying to pull him in all the way. But Ted refused to be hurried. If she wanted to be teased, by golly she was going to be teased. And when he *did* start to thrust, he was going to aim right for the place where she'd told him her G-Spot was.

Five minutes later, Reenie Richardson had her first ever orgasm.

Thirty-one

'Why is Orgasm Night going to be held in the evening?' Janet asked Jade towards the end of the next workshop – the last one in fact before Orgasm Night itself.

Estelle smiled as she saw her friend shoot a quick glance in Kate's direction. 'And don't tell me it's because it's called Orgasm *Night*, Kate, thank you very much!'

Kate spread her hands innocently. 'Wasn't going to say a thing,' she said, and everybody laughed.

'I always hold this final session in the evening because it isn't an ordinary workshop,' Jade told them all. 'It's a party, a celebration of everything you've achieved. There'll be music, games, food and drink – but the focus throughout will be sensuality, so do make an effort to dress up in a way that makes you feel good.'

'Where do orgasms fit into all of this?' Estelle asked.

'The whole evening will be building towards you having orgasms,' Jade said. 'The earlier part of the evening will be a riot of wonderful foreplay to get you into the right mood. Of course, it will be great fun too.'

'But how do you know we're all going to have an orgasm by the end of the evening?' Janet asked the question Estelle was about to ask.

'I don't know that for sure,' Jade said. 'But I have every confidence that you all will. *Every* confidence.'

When the session was over, the four women went next door to the bar to have lunch together. Estelle invited Jade along too, but she said she had to be somewhere and wouldn't be able to make it. Estelle thought it was strange that, after all these weeks, they hardly knew anything more about Jade than they had at the beginning, and she said as much to the others.

'I think she likes to be a mystery,' Reenie said. 'Helps with her image.'

There was a vibrancy about Reenie today; and no wonder – she was the second of them to have had an orgasm. She'd told them all the whole tale at the beginning of the session, and they'd all laughed at her descriptions of shaking sheds and shocked allotment holders. But really, Estelle thought, it had been a very moving story, especially when Reenie moved on to describe how next day she and Ted had gone to visit the family they'd been feuding with to propose a memorial for their dead daughter. They were going to fundraise to try to set up a community drama group to work with joyriders as Kate had suggested as well, which Estelle thought was a great idea. It seemed that at long last the feud was over, and Ted and Reenie were finally more at peace about the death of their son.

'Maybe she's got some sinister secret she needs to keep hidden,' Kate said.

'More likely she's an ordinary housewife with a beer-bellied husband and a squalling brat at home,' Estelle retorted.

'Hey!' said Reenie. 'What's wrong with beer bellies? Can be right sexy when they're bouncing on top of you, they can!'

Estelle pulled a face. 'Please!' she said.

'Reenie's right,' Kate said. 'I can vouch for them too. Although in Geoff's case, I think his is more of a bread or doughnut belly.'

Kate was also celebrating the achievement of her first vaginal orgasm this week. Geoff, she wanted them to know, was mightily endowed compared to Ian, and after the first few tries, that extra inch, she said, had 'done the business' for her.

While Estelle was pleased for both Kate and Reenie, she couldn't help wondering, despite all Jade's reassurances, whether it was ever going to happen for her, and she knew Janet felt the same way.

'I think Jade does have a secret,' Janet said thoughtfully. 'Oh, not something dark, but maybe...something sad. Now and then I've noticed, when she thinks nobody's looking, she can look...well, unhappy, I suppose. Or introspective, anyway.'

'You're the most observant out of the lot of us, Janet,' Reenie told us. 'I've never noticed her looking unhappy or introwhatsit.'

'Either that or she's happy as Larry and Janet's spouting bollocks,' Kate said with her usual helpfulness.

They all laughed, and Estelle thought back to the first session when Kate's smart alec comments had annoyed them all so. It seemed an age ago now, it really did.

'Gwen told me Jade's been living in an old caravan up on the caravan site,' Janet told them.

'*Really?*' said Reenie with a shudder. 'Poor woman. It must be freezing at night.'

Estelle frowned. 'I wonder why she's doing that?' she said.

Janet shrugged. 'Gwen says it's proof that Jade's some kind of charlatan.'

'She would,' said Reenie. 'But the proof of the pudding is in the eating, isn't it, Kate?'

Kate gave a smug smile. 'Certainly is,' she said and then looked at Estelle and Janet. 'Anyway,' she said, 'which one of you is going to be next then, eh? Maybe we should bet on it, Reenie.'

Estelle and Janet exchanged glances. Estelle guessed Janet was thinking, as she was, of their plan. They had agreed not to mention it to the others, at least not until they'd gone through with it.

'Well,' said Janet. 'Estelle's the one with the new boyfriend, so my money would be on her.'

'Estelle!' said Reenie. 'You dark horse! Come on, tell all.'

So she told them. Or the edited highlights at least. The dinner dates, the walks along the seafront to watch the sunset, the talking and the kisses...

'You mean you haven't got him into bed yet?' Kate said.

'It's only been a week, Kate, 'Reenie said. 'Give the girl a chance. It took you and Geoff years.'

As she had no answer for that, Kate resorted to pulling a face.

Estelle shook her head. 'I don't want to rush it and

343

scare myself,' she told them.

It was the truth, and she knew Mark was very conscious of how easily she could be scared too. He had told her he was happy for them to take their time, and she was grateful to him for that. Yet every time they met – and they had met for a date each and every night since the previous Friday – she knew she was getting in deeper and deeper. For her, the real leap of trust wasn't a sexual one at all. The biggest risk was in truly exposing herself, no shields, no masks, just the naked person that she was.

'Well, listen, girls,' Kate said, 'if it's any help at all, the way I finally had an orgasm this last time was by doing lots of practice at– ' She lowered her voice, '*masturbating*. When I wasn't with Geoff, I started to try out all the techniques Jade's taught us.' She smiled. 'Of course, I was *thinking* about Geoff while I did it.'

They all smiled. 'Of course,' said Estelle.

'Anyway,' Kate continued, 'this time it worked! And once I'd done it once, I found I could do it every time! So then I sort of analysed what was happening when I came – you know, what was happening with my body. And d'you know what I found?' They were all listening avidly, and it was obvious Kate was enjoying her role of orgasm expert.

'What?' prompted Reenie impatiently.

'Well, I realised I was doing something Jade told us she does: I was *bearing down*.' Kate lowered her voice still further. 'Like I was trying to have a – well, a *shit*.'

'Charming!' said Reenie.

'Doesn't matter if it's charming or not if it works, does it?' Kate retorted, and Estelle was inclined to agree.

'Doing that must change the position of your...vital bits,' Janet said thoughtfully. 'Your perineum and so forth.'

'Must do,' Reenie said, equally thoughtful. 'Though I must say I never thought of using the same action to have an orgasm as you do in childbirth!'

Once again they all cracked up, and shortly afterwards they went their separate ways.

'You give it a go, girls!' Kate encouraged Estelle and Janet on her way out, nodding her head towards their nether regions. 'That's all I'm saying!'

Janet and Estelle left the pub last. Outside they turned to face each other, smiling nervously.

'So everything's set for tonight then?' Janet asked, and Estelle nodded.

'Yes, all set. I told him to come round to mine at eight o'clock. Fiona's arriving about seven-thirty.'

'And you told him about her?'

Estelle smiled. 'Oh, yes. I told him. Well, all he needed to know, anyway. He's salivating as we speak.'

Janet nodded and gave a tight little smile that had Estelle reaching out for her. 'No; I'm OK,' she said. 'Really. See you about seven.'

* * * * *

By seven forty-five that evening, the trap was set. Estelle was dressed in some of her most sexy lingerie beneath a short red dress with a plunging neckline, which was the tartiest outfit she had been able to find. Fiona, who she had employed via the personal ads especially for the occasion, was dressed similarly

345

except that her dress was black, slit to the thigh and worn over fishnet stockings. Both of them were wearing fuck-me high heels – as Fiona called them – and loads of make-up. Estelle thought they *both* looked like prostitutes.

Now they were drinking wine and waiting for Ray to arrive. Which he did, promptly at eight.

Exchanging a last smile with Fiona, Estelle went to let him in. 'RT!' she greeted him. 'It seems ages since I saw you!'

Ray was looking a bit feverish. He was trying to take in Estelle's outfit, return her kiss and look over her shoulder at Fiona all at the same time.

'Yes, er…hi…' he said vaguely.

'Let me introduce the two of you,' Estelle said, taking hold of his hand and leading him forward. 'Fiona, this is RT. RT, this is Fiona.'

Fiona got to her feet. Below the dress, her fishnet-encased legs went on forever. She sashayed over. 'RT…' she breathed. 'How fantastic to meet you…' She began to paw his chest, looking down assessingly at his crotch as she did so. 'My, my,' she said. 'What a big boy…'

Ray seemed incapable of coherent speech. Estelle was hard-pressed not to burst out laughing. 'Why don't you two sit down?' she suggested. 'I'll go and open a new bottle of wine.'

She left them to it and headed for the kitchen space. While she was opening the wine, she looked back. Ray and Fiona were already in a clinch. Smiling, Estelle took the wine through. Ray leapt away from Fiona as if he expected Estelle to mind and loosened his tie.

Estelle poured him a glass of wine. 'Thanks,' he

346

said, quaffing it back. She refilled his glass and topped up Fiona's and her own while she was at it.

'Don't you think I've done well,' she said to Ray, 'finding Fiona?'

'Oh yes,' said Ray, looking greedily at the top of Fiona's stockings which were exposed because of the way her dress had ridden up. 'You certainly have.'

'The pleasure will be all mine, I'm sure,' Fiona drawled.

Ray put a hand on her thigh. Estelle took her cue. 'I just have to visit the bathroom,' she said. 'Back in a minute.'

Ray didn't bother to reply. He was concentrating on exploring the creamy flesh above Fiona's stocking tops.

Estelle made her way – not to the bathroom – but to the bedroom, where Janet, dressed only in lingerie, was waiting nervously on the edge of the bed. Resisting the urge to give way to hysterical laughter, Estelle tiptoed over to her and gave her a reassuring little hug.

'How's it going?' Janet whispered. 'Is he falling for it?'

Estelle grinned. 'Hook, line and sinker. You get into bed now. We'll be in very soon.'

Janet nodded, her face serious, and Estelle looked at her, feeling concerned. 'You do still want to go ahead with this, don't you?' she checked.

'Oh yes,' Janet said, sounding very definite. 'I certainly do.'

Estelle nodded. 'Good.' And she switched off the light, leaving the room lit only by one red-shaded lamp on the far side of the room.

Back in the lounge, Fiona's skirt was up around

her waist by now, and this time Ray didn't flinch when Estelle appeared. Over his head, Estelle nodded at Fiona, who instantly drew back slightly, pulling her skirt down over her thighs and standing up. 'I'm going to leave you to it for a moment,' she purred. 'Come and find me when you're both ready.'

As Fiona walked out, hips swaying, Ray didn't take his eyes off her once. If Estelle hadn't sat down on the sofa and pulled him down next to her, she knew he would have followed Fiona straight away. Taking his hand, she placed it on the zip at the back of her dress. The minute he pulled it down, the front of her dress fell forwards, revealing a transparent black peephole bra. Ray groaned and began to suck her nipples. He had done the same thing many times in the months she had known him, but as he did so now, she wondered how she had ever let him make love to her at all. She loathed him, and only the knowledge that this was absolutely the last time she would be doing anything like this with him kept her from pulling away.

'Come on,' she said after a moment, standing up and letting her dress fall to the floor. 'Fiona will be waiting.'

Ray didn't need telling twice. Stripping off his clothes as he went, he followed her towards the bedroom, arriving there wearing only his underpants and one sock. 'Fiona' was a hump beneath the dimly lit covers.

'She's pretending to be shy,' he said, dispensing quickly with the sock and underpants. 'She won't change her mind, will she?'

Estelle pulled the duvet aside and climbed onto the bed, sitting up against the headboard and patting

348

the space between herself and 'Fiona.' 'What do you think?' she asked. 'Do you really think a woman who looks like that – a woman who willingly arrives at a stranger's apartment to take part in a threesome – is going to be shy?'

Ray took his watch off. 'I guess not,' he said, and practically dived onto the bed.

Estelle pulled the duvet across him. 'Now,' she said, 'close your eyes. Fiona and I have got a surprise for you.'

Ray obediently closed his eyes. 'Fiona' wriggled up the bed to sit next to him.

'OK,' said Estelle, 'you can open your eyes now.'

And so, with his mistress seated on one side of him, and his wife on the other, Ray opened his eyes.

'Smile,' said Fiona, stepping into the room to put Estelle's digital camera to good use.

Goggle-eyed, Ray looked warily to his left and saw Janet.

'Hello, Ray,' she said.

Ray screamed. Then he leapt from the bed, trying and failing to snatch the camera from Fiona while picking up such items of clothing he happened to come across on his way out.

'You fucking bitches!' he yelled at them from the hallway, then seconds later the door slammed after him and he was gone.

Estelle and Janet looked at each other. Fiona was practically helpless with laughter. 'Take a look at this!' she said.

They looked at the shot. It was of prize-winning quality.

'Red-handed Ray,' Estelle said, and indeed, never had anybody looked so astonished or so guilty in a picture, ever.

'Well,' said Janet, after they were all dressed and Estelle had settled up with Fiona. 'That's that, I suppose. One marriage over.'

'Are you all right?' Estelle asked her, concerned.

Janet smiled. 'Of course!' she said. 'Revenge is sweet, as they say. Yes, I'm *fine*.'

Estelle wasn't convinced. 'Stay here for the night.'

But Janet shook her head and reached for her bag. 'No. You want to see Mark, and I told you, I'm fine. I can stay at my mother's house.'

'All right,' Estelle said, still feeling reluctant to let her go. 'But phone if you need to, OK? It doesn't matter what time it is.'

Janet smiled. 'OK.'

Estelle remembered the picture. 'Oh,' she said, 'and borrow my camera. You'll need to keep looking at this.'

They had one last laugh together about the picture before Janet left.

'Goodbye, Estelle. Thank you for tonight.'

Estelle reached out to hug her emotionally. 'And thank you for giving me a second chance.'

As soon as Janet had gone, Estelle phoned Mark. He came straight round. 'Are you all right?' he asked, searching her face.

It was a sign of the progress she was making that she had told all about the plan.

'Yes,' she said. 'Except for feeling very grubby. I must have a shower.'

He stroked her arm from elbow to wrist. 'Shall I make us a cup of coffee while I'm waiting?' he asked, but she shook her head, looking him straight in the face.

'No,' she said. 'Come and wash me.'

He smiled. She was glad he didn't ask her whether she was sure or not. She was glad he could tell how sure she was just by looking at her.

And so they showered together, and having Mark soap her neck, her breasts, her thighs and the cleft between her buttocks was the most erotic thing Estelle had ever experienced in her life. Mark obviously thought so too, because soon he was kissing her deeply and then they were running – still dripping wet – into the bedroom where, after a short period of fierce thrusting, Estelle Morgan had the very first orgasm of her life.

'Is that what they call a quickie?' she asked as they lay side by side afterwards, out of breath.

'Well,' said Mark ruefully, 'since it lasted all of a minute, I think it might be.'

She kissed him. 'Well, it was fucking great!' she said, and laughing triumphantly, she rolled over on top of him and began to kiss him all over again.

Thirty-two

Realising there was no way she was going to get to sleep that night, Janet knew she had a choice. Either she could mope about crying – because she was far from feeling as OK as she had made out to Estelle – or she could do something constructive.

In the end she managed to combine both activities by making a new start at clearing out her mother's belongings and sobbing her heart out all the while she was doing it. By morning there were twenty black sacks of rubbish lined up in the hallway ready to be put out for the dustmen, and she was reasonably sure she had no more tears left to cry as far as her marriage was concerned. The tears had mostly been about the waste of her life anyhow, and she certainly didn't intend to waste anymore of it.

She didn't love Ray, and it was likely that she hadn't loved him for a very long time. He was a bad habit she intended to break, along with over-apologising, settling for second best and failing to go for her dreams. Besides, today was the day for Plan Number Two.

Despite being completely exhausted, Janet arrived at work five minutes early to discover that Ray had already phoned the shop.

'I would be grateful if you could sort out your domestic discussions before you come into work,

Janet,' Carol De Ville told her, but Janet just shrugged and walked past her to stow her handbag out the back without bothering to reply. She didn't bother to return Ray's call either. Why should she? She wasn't interested in anything he had to say to her.

At ten o'clock he phoned again. Once again Carol answered it.

'Janet,' she called across the shop, 'it's your husband. *Again.*'

Janet carried on with what she was doing. 'Tell him I don't want to speak to him,' she said.

'Kindly tell him yourself!' Carol told her furiously.

So Janet walked past her boss to the phone, took the receiver from her and replaced it without speaking. Then she walked back past an astonished Carol to return to her work.

'Well!' said Carol indignantly, but the next time it rang she let it ring. But only after she had shot Janet a glare that would have caused a lesser person to keel over at forty paces.

Janet didn't care. The days when Carol De Ville could intimidate her were over, and she was counting the minutes until eleven o'clock when Plan Number Two was set to commence.

At eleven o'clock precisely, a smartly dressed man in a pinstripe suit came into the shop. Carol De Ville was instantly all smiles.

'Christopher! How lovely to see you!' she said. 'Do you have somebody to show round?'

Chris Manning, who was a local estate agent, smiled back with easy charm. 'I do indeed, Ms De Ville,' he said, and he walked past Carol to shake

Janet's hand. 'Although obviously, since Mrs Thornton works here, she's already more familiar than most with the business.' He smiled at Janet.

'That's true,' Janet said, equally charming. 'However, I know that with you showing me around I'll be able to see everything in a completely different light.' She could feel Carol's glare in the back of her neck like a deadly laser beam.

'Shall we start with the upstairs accommodation?' Chris Manning said, and Janet nodded.

'That sounds perfect,' she said.

The upstairs accommodation was presently used only for storage and was dusty and neglected.

'You'll need to use some imagination up here, Mrs Thornton,' Chris Manning told her as they walked through the back of the shop towards the stairs.

Janet smiled at him. 'Well,' she said, 'I'd be a pretty poor candidate for an interior design business if I didn't have any of that, Mr Manning,' she said.

'Indeed,' he agreed. 'But please, call me Chris.'

'Lead on, Chris.'

Janet hadn't been up to the flat very often in her six months in the shop – two or three times at the most, and even then only to dump something up there, out of the way. She certainly hadn't been viewing the rooms as a potential home the way she was now. But actually, despite the dust and the junk, they were nice rooms with high ceilings and original fireplaces that Chris Manning was keen to point out. The flat was certainly small – just a bedroom, living room, kitchen and bathroom, but if she lived here it would all be hers, and nobody else's. Janet had never had her own living space before. Doing up the flat would be almost as exciting as starting up a business.

'Are you ready to venture back downstairs now?' Chris was a nice man, quite good looking, in his early thirties, she'd say. Without a word having been spoken, something told Janet he knew exactly why she had particularly wanted him to show her round the premises. After all, why wouldn't Carol be as difficult at the estate agents as she was everywhere else?

Janet glanced at her watch. It was eleven ten – phase two of Plan Two was about to commence. 'Yes,' she said. 'I think it's the perfect time to look at the shop itself.'

It was. As they went back into the shop, John George was just coming in from the street. Carol De Ville was busy with some customers.

'The sale will include all shop fittings including the cash register,' Chris said as John elbowed his way as politely as possible past several customers who were waiting to be served.

'Excuse me, madam. Thank you so much, sir.'

At the counter he dumped a sales ledger in front of Carol De Ville with a resounding thump.

'Excuse me,' said a woman, 'we were here first.'

'I don't think so, madam,' John told her courteously. 'I was first here in 2006. And very welcome I was too in those days, let me tell you.'

'Er...shall we move on to look at the display space?' Chris said, but Janet shook her head.

'No, not just yet,' she said. 'I'd like to examine the counter area in greater detail.' And she settled down to watch.

'Very unctuous back then, our lady here was,' John said. 'Oozing charm and co-operation.'

355

Carol De Ville attempted to use some of this same unctuousness now, but her fake smile was distinctly shaky. 'John, perhaps we could discuss this at an alternative time? The shop is rather busy just now, as you can see.'

'Something in it for her then, wasn't there?' John swept on as if Carol hadn't spoken. 'Wanted to set up an account with me. An account she has never paid on time, not once in all the years we've been doing business together.'

Janet saw John take something from a bemused customer's hand and brandish it in the air. 'Take this door handle you've chosen, madam – it belongs to me. And since it belongs to me, then *I* can sell it to you. In fact, I can let you have it for twenty-five percent less than Ms De Ville can. What do you say?'

'Mr George, *please,*' Carol De Ville hissed rather desperately. Some of the customers – including the woman with the door handle – began to drift away. Others, like Janet, were rooted to the spot, enthralled by the unexpected entertainment.

The shop door opened again. Taking a look, Janet saw Michael Clark, a manufacturer of bespoke blinds from Norwich. How had John managed to track him down? She was impressed.

'Ah,' said John. 'Here's another gentleman whose account with this establishment is in arrears.'

'Five thousand pounds, to be precise,' Michael Clark said, advancing with a sheaf of invoices. 'And if the account isn't settled this morning, I shall be putting the matter into the hands of my solicitors.'

Carol De Ville looked as if she were about to explode. The small group of remaining customers looked as if they wanted her to.

'This business is currently up for sale,' she said. 'Your accounts will be settled just as soon as a buyer has been found. Now, if you'd kindly allow my customers to make their purchases– '

'I'll buy it,' Janet said.

Everybody looked her way.

Chris Manning beamed at her. 'You're interested in making an offer, Mrs Thornton?' he asked.

Janet nodded. 'Yes,' she said. 'I am. In fact, I already made Ms De Ville an offer a few days ago. That offer is still on the table.'

'Excellent,' he said, looking over at Carol De Ville. 'That is good news, isn't it, Mrs De Ville?'

The customers were all nodding. John was grinning from ear to ear.

Everybody looked at Carol. She licked her lips. 'Yes,' she said, sounding as if she'd swallowed a large quantity of razor blades.

The shop door opened again. Everybody looked round – the three customers, John George, Michael Clark, Chris Manning, Carol and, of course, Janet her-self.

It was Ray.

Disconcerted to receive so much unexpected attention, Ray came to an abrupt halt just inside the door. He licked his lips.

'Janet?' he said at last.

She looked at him. 'Everybody,' she announced to the assembled crowd, 'this is my soon-to-be ex-husband, Ray.'

There was silence. Ray looked at her. She had never seen him wear such a cowed, pleading expression. It totally failed to move her. 'Janet,

357

please,' he grovelled. 'Just let me explain. Last night meant nothing.'

'I'm a bit too busy to talk now, actually, Ray,' she said. 'I'm just negotiating the purchase of this shop.'

'*What?*'

John George chipped in helpfully. 'Janet's just made an offer,' he told Ray. 'We're all waiting to see whether Ms De Ville is going to accept it.'

Everybody's heads swivelled from Ray to Carol who was, by now, extremely red in the face. The tension was palpable. At last she spoke.

'Very well,' she said, arrogant even in defeat. 'I accept.'

It should have been a perfect moment of triumph for Janet, and for a while it was. Especially when John George gave a huge whoop of joy and lifted her off her feet to give her a huge celebratory kiss right in front of Ray.

After the fuss had died down and Janet was back at her mother's house, she phoned Estelle to tell her the good news.

'That's brilliant,' her friend said. 'Absolutely brilliant! D'you know what you'll call the shop?'

'Janet's Dreams,' Janet said without hesitation, remembering her dream.

'Perfect,' approved Estelle.

Janet smiled. 'I thought so,' she said. 'And how about you? How did things go with Mark last night?'

Estelle laughed, and just that one laugh was enough to tell Janet everything.

'My God,' she said, 'you've done it, haven't you? You've had an orgasm!'

'Yes!' confirmed Estelle delightedly. 'The very first time we made love!'

'That's fantastic, Estelle. I'm so pleased for you.' She was, she genuinely was. But even so, as Janet put the phone down a few minutes later, she couldn't help feeling envious too. Out of the four of them, she was the only one who hadn't yet scaled the heights of pleasure, and as she sat and brooded about it in her mother's house, her excitement about the shop began to crumble away.

Not only had she not had an orgasm, but now she no longer had a man to make love to, so she was even further away from it than she had been at the start of the workshops. Kate, Reenie and Estelle would all be living their lives in the glow of love and the afterglow of great sex, while she was about to become more solitary than she had ever been in her life.

Could she do it? Could she really do it? Live happily as a divorced woman? Run a business single-handedly? Cope with all the little problems of everyday life on her own? She'd never had to do it before, and her mother, Ray, Carol De Ville and even Gwen had always treated her as if she was some kind of defective. And maybe she was. Janet's Dreams would probably go bankrupt in the first few weeks and she'd end up broke, lonely *and* non-orgasmic.

Janet reached for the phone, needing to speak to somebody. But who? Her new friends were all busy having amazing sex – they wouldn't want her interrupting them with her pathetic insecurities. Debbie was wrapped up in her problems with Nigel, and besides, Janet had always resisted confiding in her daughter about her personal problems. John George? Janet smiled to herself at the thought. It was funny, but even though she barely knew the man, she

359

could imagine confiding in him. He'd been brilliant today at the shop, and she liked him a lot. He was so easy-going compared to Ray. But maybe it was a *little* too soon in their fledging friendship to confess that she was worried she would never have an orgasm.

Janet frowned, racking her brains, then suddenly remembered Jade. Of course. Why hadn't she thought about her before? Jade had smiled at her with such warmth when she'd told her she had to start standing up to people and stop doing things she didn't want to do. But she had also promised Janet mind-blowing pleasure as a result of her classes, something she had yet to deliver. Yes, Jade was exactly the right person to speak to, and thanks to Gwen's nosiness, Janet knew exactly where to find her.

By the time Janet got up to the caravan site, the sun was just beginning to set, showing the caravans in dark relief against the sky. But it was still easy to pick out Jade's caravan, because most of the other vans looked unoccupied. There was also a dirty great big black motorbike parked outside it, which it was all too easy to imagine Jade riding. Skin-tight leathers, long hair streaming behind her, the powerful throb of the engine…Yes, this definitely had to be Jade's caravan.

Leaving her car on the grass, Janet walked past the bike towards the van's door. But before she could knock, the door was torn open and there was Jade, dressed more casually than she usually was, in jeans and a jumper and smiling all over her face. 'Janet!' she said. 'How lovely to see you!'

Even though Jade was smiling and seemed genuinely glad to see her, Janet couldn't help feeling uncertain. 'I hope you don't mind me coming. My neighbour mentioned you were living here...' Janet's voice trailed off.

'Gwen of the dried-up primulas?' Jade remembered, and suddenly Janet was laughing and everything was all right.

'Of course I don't mind, Janet. Come in! I was just getting some food ready for Orgasm Night. You can help me if you like.'

Jade led the way inside the caravan and Janet soon found that when she said she was getting some food ready for Orgasm Night, she hadn't meant sausage rolls or cheese and pineapple on sticks. The table between the upholstered seating in the living space was covered in plates of very erotically suggestive food.

'What do you think?' Jade asked with a wicked smile, and Janet stood and stared.

'What are these?' she asked, looking at a plateful of halved fruit, which didn't look at all dissimilar to the view she had received when she had done her homework with her hand mirror.

'Figs,' said Jade. 'Aren't they perfect?'

Janet nodded. 'Yes, very effective,' she said, her gaze moving on to a Galia melon, halved and skinned with a cherry in the centre of each half to make it look like breasts, and then to several sets of penises and testicles constructed out of sausages and meatballs.

Janet looked at the sausages. They were bigger than the average supermarket banger. 'Impressive,' she said.

Jade laughed, but when Janet didn't join in, Jade looked at her. 'But you didn't come here to find out how my preparations for Orgasm Night were progressing, did you?' she guessed.

Janet shook her head, suddenly feeling emotional. 'No.'

'Why don't you sit down?' Jade invited her. 'I'll make us a cup of tea.'

While she waited, Janet looked around the inside of the caravan, which clearly dated from the 1970s. Jade had done her best with throws and lamps, but the carpet was chocolate brown nylon beneath the rug, the curtains were 1970s, and there was a slight smell of mildew. It couldn't be a pleasant place to live in, especially now that the nights were drawing in. So why was Jade here?

'Here you are,' Jade said, bringing the tea.

'Thanks.'

Jade smiled. 'OK. So tell me why you're here.'

Janet put her tea down next to the plate of figs. 'I wanted to ask you why you think I haven't had an orgasm yet. Only all the others have, and I've been taking your advice about standing up for myself and everything.' She thought about it. 'In fact, that's all I seem to have been doing lately.'

Jade looked at her thoughtfully. 'It takes a lot of energy, doesn't it?' she said.

Janet thought about all the plotting and the scheming. Tricking Ray with Estelle and Fiona. 'Yes,' she agreed. 'It does.'

'Sensuality isn't a race, Janet,' Jade told her. 'It will happen for you when the time's right. That may be tonight at Orgasm Night, and it may not. But it *will* happen. And in the meantime... Well, I just

362

think you need to start giving yourself permission to become orgasmic.'

Janet frowned. *Permission?* 'How do I do that?'

'Think it. Feel it. See it. Make time for it. Consciously include everything we've covered in the workshops into your life. Make sensuality the focus of your life, instead of a subject you're studying. Place yourself in the centre instead of on the outside looking in.'

As usual, Jade sounded so inspired about her subject. Even here in this run- down caravan in her old jeans and jumper. But somehow it still wasn't what Janet needed.

She licked her lips. 'Who are you, Jade?' she asked. 'Really?' And she knew suddenly that if Jade weren't open with her now, she might just turn her back on it all. She wanted to believe in her inner sex goddess and her ability to be actively sexual, but she needed more than Jade's fine words. She needed proof.

Jade spread her hands as if to indicate the caravan, the food on the table, the motorbike outside and a sparkly silver dress hanging up on a hanger from the curtain rail, which was no doubt the outfit she intended wearing for Orgasm Night. 'This is who I am,' she said. 'At the moment. But it isn't who I always am.'

Janet looked at her, remembering the first time she had been for coffee with Estelle and they had speculated about Jade's name. 'Is Jade Gate your real name?' she asked.

Jade shook her head. 'It's not the name I was given at birth, no,' she said. 'But it is who I've become. Believe it or not, I actually grew up here in

363

Norfolk.'

Janet was amazed. 'Did you?'

Jade nodded. 'Yes. But I left as soon as I was old enough. Janet, I had a very strict, loveless childhood. By the time I was a teenager, I was so damaged inside, the only way I could survive was to rebel. So I ran away, and then I did what the four of you are all trying to do at the moment: I reinvented myself. I haven't been back here since.' She shrugged. 'My partner thinks I'm crazy to try to dig up the past. If he could see the state of this place, he'd be on the first flight over to drag me home. It looked a lot better on the Internet when I made the booking, I can tell you! I have to be careful where I Skype my partner from.'

Jade sighed, her smile vanishing. For the first time that Janet could remember, she looked genuinely vulnerable. It took Janet completely by surprise, but for some reason, it also gave her a feeling of hope. Because if Jade wasn't completely perfect, if she'd made a mess of things like everyone else, then maybe, just maybe, *she* could turn things around too.

'Why did you come back?' she asked, and Jade shrugged.

'Probably because of a misguided sentimentality,' she said. 'I'm pregnant, you see, and I thought I wanted my child to have contact with his grandfather. I hoped the years might have mellowed him. But they haven't. When I went to see him, he didn't want to know. So, that's that. At least I know now.'

Jade, pregnant! Janet stared at her, noticing the carefully concealed lines of hurt in her face. Then she looked at her stomach. 'I had no idea…' she started to say, although now that she knew, she could see a soft swell to it.

'I'm only four months pregnant,' Jade said, and she smiled. 'So…new territory for me too,' she said. 'Maybe we both need to put the past behind us, eh?'

Janet smiled wanly. 'Well,' she said, 'I've well and truly burnt my boats now, so I haven't got much choice. I have to move on.'

Jade reached between the fig vaginas and the melon breasts to squeeze her hand. 'Come on,' she said, standing up, back to her normal inspiring, enthusiastic self again, 'I'll introduce you to something that never fails to make me feel as horny as hell!'

Minutes later, the powerful engine of Jade's motorbike was throbbing between Janet's thighs. Jade shouted instructions to her and when she felt ready, Janet released the clutch and began to head off across the field towards the last remnants of the setting sun.

The bike was big and dangerous. But she, Janet was in charge, and as she accelerated across the field it felt so good, she put her head back and gave a whoop of pure joy. And suddenly everything, *everything*, seemed within reach.

When she finally rode the bike back to the caravan, Jade was waiting to welcome her. 'You like?' she asked with a beaming smile.

'I like very much,' Janet grinned. 'Very much indeed. Actually, Jade, I was wondering. Could you take me somewhere on this?'

'Of course,' said Jade and, ten minutes later, with Janet dressed in Jade's spare leathers, they set off for town.

As the bike pulled up outside her marital home, Janet was unperturbed to see Ray's car in the drive. 'I won't be long,' she shouted to Jade over the noise of the bike engine. 'Just got to get something.'

'Sure,' said Jade. 'I'll keep the engine running.'

And, as Janet ran up the drive to the front door, she was gratified to hear Jade rev the engine up.

The door was flung open before she could use her key. 'What the devil – ' Ray began to say.

Janet lifted her visor up and stepped into the hall.

'Janet?' said Ray uncertainly.

'Sorry to disturb you,' said Janet. 'Something I need. Won't be a minute.' And she moved past him to run up the stairs.

When she reached the landing, Debbie's bedroom door opened and Debbie came out. 'Mum!' she said in a shocked voice. 'You look– '

Janet smiled. 'Amazing? Confident? Happy?' she supplied. 'Look, darling, I can't stop just now. My ride is outside waiting for me. There was just something I had to fetch.'

She went into the bedroom, crossed to the chest of drawers and pulled open her knicker drawer. Rummaging beneath her carefully laundered, sensible M & S white bikini pants, Janet found what she wanted.

Debbie was staring at her. 'What have you got in there?'

Janet smiled. 'Just a little present for Gwen,' she said, closing the drawer and starting to move past her daughter.

'Mum,' Debbie wailed. 'When are you coming back?'

Janet paused to squeeze her daughter's arm. 'I'll

call you soon, OK?' she said. 'Tomorrow. We'll have some lunch and talk about everything. I promise. But right now, I have to go.'

And she headed downstairs.

Ray was waiting in the hall 'Look, Janet,' he started to say, but Janet kept right on going.

She didn't need to go and knock on Gwen's door, because Gwen was right there by the bike, remonstrating with Jade about noise pollution. As Janet looked at her former neighbour in the light from the street lamp, she suddenly wondered why she had allowed let her intimidate her so thoroughly. Gwen was nothing but an embittered, bitchy bully who used make-up that was more than a little too orange for good taste.

'Janet?' Gwen said incredulously, much as Debbie and Ray had both just done. 'Is that really you?'

'Yes,' smiled Janet. 'It really is.' And she held a bag out towards Gwen: the bag containing the crotchless knickers that Estelle had given to her at the end of the lingerie party. 'Here's a little present for you,' she said. 'A little something to make your... primulas thrive.'

Then she climbed up behind Jade and they roared away into the night, their combined laughter audible over the throb of the powerful bike.

Thirty-three

Whenever Geoff thought about what was going on in the back room he had to laugh. Orgasm Night. It was priceless. And even more priceless was the fact that with the karaoke in full swing, no one in the bar had got a clue. Not even Tom.

Tom was up there now, pretending to be Tom Jones as he murdered *Delilah*, eyes screwed up with emotion as he sang. Pity nobody seemed to appreciate it. They were all drinking themselves silly or talking in that overloud way drunk people do when they don't know how drunk they are. Poor Tom. He needed a good woman to appreciate him. Geoff smiled to himself, knowing that if it were Kate up there doing her worst, he'd be cheering her on and clapping as if she were Madonna or Lady Gaga.

As Tom's song came to an end, Geoff glanced at his watch. They'd been in there for an hour and a half now. Had Kate had her orgasm yet? And if she had, had it been better than any she'd had with him so far? It better not have been!

* * * * *

Inside the back room, Kate was thinking about Geoff too. She'd thought about him when she'd made the girls laugh by putting a splodge of

368

mayonnaise on the tip of one of Jade's male genitalia snacks, and she was thinking about him now as she took her turn at making what Jade called a 'power affirmation.'

'I will continue to love and be loved,' she announced grandly from her place on the makeshift stage. She allowed her glance to rake over them all, a wicked twinkle in her eye. 'And I will shag Geoff every chance I get and twice on Sundays!'

The others all cheered, and Kate stepped down with a grin and a wave.

It was Reenie's turn to go next. Up she got, all bright-eyed and swaggering, almost tripping over on her way. 'Whoops!' she said. 'One too many gins already!'

Kate grinned. Who'd have thought she and Reenie would end up being such good pals when they'd started out loathing each other?

'Right,' said Reenie. 'Here goes. I'm going to carry on talking, that's what I'm going to do. All right, all right, I know I already do quite enough of that already, but I mean to Ted. I'm going to carry on talking to Ted. I'm going to tell him exactly what I want and exactly how I want it.' She laughed saucily. 'And I'm going to get myself a whip to use in case he ever decides not to co-operate.'

Jade clapped. Janet cheered. Kate wolf-whistled. 'I'll let you have a copy of our catalogue, Reenie,' Estelle said. 'We stock a whole range of whips.'

Then it was Estelle's turn. As she passed Reenie on her way up to the stage, they high-fived each other and Kate grinned, remembering how stuck-up and superior Estelle had once been. Now she was one of them. Though there was still something powerful about her as she stood up there, smiling at each of them in turn. The difference was, she was a complete person now instead of a brittle fake. Just like Kate herself.

'I'm going to be a better person,' Estelle said. 'A nicer employer, a loyal friend and a true and constant lover. I'm going to enjoy and appreciate commitment and I'm going to continue to take emotional risks.' She paused, smiling saucily, and Kate began to grin, anticipating something rude. 'I'm also going to rejoin the Mile High Club when Mark and I go to the Caribbean this Christmas. Except…' She held up her hand to stall their laughter, '…this time I'm going to have an orgasm while I'm up there!'

She stepped down to the accompaniment of their cheers and whoops, and then that only left Janet. Watching her climb up onto the stage, Kate felt a pang of pity for her. Poor Janet, she'd had a hard time of it lately, and they all knew she was the only one yet to have an orgasm. Though come to think of it, there was a certain glow about Janet tonight, so maybe she'd had one now after all?

'With my first profits from Janet's Dreams, I'm going to buy myself a motorbike,' Janet said, shooting a grin in Jade's direction. 'And tonight, I'm going to have an orgasm!'

Jade stood up. 'Great idea, Janet,' she said, spreading her arms wide. 'Ladies, make yourselves comfortable. Let the serious pleasure of the evening commence!'

* * * * *

Jade had brought several large cushions, and Janet

set her glass of wine carefully down on the floor and lay back on one, closing her eyes. Beneath her short, black, velvet dress she was quite naked, and when Jade told them to begin caressing themselves, Janet started by stroking her legs with slow sensuality. Her skin was pleasingly soft to the touch, and as her hand moved round to her inner thighs, she smiled to herself, remembering the throbbing power of the bike.

A woman was singing *I will survive* in the bar next door. Janet slipped one of her hands inside her dress to caress her breasts, enjoying the weight and warmth of them, nestling in the palms of her hands.

She wasn't only going to survive, she was going to thrive. She was going to make sure she had all the things she wanted in her life. She was going to have things – fantastic things – she had never even known that she wanted. She was going to have everything.

Turning slightly onto her side, Janet slipped her hand further up her thigh and imagined herself in bed in her flat above the shop. She was lying on her back, pinioned to the bed by a pair of strong male hands.

'You're so beautiful, Janet,' the man told her, looking at her body. 'I'm crazy about you…' He moved in to kiss her. It was John George, but John George with more than a touch of the pirate from Jade's erotic film.

And suddenly Janet was in that film. She was the girl in the sarong, watching the leaping dolphins. Suddenly someone looped a rope beneath her breasts and hauled her back against a muscular chest. A hand slid stealthily beneath her sarong. She opened her legs invitingly…

371

* * * * *

In the bar, Geoff was singing The Beatles' *Eight Days a Week*. Or at least, he was trying to sing it. But there was something wrong with the karaoke machine – it kept cutting out, leaving Geoff's voice hanging scarily naked in the air. Every time it cut out, he could hear the sounds coming from next door. And so he pressed on relentlessly, even after the karaoke machine had completely given up the ghost.

But no matter how hard Geoff sang, it wasn't quite enough to drown out the sound of four women... simultaneously building up to orgasm.

THE END

Also by Margaret K Johnson

The Dare Club

Aleysha, Nick, Colette and Emma are on a mission to scare themselves into forgetting their problems. But will it work?

When four very different people meet at a Lift Up course for the newly divorced or separated, there are initial tensions. Aleysha hasn't accepted the fact that her 7-month marriage is over. Nick is struggling with being a single parent. Colette is still dealing with the health problems that caused her husband to walk out on her, and Emma is a dumper, while the others are dumpees.

As the group get to know each other, Colette suggests they start a dare club. If they're cavorting several metres off the ground, or on stage, standing in a spotlight, it's bound to help them to forget about their troubles, isn't it? At the very least, they'll have some fun, and who knows? It might just change their lives forever.

Reviews on Amazon:

"I loved this book. The four very different main characters meet at a group to help people recover from relationship breakdowns and embark on a series of adventures together. They came to life for

me as I read about their ups and downs and by the end of the story, I felt as if the characters were not only friends with each other, but also with me. I had laughed with them, worried about them and cried tears of joy for them.

A good read."

"I love a book I can get straight into and the clever introduction to the people made them instant friends and companions. I loved the twists and turns and build-up which picks up a real pace as their crazy lives intertwine and their friendships grow. A thoroughly enjoyable read."

Also by Margaret K Johnson

A Nightingale in Winter

Published by Omnific Publishing

It is 1916, and The Great War is raging throughout Europe. Eleanor Martin is traveling to France to serve as a volunteer nurse. She only wants to bury herself in her work on the Front and forget her traumatic past. But when her ship is torpedoed, Eleanor has to act quickly to save an American journalist's life. As she cradles Dirk Loreson's broken body in her arms, speaking to him to keep him conscious, the possibility of a whole different future begins to open up for her.

Leo Cartwright, an ambitious artist, is also en route to the Front. A ruthless man who will stop at nothing to find inspiration for his paintings, Leo's path is destined to cross with Eleanor's. As she comes under his spell, will she find the strength to resist his demands? Will she trust her growing love for Dirk?

A Nightingale in Winter is about courage and searing ambition at a time when the very foundations of the world have been shaken.

Review:

"I love stories like this one in which all the complex threads of the plot are woven together so perfectly. The WWI setting is the backdrop Johnson has chosen, and clearly she's done her homework in that regard. I love Johnson's contemporary work. With this historical, she proves she has the skill to write wonderful stories set in other eras."

Acknowledgements

Thanks go to Soqoqo Design for the cover design, to Sarah Gooderson for her proof-reading skills and to all those who gave me feedback during the writing process. To Vicki Penrose for helping to tweak the title, and also to the cast and crew of Goddess the stage play – performed at Cambridge Drama Centre – and my friends Fionnuala Lennon and Alan Battersby who were also instrumental in the play's successful run. Thanks too to my support network, especially Graham and Alfie and my mother.

Lastly, thank you to you for reading the book, and much love to all goddesses and potential goddesses everywhere!

To find out more about Margaret you can:
Go to her website at www.margaretkjohnson.co.uk
Visit her blog at: www.margaretkjohnson.co.uk/blog
Like her Facebook page:
https://www.facebook.com/MargaretKJohnsonAuth
or
Follow her on Twitter -
https://twitter.com/Margaretkaj

Printed in Great Britain
by Amazon